4

SAMURAI CODE

SAMURAI CODE

A Jack Taggart Mystery

Don Easton

DUNDURN PRESS
TORONTO

Copy Editor: Shannon Whibbs
Design: Jennifer Scott
Printer: Webcom

Library and Archives Canada Cataloguing in Publication

Easton, Don
    Samurai code / Don Easton.

(A Jack Taggart mystery)
(A Castle Street mystery)
ISBN 978-1-55488-697-5

I. Title. II. Series. III. Series: Castle Street mystery

PS8609.A78S36 2010   C813'.6   C2009-907482-6

1   2   3   4   5   14   13   12   11   10

We acknowledge the support of the **Canada Council for the Arts** and the **Ontario Arts Council** for our publishing program. We also acknowledge the financial support of the **Government of Canada** through the **Canada Book Fund** and **The Association for the Export of Canadian Books**, and the Government of Ontario through the **Ontario Book Publishers Tax Credit program**, and the **Ontario Media Development Corporation**.

Care has been taken to trace the ownership of copyright material used in this book. The author and the publisher welcome any information enabling them to rectify any references or credits in subsequent editions.

J. Kirk Howard, President

Printed and bound in Canada.
www.dundurn.com

Dundurn Press
3 Church Street, Suite 500
Toronto, Ontario, Canada
M5E 1M2

Gazelle Book Services Limited
White Cross Mills
High Town, Lancaster, England
LA1 4XS

Dundurn Press
2250 Military Road
Tonawanda, NY
U.S.A. 14150

To our Canadian soldiers: thank you for looking after us at home and abroad. Thank you for making the world a better, and with hope, a peaceful place.

1

It was seven o'clock in the evening and the last Sunday in June when Constable Sophie White opened her locker. She had completed her first week on the job after graduating from the Royal Canadian Mounted Police academy in Regina. She was thrilled to have been transferred to the RCMP Detachment in Surrey. Less than an hour drive to Vancouver, it was one of the largest and busiest detachments in British Columbia.

She glanced at the mirror hanging on her locker door and caught her own impish grin, betraying her excitement. Combined with her young face, she wondered if it gave her a look of innocence, revealing her lack of experience. She frowned, then hardened her jaw line and tried to look stern. *Well, that didn't work! At least my uniform is crisp and clean. Everyone will respect that …*

She put her holster, containing her Smith & Wesson 9 mm semi-automatic pistol, in her locker and closed the narrow metal door. Her hands fumbled with the padlock before the sound of the click told her it was locked. She knew she was a little nervous. Before going home, she had to meet with her supervisor.

If she knew the horrific terror that awaited her, she would have wanted to curl up in the fetal position inside her locker and stay there. Her belief that everyone respected the uniform was about to be erased. Her journey home was about to become a journey to hell.

"You did well this week," said her supervisor, as Sophie approached his desk.

"Thanks, Bob," Sophie smiled back.

"Caught a fourteen-year-old kid in a stolen car," said Bob, glancing at the notes he had made. "Smoothed out three domestic disturbances and nailed one guy with two kilos of B.C. bud. Not bad for your first week," he added, matter-of-factly.

Sophie smiled again.

"You handle a car well, too," he added, focusing his attention on Sophie's face. "City traffic doesn't bother you?"

Sophie shrugged and said, "I was raised in Calgary. If I could handle the Deerfoot Trail on a Friday night when half the rednecks are going home with a few beers under their belts, I'm confident I can handle the traffic here."

A flicker of a smile crossed Bob's face before he became serious. "You are confident. But perhaps too much so, after that little incident an hour ago."

Sophie felt her cheeks flush. They had been driving through an industrial area when two cars raced away from a gravelled lane near some warehouses. Sophie had instinctively accelerated in hot pursuit. She had spun the steering wheel hard to turn down another lane in the hope of intercepting their quarry. Bob yelled for her to keep going straight, but she believed her shortcut would save valuable seconds and was anxious to show her ability. Halfway down the lane she slid to a stop at a gate blocking her path. Bob stared at her, with his arms folded across his chest. By the time she turned the car around and headed back, it was far too late to catch anyone.

Sophie sighed and picked an imaginary piece of lint from her uniformed pants. *Up until an hour ago, everything was going so great.* She swallowed and looked at Bob and said, "I didn't know the lane was —"

"But I did," interrupted Bob. "When I give you instructions, I expect you to obey."

"I'm sorry," stammered Sophie. "It won't happen again."

Bob looked at her long enough for her to feel more uncomfortable, before continuing. "You were caught up in the excitement of the chase. Next time, try to stay calm and *listen to what I say!*"

Sophie nodded, feeling the heat prickle her ears.

"At least the kids didn't finish the job," said Bob and Sophie nodded in agreement.

When they returned to the warehouse they saw where cherry-red graffiti had been sprayed on the side of the building — GRAD 20.

"You've only been here a week," said Bob. "The kids around here know the area a lot better than you do. Make it a priority to change that. Whether you're working or on days off, pay attention. Get to know your area. Learn which businesses are open late and when they close. Know which places have night janitors and which don't. Recognize those who are delivering pizzas or newspapers, and those who are casing places for break-ins. It takes time. You're new. The punks know that and will test you." Bob paused and saw that Sophie was paying close attention. Her face was still flushed, revealing her regret. "Okay, enough said. You can go home."

"Thanks, Bob." Sophie glanced over at some other officers who were running out of the office to answer a report of an injury car accident. She turned to Bob and said, "I've got some paperwork to do. Maybe I'll hang around a bit."

Bob hid his grin. *I was like that once. Never wanted to go home. The work was my life ... until I discovered that those I arrested were going home sooner than I could finish their paperwork.* He knew Sophie would learn about that soon enough. "Suit yourself, but I'm out of here. Next week we're working seven to seven nights. Believe me, if you think this last week was busy, you haven't seen anything yet."

Later as she drove her Ford Focus hatchback home, Sophie thought about Bob's remarks. She glanced at the envelope on the seat beside her. She had written to her mom and dad, telling them about her first week on the job and had tucked the note inside a Father's Day card. She felt guilty that the card was already a week late, but told herself that at least she had found the time to call.

Sophie scanned the street corners for a mailbox. *Bob's right about me not knowing the area. I don't even know where a mailbox is. No wonder the kids made a fool out of me tonight!* She checked her watch. *Only nine o'clock. Not tired yet.* With a determined look she drove back to the industrial area. *One thing is for certain ... within an hour or so, I'll know every alley, road, exit, building, and damned gate within that area!*

Sophie was about to learn that nothing about life is certain. Not even survival.

Melvin stood between two parked vans. With his hand inside his jacket, he stared at the front of the medical clinic, situated in the heart of Vancouver. It was twenty past nine and the sun was setting, but at the bottom of the skyscrapers, the shadows had already converged. *Soon it will be night.* He felt comforted. *Darkness is my friend.*

Melvin continued to stare through the glass. *Is she working tonight?* Just then he saw Dr. Natasha Taggart enter into the waiting room. He took a step forward, but stopped when she disappeared down a hall.

Natasha saw the slight lull in the waiting room as an opportunity to call her husband on his cellphone. He was also working that evening. Come to think of it, thought Natasha, he actually started work at eight o'clock this morning.

Jack answered, but immediately asked her to hold. She could hear him talking to someone in the background. *Female voice, probably Laura.*

Natasha hadn't bothered to ask Jack what was going on when he called her that afternoon to say he would be working late. He worked on the RCMP Intelligence Unit in Vancouver. Constable Laura Secord worked for him, but was also his partner. Their work was secret. At least Jack tried not to bring it home but sometimes it followed him.

Natasha felt herself tremble when she recalled how close she had once come to being murdered by some gangsters who intended to trap her husband. She intentionally pushed the memory from her mind.

She heard the female voice again and smiled. *It is Laura.* Jack was very fond of Laura, but she wasn't worried. She had also taken an instant liking to Laura, who was married to another Mountie.

She trusted Laura and knew that Jack thought of her like a sister. Most men wouldn't. Laura had long curly hair with a natural mixture of reds and gold that reminded Natasha of the leaves in autumn. She also had a body that would make any Hollywood starlet jealous. The important factor to Natasha, however, was that Laura was both intuitive and intelligent. For that, Natasha was thankful. Both Jack and Laura were seasoned undercover operatives whose lives often depended upon each other. There was no room for stupidity.

"Sorry, hon, I'm back," said Jack.

"Just called to say hi," replied Natasha. "You sound busy."

"Very. How about you?"

"It's quiet. Stuck my head in the waiting room and it's actually empty for the moment. Think I'll run out and bring a muffin back from the deli. You going to be home tonight? Should I wait up?"

"I don't know," replied Jack. "Call me when you get home. If I don't pick up, leave a message and I'll try to get back to you. I have to go. Love ya."

Constable Sophie White slowly drove past the graffiti on the side of the warehouse. For Sophie, it wasn't only graffiti. It was a sign of her failure to catch the kids responsible. *Next time I will be ready. Next ...*

For the next hour, Sophie drove through a maze of roads and lanes that dissected the industrial area. Not having seen another person or vehicle during the entire time, she was curious when she spotted headlights of another vehicle reflecting off the glass windows of a nearby building. *Hmm, kind of late for traffic to be here now.* She quickly parked her car and shut it off as she watched. *Have I been seen? Hope not.* She saw it was actually two cars, one immediately behind the other as they slowly meandered through the maze of warehouses. *They're back to finish the job!*

It appeared to Sophie that they may be checking to make sure they were alone. She felt her adrenalin surge as the cars drove toward her. She ducked down but peeked out over the dash as they continued past. She saw two figures in the lead car and the silhouette of one person in the car following. The cars slowed and turned down a side road.

Her view was blocked by a large warehouse, but when the cars did not reappear, she knew they had stopped. She smiled. They had parked within a two-minute walk of where she was. *Okay, kids. You're about to be caught red-handed.* She thought of the colour of paint the kids had used and snickered. *And I do mean red-handed!*

Briefly, she thought about her gun back in her locker ... *But these are just kids.* She was still in uniform, but decided to take out her leather wallet containing her shiny new badge and identification card. She couldn't resist flipping it open and the leather emitted a small creak. *I think I'll have the desired effect! Still, mental note. Buy myself a cellphone.* She smiled at the image she would soon present to her colleagues when she returned to the office in her car, followed by two cars with what were sure to be red-faced kids.

She got out of her car and quietly closed the door before creeping toward the warehouse. She kept to the shadows, her journey to hell coming closer with each step.

2

Natasha hurried from the clinic, stopping briefly at the employee parking lot to get a sweater from her car before going to the deli. Her silver Nissan Altima was parked next to a van and she consciously looked around before approaching her car. The clinic was located in a high-crime area and being cautious was second nature. She didn't see anyone, so she retrieved her sweater before locking and closing her car door. The light scrape of grit from a man's shoe behind her told her she was not alone.

She spun around and saw a man step out from behind the van. It was difficult to see his face, silhouetted by neon lights from behind, but she could see he had long hair and a beard. His hand was tucked inside his dark nylon raincoat. *Raincoat? Hot for this time of year. And it hasn't rained in over a week.*

"Who are you?" demanded Natasha, hoping the authoritative tone of her voice would hide her fear.

The response was an unintelligible whimper and he scurried out of sight behind the van. Natasha breathed a sigh of relief and she recalled a patient she had last treated months earlier.

"Melvin, is that you?" she asked.

There was no response but Natasha could hear him panting as his fright level increased. She made a wide arc around her car and came around the side of the van so that the lights were behind her and she could see his face.

"Melvin Montgomery! It is you! What is it? What's wrong?"

Melvin glanced furtively about.

Natasha knew that Melvin was neither an alcoholic nor a drug addict. His many illnesses were psychological. Among them, anthropophobia, also known as fear of people and fear of society.

With some people, anthropophobia would come and go, but with Melvin, it was a constant presence. He had a morbid aversion to human contact. It caused him panic attacks, shortness of breath, rapid breathing, irregular heartbeat, sweating, nausea, and an intense feeling of dread.

By nature, Melvin was gentle and much too afraid to seek help or remain in any environment where people were nearby. It was not an easy life. A life that forced him to live in a doorway in an alley, his existence dependent upon a few select Dumpsters behind the area restaurants.

Natasha had encountered and befriended him before. The first time she had helped him, he had made it as far as the entrance to the waiting room, but when he saw the other patients, he wouldn't come in. The receptionist became alarmed at the sight of a vagrant with an old green sleeping bag draped around his shoulders loitering outside. She notified Natasha, who went out and discovered he was suffering from an infection caused when he was bitten on his chest by an injured cat that he found. She allowed him to enter through the rear fire-escape door.

A few days after that, Melvin returned after someone roughed him up and stole the antibiotics she had prescribed. His trust for her had grown enough that he had stepped inside to let Natasha re-examine his chest in the corridor. *Maybe tonight will be easier,* she thought.

"It's okay," said Natasha. "I see you've been waiting for me. I'm here now. It's okay. Are you hurt?"

Melvin stared at Natasha for a moment before slowly taking his hand from his raincoat and holding it out. Blood seeped from a dirty rag wrapped around his hand.

"Looks like I better take a look at that," said Natasha. "What happened?"

"I fell," mumbled Melvin. "In a Dumpster. A piece of tin," he added for explanation.

Natasha sighed, not so much at the injury as to the predicament that caused it. "You should come inside so I can have a better look. You might need stitches."

Melvin looked at the clinic and shook his head, retreating farther into the shadows as two people strolled by on the sidewalk.

"It's okay," said Natasha. "There is nobody inside the waiting room. I'll walk ahead and make sure we're not bothered."

Minutes later, Natasha had achieved some success as Melvin followed her into the clinic, but before she could examine him, he sought refuge in the rear washroom.

As the minutes ticked by, Natasha heard the receptionist talking to some newly arrived patients.

"Melvin?" she said quietly. "You have to come out. You can trust me. I'll make sure nobody hurts you, but you —"

The door unlocked and Melvin stepped out. He glanced around and saw Natasha was alone. "I wasn't hiding from you," he whispered, glancing nervously down the hall. "I saw you were scared of me when we were outside. I know I don't look so good. I'm sorry."

Natasha saw that Melvin had wet his hair and slicked it back from his face in an attempt to look nicer. She smiled and said, "You did scare me, but that was before I knew it was you. I don't need to be scared of you, do I?"

Melvin looked concerned, shaking his head, then caught Natasha's smile. He gave a small smile out of embarrassment at the irony of the situation and lowered his head.

"Think you could handle coming inside an examination room with me?" asked Natasha.

Anguished, Melvin looked into the small room, but nodded and entered. Once inside, he allowed Natasha to treat his injury.

Natasha spotted a clump of cat hair on Melvin's coat and said, "By chance, that wouldn't happen to be from the same cat who bit you before?"

Melvin shyly nodded and said, "I adopted him. I call him Winston."

"Good name," replied Natasha. "Last time we talked you mentioned he had just lost his front leg. How is he doing?"

"That was when we first met. He had crawled up into the engine compartment of a parked truck to keep warm. When the guy came back and started his truck and drove off, I think Winston caught his leg in the radiator fan, but he's better now, thanks."

"You said he took off after he bit you. Did he come back again later?"

"No, it took a few days of looking but I found him a few blocks away. He didn't mean to bite me. He was just hurting. We're friends now."

"Does he have trouble getting around?"

"He can run faster than me," replied Melvin. "He is also afraid of people. Especially cars and trucks." Melvin smiled at Natasha and added, "Yeah, I know what you're thinking. Winston and I are kind of the same."

Natasha's smile revealed that Melvin had read her thoughts correctly.

"At night, he crawls into my sleeping bag with me and sleeps curled up on my chest."

"The piece of tin you fell on left quite a cut," said Natasha, changing the subject. "I'm sure it's painful."

"Yeah, but don't worry. I won't bite you," grinned Melvin.

* * *

Mad Dog scanned his rear-view mirror one last time before pulling in behind the warehouse and parking. Snake and Looner, who were in the car in front of him, had also parked. Mad Dog shut off his headlights and sat for a moment, peering around in the darkness. He lowered the car window and listened. He saw Snake get out of his car and stand scanning the area, as well. Looner was less cautious and gave Mad Dog a friendly smile as he approached.

"Let's do it," said Looner.

"Shut the fuck up and listen for a moment," said Mad Dog.

Looner listened briefly and said, "I don't hear nothin'."

After a pause, Mad Dog replied, "Me either, but after this afternoon, I ain't takin' no fuckin' chances. You search 'im good?" asked Mad Dog, with a nod of his head toward Snake.

"Yeah, real good," replied Looner. "He ain't gonna rip us. It's only you and me that got pieces," he said, patting the butt of the .44-calibre semi-automatic pistol stuck in his waistband. "Besides," added Looner, "I trust him. Can't say as I feel the same about Pete and Bongo, though."

Mad Dog tried to qualm the rage he felt in order to think. It had been a bad couple of days. Less than three weeks out of prison for serving most of a four-year sentence for armed robbery and he was nearly arrested again yesterday afternoon. *What the fuck happened?*

He replayed yesterday's scenario over again in his head. He had already picked up his stash of killing machines. Two Mac-10s with silencers, two Uzis, and three Desert Eagle .44-calibre magnum semi-automatic pistols. As planned, he was to deliver them to everyone two hours before the armoured truck arrived.

Mad Dog was on his way when things fell apart. He spotted the same car that ran a red light behind him the day before. Checking a piece of paper in his pocket confirmed that the number he had scrawled down was the same plate. He exchanged eye contact with the pig driving the car. The pig knew he had been burned and tried to cut him off in traffic. Mad Dog knew he had been extremely lucky. *Lucky that I got a good memory for numbers. Lucky to get away.*

Immediately he called Snake and Looner on their cellphones. He was in time to warn them. Pete and Bongo were not so lucky. *So how did the pigs find out about it?*

The plan to rob the guards from the Brinks armoured truck was something he had thought about constantly during his last year in jail. It was all he and Looner had talked about. The other men were hand-picked later. Looner had been released two months ahead of him. *Did Looner say something to earn an early release? Then again, he's so stupid, he could have let it slip accidentally.*

Then there were Snake, Pete, and Bongo. Snake came recommended through Ophelia, a hooker he knew and trusted. Pete and Bongo were guys he had met in a bar. Both said they were addicts. He believed they would want the money as much as he did. Were they really arrested? Or was one of them the rat? There was his own girlfriend, Julie. She had visited Mad Dog regularly when he was in jail. *Was it her? Had she found someone else when I was inside …? Naw, the bitch loves me.*

Mad Dog warily glanced at Snake and Looner. Now it was every man for himself. Unlike Looner, he didn't trust anyone … including Looner, who was too stupid to know the pistol Mad Dog gave him wasn't loaded.

Snake was another story. He was smart and Mad Dog knew he hadn't earned his nickname by being nice. Now survival was the name of the game … and being around someone like Snake made him nervous.

No place was safe and he was broke. Except for one thing. He had a trunk full of a very valuable commodity. With luck, he and Julie would get enough cash to slip into the States and make their way to Mexico. Snake knew some bikers willing to pay top dollar. *The trick is to sell the guns and get the money without being shot or robbed by either Snake or the bikers.*

Mad Dog was happy with the scenario that had been negotiated. Julie and Snake's girlfriend would both wait in a motel. Snake would pick up Looner, who would search Snake and his car, just to keep him honest. Looner would take Snake to meet Mad Dog, who would give him the guns, except for two Desert Eagles that he and Looner carried. He would keep one for his run to Mexico. Looner would keep the other.

When Snake got the guns, he was to call his girl-friend, who would then call the bikers to bring the money to the motel. Julie would turn over the ammo for the guns and the bikers would take Snake's girlfriend as a hostage until Snake delivered the guns to them.

Mad Dog glanced up at the sky as he walked to the rear of the car. There was a full moon, which pleased him. He knew a remote road behind Cultus Lake that would take him close enough to an area where he could walk through the bush and cross the border into the States. It would be better if he didn't have to use a flash-light. He had used the route before when he had helped his brother import cocaine. With luck, he and Julie would be in the States within the next couple of hours.

He and Looner were to part company near the U.S. border. Looner would drop him and Julie off and take the car. Looner's plan was to hide out with a girl-friend in Prince George. Mad Dog knew Looner would be caught sooner or later, but it would help him if the cops didn't find a stolen car ditched near Cultus Lake and put two and two together.

Snake wasn't talkative about his plan to escape. *Likely crawl back into the same hole he came out of and wait until the heat died down.*

Mad Dog took a deep breath before popping the trunk as Looner and Snake gathered around to look inside.

"As promised," said Mad Dog, fingering the butt of his .44 as Snake bent over to examine the guns.

A woman's voice screamed behind him, "Police! You're not going anywhere this time!"

Constable Sophie White saw three men spin around to face her. She gasped when she saw two of them were pointing pistols at her. One man straightened his arm to shoulder height, aiming it at her face as his finger started to squeeze the trigger.

3

"Wait!" Snake yelled at Mad Dog. "The pig-bitch doesn't even have her piece out. There could be more of them," he said, glancing around nervously. "If there's others, she could be our ticket out of here!"

Mad Dog stared at the young woman in front of him as she dropped her police identification on the ground and slowly raised her hands. *Something sure as hell don't make sense! How come there ain't an army of pigs with guns?*

"Why is she here by herself?" asked Mad Dog before looking at Sophie and demanding, "What the fuck are you doing here? How did you know we were here?"

"I … I don't know who you are," she replied, her voice barely audible. "My, my partner and I were on our way home. I left my gun and portable radio in the car with him."

"Why are you here?" snarled Mad Dog.

"I just, I mean, we … there were some kids who were vandalizing some of these buildings earlier tonight. We were checking it again on the way home."

Mad Dog stared at her silently for a moment and then said, "I think she's lying. If she had a partner, why isn't he with her?" He glanced at Looner and said, "You want to shoot her?" Remembering that Looner's gun was empty, he added, "Never mind. Fuck it, I'll do it!"

"Hang on," said Snake. "I don't wanna get busted for killin' a cop if I don't need to. Do that and the cops will be huntin' us down for as long as we live."

"We got no choice," said Mad Dog. "The pigs will figure out who we are. Besides, she's seen our cars. I don't have time to rip another one off. Too risky under the circumstances. I gotta get outta here. There's no fuckin' way I'm goin' back inside."

"We just got here," observed Snake. "She's gotta be parked close. Find her wheels. We'll tie her up and lock her in the trunk of her car."

"Tie her up with what?" asked Mad Dog.

"If we don't have somethin', then I'll rip some wires out from under the hood of her car. We'll be long gone before anyone finds her."

"We ain't got time for that," said Mad Dog.

"Fuck, what will it take? Five minutes?" Snake looked at Sophie and yelled, "Empty your pockets, pig!"

Sophie's keys fell to the ground. "My car is over there," she pointed. "I'm alone," she confessed, meekly.

Mad Dog paused, but looked at Snake and said, "Okay. Five minutes max. Looner, grab the keys and bring her car here."

Looner did as instructed and a couple of minutes later, he pulled up in Sophie's Ford Focus and got out.

"It's a fuckin' hatchback!" said Mad Dog. "I sure as fuck ain't leavin' her in no hatchback! At least, not alive!" He was still a short distance away from Sophie, but before he could take proper aim, Looner pulled the pistol out of his belt and stepped between and said, "Want me to do it, Mad Dog?"

"No, I'll do it," replied Mad Dog. "Next time can be your turn. Open up the door to her car and make her get in the back seat. You get out of the way, too, Snake."

Looner opened up the car door and clicked the lever on the seat with the barrel of his pistol, allowing the front seat to spring forward, before stepping back.

Snake moved closer to Sophie and said with a sneer, "Guess it ain't your lucky day, is it pig? Guess it's nighty-night time for —" He stopped, his eyes ogling her body. "Holy shit!" he said, running his fingers up the side of her ribcage. "You're a fine piece of meat, ain't ya?"

Sophie stared back. She was shaking and she felt the need to vomit.

Snake gave an evil grin and added, "Maybe it's your day to get lucky." He looked back at Mad Dog and said, "I ain't never fucked a pig before!"

"I don't have time for that," said Mad Dog. "Get out of the way so I can do what I gotta do."

"You don't have time for that?" said Snake, letting out a short laugh. "Oh, baby, I always got time for that!"

Before Mad Dog could reply, Snake spun around and buried his fist deep into Sophie's midriff. She slumped toward the ground as Snake grabbed her.

"Snake, what the fuck you doing?" asked Mad Dog.

"Puttin' her in the back seat," Snake replied, "like you said," he added, tossing Sophie into the back of her car. He glanced at her as she was squirming and gasping for breath. "Bet it isn't your first time in a back seat with a man, is it, my little pork tenderloin?"

Snake turned to Mad Dog and lowered his voice and said, "Come on, give me a piece. I'll have a little fun with her. Won't take me but a minute or two. Then I'll shoot the bitch and torch her and the car."

Mad Dog hesitated. He was about to say no, but it occurred to him that lady luck had handed him an ace he could keep up his sleeve to guarantee his freedom. If he was caught running the border tonight, even with the attempted armed robbery yesterday, being able to hand over a cop-killer would be the best "get out of jail card" he could ever have. *The only trouble is I gotta make sure I don't let Snake shoot me, too, and take the guns or money for himself.*

Mad Dog smiled and said, "Looner, toss him the other .44." He then ejected one bullet from his gun and said, "Give him that." He glared at Snake and said, "One bullet only!"

"That's all I need for that little pig," said Snake.

Sophie watched from the back seat of the car. Any hope she had of grabbing Snake's gun and gaining her freedom was dashed. *Even if I get the gun ... one bullet, three men ... my only chance is to convince them not to kill me.* She looked at their faces and knew that was unlikely. *I'm going to die and there's nothing I can do about it!*

Seconds later, Snake cautiously picked up the gun. Looner followed Mad Dog's lead and also pointed his pistol at Snake.

Snake grinned and said, "Come on guys, after what we've been through together?"

"It's because of what we've been through," replied Mad Dog. "Besides, I know your rep. Hurry up. When you're done, shoot the pig, then call your ol' lady and tell her ya got the guns. Don't torch the car until after Looner and I leave. Now … hurry the fuck up!"

Sophie cringed back in the seat as Snake leaned in.

"Lie on your back with your arms underneath ya!" ordered Snake. "I don't want ya grabbin' at no gun!"

Sophie did as instructed and Snake crawled in on top of her while pointing a gun at her face. She felt his knee force her legs apart and was conscious of the gun beside her temple.

"Please, don't," she pleaded. "I'm a cop. Think about it. You hurt me and you go away for life. Just take my car keys and drive off."

"Ya know somethin'," said Snake, "actually, I'm a nice guy. If it was me, maybe I would. But my friends … well, they ain't gonna let that happen, so ya may as well enjoy it. Treat it like it's your last!"

Sophie heard Looner chuckle at Snake's comment. In her mind, she thought it odd that she sensed a partial satisfaction by thinking that DNA might be found inside her body. *I'm going to be raped and murdered … and I'm thinking about DNA …*

"Give me a hand, will ya Looner?" yelled Snake, while leaning back and tugging on Sophie's belt.

"Grab her fuckin' pants by the cuffs and help pull 'em off for me!"

Sophie felt Looner yank her shoes off and toss them in the front seat. Snake leered at her and said, "Now if you're real co-operative, maybe I'll decide you're worth livin'."

As he leaned closer she could feel his warm and moist breath on the side of her neck and then her ear.

Looner leaped back as Snake cried out.

"You fuckin' bitch!" screamed Snake.

"What happened?" asked Looner.

"She kneed me in the nuts!"

"Jesus fuck," said Mad Dog. "Shoot her. Enough is enough."

Sophie was dazed, confused, and in shock as Snake pointed the gun at her face. He looked unafraid and calm, as if he had done this many times before. She closed her eyes and felt one of his hands choke her jugular as he held her head still.

The car echoed to the sound of the explosion and both Mad Dog and Looner watched as Snake backed out of the car. His hands and face were splattered with blood. He looked at Mad Dog, gave a wicked smile and said, "I thought pigs would squeal more than that. Bet she would have if I coulda fucked her before blowin' her face off!"

Mad Dog peered in the back seat at Sophie's body, curious what damage a .44 magnum would do. Now he knew. Her face was drenched in blood.

"Ya got a rag for me to wipe my hands?" asked Snake nonchalantly. It occurred to Mad Dog that it was the same tone of voice a person might use to ask for a napkin after eating fried chicken.

"The pieces are wrapped in rags," Mad Dog reminded him. "I'll grab ya one of 'em. Better wipe your face, too."

Seconds later, the weapons were loaded in the trunk of Snake's car and Mad Dog listened as Snake called the motel to speak to his girlfriend. "Done deal. Got 'em all. Went as smooth as your silk undies."

Mad Dog glanced at Snake and the Ford Focus in his rear-view mirror as he and Looner drove away. *Smooth as silk? Snake's nickname is perfect. Cold-blooded reptile.*

A short time later, Mad Dog breathed a sigh of relief when Julie answered the door at the motel and gestured to the money she had piled on the bed.

"You count it?" asked Looner, running past Mad Dog to look at the money.

"Three times," she replied.

"Snake's ol' lady?" asked Mad Dog.

"She's got their cut and a biker took her away. Hope Snake loves her enough to deliver. Otherwise she'll be workin' on her back forever to pay for it."

"Who cares," replied Mad Dog. "Pack up. We're leavin' —"

Mad Dog's words were lost at the sound of breaking glass as the first of three percussion grenades came through the motel window. The explosions left them all in a momentary state of shock and confusion.

Seconds later, Mad Dog looked up at the RCMP Emergency Response Team from where he was hand-cuffed on the floor. "Who's in charge? I need to talk to someone who works on murders."

Looner looked at Mad Dog from across the floor and said, "What the fuck ya sayin'? Get a lawyer! Don't talk to nobody!"

Mad Dog smiled and said, "Don't worry about it. We don't need a fuckin' lawyer. The three of us will be free by morning. I guarantee it!"

4

Sophie stared up at the ceiling of the car as she replayed what had happened. Snake had crawled in on top of her, trying to undo her pants while pinning her arms with his knees as he waved his pistol at her face. *I did try to knee him in the nuts … but he was expecting it and turned sideways. Whispers to me to play dead and starts choking me so hard I can't breathe … before smashing my nose with the butt of the gun. Then screams like I hurt him and pulls the trigger — Doesn't make sense.*

The car door opened and Sophie could hear Snake talking. She closed her eyes and realized he was talking on his cellphone. *He thinks I'm dead! The bullet went through my hair … but the blood from my nose got smeared all over my face by his hand when he pushed himself out … he thinks he shot me in the face and that I'm dead.*

Sophie lay still, trying to control her breathing. Despite the ringing she had in one ear, the sound of her heartbeat seemed to echo loudly inside the car. She heard Snake's voice as he tilted the driver's seat forward.

"Good. Let me know when it's a done deal," he said. Sophie heard the call end, but his phone rang immediately.

She felt a trickle of blood running down the back of her throat and into her lungs. She felt the need to cough. Her body demanded air and she willed herself not to breathe. *Focus on something different. I can't! I have to breathe!*

"Oh, hi, honey," she heard Snake say. "You just get home? Sorry I can't talk. Have to keep the line clear so — no, wait, actually I'm glad you did call."

Sophie tried to swallow, but let out a small cough instead. *Snake quit talking! He heard me! My only chance is to grab him!* She sprang to attack. Snake saw it coming and casually let the front seat drop back into place while stepping back. She was trapped. *Too late to fumble for the seat release. I'm dead!*

Snake looked at her and held up one finger for her to wait a moment as he spoke into the phone. "I've got a police woman with a broken nose ... No, not Laura ... No, I don't expect you to look at it. We're way out in Surrey ... Uh, huh. Tell her to sit up and pinch the lower part of her nose for ten minutes. Got it. While she's doing that, I'll take her to Surrey Memorial. Listen, I should go. She's upset. Love ya."

What the hell? Sophie thought.

* * *

Mad Dog was placed in an interview room where he was introduced to Staff Sergeant Randy Otto and Corporal Connie Crane, both members of the Integrated Homicide Investigative team, or I-HIT, as it was more commonly known.

Mad Dog smiled with satisfaction, quickly waived his right to a lawyer, and gave a detailed statement of his plan to rob an armoured truck. He also said he bought the guns in the United States and smuggled them across the border on foot. When he finished signing the statement, he leaned back from the table and said, "Time for a little bombshell for ya. The stuff I just told you about is chicken feed."

"Really?" said Connie, raising an eyebrow. "You think with your record that conspiracy to commit armed robbery is chicken feed?"

"Oh, yeah," said Mad Dog smugly. "That is definitely chicken feed. Somethin' else happened after I got away from ya yesterday."

"Oh?" asked Connie. "What would that be?"

"A murder," replied Mad Dog.

"We're listening," said Randy, sounding bored and glancing at his watch.

Mad Dog smiled. "You don't look impressed." He snickered and added, "That's 'cause you don't know who was wasted yet." He leaned forward, savouring the moment, while drumming the fingers of both hands on the desk, waiting to hear their pleas for more information. Neither Randy nor Connie responded. The drumming slowed and eventually stopped.

Mad Dog leered silently for a moment, chuckled, and smacked his palms together, emitting a loud clap before using his hands to take an imaginary shot at Randy and Connie. "Bang! Bang! It was one of you!" he blurted out.

Neither Randy nor Connie showed any emotion as Mad Dog anxiously looked back and forth at them both for a response.

"Bang, bang?" said Randy, looking at Connie.

She shrugged in response. "We're both fine," said Connie.

"You guys don't understand!" said Mad Dog. "Not you! Another cop. It just happened. You don't know about it yet. A woman cop near some warehouses in Surrey. She was murdered. I saw the guy shoot her!"

"What do you think?" asked Connie as she looked at Randy.

"Not interested," replied Randy.

"What the fuck?" yelled Mad Dog. "What do ya mean you're not interested? I ain't bullshittin' ya. Everything in my statement is true! You let us walk and I'll give ya a cop killer. Fuck, I could probably even call him and set him up for ya!"

"Appreciate it," said Connie, "but after careful consideration, we're not interested in letting you off to catch this other guy."

Connie and Randy could no longer control their mirth, which did nothing to ease Mad Dog's enraged response as he snarled and sputtered, demanding that a car be sent to the location where he swore the murder had taken place.

"You have never really been formally introduced to Snake, have you?" Connie finally asked.

"You already know his name!" said Mad Dog, startled that the ace up his sleeve had already been discovered.

"His real name is Corporal Jack Taggart," said Connie. "He is an undercover RCMP officer."

Mad Dog's mouth hung open in disbelief as Randy pointed a finger at him and said, "Bang, bang."

Mad Dog swallowed in disbelief. "You let an undercover cop kill another cop?"

Randy rolled his eyes and turned to Connie and said, "I want his girlfriend charged under section 153.1 of the Criminal Code."

"What section is that?" asked Connie.

"Having sex with a person with a mental disability."

Corporal Jack Taggart and Constable Laura Secord took several sophisticated and deadly weapons out of the hands of criminals. The catch-and-release program of the justice system saw several more offenders retagged and held again. At least for the moment.

Neither Jack nor Laura knew that the next night, a person using a cheap pistol would commit a murder that would ultimately carve permanent nightmares into their brains for as long as they each lived.

This murder involved someone not known to the

police. A dedicated professional who was known only to a select few of Vancouver's top organized crime figures. They privately referred to him as The Enabler. His real name was Kang Lee.

5

Kang Lee checked his watch as he arrived at the Avitat Lounge at the South Terminal of the Vancouver International Airport. The northern windows offered a view of the runway generally utilized by private aircraft. *I'm right on time. As it should be. Punctuality is a window to a man's character and integrity.*

He adjusted the Thai-silk handkerchief in the breast of his Liana Lee cashmere silk suit: a suit he'd had tailored for himself last year after a visit to Lee's store on New York's Lexington Avenue. It was a gift to himself for his fiftieth birthday. With a price tag of over eight thousand dollars, it was his favourite suit. *Displays elegance and grace.* He knew he was partially persuaded to purchase it from Lee, because she, like himself, was originally from Korea. That they coincidentally shared the same surname was not important, as Lee is the second most common name in South Korea.

His shoes, made by Salvatore Ferragamo, were a mocha crocodile with a price tag of fifteen hundred dollars. His watch, the Leman model made by Blancpain, with its crocodile strap and eighteen-karat-gold clasp, cost considerably more than his suit and shoes combined.

His head was shaved, further accenting the one-karat diamond stud protruding from one earlobe. Although he was short by Western standards, barely reaching the height of many men's chests, his confidence and manner exuded a strength that caused most people to instinctively make way for him.

His ensemble helped to make him feel powerful amongst men. *Is it wrong to dress in a manner that demonstrates my real power? Of course not!*

As he waited, he thought of the reason why his boss was coming to meet him. The number two man in their organization had recently died of a heart attack while being entertained by two women in a thermal hot springs. *Not a bad way to die … if you must die. And so it comes to pass that one man's loss is another man's gain.*

He knew he was being considered as a replacement. His only real competition was a man who worked out of their office in Palermo. *Like me, he lords over a few of that country's top crime bosses. Of course, they don't realize it. They think we only enable them in their pursuit for wealth and power … when will they realize that we also control the strings that decide their very existence?*

He brooded when he thought about his competition. In some ways, it wasn't fair. Italy had been established with the appropriate networks dating back hundreds of years. *Some families there have become multi-generational in their acceptance of graft ... or the knowledge of what will happen should you refuse. It is natural that Italy would produce higher revenue. By comparison, Vancouver is brand new ... I have only been here four years ...*

He paused to look out the window and take in the dynamics of the airport. *But the potential is astronomic!* He smiled. *Surely it has been recognized that I have done well? I have seen that our interests are well established with smuggling immigrants, protection, heroin, ecstasy.... It is more challenging to set up new pathways. Any accounting clerk could run Palermo. My assignment demands tact and presence of mind. Convincing local syndicates that I am not competition, but someone with the connections to greatly enhance their revenue by lowering the risk of police or customs interference. It takes time. The boss must understand that?*

He glanced out the window and saw his boss's executive jet touch down on the runway. The jet was a Falcon 50EX. Its three powerful engines were capable of reaching intercontinental destinations while travelling at Mach .80. It was also designed to use backcountry airfields with shorter runways when necessary. Lee had been on the aircraft when his business called for such a backcountry rendezvous — places where customs officials were often no more than hired peasants with uniforms — people who could be bribed for as little as a bottle of whiskey or a carton of cigarettes.

He knew that his boss's bodyguards; Da Khlot and Sayomi, would be on board the jet. *I should have such people*. Lee smiled, recalling Da Khlot's nickname for his boss: The Shaman.

Da Khlot, born into a mountain tribe in Cambodia, really believed that their boss had mystical powers. Control of the spirits. Either for the good of a community ... or to wreak terror. Control of anything he desired. Lee knew that shamanism was still popular in Korea as well. Usually a shaman was a woman, but not always. *Perhaps Khlot is right ...*

The jet rolled past, its three engines screaming like banshees, as if protesting their shackled entities to the jet and their subservient existence to the man inside.

Lee caught his own reflection in the glass superimposed over the jet. *Having to live in Vancouver ... am I really only a big fish in a small pond? When will ... The Shaman ... allow me to return home and fulfill the destiny that is surely mine to —*

He lurched forward as a duffle bag connected with the back of his head. A heavy-set woman hurrying past with the bag slung over her shoulder stopped.

"Sorry, kid. Are you okay?" she asked apologetically, turning around. Realizing her second blunder, she said, "I mean ... sir. Sorry, I thought you were ... I just caught you out of the corner of my eye. Are you okay?"

"I am quite all right," replied Lee tersely, while straightening the neckline of his suit jacket. "Perhaps if you were more punctual, you wouldn't have the need to rampage around the airport like a fat cow with cataracts!"

* * *

Da Khlot glanced out the window of the Falcon 50EX as it approached the terminal. He was a long way from his birthplace in the jungle of Cambodia.

Life had not been kind to Da Khlot. His fourteen-year-old orphaned mother was raped and he was an unwelcome outcome of that atrocity. He was eleven years old in February 1975, when his mother died after stepping on one of an estimated 5 million land-mines left in Cambodia from a host of warring factions. It was the same year the Khmer Rouge came to power and he was promptly taken in as a soldier for that regime.

Over the next four years, the Khmer Rouge, under the command of Pol Pot, were responsible for an estimated 1.5 million deaths of their fellow citizens. A large number for a country that had a population of only 7.5 million.

Along with other newly recruited soldiers, Da Khlot was taken to open pits containing bound and captive people who had been deemed enemies of the country. He and other newly recruited children were given pickaxes and made to kill the prisoners before they were buried in mass graves. Some of these enemies were Da Khlot's neighbours. People who fell into the category of professionals and intellectuals ... or anyone wearing eyeglasses, for that matter, as they were deemed by the Khmer Rouge to be literate and thereby a threat to the new regime.

Da Khlot was told that by using pickaxes they would save bullets. In the beginning, he, along with other children, cried as much as the victims, but fear drove them to obey. Eventually the tears dried up along with any emotion he felt. Obeying came without question.

In December 1978, Cambodian forces invaded Vietnam. They were repressed and Vietnam retaliated by invading Cambodia and seizing the capital, Phnom Penh. As a result, the four-year reign of terror by the Khmer Rouge was toppled, but the resistance movement of the Khmer Rouge continued to fight on in western Cambodia from bases hidden in Thailand. The Khmer Rouge were "unofficially" aided by the Thai Army and the United States Special Forces. Diamond and timber smuggling were used to bring in money to supplement their needs.

In 1996, Pol Pot signed a peace agreement officially ending the movement. By then, Da Khlot had become a high-ranking guerrilla leader with twenty-one years of experience at torture and murder. Although he was an expert marksman, he was particularly renowned for his ability with a knife.

Da Khlot knew the spot on the back of a person's neck in which to plunge a knife and cause instant paralysis. The victims would collapse in a heap, but their eyes revealed their horror as their brains wondered how long Da Khlot would let them live — sometimes hours, sometimes longer, depending on the impression Da Khlot wanted to make on other prisoners.

To obey and kill without question. It was all Da Khlot really knew how to do, but during the late 1990s his profession was quickly coming to an end.

Many of the top Khmer Rouge leaders were being captured and imprisoned for war crimes and crimes against humanity.

It was Da Khlot's knowledge of the smuggling routes and vital contacts that allowed him to survive in the jungles for nearly seven years. He had a rudimentary knowledge of English — the universal language of understanding in the higher echelon of a trade, where numerous ethnic groups did business together. Heroin was soon added to the smuggling list and the money was no longer being taken by the Khmer Rouge.

For a while, Da Khlot thought fate was smiling kindly upon him. Then, in July 2005, he was arrested near the Thai border by Cambodian Special Forces soldiers. Under armed escort, he was brought to a small airfield to be flown to Phnom Penh, where he knew he would eventually be executed for his crimes.

As he sat handcuffed and in leg irons in a small office awaiting transport at the airfield, he counted the number of Special Forces soldiers guarding him. *Six! True, I am a large man. Perhaps even bigger than most Westerners. But six! A child with a pickaxe could do what it takes six of these men to do …*

Jubilant, these men knew the prize they had caught and were taking no chances. By tomorrow, he would be front page news. *Now it is I who kneels in the pit. Waiting and listening to the screams as my turn approaches. Perhaps I will be lucky enough to throw myself out of the helicopter. Cheat them of the torture of waiting.*

He did not hear the expected rhythmic beat of an olive-drab Soviet-made Mi-8/17 helicopter from the

Royal Cambodian Air Force arrive to whisk him away. His salvation arrived — in the form of a Falcon 50EX jet.

The impossible was made possible. A man of unlimited influence had arrived. A man capable of changing one's destiny.

The top soldier bowed when the newcomer emerged from the jet and Da Khlot was taken from the room and paraded in front of the newcomer. Then it happened. This man, this shaman, told the soldiers they had made a mistake. Da Khlot had never been fingerprinted. Confirmation of his identity was strictly visual. *At least, that was the official version,* thought Da Khlot wryly. *I wonder how much was paid for my release?*

It was Da Khlot's first ride in an aircraft, let alone a luxury jet. He was also given a new job. He was told he was to be a bodyguard.

Da Khlot soon learned that he was much more than a bodyguard. He was used to quietly fulfill The Shaman's wishes in some of the countries they visited. He was of particular use in countries where guns were not available due to the annoyance of certain customs regulations.

Much like my early days as a soldier … bullets are not always available. It does not matter; I am an expert with a knife — or even a pickaxe.

Da Khlot never questioned The Shaman's orders or why someone was chosen to enter the spirit world. Khlot lived by a motto from his days with the Khmer Rouge: *To keep you is no benefit. To destroy you is no loss.*

Da Khlot wiped his sweaty palms on his pants. He was seated facing the cockpit at the rear of the plane. Despite his unwavering faith in The Shaman, he was never comfortable in the air. *After all, it is I who is mortal …*

"Feel better?" asked Sayomi. A stifled smile betraying her amusement.

Da Khlot stared passively at Sayomi, who was sitting in another overstuffed lamb's leather seat facing him. *She is like an annoying mosquito in the jungle who finds a hole in the net over where I sleep. Why does this spoiled young Japanese woman take such delight in my discomfort?*

"Ignoring me, are you?" she chided, tossing her long black hair over her shoulder with a flick of her head.

She is beautiful … when she is quiet. Does she think she is better than me? Yes, she has a third degree black belt in kick-boxing … capable, she says, of breaking a man's neck. But even she admits she has never killed. Who is she fooling? Herself? Her being a bodyguard is only polite address for her real function. That of being The Shaman's mistress. Any whore could fill that role —

"Perhaps your ears don't work so well anymore," suggested Sayomi. "I asked if you were no longer afraid?"

"I am not afraid," replied Khlot, staring back, his face without expression. *You grow older every day. Your beauty fades with the knowledge of who you become. Perhaps soon, another young woman will catch The Shaman's eye and he will decide that to keep you is no benefit …*

Da Khlot abruptly turned his attention to The Shaman, who glanced back from his seat near the front of the plane. A slight nod from The Shaman commanded his presence.

"Don't forget to bow," teased Sayomi. "Otherwise the next person you may be ordered to kill for not showing respect could be yourself."

Da Khlot ignored her as he quickly made his way forward, bowed respectfully, and took a seat across from The Shaman.

The Shaman, eyes focused on his laptop, finished reviewing the latest news posted on the Internet by Canadian newspapers; including the *Vancouver Sun*. Keeping up to date on the latest news from the countries he visited had become a ritual. Any articles of interest, such as pending court decisions regarding the legality of criminal proceedings or sentencing practices, were kept for reference. Over the last few years, he was constantly encouraged by what he read concerning British Columbia.

The Shaman looked gravely at Da Khlot and said, "This mission is of the utmost importance."

Da Khlot remained stoic. *Are not all of The Shaman's missions important?*

"Your duty as an observer on this mission does not mean that I have lost faith in you. Quite the opposite. Loyalty is what it is all about. Do you understand?"

Da Khlot nodded, although he didn't really understand.

"I expect that tomorrow night you will need to wear your new suit," said The Shaman. "Make sure you do not lose a button on the suit jacket," he added, with a smile.

Da Khlot did not question why his new suit was equipped with a hidden video camera and a lens that looked like a button. *I am but a soldier. I obey. Tomorrow night someone will die. It does not matter why.*

Natasha awoke at the sound of Jack's key unlocking the front door to their apartment. She leaned over and turned on a bedside light, before quickly brushing her shoulder-length black hair with her fingertips.

"You're awake," said Jack, sounding pleased, as he entered the room.

"Couldn't sleep," replied Natasha. "Got turned on reading a sexy article and decided to wait up."

Jack glanced at a copy of *Canadian Medical Association Journal* on the bedside table. "Pretty hot stuff! Are you going to give me another night class in human anatomy?"

"The thought crossed my mind."

"Think you can wait until I shower?"

"You'll need another one when I'm done with — hey! That's blood on your shirt."

"Not mine. It's from that policewoman with the broken nose I told you about. She's okay, other than looking like a racoon. Now you know why I need to shower."

"Everything go okay?"

"Yes, it went fine. Some bad guys went back to jail tonight."

"Good. Go shower. I'll stay awake, but don't take too long."

"Do you mean you'll stay awake while I'm in the shower ... or after?"

Natasha replied by throwing a pillow at him.

Jack chuckled, caught the pillow, and threw it back. Then something else caught his attention. He picked up an imitation red rose off of their dresser. Its stem and leaves were green plastic and the red flower was made from silk. The flower was extremely faded and it was obvious it had spent many years in the sun. "What's this?" he asked, placing one hand over his heart as if overwhelmed by her thoughtfulness.

"That's not for you! A man ... it was given to me."

"Is that a fact?" Jack raised an eyebrow and added, "Well, although it is a symbol of love, I think I should warn you, that it is imitation only. Whoever the rogue is, I suspect his feelings for you are likely about as genuine as this rose."

"Oh, I don't know," replied Natasha. "I believe his feelings are sincere."

"Really?" replied Jack, sounding intrigued as he examined it more closely. "By a small piece of broken eggshell on the underside of one leaf, I would guess that you had breakfast with this new lover of yours?"

Natasha laughed and said, "Okay, I confess. It was under my windshield wiper when I left work."

"A secret admirer," said Jack. "This is getting more interesting all the time."

"Not so secret," replied Natasha. "A grateful patient who is too shy to deliver it personally. His name is Melvin."

"Should I be jealous?" asked Jack, pursing his lips

in an attempt not to smile.

"Depends on your performance after your shower," replied Natasha, sounding mischievous. "And how quick you come to bed. Not to mention, as I recall, it is you who tends to fall asleep all too soon sometimes."

"I'll be fast," said Jack, placing the rose back on the dresser. "Laura and I want to be at work by eight," he added, while setting the alarm clock.

"By eight! That's only five hours away. Can't you sleep in a little longer? I thought you were working afternoons on Monday. I don't go in until after lunch."

"Sorry, hon," replied Jack, letting out a sigh. "Our new boss starts tomorrow. Staff Sergeant Rosemary Wood. I should be there to greet her on her first day. I'll take Tuesday morning off. I promise. I'll even bring you breakfast in bed."

"You better."

Jack undressed and then disappeared into their ensuite.

"What is she like?" Natasha called after him. "Do you think she's going to be okay?"

"Who?" asked Jack, his mind reflecting back to earlier in the evening and the look of terror on the face of a petrified young woman in the back seat of a car.

"Your new boss. Didn't you check her out? You said she was coming in from Toronto."

"Oh, her. I never heard her name until last week. Don't know much about her, other than she worked on terrorism."

Natasha heard the sound of the shower come on,

but Jack yelled back, "I did hear she got in trouble over an illegal search of some office."

Natasha caught the tone of Jack's voice. *He sounded happy. Why would that please him?* She paused a moment and understood. *Birds of a feather …*

She rolled over and caught a glimpse of the full moon shining in around the edges of the drapes. She flicked off the bedside light and got up and opened them. It was a clear night and the moon shone brightly into the room. *Definitely more romantic.*

The moonlight cast an elongated replica shadow of the rose on her dresser. Lying in the shadow was a silver necklace, the moon illuminating its singular large pearl.

Jack had received the necklace as a gift from a man he once helped. *Somehow, the two gifts seem to go together.* She looked out at the night sky. *The world can be a wonderful place. People can be so kind. So much life and beauty.*

But within the next twenty-four hours, Natasha's mood would change — when the man she cared for was beaten, kidnapped, and murdered.

6

It was quarter to eight in the morning when Jack and Laura arrived at work, but not as early as their new boss, who had arrived an hour earlier. Staff Sergeant Rosemary Wood beckoned them in to her office and introductions were made.

Jack guessed she was about six or seven years older than he was, putting her in her early to mid forties. She was tall, and judging by her build, he suspected she ran marathons. Her hair was blonde and cropped. He sensed she was studying him with some curiosity. It should have made him nervous, but the hint of bemusement on her face told him not to worry.

"Do you prefer we call you Staff?" asked Laura.

"I prefer Rose," she replied. "Please, both of you take a seat. Make yourselves comfortable."

"Named after Rosewood?" asked Jack, as he sat down. "That small town in Florida where the Ku Klux

Klan massacred people back in the 1920s."

Rose smiled and said, "I prefer to think my name is symbolic with rosewood, the type used in musical instruments."

Jack smiled. *Good, she has a sense of humour.*

"Checking to see if I have a sense of humour, are you?" asked Rose.

Jack felt slightly taken back. *Okay, lady. One point for you.* He gave a quick grin in response.

"Do you two always come in so early?" asked Rose. "I'm aware that you both worked an undercover operation over the weekend and worked late last night. I didn't expect to see you today."

"We had planned on working an afternoon shift, but thought we should honour you with our presence for your first day here," replied Jack.

"I see," she replied. "A couple of brown-nosers."

Jack chuckled and replied, "If you think that about us, I suggest you ask our previous boss. He might disagree."

Rose smiled and said, "That would be Staff Quaile. Yes, I heard about your relationship with him."

"You've done your homework," said Jack.

"It wasn't hard. Rather curious, really."

"Oh?" asked Jack.

"Are either of you aware of where I was supposed to be transferred to?"

"I only know that you came from Toronto and worked on terrorism," said Laura.

"Yes. The Integrated National Security Enforcement Team, or INSET as it is called. Up until a week ago I thought I was being transferred to Commercial Crime."

"I heard that there had been a last-minute change," replied Jack. "I didn't hear why."

"I thought I was being transferred under a cloud. Back east, I was criticized by the brass for gathering intelligence at a commercial location. They said it did not meet the judicial criteria in regard to a search."

"Searching a place after office hours without a warrant?" suggested Jack.

Rose stared at him for a moment before replying, "It seems you've done your homework, as well."

Jack shrugged in response.

"For the record," continued Rose, "my watch was wrong. I didn't realize the office was closed for the night as opposed to an employee having stepped out for a moment. It didn't help that someone left the door unlocked. It could have been by the same janitor who was sleeping in an office across the hall and happened upon me. It complicated matters further when he later decided to call headquarters to verify my credentials."

"I see," replied Jack.

"I bet you do," she said, with a face that made Jack think she played poker. He mulled over her choice of words to describe the unlocked door. *It could have been by the same janitor ... meaning in theory, it could have been ... but sure as hell wasn't.*

"Did they say why they changed the transfer?" asked Laura.

"That is the curious part. Last week, when I got a call from Staffing, they sounded a little miffed."

"Miffed?" asked Laura.

"Staffing said Assistant Commissioner Isaac intervened and I was being re-routed to Intelligence. Rather unusual to have someone interfere with Staffing like that. Do you know anything about it?"

"No," replied Jack.

"Last Friday afternoon I was called in for a short meeting with Isaac."

"Oh, really?" said Jack, feeling like the cup of dark-roasted black Starbucks coffee he had on the way to work wasn't such a good idea for an empty stomach.

"Yes, really," replied Rose, staring back at him.

"Guess he wouldn't have called you in on a day off just to welcome you to the section," said Jack, fishing for more information.

"He welcomed me, but spent most of his time discussing you," she replied. "I had the distinct impression he feels — well, let's just say he feels you need a little more experience at testifying in court."

Jack was confused. "We're on an Intelligence Section. We're supposed to avoid court when we can, gather intelligence, and turn the results over to the appropriate section to investigate further. They're the ones who normally make arrests, seize evidence, and go to court."

"I'm aware of that," replied Rose. "However, Isaac is concerned that it is the coroner who most often receives the results of your work."

Laura looked down ostensibly to examine a hangnail.

"Oh, that," replied Jack, sounding casual. "There have been a couple of individuals I was working on who fell victim to the people they were associating with. Isaac once suspected I had something to do with the death of a man in Mexico. The man was someone I was working on. I happened to be in Mexico on my honeymoon at the time. Isaac looked into it and discovered that the death was the result of an accidental drowning. He apologized to me personally once he discovered his error. I'm surprised he would mention it. It was simply a coincidence."

"So he told me," replied Rose. "How interesting you should use the word 'coincidence.' He said you could be nicknamed 'The Coincidental Corporal.'"

"What are —" Jack started to say defiantly.

"Hold on," interjected Rose, putting her hand up for him to stop. "Laura, this is obviously making you uncomfortable. Would you mind leaving us for a moment? I'll want to talk with you later."

"What are you trying to say?" asked Jack, as soon as Laura left the office. "What is Isaac insinuating?"

"Oh, I don't think he was insinuating," said Rose, pursing her lips, eyes locked onto his.

Jack returned her gaze and decided not to respond to that comment.

"He revealed only the facts as he knew them," she continued. "No evidence of wrongdoing on your part was noted, although he tended to overuse the phrase 'by coincidence' when describing you. In fact, he made it clear that there has never been any … what's the word he used? … oh, yes … credible evidence or confirmation of any wrongdoing on your part."

Jack sighed and took a moment to mull over what

he had been told before asking, "What is he suggesting? Where do I stand with him?"

"I did get the distinct impression that it would make him happy if you brought one in alive."

Jack nodded silently.

"You should also know I wasn't asked to rat on you."

"Thanks. Nice to know."

"But he did make it clear that he goes by the book and would take immediate action if any evidence of wrongdoing came to light."

"Fair enough. I would expect nothing less."

Rose snickered.

"What's so amusing?" asked Jack.

"That is exactly what Isaac said you would say."

Ouch! "So, where do I stand with you on all this?"

Rose smiled and said, "By *coincidence*, I had said exactly the same thing as you — that I would expect nothing less."

"Glad we're on the same page," replied Jack.

Rose didn't immediately reply, but, after straightening a pile of reports on her desk, she looked at Jack and said, "It is evident to me that the work you do is exceptionally dangerous. Considering what I heard, how is it you've never taken stress leave after all you have been through?"

"As per policy, I meet with the department psychologists," replied Jack, defensively. "They continue to give me a clean bill of health."

"So I've been told. You've never even been recommended for a brief sabbatical from undercover duties. Very unusual, considering how long you've been doing it."

Jack shrugged and said, "Apparently they think I'm suited for it."

"I know the training and selection criteria for undercover operators is good," continued Rose. "I volunteered for it myself once, but failed to make the cut. I've done some minor stuff. Portraying a girlfriend the odd time, but never any real undercover operations."

"The training for UC is pretty good," said Jack.

"Still, it's not that good," replied Rose. She eyed Jack curiously and said, "Taking that into account, coupled with the continuous lack of any concern by the Force psychologists, I understand your training, or should I say, your self-preservation skills, started as a child."

"It was my understanding," replied Jack irritably, "that my conversations with the psychologists were to be kept strictly confidential."

"No, you're correct. I didn't talk to them," said Rose, as she sighed and her eyes softened. "I was simply speculating. As your boss, I am concerned about your emotional health as well as your safety. If you need a break, let me know. It doesn't have to be official. It will stay between the two of us."

"I feel fine, thank you." Jack then added, "You're exceptionally intuitive. I'm surprised you didn't make it as an operator."

"I lack the ability for fast imaginative responses in unexpected situations," replied Rose. "I have a tendency to overanalyze. As far as being intuitive goes, thank you." She watched Jack carefully and added, "It may help that I have my masters in psychology."

She expected to see the usual signs of discomfort that people initially felt when they learned of her psychological training. *Fear of being analyzed or having someone guess their deepest secrets.* It didn't appear to faze Jack.

"Good for you," he replied. "Explains why you clued in about my self-preservation skills developing as a child. Your terminology was the same as the Force psychologists. It is true. When I was a child, report-card time in our house or anything to do with school for that matter, was a nightmare. As a preschooler, I would watch my father flip through a school textbook and ask my older brother questions. If he didn't know the answer, my father would backhand him out of his chair, make him set the chair up again, sit in it, and then ask him the same question again. Not exactly the best teaching method. Explains why my brother left home when he was fourteen."

"And then it was your turn to sit in the chair?"

"What I did, from about the time I was ten or eleven, was pretend to be mildly mentally challenged. My father believed it and I avoided the punishment that was handed down to my brother." Jack sighed and said, "So, I guess you're right. My self-preservation skills did start as a child. Not just learning to lie, but to watch someone, to know when they are about to strike with little warning, as my father would do. Childhood lessons serve me well in what I do now."

Rose gave a grim smile and nodded.

"So why did you become a police officer instead of a psychologist?" asked Jack.

"Thought it would be a more hands-on approach to helping people. Why did you become a police officer?"

"I hate bullies."

"Bullies like your dad?"

Jack nodded. "He was physically and emotionally abusive. Also a pedophile. As he grew older, he also took delight in making people angry. Guess it was another way to make himself feel powerful."

"Wow … you seem pretty open about it."

"It is my belief that if people would stop keeping stuff like that secret, it would save a lot of children from a lifetime of horrible problems. I didn't find out about his pedophilia until he was practically on his deathbed. Not enough time to put him through a trial."

Rose nodded.

Jack then made pretence of looking around the walls of her office.

"What are you looking for?" asked Rose.

"A picture of Sigmund."

Rose smiled and said, "Personally I think Freud is overrated."

"Carl Jung?"

"Don't care for him, either. My doctrine is more in line with a man called Adler."

"Good old Alfred," replied Jack. "I agree. Jung is too spiritual for my liking."

"You also have an education in psychology," said Rose, meaning it more as a question than a statement.

"No. Just light reading. Clinical works of Alfred Adler."

"You call that light reading?"

Jack shrugged and said, "It's been awhile. I only skimmed through it."

"The Force shrinks never had a chance with you, did they?" she said, accusingly.

Jack grimaced and said, "Their intentions are good. I believe in the program, but I warned them that many of the good operators are still fooling them."

"You included?" she asked.

"No. Like I said, I believe in the program. I am as honest as you would be."

"As I would be?"

Jack smiled and said, "Some things they don't need to know about."

"Really? Care to expand?"

"Uh, let's see, situations comparable to a watch being faulty and an office door left unlocked."

Rose paused. *Okay, time to change the subject.* "I see, well ... I do want you to know that although I'm not sure why Isaac transferred me here, I am happy with it. I'm not the Commercial Crime kind of girl." Rose paused and added, "Guess 'girl' is politically incorrect these days. I should say woman, but the older I get, the more I prefer girl."

Jack smiled. "Perhaps with your background, Isaac decided you are better suited for these duties. To keep an eye on me in case I start looking for a clock tower to climb."

"I guess time will tell, won't it?" she said, giving

a slight grin. "I anticipate that I will earn my pay. Speaking of which — better bring Laura in. I have something to talk to both of you about."

Rose watched as Jack stepped out of her office. *The Force shrinks weren't the only ones who never had a chance with you. No wonder Isaac rolled his eyes when I asked him about the results from the Internal Affairs investigations.*

Jack went across the hall to retrieve Laura. "Everything is okay," he whispered. "I'll fill you in later."

Rose waited until they both returned and said, "I should let you know that my first phone call this morning was a complaint from some inspector out at Surrey Detachment." She looked directly at Jack and said, "He told me you attacked one of his officers last night and broke her nose. Constable Sophie White."

Jack frowned. *Great way to start off ...* "There were extenuating circumstances," he said grimly. "I was in an undercover situation. My notes on the matter are in my desk drawer. I can get them for you."

"I know," replied Rose, "I've read them."

You read them? thought Jack. *Note to self: watch where I leave stuff.*

"I wanted to nip this in the bud before it went any further," continued Rose. "While I was reading your notes, the second call I took this morning was from Constable Sophie White. She wanted to thank you for saving her life."

"Oh? Well ... that's good."

Rose remained passive.

"Isn't it?" asked Laura.

Rose replied, "I called the inspector back and informed him that what you did was a basic under-cover strategy known as the Sophie Solution."

"You what!" exclaimed Jack.

Rose laughed and said, "Not really. Still, I'll leave it to your imagination as to how embarrassed he was when I did call back. He wasn't aware of all the details." Rose leaned forward, clasping her hands on her desk before saying, "Good work last night. Both of you." There was no doubt she meant what she said.

Jack and Laura nodded silently.

After leaning back in her chair, Rose continued, "Your report said you were originally introduced to Mad Dog through an informant."

"That's right," replied Jack.

"How about the threat level to him or her?"

"The informant is safe."

"Good enough. You seem confident about that?"

"I am," replied Jack, quietly, in a tone that betrayed some sadness to Laura's ears. It crossed her mind to ask him about it later, but decided against it. Jack was extremely protective about his informants. If he wanted to tell her something, he would do so without her asking.

"So what is next on your agenda?" asked Rose.

"We would still like to do a little follow-up on the guns we seized. Track Mad Dog's phone tolls and see if we can figure out who in the U.S. supplied them to him. Might be able to tip off the Americans and have them put a stop to it."

"Illegal guns being smuggled into Canada is a pri-ority. Keep me up to date."

Once back in their office, Laura said, "So? What's your first impression of our new boss?"

"She seems okay." Jack then filled her in on the conversation he'd had with her.

"Sounds honest," said Laura when Jack had finished.

"There is one other thing you may wish to keep in mind," said Jack. "Remember her comment about reading my undercover notes?"

Laura nodded.

"I keep them in my desk drawer ... my locked desk drawer."

"Oh, man. You mean she picked —"

"Must have accidentally left it unlocked," interrupted Jack. "Like that office door in Toronto," he added with a grin.

"I see," said Laura, frowning. "I don't know if that's a good thing or not."

"At least she's honest about it."

"I guess. So, you trust her?"

"Not particularly. Too soon to know, but my initial feelings are good."

"Not exactly someone you would call a good friend yet?"

"No. She is our boss, so I don't ever see her becoming a good friend. Her position demands otherwise."

"But you're my boss and I thought we were good friends?"

"Without question. But we're also partners and don't normally have to answer directly to Isaac. If Rose is good, I feel an obligation to protect her from knowing something she could be criticized for."

"I hear you. So, what do you want to do now? Personally I feel like getting out of here and grabbing a cup of tea someplace. My treat. Buy you a coffee?"

Jack sighed and said, "I need to visit a friend receiving hospice care. Won't take long. Maybe an hour."

"Is it anybody I know?"

Jack shook his head and said, "You've never met her. An old informant." Jack paused before continuing, "At this point there is no harm disclosing her identity. She's a ... or was, a hooker by the name of Ophelia." He took a deep breath and slowly exhaled before saying, "Well, not that old I guess. Cancer," he added, for explanation. "Maybe two weeks left at the most."

"Is she the one who introduced you to Mad Dog?"

Jack nodded and said, "I want to let her know how it went."

"She did good, turning you on to that crowd."

"She also turned in the guy who robbed and murdered that eighty-eight-year-old war veteran in his house last year."

"That was the one I was on!" exclaimed Laura. "The UC where you brought me in pretending to be your girlfriend."

"Ophelia doesn't have anybody in her life. I owe her."

"Want me to go with you?"

"No, but thanks, anyway. I will take you up on your offer to buy me a coffee first. Right now I could use a cup."

* * *

Jack enjoyed his coffee break and found the light conversation he had with Laura relaxing. He wouldn't have relaxed, if he had known that in the early hours of the following morning he would be using his 9 mm to kill an innocent victim in a back alley.

7

It was ten o'clock in the morning when Kang Lee arrived at the Pan Pacific Hotel in downtown Vancouver for a private meeting with The Shaman.

Lee sipped his espresso while seated on the balcony of the Jade Suite, located on the sixteenth floor. The Shaman, seated next to him, took a moment to gaze out over Vancouver Harbour. The view was exquisite and included the Lions Gate Bridge and the mountains.

Normally Lee would have enjoyed the view, but he had other things on his mind. *Have I been selected to number two position or not?*

The Shaman, still wearing the hotel bathrobe, took a swallow of freshly squeezed orange juice. After putting the glass down, he ran a hand through his thick, dyed-black hair that he kept trimmed to collar length.

The bathrobe concealed a body that Lee knew was tall, athletic, and agile. The Shaman had a passion for *kenjutsu*, a military art form originally created in Japan during the fifteenth century, primarily designed to instruct samurai in the use of swords. He had reached the highest level attainable in the sport, that of *kyoshi*, which made him a master. Overall, the muscular tone of his body, coupled with his agility and appearance, made him look much younger than he was. It was only the ruggedness of his face that betrayed his age of fifty-two.

"So, tell me," said The Shaman, "in regard to the immigrants we have brought in, have any new pathways come to light?"

"Two new situations within the last month," replied Lee. "A man who gained a position in Pacific Rim Oil and Gas has some valuable inside information that will benefit us greatly on the stock market. He asks that we arrange for more of his relatives to come to Canada."

"It will be done. The other?"

"The president of another company, Eagle Eye Drilling and Exploration, is having an affair with his personal secretary. The president is married with two children. The personal secretary is a young man we brought over two years ago. Neither the president's wife nor the company executives know that the president is gay, let alone prone to pillow talk about private company business. We have collected enough information to make the company's next stockholder meeting extremely ... shall we say, newsworthy?"

"Do you anticipate another advantage on the market, perhaps by selling short? Or will he be approached to pay by some other means for our silence?"

"The company may be on the verge of a major discovery. It is still being analyzed. I should know more within a week as to which way to approach the situation."

"Excellent. And our other ventures ... the intrepid Canadian. How is he doing?"

Lee smiled. The intrepid Canadian was Arthur Goldie, who oversaw the distribution of heroin once it arrived in Vancouver. Goldie had come a long way since he first came to their attention back in the early 1990s. That was when Goldie first wanted to import heroin from Burma to North America. Goldie had met personally with warlords overseeing the poppy plantations in Burma in an effort to extract what he thought would be the lowest price. The Shaman admired him for his courage at the time. Lee believed that Goldie was less courageous than he was naive.

Lee smiled to himself at how simple it had been to convince Goldie to pay a percentage of his profit to them. He first befriended Goldie at a hotel in Rangoon. A day or two later, Goldie was arrested at a Burmese checkpoint and his first shipment of heroin was seized. Lee stepped in as a sympathetic friend with high-level contacts. Soon, Goldie and his shipment were both on their way again.

Goldie was readily willing to pay a commission to guarantee the safe passage of future shipments. He never realized that the same people who sold the heroin also sold the information to The Shaman. It was The Shaman who paid the majority of the real salary earned by many of the police, military, and immigration officials in Southeast Asia.

In effect, The Shaman was often able to control which shipments would pass and which ones wouldn't. In time, with the continued safe arrival of his goods in Vancouver, Goldie profited more than ever and his shipments increased in proportion, as did the commissions he paid out.

Now Goldie was no longer a micromanager. He owned a couple of antique stores, as well as a nightclub. Both types of businesses served to launder his money and to insulate him from the annoying tentacles of law enforcement. He had reached the point where he could sit back and collect commissions himself from the executive members of other crime families who also frequented his nightclub, bolstering his profit margin even higher.

"As you know by the increasingly large shipments and commissions, he is doing well," replied Lee.

"From what I have read," replied The Shaman, "in British Columbia that should be rather easy and relatively stress-free. Low risk and high gain."

"There is some risk. Last year the national police, the RCMP as it is known, made several dozen arrests in regard to bikers. Many were charged with selling cocaine. The police in Canada are not as easily persuaded to turn a blind eye. Bribery is relatively rare."

"Still, is it not true that judicial sentencing practices in British Columbia make it irrelevant? I am familiar with the arrests you mention. It will be interesting to see how long those arrested will actually spend in jail. From what I've read so far, it shouldn't be long. What does interest me is that the arrests were the result of a police informer who was a member of the gang. I have heard a rumour that the courts may not accept the evidence of the police informer because he broke the law while working for the police. An abuse of process it is called."

Lee thought about it briefly and a smile crossed his face. "If the court rules favourably, it would certainly make it easy to identify any informers in our midst. They would be unable to behave or perform their duties as directed."

"Exactly. It is something we will follow. I wish the bikers luck."

"Even if they are our competition?" asked Lee seriously.

"We do not sell cocaine," replied The Shaman, with a shrug.

Lee nodded. *No, not yet. When we are stronger and the time is right, then —*

"So, back to Mister Goldie," continued The Shaman. "How is his progress outside of British Columbia?"

"Through his contacts, he is opening up more distribution channels all the time. Much of Western Canada and recently Seattle are beginning to add to our investment strategy."

"What about the eastern seaboard?" asked The Shaman. "That is where the population is based. I expected our man in Palermo to have had the contacts in New York, but the Italian mafia there has lost all honour. Respected crime bosses are arrested almost daily and continue to cheerfully sing to the police in exchange for leniency. So much for *omertà*. I would like to discover a new path."

"I understand," replied Lee. "I have approached Mister Goldie on this matter, but he indicates it is a slow process. Competitive organizations in Ontario and Quebec have been receiving their shipments from Afghanistan. I thought the lack of stability in Afghanistan would have crippled that front, but apparently not."

"The opposite, I should think," said The Shaman. "Heroin will be sold more than ever so that the various factions will have money for arms."

Lee nodded politely in agreement.

"And our Chinese friend, Mister Wang, appears to be doing well?"

"Yes," replied Lee.

Hui Wang was originally from Hong Kong, but had moved to Vancouver. His role was similar to Goldie's, except that he oversaw the distribution of ecstasy and methamphetamine, or crystal meth, as it was known on the street. Wang had also insulated himself well and owned a restaurant and a specialty store that sold imported bamboo furniture. Both served to give him an aura of respectability, as well as launder his money.

"You have done very, very well as our emissary in Canada," said The Shaman.

"Thank you," replied Lee, trying unsuccessfully to read what The Shaman was thinking.

"As you are aware, there is a position I need to fill at home. It is unfortunate that my most trusted employee, in essence, the vice-president of our organization, succumbed to heart failure." The Shaman paused to swallow more orange juice.

Lee waited. He was not offended that he was not the most trusted employee. At least, not yet. The Shaman compared their organization's protection to the skin of an onion. Comprised of numerous layers, the closer you came to the heart of the company, the more scrutiny and tests there were to ensure ultimate protection.

The Shaman placed his glass down and turned to Lee and asked, "Would you like to return and fill that position? To once more live under the same roof as your family?"

Lee's broad smile gave his answer before his words announced, "It is my dream!"

"Then it shall be."

"When do you foresee this taking place?" asked Lee, trying to contain his glee and maintain the proper dignity in his voice.

"That is the problem at the moment," replied The Shaman. "I have a candidate in mind to fill your position at the investment company, but the person I am considering is not experienced in the commodity market like you are. With the rapid expansion of our influence here, I think we need to separate the two ventures. What we need to find is a suitable replacement for you to oversee our eastern commodity distribution."

Lee nodded. He knew the commodities referred to were heroin, ecstasy, and methamphetamines.

"Canada is a different culture compared to our European and Asian markets," continued The Shaman. "Now that you have set up the proper framework, I think it is better to have someone who was born to this culture or has lived here for many years to replace you.

Such a person would know who to recruit in Canada and would also be more familiar with their family history."

Lee knew that "family history" meant the personal knowledge of who and where families lived — knowledge that would ensure the strict obedience of new employees if they did not wish any harm to befall their family. He thought briefly about his own wife and their two daughters. He had seen little of them since working in Canada. *Of course, their safety is not an issue. My loyalty is absolute … and I have brought them great prosperity.*

"Providing, of course, that such a person existed and was qualified," continued The Shaman. "If you have a potential candidate, then I would suggest that after the appropriate security checks, some testing and training, six months would be appropriate for you to leave Canada."

"I have such a person in mind," said Lee.

"And would that be Mister Wang? He came to Canada as a young man, and with his associates he undoubtedly has connections across North America."

Lee shook his head. "Mister Wang has eastern connections through the Big Circle Boys and the Sun Yee On triad, but, like Mister Wang himself, they seem reluctant to conduct business with Westerners. I do not believe Mister Wang is ready to advance to my position. In my opinion, he still associates too closely with individuals who could arouse police curiosity."

"Do all his associates adopt gang names? Do they not realize the target they then present to the police? I know some feel the name coupled with the reputation will promote fear and inspire compliance, but the risk of identifying one's membership to the police outweighs that advantage."

"Mister Wang has contacts with some new gangs who choose not to adopt a name for that reason. It is a step in the right direction, but even Mister Wang admits that their philosophy of dealing only with Asians is still prevalent. I have spoken to him about it, but I am afraid that he tends to feel safe around these people. They are Asian, like him, and tend to shun Westerners. No, for what you suggest, if we are to influence the eastern market, we need a Westerner to open the door. For that, I would recommend Mister Goldie."

"Ah, the intrepid Canadian," replied The Shaman. "I wondered if you felt he would be worthy."

"He has many connections," replied Lee. "Furthermore, he has never been convicted of any criminal acts. He is welcome to travel anywhere, including the United States."

"He is like you," observed The Shaman, "in that you have no criminal record."

"Somewhat different," noted Lee with a smile. "Goldie, like Wang, controls a large gang of barbarians. The drug business is different than our other, more corporate, enterprises. Goldie and Wang did not make their way to the top by relying entirely on their intelligence. They are both personally familiar with the use of … lethal persuasion."

"So, his resumé is different from yours in that you have never had to soil your hands with another person's blood," said The Shaman.

"I suppose so," mused Lee, "but I do respect his intelligence, nevertheless. He has never been convicted and it has been years since the police even came close to catching him. And that was not in Canada. Since then, like your past analogy of the onion, he has developed many layers of protection."

"Despite what you think, if he is to fill your position, he will not do so without proper screening, including a polygraph."

"Most certainly. As you have taught me about the onion — the closer you are to the middle, the more intensity exists. If you do not wish to fly someone in, here in Vancouver are several firms that offer the services of lie detectors for corporations."

"We will decide at the time, but you will mention it to him within the next few days. I will be spending a week golfing at Crown Isle in Courtenay on Vancouver Island. I hope it is as luxurious as the Internet makes it out to be."

"I have never been there."

"Perhaps next time I will invite you to accompany me."

"Thank you."

"Now, we will meet again next week before I leave Canada. I will wish to know how Mister Goldie reacts to our proposal and the security measures we require. He knows a great deal about us. If he refuses, I would see it as a serious problem."

The Shaman's eyes glanced through the glass window of the balcony to where Da Khlot was seated inside before adding, "Should that happen, as Mister Khlot has said, to keep him would be of no benefit."

"I see no reason that he would refuse. I didn't," added Lee with a smile.

"No, you didn't. And if all goes well, you will be stepping through the last layer of the onion yourself. The protection will be for you as much as for me."

"He will be scrutinized carefully," said Lee. "If he passes, would you like to meet him in person?"

"He will be your responsibility. I see no necessity for him to know my name. I'm sure that in time, with the transactions involved, he will figure it out, but I see no advantage in personal contact. His placement is your decision. I hope you have chosen wisely. Your life will depend upon it."

Lee nodded sombrely.

"Now, this brings us to another small matter that needs to be discussed. Trivial, but requiring prompt attention." The Shaman paused, smiled, and said, "Like peeling the onion, I hope it does not bring tears to your eyes."

Da Khlot hurried to open the door to the balcony when The Shaman and Lee stood up, signalling an end to their meeting. Lee's face did not portray the jubilance of a man who had been promised a promotion. His eyes appeared distant and his jaw was set with determination as he hurried out of the suite.

Da Khlot looked at The Shaman, who returned his gaze and said, "Tonight you wear your new suit."

8

It was two o'clock in the morning when Corporal Connie Crane arrived at Coquitlam River Park, where the murder had been reported. She was the second member of the Integrated Homicide Investigative team to arrive.

Several marked and unmarked police cars lined the side of the main road, and yellow police tape sealed off a small, gravelled parking lot leading into the park. Inside the park, floodlights running on generators were being turned on, sending an array of light and shadows through the trees.

She parked behind a patrol car and approached two uniformed officers standing near the tape.

"I'm with I-HIT," she explained, reaching for her badge inside her windbreaker. "Do you know where my partner —"

"Over here, CC!" yelled Dallas, answering her question.

Connie ducked under the crime scene tape and approached Dallas. He was a new addition to I-HIT and this was only their second case together. He was a blood-splatter expert, which was a field of expertise unto itself. CC felt he had distinguished himself on their first case and was glad to be paired up with him.

"Sorry I'm late," she said. "Accident on the Port Mann. What have we got?"

"Adult male, still warm. Multiple gunshots. Empty 9 mm six-shot semi-auto pistol beside the victim. Whoever did it made no attempt to hide the gun."

"Where's the body?" asked CC.

"Less than a minute walk along that path," replied Dallas, pointing to a trail leading from the parking lot. "Face down beside a small creek."

"The parking lot doesn't look well used," noted Connie. "Couldn't hold much more than five or six cars. Who reported it?"

"A young couple who came to park and make out. They got into an argument and ended up going for a walk. I think what they saw took their mind off the quarrel. They didn't see anyone and there were no other vehicles."

"How does the couple look?"

"I don't think they had anything to do with it. They've given statements. I did a quick statement analysis ... appears truthful."

"Victim a dealer? Into drugs?"

"Don't know. He looks and is dressed like a street person. Also had a relatively fresh dressing on one hand. Looked professional. I'm betting he received medical treatment recently. I patted him down for a wallet, but there wasn't one. No identification that I could find yet. Maybe when we print him —"

"Robbery?" said CC.

"Don't think so. It was more like a kidnapping and execution. The guy's hands were bound behind his back with duct tape. His mouth was taped, as well. So were his ankles, but I found a piece of duct tape in the parking lot. Looks like he managed to get most of the tape off his ankles while being transported. I think he was dragged out of a vehicle and dumped on his back on the ground. Someone tried to shoot him in the face but the bullet took a chunk out of his ear. The victim rolled in panic. I think that's when he freed the last of the tape on his ankles and got to his feet and bolted. Later he took another bullet through his thigh, one in his back, and then one to the back of his head. The last one was at such close range that the muzzle likely touched the back of his head before the final shot. Pretty cold thing to do."

"No shit."

"I checked the gun. Looks like all six rounds were fired."

"So whoever murdered him was a lousy shot. Probably missed him with two rounds altogether."

"Could be. Something peculiar, though. The victim had a large garbage bag over his head and torso."

"How was he able to run so far down that path?" asked Connie.

"It wasn't the dark-green type of bag. Made of clear plastic. The type you would use for disposing of leaves and stuff in the fall."

"Someone figured it would help eliminate DNA from their vehicle."

"That's what I figure. The victim was coughing up blood before he got here. The inside of the bag was sprayed from blood coming out his nose."

"Maybe the bullet in his back went through a lung."

"No. Wait until you see the bag. There was quite a bit smeared around inside. I think the bullet in his back was followed in short order by one to the skull."

"What's your guess on why he was bleeding prior to arrival? Think he was punched in the face?"

"No, it's not a broken nose. I've seen this type of blood pattern before. My guess is someone took a bat or pipe to his ribcage to subdue him. Autopsy should confirm it, but I bet one of his lungs is punctured with a broken rib."

"A tough way to die."

"Yeah. I bet he knew it was coming. Slow and painful way to go. I've uncovered the route the victim took after arriving and have a theory from what I've seen. Where do you want to start? At the body or do you want me to show you the evidence leading to the body?"

"May as well start at the beginning. If he was bagged, I doubt that there is much blood in the parking lot."

"There's always some when someone is shot. Bagged or not."

"Too dry for foot or tire tracks," said CC, thinking aloud.

"This is the beginning as I know it," said Dallas, pointing to an area in the gravelled lot. "You can see a double set of scuff marks in the dirt. Like a bounce followed by short drag marks that match the heels of his shoes. My guess is he was dragged out of a van by two people. If it was a car —"

"He would have been lifted from the trunk. There wouldn't be these patterns in the gravel from being set down."

"Exactly."

"Thought your specialty was blood?"

Dallas smiled and said, "If you look closely, you'll see a little blood smeared in the gravel."

"Got it," said CC.

"The pattern is repeated about two shoulder widths away and then repeated a third time."

"What the hell? You're right."

"Let me take you through it," said Dallas. "He was dragged backwards out of a van and dumped on the ground. Someone tried to shoot him in the face, but he likely saw it coming and moved. The first shot took out a piece of his ear and tore the garbage bag. He then rolled two complete turns, leaving blood from his ear about two shoulder widths away on each roll." Dallas looked at CC and said, "Are you with me so far?"

"Hang on," said CC, clasping one hand over her ear and then stepping sideways while spinning around to simulate a roll. "Got it. Explains the gap in between."

"Exactly. And here we have a small ball of duct tape. I think he got that off while being transported and it probably stuck up inside his pant leg. He still has a short piece of it on his ankles, but I figure he was kicking in his panic. His legs broke free at this point and he got to his feet and started running."

CC then followed Dallas a short distance down the path, where he used a flashlight to point to a new blood trail that was easily visible.

"Here is where he took one to the inside of his thigh, but kept running," explained Dallas. "By the large amount of blood, I'm sure the bullet hit his femoral artery. If whoever murdered him hadn't finished the job, he would have bled out pretty quick."

CC paused to envision the nightmare. *Beaten with a bat or pipe ... broken rib through your lung ... bound in duct tape ... kidnapped and laying on the floor of some van ... dragged out and shot in the face ... escape while more bullets are flying ... trying to run with your hands tied behind your back ... shot through the thigh ... staggering ... unable to gasp for air through your mouth ... shot in the back ... face down in the dirt ... feel the gun on the back of your head —*

"And here," said Dallas, waving his flashlight beam over a spray of dark red blood in a contrasting splatter against the bright green leaves on a bush beside the trail, "is where he took one to the back. See where the blood from his leg changed direction? He spun around, staggered, and went down."

CC looked at the man lying face down along a short embankment beside a small creek.

"The killer then put the last shot into the back of his skull," continued Dallas.

CC paused and looked around. She knew that Dallas thought she was searching for clues. In reality she was trying once more to grasp the inhumanity of the human race. She sighed and looked at Dallas and said, "Guess it leaves us with who and why. Also, who is the victim? You said you checked for a wallet?"

"I only patted his front and back pockets. Nothing. Maybe he has it in his jacket. I didn't want to move anything until the Forensic Identification Section does their thing."

"I want to identify this guy. I'm not going to wait for FIS," said CC. "I'll be discreet. The sooner we can ID him the better." She bent over the victim and gently started to roll the body over on the side, but her attention was diverted to a shadow cast by a fern growing out from the side embankment on the other side of the body. "Dallas, over there!" said CC. "Under the fern … see it? In the shadow. There's something there."

Dallas pushed the fern aside and shone his light. "Bingo! We've got a footprint." Dallas squatted and examined it closer. "Too smudged to match, but gives us an idea of size."

"Maybe the couple who found him," suggested CC.

"They said they didn't come down off the trail. Plus she was wearing short heels and he is big. I'm betting size ten-to-twelve range. This is much smaller. Not the vic's. Maybe a woman?"

"Pretty wide for a woman," commented CC, turning her attention back to the body. "Hang on, hand me your light."

Dallas passed CC his flashlight and saw her direct the beam through the front of the clear plastic bag that was still covering the head and upper torso. She then squinted, peering closer through the bloodied plastic and reached her hand inside and took out a prescription pill bottle from the victim's shirt pocket.

"Son of a bitch," she muttered.

"What is it? Got something?"

"Yeah, we got something all right. Do you know Corporal Jack Taggart from the Intelligence Unit?"

"No," replied Dallas, bending over for a closer look at the pill bottle.

"His wife is Doctor Natasha Taggart," replied CC, covering her eyes with one hand as she unconsciously massaged the sides of her temples.

Dallas paused for a moment, glancing at CC. "Do you want me to call her?" he asked.

Connie sighed and said, "No, I will."

"What's the problem?"

"I don't know," replied Connie, "but with Jack, there is guaranteed to be one."

9

It was 3:30 in the morning when Jack awoke and answered his phone. He listened as Connie briefly gave him the details of the murder.

"And no identification?" said Jack.

"Nothing except a prescription pill bottle listing Natasha as the prescribing physician. It's soaked in blood. The last name looks like Montgomery."

"Hang on, I'll wake her," said Jack.

"I'm already awake," said Natasha. "Overdose?" she asked, taking the phone from Jack who shook his head in response.

Natasha listened in shock and disbelief, her ears hearing the words, but her mind acting fuzzy and numb. She heard herself speak. She sounded professional, but it was as if someone else were saying the words ... putting her brain on hold for the real flood of emotion that would follow moments later. She passed the phone back to Jack.

"Natasha thinks he lives in an alley close to her clinic," said Connie. "She thinks she can recognize his sleeping bag and is willing to help us. Think you could drive her and meet us there? We want to find out where this guy was grabbed as soon as we can."

"We're on our way," replied Jack. "Give me your cell number." Jack hung up and looked at Natasha. She was sitting on the bed with her knees drawn to her chest, holding the plastic rose.

"Someone murdered Melvin," she sobbed. "Why? Why would anyone do that? He was harmless. A gentle person. Why shoot him?"

"I don't know. Come on, we need to get dressed."

Minutes later, as they rode the elevator down to the parking garage, Natasha turned to Jack as anger started to overcome grief. "Why?" she demanded. "Why would anyone do this?"

"CC is a good investigator. Very thorough. If anyone will find —"

"Don't you patronize me! I know how these things work."

"What are you talking about?"

"Melvin isn't some la-de-da member of society. People like him disappear all the time. Who out there really cares? I'm the only friend he had," she added, with a sob.

"Melvin didn't disappear. He was murdered. It will be investigated as closely as if he was the mayor."

"Yeah, right," muttered Natasha sarcastically.

Jack hugged her as he sighed and said, "Melvin doesn't sound all that different from who I was visiting today — Ophelia. I told you about her."

Natasha paused, swallowed and said, "You're different. So am I. Who else has visited Ophelia?"

Jack grimaced and shook his head.

"Exactly. And I'm the only one who Melvin could ever turn to."

"That may be, but CC is a good investigator. She'll do her best to solve it."

They drove in silence, and were almost at the alley when Natasha asked, "Is she as good as you?"

"Who?"

"Connie Crane. Is she as good as you?"

"When it comes to homicides, I bet she's better. Homicide is her field of expertise. Mine is organized crime."

"How do you know it isn't organized crime if you don't look into it?"

"Honey, come on. Think about it. What you have told me about Melvin. It doesn't make sense to involve organized crime figures."

"Right. Proves what I was saying earlier. All this crap about it being looked at as closely as if it was the mayor. That's what it is. Crap!"

"I'm not feeding you crap. You know me better than that," said Jack quietly.

They slowly drove up and down several alleys before spotting a crumpled green sleeping bag lying in a pile near the bottom of a wooden hydro pole.

"That's it, I'm sure," said Natasha.

"We'll just wait in the car until I-HIT gets here," said Jack.

Moments later, Connie was the first to arrive, and Jack and Natasha got out of their car to greet her.

Connie used her flashlight to closely examine the area while Jack stood with his arm wrapped around Natasha. Her beam caught a sheet of plastic the wind had blown against the side of a Dumpster a short distance away.

"Bet he used that to try and keep dry," said Connie. "When the rest of the team gets here we'll bring that in and print it for —"

The mournful cry of an animal in distress erupted briefly and went quiet.

"What the hell was that?" questioned Connie.

"That could be Winston," said Natasha. "Melvin had a cat named Winston."

"It sounded like it came from around here," said Connie, walking over and gingerly lifting a corner of the sleeping bag. The sound erupted again. Louder and in more pain.

Jack, Natasha, and Connie bent down to look as Connie shone her flashlight inside the bag. Winston lay inside, his eyes blinking at the light. His head twisted and turned as he tried to get away, but his legs didn't move.

"I'll get him to a vet," said Jack.

"His back and spinal cord are broken," said Natasha. "He needs to be put down."

"It's only 4:30," said Connie. "You won't get a vet much before nine."

Winston uttered another long low mournful sound, ending only when he sneezed and coughed up more blood.

"We think the victim was beaten with a bat," said Connie. "Must have been when he was in his bag. Bet the cat got in the way."

"Oh, God," cried Natasha, standing up and returning to their car where she sat inside, holding her head in her hands and crying.

"Shit," muttered Connie. "Tell her I'm sorry, will you? I thought as a doctor it wouldn't affect her like this."

"Melvin was sort of a special patient," sighed Jack. "You'll be here for a while. I'm going to take her home. We'll fill you in on the details later."

Connie watched as Jack got in the car and spoke with Natasha. Seconds later, he returned.

"Winston is in critical pain," said Jack. "He needs to be put down. The sooner the better."

"He howls all the more when I move him," replied Connie.

"I know. I think you should shoot him now."

"Me? Forget that! I'm not doing it. Besides, someone will hear the noise and call nine-one-one."

Jack looked back at Natasha and took a deep breath and slowly exhaled. "I'll do it," he muttered.

"This is a crime scene! You can't just go and shoot —"

"Explain that to Natasha. Besides, you'll want Winston's body for DNA. Maybe find his fur on the killer. Don't worry, I won't screw anything up."

Connie watched as Jack retrieved a piece of cardboard and an empty plastic litre pop bottle from the dumpster. Moments later he eased Winston out of the sleeping bag and onto the cardboard and carefully dragged him over beside the wooden hydro pole.

He stood silently and looked at Natasha. She stared back for a moment before nodding.

Jack looked down at Winston and said, "I'm sorry, little guy. I really am." He took out his 9 mm and shoved the barrel into the empty bottle and knelt down, lining up Winston's head and using the wooden hydro pole as a backdrop.

Winston sniffed the bottom of the plastic bottle and looked at Jack. *Oh, don't do that … It's as if you trust me, like you think I am going to help you. Goddamn it …*

The bottle muffled the sound of the explosion, but it was still loud enough to cause Natasha to jerk and once more cover her face with her hands.

"I'll take it from here," said Connie, quietly. Jack didn't reply and she saw him close his eyes briefly.

"You okay?" she asked.

"No, I'm not okay. I feel sick about what I just did."

"It was the right thing."

"What happened to Melvin and what happened to Winston was not the right thing," replied Jack, before going back to his car.

Neither Jack nor Natasha spoke until they returned to their apartment and parked the car.

"Somebody is going to pay for this," said Jack. His voice was almost a whisper, but his intention was clear.

* * *

It was 10:30 when Rose arrived at work. Her jaw was still frozen from an early-morning dental appointment and she was taking off her jacket as Jack entered her office.

"There was a homicide last night. An indigent person by the name of Melvin Montgomery. He was kidnapped from downtown Vancouver, tied in duct tape, and murdered in a park out in Coquitlam. I'd like to poke my nose into it a little bit."

"Good morning to you, too."

"Sorry. Good morning. I got your message that you would be late. How're your teeth?"

"The ache is gone. Turns out I'll need a root canal. So, you were saying an indigent person was kidnapped and murdered. Odd. What group do you think is behind it and why?"

"Well … to be perfectly honest, I —"

"I suggest you always be perfectly honest with me. Why are you interested in it?"

Jack paused, and said, "The victim was known to my wife. She's a doctor and had been treating him. They found a prescription on the body. Corporal Connie Crane is the lead investigator. She called Natasha at 3:30 this morning." Jack told her what had transpired.

"Why kidnap a homeless person and drive him all the way out there to kill him?"

"That's what I'm trying to figure out. Melvin even had a garbage bag over his head. Connie said the weapon was a cheap Saturday night special they found at the scene. Nothing makes much sense at the moment. Maybe the victim was in line to inherit some money. So far, it doesn't look like it."

"Doesn't sound like it would fit our mandate."

"It likely doesn't."

"But you would like to stick your nose into it regardless? More of a favour to your wife?"

"Yes."

"I see." Rose was quiet for a moment before asking, "Have they traced the gun?"

"I called a few minutes ago and spoke to another investigator by the name of Dallas. He said it was made in the U.S. and owned by an elderly man in Georgia. He died of old age four years ago and his property was turned over to his son. The son said he found a second handgun purchased by his dad, but not the first one. It was never reported stolen and the family has a solid reputation in the community."

"So, how did it end up in Canada?"

"Your guess is as good as mine. I-HIT sent it to the lab to see if it has been involved in any other cases. It will take a week or two before we find out. Longer yet for the U.S."

Rose nodded and said, "After all the other cases you have been involved with, this seems rather mundane."

Jack shrugged. "Yesterday you told me if I ever needed a break, to let you know. Maybe this is it."

"Do you think I-HIT would mind having you poke around?"

Jack sighed and said, "Connie might not like it. CC

is good, but our paths have crossed before and she never seemed overly appreciative of the methods I used."

"Isaac spoke to me about those cases. Perhaps Corporal Crane would have been more appreciative if you had left her someone to take to court, rather than someone hauled off in a body bag."

"That —"

"I know. Was a coincidence."

"Exactly," said Jack, feeling uneasy.

"Does the victim have any personal relationship with anyone you know, other than being treated by your wife on a professional basis?"

"No. My wife took it hard ... losing a patient. She felt sorry for him, but that's it."

"Well, as you obviously know, gun smuggling into Canada is a top concern. The seizure of the weapons that you and Laura were responsible for over the weekend illustrates the need for our involvement. Would you be content to limit your field of investigation to the gun for the moment and let I-HIT handle everything else? Until such time, of course, that circumstances or information indicates otherwise?"

"Definitely," said Jack, with a smile. "Do you think you can convince the powers that be that a Saturday night special falls in our mandate?"

"Leave that to me. Do you know Connie Crane's boss? What is he or she like?"

"It's Staff Sergeant Randy Otto. In a nutshell, I'll tell you what I know. He's a good guy. Very experienced policeman. Cares about his people ... but is also the type to see the big picture. The only bad thing I can say about him is he prefers Scotch over martinis and demands that the Scotch not be pedophilic."

"Pedophilic Scotch?"

"Has to be well-aged," replied Jack with a grin.

"Sounds like you know him well."

"Got to know him over the murder of a Vietnamese girl. I really respect him."

"I'll give him a call first, then mention it to the brass after. It would also be helpful if you could find out the proper description of the pistol. I doubt that the brass would know the difference between an Uzi and a wobbly Webley, but describing it as a 'Saturday night special' won't exactly impress them."

"I already asked. It's a 9 mm six-shot semi-automatic made by Bryco Arms in the U.S. Bryco used to be well known for making the most Saturday night specials used by criminals. They sold for under fifty bucks. A lawsuit in 2003 finally put them out of business."

"Good. That sounds better. So we've got a weapon from a notorious gun manufacturer in the U.S. catering to criminals, and now has been used to commit a murder in Canada. Don't worry, I won't have any trouble pitching it. You get any flack, direct it my way."

"Thanks, Rose. I appreciate this."

"No problem."

Jack was leaving when Rose said, "Jack!" She waited until he turned to face her before lowering her voice and saying, "If you solve it, I'd appreciate it if the bad guy makes it to trial."

Jack nodded quietly and left.

* * *

Two hours later, Jack and Laura received a visit to their office from Connie Crane.

"Okay, Jack! What the hell gives?" she shouted as she strode in.

"Hi, CC. Haven't you gone to bed yet?" replied Jack.

"Don't give me that shit! I talked to Dallas. Why are you sticking your face into my homicide?"

"Because I told him to," said Rose, walking in behind her.

Jack quickly made introductions and CC cast a suspicious glance at Jack before turning to Rose and saying, "Why? What business is it of yours?"

"International gun smuggling," replied Rose.

"International gun smuggling!" replied CC. "Jesus, this is just kids! Not organized crime!"

"Kids?" asked Jack.

"Yeah, we found a footprint made by the perp. Not clear enough to match to a shoe, but from the size of it, we think it was a young teenager. We've already got the school liaison officers checking out the youth gangs."

"The gun was left at the scene," said Jack.

"So what?" replied CC.

"Most kids would value a handgun. Dropping it at the scene is something a pro would do."

"A pro? That's a laugh. Sounds like you need some sleep. This is just some kids who used a cheap pistol to whack a wino. A thrill kill, that's all."

"A thrill kill?" replied Jack. "Why drive him all the way out there for that? Except for the victim, the hit matches a lot of organized crime type hits."

"Organized crime! Get off it! This isn't *The Sopranos*! I don't see what business it —"

"Cool the attitude," said Rose quietly. "We are all on the same team. Gun smuggling from the U.S. into Canada is a major concern. Perhaps you aren't aware of it, but our office was instrumental in seizing several automatic weapons last weekend."

CC paused and said, "Sorry. And yes, I'm aware of that case. Randy and I talked to Mad Dog about it after he was arrested." She glanced at Jack and Laura and added, "Good going, by the way." She turned to Rose and said, "But this is different. No Mac-10s and Uzis here."

"Maybe you're right," said Rose. "But if it is a juvenile gang, let's put a stop to them before they do become *The Sopranos*. I really don't see what the problem is."

CC eyed Jack suspiciously. *With you, there is always a problem.*

"Our office will concentrate on following the trail of the gun and your office can handle everything else," continued Rose.

"Okay," sighed CC. "You work on the gun. Good luck. I think you'll find it to be a dead end, but if you do discover something, I expect to be notified immediately."

"Naturally," replied Jack. "By the way, Dallas told me Melvin had a clear garbage bag over his head and upper torso. Kind of unusual."

CC pulled up a chair to sit in while Rose perched on the corner of Jack's desk.

"Kids watch a lot of *CSI* these days," replied CC. "Maybe they thought it would stop us from finding any DNA in their van."

"Van?" asked Rose.

"No witnesses to anything, or tire tracks. We're guessing he was hauled out of a van by the way his heels were dragged in the parking lot."

"Why would anyone kill Melvin?" asked Laura.

"Kids ... no conscience," replied CC. "Probably their way of getting an adrenaline rush."

"You seem certain that it was kids," said Jack.

"We're checking into the possibility that it was someone who knew him, but it doesn't look like it. The cheap pistol found at the scene was sold to some guy in the States who didn't have a record and has since died of old age. I meant it when I said good luck on finding anything out about it."

"We'll give the gun a shot," replied Jack.

"I'm so tired, I actually think that is funny," said CC. "But I'm sure we'll discover the murder is connected with a youth gang. Kids won't keep it a secret for long. Eventually somebody will talk."

"Yes, or eventually someone else will be murdered," suggested Jack.

"Yeah, well, there is always that possibility," said CC, getting up to leave. "Nice to have met you, Rose. Sorry if I sounded off before. I haven't had much sleep."

Jack followed her into the hallway and said, "Listen, CC. I don't have any intention of looking over your shoulder. I only want to help out a bit."

"Help out a bit? Yeah, I've heard that one before. Can you blame me for being a little paranoid? Last night I find Natasha's name on the victim. An hour later I watch you kill a cat at the crime scene. Speaking of which, that really shook you up, didn't it?"

"It bothered me," admitted Jack.

"I know. You were shaking afterwards." Connie shook her head and said, "You're a hard guy to figure out sometimes. Which is why I'm not exactly ecstatic that you'll be part of the investigation. I've been down this street before and it wasn't pretty."

"This is different. All I want to do is lend a hand. If I can trace the gun it might help."

"So you don't know Melvin Montgomery? Never met him?"

"No. He was only a friend of my wife."

"A friend?"

"I mean, patient," Jack hastened to say.

CC gave Jack a hard look. *Oh, fuck.*

10

The next week drifted past with Jack and Laura getting bits and pieces of the information they sought through the police in Georgia in an attempt to track the pistol. There wasn't much. They learned that the gun was bought new eleven years ago by a man who lived in Savannah Beach, Georgia. The man had no criminal record and was sixty-four years old when he bought the gun. Records showed he bought a second handgun two years later — a Smith & Wesson revolver.

The revolver was now owned by the man's son and he was interviewed by the police. The police learned his mother died of ovarian cancer when his father was sixty-seven. Four years ago his father died of a heart attack and the son inherited all of his father's belongings. The son said he only found the Smith & Wesson in his dad's belongings and had no idea what happened to the other pistol. The police said the family was respected in the community and they believed the son was telling the truth.

"What do you think?" asked Jack when Laura finished reading the report they had received from Georgia.

"Doesn't look good," replied Laura. "I wonder what prompted him to wait until he was sixty-four to buy a gun? Bet his house was broken into," she added.

Jack shook his head. "No, I checked. He lived there all of his life. No reported break-ins before or after his gun purchases."

"Joined a gun club?" suggested Laura.

"Not that, either. I do have another theory."

"Which is?"

"He bought it shortly before turning sixty-five. What do a lot of people do when they turn sixty-five?"

"Retire, buy the biggest car they can find, and drive it slowly up and down the street in busy traffic."

"Exactly!" replied Jack.

"You mean I'm right? What's that got to do with it?"

"They retire and travel. They're Americans. Think about it. Remember that motto from an old TV Western? 'Have gun, will travel'!"

"Guess I'm not that old, but I get your point. And when he was sixty-six he bought a second gun because —"

"He lost his first one or it was stolen. But why didn't he report it?"

"Because he brought it someplace where he wasn't allowed to bring it?"

"That's my guess. I'm going to call the son myself."

"Today's the fourth of July. American Independence Day. He might be home."

Laura listened as Jack dialed and then spoke.

"Yes, sir. That's right. A Mountie from Canada.... Yes, I know the police spoke with you ... no, actually I've never ridden a horse ... yes, I'm a real Mountie. ... Thank you, I like to think my English is pretty good, too. It is mostly only one province, what you would call a state, that speaks French.... Um, about seventy Fahrenheit right now ... no, I'm not spoofing you ..."

Laura watched as the conversation continued and listened to Jack when he asked the questions he wanted answered.

"A motor home, did they? To Niagara Falls, Canada, in early September ... ten years ago." Jack smiled and gave Laura the thumbs-up sign. "I see, well, that is unfortunate. I hope it didn't ruin the rest of their holiday."

When Jack hung up, he gave Laura the details she had already heard, plus he said, "They only stayed one night in Niagara Falls because someone vandalized their motor home. He said they were upset about it and returned to the States the next day."

"In other words, if whoever did it got caught with their gun, they didn't want to be around to face the music."

"You got it. He remembered asking them if anything had been stolen and said they were a little vague about that."

"So we have a pretty good idea on how the gun arrived in Canada," said Laura. "Now what?"

"Start tracking down places where you would stay with a motor home in Niagara Falls and see if there are any records of break-ins ten years ago. Other people could have been robbed and reported it. Maybe there were suspects or arrests."

"Heck of a long shot. Also not what you would call organized crime."

"I know, but Natasha is afraid it will fall by the wayside. I promised her I would look into it. Besides, I think we both could use a bit of a break from —" Jack stopped to answer his phone. It was CC and he quickly jotted down notes as he spoke with her.

— Ten years ago (September) gun used in a coffee-shop robbery in Regina. Bullet fired in ceiling.

— Nobody hurt. Small amount of $ taken. Suspect in his 40s, wearing ball cap, swarthy complexion — mole below left eye.

— Four years ago (August), a suspected drug dealer (Bernie Wingham) in Trail, B.C., was shot in the knee at his house. Bernie would not co-operate with police. No suspects.

— Two years ago (April), gun used in a mugging in Vancouver. Two men tried to rob an employee of an antique store of the day's

receipts when he stepped out to go to the bank. Victim shot through the arm. Bullet went through a window of a restaurant half-way down the block and lodged in a wall. Police were inside having dinner. Suspects got away in a car with stolen plates. Both with collar-length black hair, tall, early 20s.

— Same gun used to murder Melvin M.

"So, somehow I think the gun ended up in the hands of some kids," said CC in conclusion. "I'll send you copies of the reports I have on what I just told you. Maybe it was someone's older brother who tried to rob the antique store."

"Wasn't this Bernie character in Trail re-interviewed after the antique store mugging?" asked Jack. "It sounds like blind luck that he didn't get killed."

"He was re-interviewed, but wouldn't co-operate. Too afraid. Four years ago he was growing and selling pot. The members in Trail think he's gone straight. He has since married and has two toddlers. The guy hobbles around with a permanent limp. I guess he counts himself as lucky to be alive."

"So, now that he is married, he is even less likely to risk talking."

"For sure. I just got off the phone with one of the members in Trail who tried to talk to him last time. Basically had the door slammed in their face. Now that the gun was used in a murder, I'm not optimistic that it will alleviate his fear at all. I guess we could try again but I think we're wasting our time."

"Do you mind if Laura and I try?"

"Fill your boots."

"Does Bernie still live in the same house as when he was shot?"

"Yes. The member mentioned that the house used to be a junk heap, but now that Bernie is married, he actually has a white picket fence and flower beds. Why? What are you thinking of?"

"I'm thinking I've been drinking too much."

The following day, it was suppertime when Jack and Laura approached Bernie Wingham's house in Trail.

Jack did up the top buttons of his golf shirt on the way to the house and whispered, "How do I look?"

"Like you're on your way to church," replied Laura.

"Good, I'll ring the bell and be right back."

A moment later, Bernie's face appeared in the door window. He saw Jack and Laura facing each other at the bottom of his porch steps and opened the door.

Jack was talking quietly and solemnly to Laura, but his words could be overheard. "God grant us the serenity to accept the things we cannot change, the courage to change the things we can, and the wisdom to know the difference."

"It's time," replied Laura, glancing up at Bernie. "I'll wait here. Go do it. Your eighth step."

"What are you guys? Jehovah Witnesses? I'm not interested!" said Bernie through a half-opened door.

"Bernie, no, wait!" said Jack.

"You know my name? Who are you?" asked Bernie, limping out onto his porch. "What do you want?"

"I came to make amends," said Jack, walking up the stairs to meet Bernie. "It is an important step in the program."

"Amends for what?" asked Bernie. "What program?"

"My name is Jack," said Jack, offering his hand.

"I said what do you want?" asked Bernie, ignoring the intended handshake.

Jack sighed and looked to Laura as if for support. She nodded encouragingly, and he turned to Bernie, and said, "I'm an alcoholic. I'm in recovery."

"What the hell does that have to do with me? Did my wife put you up to this?" he asked, glaring back into the house.

"No. This isn't about you. It's about me. I came to apologize."

"For what?"

"It was my idea to have you kneecapped four years ago."

"Jesus fucking Christ!" roared Bernie.

"Please, let me explain," pleaded Jack, after giving Bernie a few seconds to recover. "I used to drink a lot back then."

"Maybe you drank too much … because I don't ever remember seeing you before," said Bernie suspiciously. "And who's she?" he asked, with a nod toward Laura.

"She's my sponsor."

"Yeah? For her, I'd join AA myself." Bernie then glared at Jack and said, "I'd definitely remember her ... and I ain't never seen you before, either."

"You probably haven't. I scored some weed once from a guy who made me wait in the car while he came to see you. Later, I got to thinkin' that you must have a lot of money."

"So you put Angelo and Dominic up to it?"

"I was so drunk back in those days, I hardly remember much." Jack looked around at the yard and said, "I wasn't even sure if it was the right place. Somehow I thought it looked different. I don't remember the fence."

"How did you know them?"

"Know who?"

"The brothers. Angelo and Dominic. How did you know them?"

"Is that their names? I don't even remember. I met them in a bar and one thing led to another. As I recall, I thought they may have already known you."

"Yeah, they did. But ... you're telling me that it was your idea to rob me?"

"Sorry about that," said Jack, hanging his head in shame. "I didn't think anyone would get hurt. I stood six and was supposed to beep the horn if the cops were coming. It seemed like a good idea when we were drinking."

"Jesus Christ," sputtered Bernie. "Do you know I'm forever gimped now?"

"I didn't know, man. I'm really sorry. Guess I should find Angelo and Dominic and apologize to them, too. I remember stealing their car radio a few days later."

"You what? Jesus, you're lucky they didn't kill you." Bernie paused and muttered, "Fuck, I should never have told you their names." He cast a worried look at Jack and said, "Forget about them if you want to stay alive."

"Stay alive? Why? Are they dangerous?"

"Dangerous! What the fuck do you think? Look at my leg!"

"Oh ... yeah."

"Not only that, the cops were around a couple of years ago, asking questions. The same gun was used to shoot somebody in Vancouver. More than that, two years ago Angelo and Dominic killed some guy in Vancouver."

"With the same gun?" asked Jack.

"Nope. Sliced him up instead. I don't think the cops ever did connect them with the gun."

"Who did they kill two years ago? What guy?"

"Don't know, but the cops have been looking for them for that. Let's just say that Angelo and Dominic aren't the forgiving type and wouldn't appreciate being found. My advice is to keep your yap shut and get the fuck off my porch."

"So, you forgive me?" asked Jack, giving himself a self-satisfied smile.

Bernie's face turned red and he said, "Do I look like I fuckin' forgive ya?"

"Oh ... guess not. Sorry, I thought you did because you warned me about Angelo and Dominic."

"I don't give a fuck about you! I just don't want you to do something that might bring Angelo and Dominic back to see me."

Jack hung his head and turned and walked back down the steps while Bernie glared at him from the porch. Laura placed her arm around Jack's shoulder to console him as they walked back to their car. In reality, she hoped that the shaking of their shoulders from snickering would be mistaken for grief.

"Hope ya end up back on the bottle!" yelled Bernie, as they drove away.

Twenty minutes later, Jack and Laura met with Constable Sarah Hundt in the Trail RCMP office. Sarah knew immediately who the brothers were. "There are Canada-wide warrants on them for murder," she said. "Going back two years. Their mom still lives in Trail. We've still got their photos up on the bulletin board. Hang on and I'll get them and pull the files."

Like both their parents, Angelo and Dominic had lengthy criminal records with numerous offences for violence, robbery, and possession of stolen property. A Vancouver RCMP Drug Section informant had linked them to the torture and murder of a high-level heroin dealer in Vancouver two years prior. The heroin dealer bled to death from multiple slash marks made by a knife while he was tied to a chair. A search was made for the brothers, but they had vanished and the informant was unable to obtain any further information.

"Two years ago was about the same time that gun was used to rob an antique store," commented Jack, while reaching for his own file to cross-reference when the antique store was robbed. He felt a rush of excitement as he compared the details. "The heroin dealer was killed on the same day and only a couple of hours before the robbery of the antique store!"

"That's no coincidence," said Laura.

"You've got that right," replied Jack. "I'm betting the torture of the dealer was to get info on something. Either money or dope. The owner of that antique store was not an innocent victim. They wouldn't have had to torture someone for that. Angelo and Dominic were after him for a lot more than the day's income from the store."

"We need to find Angelo and Dominic," said Laura, turning to Sarah. "Where does their father live?"

"He died six years ago, drunk behind the wheel," replied Sarah. "They didn't have any other kids except Angelo and Dominic. The mom still lives in town."

"So Dad died and the kids got the gun to carry on the family business," said Jack.

Laura nodded in agreement.

Jack pointed to a file in front of him and said, "The mother, Giorgetta, her record includes convictions for prostitution in Hamilton, Ontario."

"Hamilton … practically next door to Niagara Falls," replied Laura.

"Angelo and Dominic's criminal history is all in B.C., but the parents' criminal history is largely out of southern Ontario," noted Jack.

"When did the family move to Trail?" asked Laura.

"Our first record was a noise complaint ten years ago," replied Sarah.

"Do you still have a picture of the father?" asked Jack.

Sarah nodded, then dug through a file and handed Jack a picture. Jack smiled and handed it to Laura. A mole was clearly visible under the father's left eye. "We've solved who robbed the coffee shop in Regina," he said.

"So that was when the family was moving west and picking up money for their travelling expenses," replied Laura. "So, where to now?"

"Took us all day to get here and tomorrow will be wasted getting home. Let's make it two for one and knock on another door. With Giorgetta's background and desire to protect her sons, she'll be paranoid, but we have nothing to lose."

Jack and Laura both smiled at Giorgetta as she peered out a side window of her house before opening the door.

"Hi," said Jack. "We're friends of Angelo and Dominic. Are they around?"

"My boys don't live here no more," replied Giorgetta, suspiciously. "Who are you? What do you want?"

"We're friends of theirs. Met them in Vancouver a couple of years ago before I moved to Cranbrook. I owe them some money for some stuff they gave me to fence ... I mean, sell, in Cranbrook. They gave me your address and said I could always contact them through you."

"Yeah? Is that a fact? When did you last talk to them?"

"Sometime last fall when they called me. They didn't say much on the phone, but are anxious to get the money I owe them. I've got it now."

"You're a fuckin' liar!" replied Giorgetta, spitting out the words.

"What?" replied Jack in surprise, while wiping his face with the back of his sleeve.

"You're a fuckin' liar! My sons have been dead for over two years!" She looked at Jack in disgust and said, "You fuckin' cops … they may have been troubled boys, but they always called on Mother's Day, even when they were in jail. They haven't called in over two years. I know they're dead. So, fuck off, cops!"

11

It was mid-morning on Thursday when Kang Lee spoke briefly with The Shaman as they walked toward the Avitat Lounge at the South Terminal of the Vancouver International Airport. Da Khlot and Sayomi trailed behind, out of earshot.

"I wish you a pleasant flight," said Lee. "I look forward to the day when I shall accompany you home."

"The day will arrive soon enough."

"With Mister Goldie's eagerness to fill my position, perhaps it could be sooner than six months? He is intelligent. I am sure he will learn fast."

"And Mister Wang? Any indication that he was unhappy because he wasn't chosen?"

"Not at all. He is happy in his own pond and agrees that Mister Goldie is better suited. In fact, when I met with them both, Mister Goldie displayed dismay at being slow in developing the market back east.

Mister Wang volunteered that a couple of his associates would be moving to Montreal and might later be in a position to assist Mister Goldie. Their spirit of co-operation with each other and our organization appears to be good."

"And what about Mister Goldie's replacement? Do you think Mister Wang is capable of handling both functions?"

"No, Mister Wang indicates that he is busy enough. However, Mister Goldie says he has several reliable people in mind to choose from who would be suitable."

"People he says are reliable depend upon his own reliability," said The Shaman.

"He did not hesitate when I told him he would be required to take a lie detector test."

"And, I presume, with the knowledge he will have acquired about our corporation, he knows what would happen should he fail such a test?"

"He does."

"Still, Mister Goldie is not a family man. Something I consider an important asset to ensure loyalty. With him, I foresee an annual lie detector evaluation, combined with further assignments to ensure his sincerity. In the meantime, six months is not long. Haste brings mistakes. You must be absolutely certain he is the right man for the position before you vacate it. If he is not the right man, then we will find a new one. I would find no fault with you should such a decision be necessary *prior* to the six months."

Lee nodded quietly.

"I know you are anxious to return to your family."

"That is true," lamented Lee.

"You know they will continue to be watched and well looked after. I recognize that you have worked hard. Your family has been rewarded accordingly. Do not spoil what you have," added The Shaman with a subtle glance behind him, "by making a mistake."

"I understand," replied Lee, envisioning Da Khlot's expressionless dark eyes watching his own family. The family he longed to be with.

It was late Friday afternoon when Laura dropped some documents onto Jack's desk. "Your theory may be right," she said. "Company checks — take a look."

Jack looked at the documents and saw that two antique stores were owned by an Arthur Goldie, who also owned a Vancouver nightclub called Goldie Locks. It was Goldie's employee who had been shot in the arm two years ago. Neither the employee nor Arthur Goldie had any criminal record.

"I talked to the narcs," said Laura. "They told me they currently have an ongoing undercover operation targeting heroin at the ounce level. Last week, one of the operators bought a quarter-pound from a dealer by the name of Jojo. The narcs followed him after the order was placed and he went to the Goldie Locks nightclub for a few minutes. He then met the operator an hour later at a McDonald's restaurant and did the deal."

"Did they see who Jojo met in the nightclub?"

"They said he met with numerous people. The narcs couldn't tell who was involved with the deal."

"Could be a coincidence," said Jack. "Maybe Jojo went to see who was around to party with him after his sale."

"You won't think it's a coincidence after you read these next reports," said Laura, handing Jack some more papers.

Jack scanned the reports and saw that Goldie Locks nightclub had come up in numerous wiretaps and drug investigations over the years as a common meeting spot for several high-level heroin dealers, *including the heroin dealer tortured and murdered by Angelo and Dominic.*

"Love it!" said Jack, with a smile. "Too big of a coincidence for Angelo and Dominic to torture a drug dealer and rob an antique store later the same day. Especially when both places are owned by the same person. In my books, Arthur Goldie is dirty."

"Proving it will be another story," said Laura.

"Angelo and Dominic tried to rob some people connected to the big league," mused Jack. "My guess is the antique store employee is, or was, a money bagman for the organization. In fact, with him making the store's deposits, you can bet that his real job is to transport drug money. Our two Italian brothers found out that the dealer they tortured had just done a deal. Maybe they were hired for protection by whoever was doing the buying. Bet they grabbed the dealer later and when he didn't have the money, they tortured him to find out who did. The dealer then gave them the name of the bagman from the antique store."

"You could be right on that account," said Laura. "I agree we could be on to something big as far as drugs go, but how did the gun used by Angelo and Dominic end up being used to kill Melvin? And why?"

Jack paused as he scanned the reports again, hoping an answer would jump out at him. It didn't. "I don't know," he said. "If the brothers are dead ... and after talking with dear old mom, I tend to think they are, then —"

"Maybe she lied and said they were dead so we would stop looking."

"Didn't get that sense, did you?" asked Jack.

"No," admitted Laura. "She seemed genuine. Plus the brothers aren't all that bright. If they were alive, I think they would have been located."

"I agree. Following that logic, I think they're dead because of who they tried to rob. Their bodies haven't been found, which means whoever killed them may have inherited the gun. If their bodies were dumped in an alley, then anyone could have come along and picked over the remains like vultures. We need to find out who killed them."

"Any ideas how?" asked Laura.

"Find the employee from the antique store and put a bullet through his other arm. See who comes after us."

Jack saw Laura's concerned look and quickly added, "Don't take me seriously! I'm joking."

"Oh, man. Good ... I wasn't sure. It's hard to tell with you."

Jack chuckled and said, "Of course I was joking." Then his face became serious and he said, "You know, it would probably work."

"Jack!"

Jack grinned and said, "Okay, okay. Plan B. How about we look at Arthur Goldie and his businesses and see if we can confirm our suspicions?"

"Shake the tree and see who falls out. Get an informant or something. Maybe the narcs will help out."

"Exactly. Even if we are off base on who killed Melvin, either way, these guys could be good targets. I'll talk with Rose and let —" Jack stopped to answer his cellphone. It was a nurse from the hospice.

"Appreciate ya comin'," said Ophelia, staring up from her hospital bed at Jack. Her normal raspy voice sounded even worse. She tried to wiggle to a better position, so he adjusted her bed to raise her upper body, but suggested she lay still while he pulled up a chair.

"I should have come here sooner," she said. Her voice crackled as she spoke, making her words difficult to hear. "The morph' they're giving me isn't bad."

"That's good," replied Jack. "Have you managed to steal any so you can sell it on the street later?"

A smile flittered across her face before she became serious. She stared at Jack for a moment before saying, "Guess you know this is the last time you'll have to come and visit."

"I don't have to come here," said Jack. "I'm here because I want to be here."

"Yeah, well, I appreciate it. You being a cop, too. Go figure."

"You're not a bad person, Ophelia," said Jack. "You're sick, but you're not bad. I'm sorry that life dealt you the hand it did."

"Win some, lose some." Ophelia coughed several times and briefly nodded off. A minute later she awoke with a start, perhaps afraid that she wouldn't awaken. She was relieved to see that Jack was still there. "Lucky I'm dying in here rather than out on some pig farm. Things could be worse."

Jack nodded, but for Ophelia he knew that things were never a lot better, either.

"So, how come you do come to see me? You don't owe me nothin'."

Jack looked intently at Ophelia and said, "I respect you for the kind of person you are. You're the type who worries about people. For the kind of life you've had, it would be easy to use it as an excuse, but you don't."

"There's somethin' you're not tellin' me."

"You're a good person."

Ophelia blinked her eyes a couple of times and said, "Thanks for seein' me."

"It's no problem seeing you. My office isn't that far away."

"I don't mean that. I mean for *seein'* me." Ophelia coughed some more, but didn't take her eyes off of Jack's face. She knew he didn't understand. "Let me tell ya somethin'," she said. "My last day on the street before you brought me in, I was feeling pretty sick. Just leaning against a doorway, too sick to turn a trick. Some lady walked past me with a boy, about five years old. The boy could tell I was sick and said, 'Look, Mommy!' The lady gave me a disgusted look, you know, like I was a pimple on the ass of society. Then she said, 'Don't stare, honey. That's just nobody.'"

Jack stared at Ophelia, putting himself in her place.

"Guess what I'm tryin' to say," continued Ophelia, "is people who got it don't give a shit about people who don't. We're nobodies."

"I think you're somebody."

Ophelia's face softened and she looked at Jack and said, "I've seen that in you. You're different than most people. Guess what I'm asking is why?"

Jack swallowed, not sure how to respond.

"Come on," prompted Ophelia. "I'm gonna croak before morning. It ain't like I'm gonna tell anyone."

Jack took the time to take a deep breath and then slowly exhaled. When he finished he said, "I had a sister who died of alcoholism — although that is like saying a bullet killed you instead of the person who pointed the gun at you and pulled the trigger."

"So, who pulled the trigger?" asked Ophelia. "Your father?"

Jack nodded and said, "You're pretty perceptive."

"Perceptive!" snorted Ophelia. "Try experienced."

Jack sighed and said, "Well, you're right. Amongst other less than desirable traits, my father was a pedophile. When my sister escaped from home, she lived alone in a grubby trailer and was always taking in stray animals to look after. A friend of mine once saw her on the street and thought she was a homeless person. Basically, she was." Jack stared at Ophelia for a moment, before acknowledging, "Maybe she is one of the reasons I look at some people differently. I don't know. Some days I feel like I've seen too much suffering. Too much injustice."

Ophelia reached toward Jack's hand, so he leaned forward so she could hold it. Her grip was firm, but her flesh felt cold. Her organs were shutting down, including her heart.

"Thanks for telling me," said Ophelia. "It was something I was always curious about. Helps explain why you let me get away with settin' that guy up to be whacked with a tire iron that night."

Jack shrugged and said, "That guy was going to turn a trick with a twelve-year-old kid. I don't feel bad about letting you get away with it because of who you are inside. You've made a few slip-ups here and there. Who hasn't? We're all human. But in my books, you're somebody. Somebody who made a positive difference in this world."

He realized her grip on his hand had loosened. She was dead.

He never knew if she heard his last words or not.

12

It was Monday afternoon and the meeting in the boardroom was attended by investigators from I-HIT, the RCMP Drug Section, and the Intelligence Unit.

Jack and Laura gave an account of their findings, leading up to their theory about what happened to Angelo and Dominic.

CC rolled her eyes and said, "Thanks, Jack. I knew bringing you into this would add to the body count. Now you're telling me that it's not only Melvin Montgomery who was murdered, but you're saying we've got two more bodies out there that we haven't found yet?"

"Sorry about that," replied Jack.

"Ah, it's okay," replied CC. "Was just spoofin' ya. The both of you did good. Filled in some missing pieces of the puzzle. And as far as the bodies go, if there are any, unless we end up finding them on our turf, it could be Vancouver PD's responsibility. I'll bring them up to date on it later, but without any bodies, I'm not sure what they'll do. Maybe they'll interview the employee from the antique store."

"Tell them to hold off on that," said Jack. "I doubt they would get anything and the police attention could heat up the narcs on their UC operation."

"I agree with Jack," said Sammy, who was one of the investigators taking an active role in the under-cover operation.

"Not a problem," replied CC. "I'll hold off. But where do you propose we go from here?"

"What about a wiretap?" suggested Jack, looking around the room.

"I'll check with Crown," replied CC, "but I think it is highly unlikely that we have the grounds to get one. How about getting one for drug trafficking?"

"We've got one on Jojo," said Sammy. "So far he's the biggest fish we've caught and even he is small com-pared to what we know about some of the big players who frequent Goldie's. As far as the wire on Jojo goes, it hasn't been all that productive. He likes pay phones followed up with a lot of heat checks before meeting anyone face-to-face. Even after the heat checks, if we're lucky enough that he hasn't spotted our surveillance, when he does meet someone, he has a habit of meeting several people over a space of a few minutes in places like restaurants, nightclubs, or bars. That makes it dif-ficult to figure out which person is of importance and which one is just a casual acquaintance. With what we have so far, there are absolutely no grounds for us to get a wiretap on anyone else."

The conversation continued for several minutes, but eventually it was decided that Drug Section would continue with their undercover operation in the hope of gaining grounds to apply for a wiretap on people connected with Goldie Locks. Jack and Laura would start doing surveillance of Goldie and his nightclub to see what they could learn.

"Keep me informed of all the players," said CC. "If you do get a wire, maybe we can match somebody up with a younger brother affiliated with a youth gang. Or someone with a kid demented enough to murder a homeless guy."

"The kid had to be old enough to drive a van," said Sammy. "Makes him sixteen, at least."

CC laughed and said, "You ever been to Surrey? Half the stolen cars are taken by kids a lot younger than that. The footprint we found at the scene could be from a twelve-year-old."

"Good point," said Sammy, shaking his head.

"How long before you think you'll bring the UC op to an end?" asked Laura.

"We're already halfway through July," replied Sammy. "We're supposed to have things wrapped up by the first week of August at the latest." Sammy looked apologetic as he glanced at CC and added, "I have to tell you, it doesn't look good that we'll connect with any of the big players. Our budget can't afford the hundreds of thousands of dollars it would take to buy at their level. They deal multi-kilos. We have a budget that is at the ounce level."

"Don't worry about it," replied CC. "It's a hell

of a long shot, anyway. Even though Jack and Laura did trace the gun to Goldie's doorstep, it doesn't mean that anyone he knows had it. Angelo and Dominic may have tossed it before they … well, disappeared."

Jack and Laura looked at each other and she gave a subtle shake of her head. Jack thought the same way. *If Angelo and Dominic didn't toss away the gun when they kneecapped Bernie, they likely didn't toss it away over shooting someone in the arm. And what twelve-year-old kid would throw a gun away?*

Laura saw Jack smile at her. It was a smile she had seen before. *He's got a plan.*

It was eight o'clock Tuesday night when Jack found a place to park in an alley one block down from the rear door of the Goldie Locks nightclub. He rested the binoculars on the steering wheel to hold them steady and was able to see Goldie's car parked behind the nightclub. It was a new Aston Martin V8 Vantage Roadster with a custom gold paint job, complete with vanity plates reading GOLDIE. Laura was in another car, and found a place to watch the front of the nightclub.

An hour went by before Arthur Goldie appeared out the back door of his club. Jack noted that Goldie's physique made him relatively easy to see. He was a tall man with a thin body, which made his hands, feet, and head look extra large and gangly in comparison. He was forty-three years old and kept the hair on the sides of his head shaved short, but had a mop of thick brown hair on the top of his head. He was dressed in khaki-coloured slacks and an open moss-green windbreaker that revealed a canary-yellow golf shirt underneath.

"We've got action out back," radioed Jack. "Looks like he'll be eastbound in the alley."

"I'll see him when he comes out," replied Laura.

"Keep it loose," cautioned Jack. "I don't want him to see our faces yet."

"It'll be real loose, out of sight, if he steps on the gas with what he's driving," replied Laura. A moment later she said, "Okay, got him. Turning north from the alley. What's he got on the top of his head?"

"Just his hair," replied Jack, while turning north on the street one block west of Goldie before making a quick right on Robson Street to catch up.

"Looks like a dead rat."

"Think the rat is under the hair."

"Copy that," snickered Laura. "Okay, he's picked up a ruby coming on to Robson. No indicator on, looks like he'll be going straight through."

Jack glanced at Goldie's club as he drove past and then entered the left turn lane at the next light. He spotted the Aston Martin to his right where it was still parked, waiting for the light to change.

For the next ten minutes Jack and Laura followed Goldie. Eventually, he parked in another alley behind a restaurant before entering through the rear door. Unlike many criminals Jack had worked on, Goldie seldom checked his rear-view mirror and did not drive in a manner to detect if he was being followed. *Is he really an innocent business man? Or does he feel safe because he thinks he is so immune and protected by others who do the dirty work?*

"Keep an eye on his wheels," radioed Jack. "I'm going on foot to walk past the front of the restaurant to see if I can spot who he's meeting. He either owns the place or has to be on good terms with someone to walk in through the back. I'll call you on your cell."

Jack glanced in through the front windows of the Wang Hui Chinese Restaurant as he strolled past. He didn't spot Goldie, but did see a group of Asian men sitting around some tables that had been pushed together. By their boisterous mannerisms and the way they were dressed, Jack had the distinct impression that they were gang-affiliated ... and not the boy scouts. He spoke to Laura on her cell and relayed his observations.

"Sounds interesting," replied Laura. "Want to start scooping licence plates? Maybe find out who —" her words broke off suddenly. "Hold it, Goldie's out again and chatting in the alley with some guy. Short, barrel-chested Asian wearing black, baggy pants, and a red golf shirt. Maybe forty to fifty years old."

"The restaurant is Chinese," said Jack. "Bet it's the owner."

"Okay, that was quick," continued Laura. "Goldie is back to his wheels and the red golf shirt went back inside the restaurant. Your call. Want me to stay with Goldie?"

"No, let him go. I don't want to heat him up. Let's watch this place and see if we can figure out who the clientele is and what is going on that would require a back-alley meeting."

Over the next couple of hours, Jack and Laura recorded numerous licence plates of people coming and going from the restaurant. They also noted a pay phone outside the restaurant was used frequently by the clientele, some of whom clearly had cellphones.

By noon the following day, Jack's and Laura's desks were piled high with paper. They identified the owner of the restaurant as Hui Wang, who named his restaurant in the Asian fashion of Wang Hui Chinese Restaurant by using his surname first. It was also discovered that Wang was the owner of a furniture store called Wang's House of Bamboo.

What Jack found of particular interest was that Wang had been charged for trafficking in crystal meth several years earlier, but was not convicted after someone else claimed ownership for the drug.

Laura glanced at the mug shot of Wang and confirmed that he was the man in the red golf shirt.

Jack discovered that he was partially right in that the clientele belonged to a gang. In fact, there were three different Asian gangs represented by the clientele. The Big Circle Boys, Sun Yee On triad, and some who had been listed by the Vancouver Police Department's Anti-Gang Unit as belonging to gangs who were unnamed. Their criminal records included: attempted murder, kidnapping, assault, extortion, pimping, auto theft, identity and credit card theft, and drug trafficking.

"Except none of the drug trafficking is heroin," said Jack, looking at the different records. "These guys are all into ecstasy and meth. If Goldie is involved with heroin, then he's visiting the wrong crowd."

"Maybe Wang plans on adding to his menu," suggested Laura.

"Maybe, but something doesn't sit right," replied Jack. "Goldie seems much more sophisticated. The Chinese we saw were basically a bunch of hoods strutting around like Hollywood gangsters. They all seem close-knit. To me, Goldie doesn't fit in."

"He must somehow. He met with Wang in the alley."

"You've got a point there. I'm going to call Sammy and see how they feel about approaching some of the dealers associated with Wang. Those guys are punks in comparison to the players who hang out at Goldie Locks. If heroin is about to be moved through there, it might be an opportune time."

Drug Section was glad to assist, and over the next few nights they managed to get an undercover operator to meet some of the Chinese associated with the restaurant. By the following Monday, another meeting was held amongst the investigators in the boardroom.

"Good news, bad news," said Sammy. "The good news is that Jack and Laura gave us a hell of a good tip on the Chinese restaurant. We've got two operators in with some of the bad boys connected to there. One operator is Chinese. She is being offered large quantities of ecstasy and crystal meth. She scored a sample of the meth and it is high quality. I tell ya, the bad guys are tossing weights and numbers around like it was the Toronto Stock Exchange. Anything goes, providing you've got the cash. We've also seen Wang using the pay phone out front. We've submitted a new operational plan to start a new UC there and I think we'll have a wiretap up and running on Wang that will include the pay phone out front."

"How long to get wire?" asked Jack. "With the action you're talking about, I imagine it will take you a month or so to push the paperwork through."

Sammy smiled and said, "Normally, yeah, but we got the Asian Heat on board with us."

"Asian Heat?" asked Jack.

"That's what I call her," replied Sammy. "She's of Chinese ancestry and is attached to the Asian Based Organized Crime Unit within our office. Tina is a real pit bull when it comes to catching bad guys. Before joining the Force, she was a loans officer in a bank. She's good with the paperwork. Don't worry, we'll get the wire. We'll also bug his car if we get the chance."

"Tina sounds like someone we could use in our office," Jack said, looking at Laura.

"Hands off!" replied Sammy. "I shouldn't have told you about her."

"You said earlier that there was some bad news," interjected CC.

"Our operators have been turned down flat when

it comes to heroin. Maybe Arthur Goldie isn't into heroin. Maybe it's his clientele who is."

"Then why the back-alley meeting?" asked Jack.

Sammy shrugged and said, "It's summer. The restaurant kitchen was probably hot and steamy. Outside would be cooler."

Jack shook his head and said, "If he's innocent, why not phone? He drove all the way over for a two-minute chat."

"Well ... whatever, but with a new UC in the works on ecstasy and meth, we're going to be shutting down the heroin operation soon. Maybe we'll get Wang talking to Goldie, but as it stands now, as far as the heroin operation goes, we hope to set up the final buy and bust within the next two weeks."

"Mind if Laura and I start a little UC of our own in Goldie Locks?" asked Jack.

"Uh ... hang on, Jack," said Rose. "Are you proposing that you and Laura start buying heroin? We also don't have a budget for that."

"Not buying heroin," replied Jack. "Just an intelligence probe. Basically go in and watch. See who's who in the zoo. Might claim a few drinks, but nothing too expensive."

Laura glanced at Jack. *A few drinks, a few laughs ... nobody gets hurt ... right, Jack?*

"That I can approve," replied Rose, "provided we're not interfering?" she added, looking at Sammy.

Sammy shook his head and replied, "Not at all. It could help us. If Jack and Laura can figure out who is who in there, next time we score from Jojo they might be in a position to figure out what is going on if he shows up at the club after."

"Keep us in the loop," said Jack. "We'll start going inside and getting acquainted."

"As long as you don't cause us any heat before we're done with our operation."

Jack smiled. *That is exactly what I intend to do.*

13

It was Wednesday and relatively quiet at eight o'clock at night when Jack and Laura walked into Goldie Locks. The nightclub was tastefully decorated with well-spaced leather furniture and dim lighting. Classical music played softly through speakers and it, along with the expensive drink menu, ensured that the establishment catered to the over-thirty crowd — over thirty and wealthy.

A bouncer, who Jack figured had a taste for steroids, nodded politely to them from where he stood near the front door. He had short, blond hair trimmed in a buzz cut and wore a tan-coloured suit with a bright pink tie. His colleague, who looked like he could have been his twin brother, was dressed in a similar fashion and loitering near the bar where he was flirting with a waitress.

"Looks nice. How do you want to play it?" whispered Laura, as they made their way inside.

"Classy, wealthy, and friendly for now," replied Jack.

"And later?"

"Once we get in with Goldie, he should be impressed by who he thinks we are. Then maybe we'll add a touch of intimidation or psychotic behavior to the recipe. Keep him a little off balance ... but interested. He's used to being in charge. I want him to like and respect us, but we've got to keep control."

Jack and Laura took a seat together on a white leather sofa facing an etched-glass oval coffee table.

"Martini, gin," ordered Jack, to the young woman who quickly arrived to serve them.

"Bombay or Tanqueray?"

"I prefer Tanqueray Number 10, but if you don't have Number 10, then Bombay."

"Sorry, we don't have Number 10, so Bombay it is. And you, madam?"

Laura frowned and replied, "Bellini."

Jack saw Laura glare at the waitress as she left to get their order. "Okay, what's up?"

"What's up," seethed Laura. "Didn't you hear what she called me?"

"I thought she was polite?"

"She called me madam. I've never been called that. Do I look that old to you? I'm not even thirty-four yet. Do I look older?"

Oh, Christ. "Maybe she thought you owned a brothel," offered Jack, hoping to make light of the situation.

"I bet it's my makeup," replied Laura, sounding concerned. "I was running late and in a hurry. I'm going to the ladies' room," she added, abruptly leaving.

The cocktails arrived before Laura returned and Jack asked the waitress her name.

"Patty," she replied with a smile.

"Pleased to meet you. My name is Jack. My girlfriend Laura and I recently moved here from Edmonton. Have you been working here long?"

"Just started the end of June. Only for the summer. I'm going back to Simon Fraser in the fall. Getting my degree in education."

"Good for you. Waitressing and dealing with the public is a learning experience. Something that will come in handy when you're a teacher."

"Hadn't thought of it that way," replied Patty.

"Speaking of which," continued Jack, "between you and me, Laura hated being called 'madam.'"

"I'm sorry, I —"

"Not a problem, but perhaps mention to her that you noticed she looked upset and —"

"I upset her?"

"And that you feel awkward being ordered to call all women by that —"

"The boss didn't order us. I just —"

Jack put up his hand, gesturing for her to stop. "It would enhance your tip if she thought you were following orders from the boss."

Patty paused and then smiled. "I'll take care of it," she said.

Jack noticed Patty go up to Laura as she was returning from the ladies' room.

"It wasn't me," said Laura happily as she sat down.

"Wasn't you what?"

"The waitress. Her name is Patty. She was only following orders on calling women 'madam.'"

"Go figure."

"I asked her about her boss. She said she didn't really know Mister Goldie all that well yet. I asked her if he ever mingled with the customers and she said, sometimes. I said if he did, he would soon find out that calling young women 'madam' was not a good idea."

"I bet they change their policy," replied Jack. "It's good he mingles. Just have to get him to mingle with us."

Good undercover operatives are friendly by nature. Within a couple of hours, Jack and Laura were on a first-name basis with most of the staff.

On Thursday night, Jack and Laura returned to the club. Patty was quick to serve them, no doubt appreciating the fifty-six-dollar tip she received on top of the forty-four-dollar bill for the two martinis and two Bellinis she served the night before. The bartender, Purvis, also appreciated Jack's added tips in appreciation of what he deemed "the perfect martini." He waved to them both when they came in.

Jack took a jar out of a plastic bag and handed it to Patty and said, "Give this to Purvis, will you?"

"Olives?" asked Patty in bewilderment, staring at the jar.

"His martinis are excellent, but the olives he uses are getting old. Also, mention to him that I prefer three olives."

Later that night, Jack and Laura saw Goldie make an appearance. Purvis spoke to him from behind the bar and Jack saw Goldie glance in their direction.

The next martini was on the house. When Jack and Laura left that night, they were being treated like prized regulars by all the staff.

It was ten o'clock on Friday night and Jack and Laura were looking for a place to park at Goldie Locks when Jack received a call from Sammy.

"Interesting call on the pay phone this afternoon," said Sammy. "We just got it translated. Wang called another Chinese man by the name of Woo. We don't know Woo's full name yet. The number is registered to an auto body shop. It sounds like Woo is moving to Montreal and Wang told him to try and find a new connection out there for his friend who owns the nightclub. Wang has to be talking about Goldie."

"Connection for what?" asked Jack.

"Didn't say."

After hanging up, Jack recounted the conversation to Laura.

"So, what do you think?" asked Laura.

"Let's get Goldie to tell us what it's about."

"Really? And how —"

"On the sidewalk!" said Jack quickly, turning Laura's attention toward the front of Goldie Locks.

Laura saw Goldie, in his familiar moss-green windbreaker, and Wang both walking down the sidewalk.

Wang checked his watch and said something to Goldie, after which both men hurried their pace.

"What do you think?" asked Laura, with her hand on the door handle.

"They're late for something. Would be nice to find out what. Go for it, but don't be seen or Goldie will for sure recognize you from the club. I'll call you on my cell. I'm going to give Sammy a call first and see if he knows anything."

Once Laura exited the car, Jack dialed Sammy on his cellphone. "Sammy ... Jack again. You ever get a bug in Wang's car?"

"Yeah. Went into his garage behind his house last night and did it. Nothing on it yet. We didn't have time to put in satellite tracking. The asshole turned his lights on. Probably going to the bathroom, but we decided to bolt."

"He's walking with Goldie near Goldie Locks. You don't know anything?"

"Nope. We heard him in his car. Just the radio on and traffic noise. No indication he was with anyone or where he was going. Sounds like he parked it about fifteen minutes ago."

"If you hear something, give me a call."

Moments later, Jack realized that walking would be faster than driving as he sat in a long line of traffic. He looked for a place to park as Laura discreetly followed the two men around a corner and out of sight down the next block.

Meanwhile, Laura was relieved to see that both men were in a hurry and that neither one took the time to look behind them. She didn't look behind herself either, otherwise she may have noticed a third man who stepped out from an alley and followed her down the street.

Partway down the block, both Goldie and Wang stopped and turned to talk with one another. By the way Goldie was gesturing with his hands, Laura presumed they were having some type of disagreement.

Despite it being the third week of July, the weather was cool from the nightly wind that came in off the ocean to replace the heat rising from the tall buildings. Laura pulled the collar of her jacket snugly around her neck and took momentary cover inside a convenience store. She pretended to browse along a magazine display while watching Goldie and Wang through the front window as she whispered to Jack on her cellphone.

The man following Laura stayed back in the shadows, watching and waiting for her to come outside. A lane emerged between tall buildings onto the street a few paces down from the convenience store. The area was dark, and for the moment, deserted. He knew it would be a good place to attack and then escape.

"Okay, they're starting to move again," whispered Laura. "Where are you?"

"About a block behind," replied Jack, jogging past some pedestrians. "Be there in a couple of secs and I'll take the opposite side of the street."

Laura saw that Goldie and Wang had moved to the end of the block and were standing at the corner.

"Looks like they're waiting for someone," whispered Laura. "Maybe getting a ride. I'll see if I can grab a plate."

"Not too close," warned Jack.

"There's a lane between me and them. Pretty dark. I can hide in there. They won't see me."

Seconds later, Laura crept into the shadows, barely visible by the corner of a building as she watched Goldie and Wang, who seemed intent at looking at the cars going past them.

"Not a fuckin' word bitch!" a man hissed, grabbing Laura by the shoulder.

Laura gasped as she was brutally spun around with her back slamming up against the cement wall of the building. A man loomed over her, holding a syringe close to her face.

"Your purse, lady, or I jam this in your fuckin' throat!"

"KEEE-AI!"

Jack heard the sound of Laura's vicious, paralyzing yell from across the street and looked over, as did both Goldie and Wang.

It takes the human body approximately two seconds to physically respond to a given stimulus. In those two seconds, Laura delivered three karate punches. Her arms moved in opposite unison to each other. As one fist pulled back, the other struck. Her training caused her reflexes to automatically give her knuckles a last-second twist upon impact for a bone-crunching finish. Her first blow was delivered to the man's solar plexus. His body was in the act of doubling over when her second punch collided with his Adam's apple. His head snapped back and he emitted a rasping, choking gurgle as his feet staggered back to maintain his balance. Her third punch to his scrotum caused him to plop on the sidewalk like a wet sack of cement.

Jack raced across the street, dodging cars as he went, but did not arrive until a couple of seconds after Goldie and Wang did.

"Are you okay?" asked Goldie, staring down at the man who was emitting a sickening moan while lying curled in a ball on the sidewalk with his hands between his legs.

"Uh … yes, thank you," replied Laura.

"Sweetie! Are you okay?" asked Jack, as he arrived, still panting for air. "Did he hurt you?"

Laura caught the subtle shake of Jack's head. *Guess he doesn't want me to act scared.*

"What happened?" asked Jack.

"I, uh …" Laura glanced at Goldie and Wang, who were giving her odd looks as they glanced back and forth at her and the large man moaning on the sidewalk. "I was going to go to the store, you know, for … personal stuff, before meeting you at the club. Then this guy grabs me and hustles me into an alley and tries to rob me. I'm okay. How did you get here so fast? Did you see him following me?"

"No," replied Jack. "I got to thinking that you shouldn't be out here alone at night and started walking to catch up to you. Are you okay? Bet you could use a drink?"

"I'm okay. Think I could use a couple."

"Do you want me to call the police?" offered Goldie, bringing out his cellphone.

A diamond embedded in Goldie's front tooth sparkled as he spoke. It served to remind Jack further about the discrepancy in life between people like Goldie and Melvin.

"No police!" snarled Jack. His response drew the action he hoped for. A surprised look crossed Goldie's face and he glanced knowingly at Wang.

"I mean, it's okay," Jack added, pretending to gain his composure. "It looks to me like he learned his lesson. Thanks, anyway."

As Goldie and Wang turned to leave, Goldie overheard Jack say to Laura, "Have you got a jackknife in your purse? I'm going to cut his nuts off."

"Hang on, honey, I'll look," replied Laura. "Sorry," she replied a moment later.

"Guess I'll stomp his brains out instead."

"Oh, honey … don't," pleaded Laura. "You'll get blood all over your pants and someone is liable to call the police. Besides, he might have AIDS. Come on, forget about it. I want a drink."

Goldie and Wang's mouths both gaped open as Jack and Laura held hands while casually browsing in store windows as they sauntered away.

When they were around the corner, Jack turned to Laura and said, "Keee-ai? Is that what you call discreet surveillance?"

"I'm sorry," she replied. "He scared me. I acted without thinking. Next time I'll scream like a little girl or pretend to faint."

"Too late to act that way around these guys now. Don't worry, it worked out."

Laura snickered and said, "Did you see them turn around and the looks on their faces when you asked me for a jackknife? By the nod you gave me, I presumed you wanted me to go along with it."

"I did. Imagine what they think of us. Goldie is bound to be curious."

"Curiosity killed the cat."

Jack paused, remembering Winston.

"I'm sorry," said Laura. "Stupid thing to say after what you had to do."

"Forget about it," replied Jack. "By the way, I saw a syringe lying on the sidewalk."

"That's what he threatened me with."

"Bastard deserves to have his nuts cut off."

"That would be cruel," said Laura seriously. She thought about it for a moment and added, "I could see him being euthanized, but not tortured."

"Euthanize him!" exclaimed Jack with a laugh. "You mean, whack the son of a bitch!"

Laura frowned and replied, "Well, yes, but euthanasia sounds nicer."

Goldie and Wang weren't the only persons to hear Laura's yell and see her response. Kang Lee looked out the open window of his car and gestured for Goldie and Wang to join him. His thoughts were on Laura. He would never forget her face. *Beautiful, but dangerous. Like a Western version of Sayomi ... Where did she learn to fight like that?*

14

"What was that all about?" asked Lee through the window as Goldie and Wang walked up.

Wang gestured with his thumb and said, "The guy lying curled up on the sidewalk tried to rob that couple who just walked away. Or at least, he tried to rob the lady."

"Interesting lady," noted Lee.

"They're customers in my club," replied Goldie.

"Better hope they don't say much," offered Wang. "Not good for business."

"They didn't seem all that concerned," mused Goldie.

"Enough of that," said Lee, sounding irritated at the chatter. "I feel like sushi. There's a place I want to try called Azuma. On Denman near Comox. Meet me there. I have other business to attend to after."

Moments later, Jack received a call from Sammy who said, "Sounds like Wang is back in his car. Got somebody with him. No idea where they are or where they're going ... hang on ... they're both laughing about something. Want to stay on the line and see if we can hear where they're going?"

"I think he's with Goldie," said Jack. "Sure, I'll hold."

A few minutes later Sammy reported that the car was shut off and he heard Goldie and Wang leave. "Want me to hold the phone close to the speaker and play back what they were laughing about?" asked Sammy.

"Go ahead."

Jack heard the recorded sound of a car and Goldie saying, "You see how that chick dropped that guy? Man, he hit the ground like a rotten tomato!"

"It's where she nailed him that makes me cringe," replied Wang. "I almost feel sorry for him."

"I didn't feel sorry for him until her boyfriend was going to cut his nuts off. Then I would have felt sorry for him!"

Laughter was heard and Goldie continued, "Did you hear what that woman yelled?"

"Sounded like *karate*."

"She moved so fast I wasn't sure what she did, but I think she kneed him in the nuts or something."

"You say they're customers of yours?"

"Just lately. Haven't seen them before this week."

"Better not screw up her order. Especially if the boyfriend finds a jackknife."

Sammy then came back on the phone and said,

"Don't know what that was all about, but that was basically it. I'll call if anything else crops up."

Norimaki sushi rolls did not appeal to Goldie, but he ordered them, anyway. He did not like any sushi for that matter, but had decided that these were the least unpleasant. At the moment, any complaints from his taste buds had taken a back seat as he watched Lee's face for a response to the suggestions that he and Wang had made. When the response was not immediate, Goldie added, "The two of us have talked about it. We would not be in competition with each other. Both products would have different distributors."

Lee slowly chewed a mouthful of eel while he thought of a response. Eventually he swallowed and turned to Goldie. "So," replied Lee quietly, pointing the ends of his chopsticks at Goldie's face, "You think it would be easy to add cocaine to your portfolio?"

Goldie nodded and said, "I'm often approached by my people. It is a highly enriching commodity."

"A commodity for which we cannot offer protection," said Lee. "Has it been that many years ago that you forget what that is like? Do you not remember how you felt, sitting in a hot and steamy customs office in Burma? Your clothes soaked with the sweat of someone who believed his life to be over?"

Goldie was silent as he recalled that fateful day.

"Operate within the confines of protection," continued Lee. "We have been over this before. Our organization cannot guarantee your protection in South or Central America."

"I know, I know," replied Goldie. "It's just that it is so damned lucrative."

"Are you not making lots of money? And much more so, if the doors to eastern Canada open, allowing easy access to places across the border like New York. Why take the risk of investing money in a climate that is not secure?"

Goldie sighed. "Perhaps you're right," he added, begrudgingly.

"Of course I'm right," replied Lee. "Besides, it is my understanding that Satans Wrath controls most of the Canadian market for cocaine. They would demand you deal through them. With that would come more risk."

"That is precisely why my idea is more logical," said Wang, catching the sudden glare he received from Goldie. "What I proposed does not require import. Quite the opposite."

Lee shook his head and said, "What you propose is farming."

"It is not farming," protested Wang. "Hydroponics. B.C. is providing the best marijuana in the world. Why shouldn't I get a cut of it?"

"It is still farming, is it not?" replied Lee. "Indoors, perhaps, but still farming. With that comes land for the buildings and an army of people to manage the crops. Deliveries are both bulky and smelly. Such operations last only a matter of time before gaining police attention. With your army of farmers, how do you ensure obedience or loyalty? How long before one of the hoodlums you employ turns on you?"

"But the risks are low," said Wang. "British Columbia does not send marijuana dealers to jail ... at least rarely and then not for long."

Lee smiled and admitted, "The penalty for *any* crime in B.C. is low, which is why we have opened up operations in Vancouver. But it is not the risk of incarceration that I am warning you about. The risk is having the police seize all your assets once the criminal offence has been proven. Are you willing to see the undoubtedly large nest egg you have made suddenly taken from you because of greed?"

Wang glanced at Goldie for a sign of support, but did not see any. If anything, he felt that Goldie was anything but supportive. *Now he nods his head as if to say "I told you so"?*

"It is not only your life you are risking," continued Lee. "That market is largely controlled by the Vietnamese. You may be inviting conflict with —"

"Cannot the organization influence the Vietnamese?" asked Wang.

Lee paused, irritated at being interrupted. He took a deep breath before continuing in a conciliatory manner. "With the Vietnamese in Canada, there are many ... undisciplined ... individual enterprises. It would be too labour-intensive to extend our influence to so many independent small groups. The effort of locating their families in Vietnam to ensure compliance would not be worthwhile. There is also a more important consideration. You know how the police work. They usually go up the corporate ladder. Should you be arrested, even for what in B.C. is taken as the trivial offence of trafficking in marijuana, our organization would never accept you into our fold again. There would be no starting over with us."

"I would never tell the police about you," said Wang. "You know that! We are very careful. Arthur and I don't even use your real name in conversation. We only refer to you as 'The Enabler.' I would never divulge your identity. Ever."

"My boss is also very careful," replied Lee. "You refer to me as 'The Enabler?' Well, I refer to him as 'The Shaman.' He is brilliant in such matters and I also would never make the mortal mistake of divulging his name. That said, I have already discussed with him the idea of expanding into the areas you have both suggested. He declined for the same reasons I gave you. If you wish to go out on your own into that market, then do so with the realization that you will be entirely cut off from our organization."

Wang let out a deep breath and said, "No, I do not wish to do that." He glanced at Goldie and added, "It was an idea we *both* had. Something *both* of us thought we should discuss with you."

Lee caught the edge in Wang's voice. *Is there petty jealousy over my decision to have Goldie fulfill my position? I assured The Shaman that there wasn't ...*

"It is good that we exchange ideas," said Lee. "For example, your suggestion about that person you trust who is moving to Montreal."

"Woo," replied Wang.

"His name to me is not important. What matters is your desire to help our organization. The Shaman would prefer that Arthur take on my current role as he was born in Canada and is more familiar with the culture. However, you have shown that you are not only above petty jealousy, but that you were willing to offer Woo's services to Arthur. A fact I have brought to the attention of The Shaman himself."

"Thank you," replied Wang, his smile revealing his delight at being praised.

"Kingdoms are built by the strengths, work, and ideas of many," continued Lee. "The closer you get to the king, the more protection is needed. You have both done well and have earned the right to stand within the castle walls. At this point I would suggest that it would not be wise for you to go out and cross the moat into unsafe territory." Lee pinched another piece of eel between his chopsticks and raised it toward his lips before pausing and asking, "Agreed, gentlemen?"

Goldie raised a cup of sake to show his compliance. He was quickly joined by Wang. Lee nodded and did likewise to make a silent toast.

Lee smiled when they resumed eating. Naturally, he did not mention the most important reason he did not want Goldie and Wang investing elsewhere. Spreading the money around would have an adverse affect on the amount of commission received from the products that The Shaman did control.

* * *

Jack awakened late Saturday morning and was glad that both he and Natasha had the day off. They were into the third week of July and the weather could not have been more beautiful.

Breakfast consisted of sitting in their housecoats eating croissants and drinking black coffee on their apartment balcony, which overlooked the city. Neither talked of work. For many couples, such a Saturday morning breakfast may have been normal, but neither Jack nor Natasha led normal lives. Love and intimacy too often took a back seat to the pressures of their careers.

"Come on," said Jack, when they finished. "Get dressed. I'm taking you someplace special."

"Someplace special?" asked Natasha, raising an eyebrow.

"You'll see," Jack replied. "This is our day. I want it to be special. Today the world can wait. It'll be just you and me."

At one o'clock Natasha found herself holding Jack's hand as they strolled across the Capilano Suspension Bridge. The location had a special meaning. It was not only that the view of the Capilano River, 230 feet below, was spectacular. It was because this was where Jack had given Natasha her engagement ring almost two years earlier.

At the centre of the bridge, Jack turned and hugged Natasha as his lips softly caressed hers, kissing her long and tenderly.

"I love you so much," he whispered. "For me, my life really began on this spot the day you accepted the ring."

"And if I had said no, would you have jumped?"

Jack stepped back and looked at her for a moment before saying, "Hell, no. I'd have pushed you off!"

Natasha laughed and said, "You're so damned romantic. You certainly know how to sweet-talk a girl." She looked intently into his eyes and her smile faded.

"What is it?" he asked.

"Remember when we agreed to be married for two years before starting a family?"

Jack nodded.

"Don't you think it's close enough to two years to start trying?"

Jack felt a sense of shock. *Has it been two years already?*

Natasha saw the look on Jack's face. She stepped back and felt her eyes water. "What? You've changed your mind?"

Jack paused and said, "I have to admit, the idea really scares me."

"A fine time to be telling me this now! Why didn't you mention it last time we were on this bridge? I wouldn't have accepted the ring."

"I haven't changed my mind. Just give me a moment."

"If you really want children, why do you need a moment?"

"I'm afraid."

"Afraid of what?"

"Afraid I won't make a good father because of my own upbringing. I didn't have much of a role model. Sometimes I feel like I don't know how to act around children."

"I would never allow you to treat our children badly."

"I know … and I want children. I'm just a little afraid. You caught me off guard."

Natasha stepped closer and gently kissed him before saying, "The fact that you worry about that makes me think you'll make a great dad. I'd never allow you to be any other way."

Jack smiled. "I know," he replied. "I have complete faith in your ability to be a good mom … and a wife."

"So, no more birth control?"

"No."

"Good, we've done enough practising," replied Natasha with a grin.

"Hey! We should always practise. Every chance we get."

Natasha giggled and said, "Okay. I hear that practise makes perfect. I could go along with that."

"Good. Let's have lunch."

A few minutes later, Jack found a secluded spot amongst some towering Douglas fir trees and spread out a blanket before opening a small cooler. Lunch consisted of spiced Dutch gouda cheese, French bread, strawberries, a chilled bottle of Pinot Grigio, and dark chocolate squares for dessert.

Natasha felt Jack's warm embrace again as they lay with their legs entwined upon the blanket. "You plan on seducing me now?" she asked, feeling his kiss and warm breath upon the nape of her neck.

"The thought crossed my mind, unless you want to see if we can get the bridge rocking."

"Exhibitionism isn't really my style. No, I think this —"

Jack groaned and picked up his cellphone to look at the number of who was calling. "I'm not available," he muttered and let the call go to voice mail. "Now, you were saying?" asked Jack with a smile, pulling Natasha closer.

"I was suggesting we may have enough privacy —"

Jack swore softly and glanced at his phone again. This time a text message said URGENT!

"Sorry, hon, I better take this." Jack sighed.

His call to Sammy was short. Sammy concluded the conversation by saying, "Sorry for the delay. The monitors didn't get around to listening to it until now. CC is on her way in, too."

Jack hung up and turned to Natasha and stared a moment without speaking. He could see the tears form in her eyes.

"You promised," she said quietly. "You said it was going to be our day."

"It's about Melvin," replied Jack. "We've got a lead."

Natasha's open mouth showed her surprise. Her sorrow gave way to anger. "Go get 'em," she said angrily.

15

Jack, Laura, and CC crowded around Sammy as he replayed a second conversation held in Wang's car between Wang and Goldie.

"So what do you think of the meeting tonight?" asked Wang.

"It went about how I expected," replied Goldie.

"How you expected?" replied Wang, his voice sounding angry. "Wish you would have told me that up front. I thought you caved in too easy. You sure as hell didn't try to back me up!"

"Trouble in paradise," said Jack. *Divide and conquer ...*

Laura caught his grim smile. *Oh, man ... that means trouble ...*

"He raised some good points," continued Goldie. "I agreed with him. Nothing wrong with admitting when you're wrong."

"Were we wrong? Or are you sucking up to him because he plans to promote you into his position? You want to become the new Enabler."

"Fuck you," replied Goldie. "I'm not sucking up to anybody. The Enabler was right about what he said. Why rock the boat? We've got a good thing going. Maximum gain with minimum risk. As he said, if you don't like what you have, then branch out on your own. Just be prepared to accept that you'll be operating in a theatre without protection."

"Who the hell is this Enabler guy?" whispered CC.

"Don't know," replied Sammy.

"I still think The Enabler is looking after his own interests, as well," grumbled Wang.

"Oh, definitely. I totally agree. But in reality, his interests become our interests."

"Yours, maybe, once you're in his position. You'll be making the commission that he is getting now."

"True, but you'll still be making a good cut on your end. Besides, if your man Woo ever gets his ass moved to Montreal and can find someone to move product there, then I'll make sure you get a percentage of everything distributed on that end. That's if you could ever convince him to deal with us round-eyes."

"I don't know about that, but if he does, then you better be dividing the noodles my way." The sound from inside the car was partially obliterated by the sound of squealing brakes. "Hey! You fucking moron! Signal next time!"

"You know I will," continued Goldie. "That is what The Enabler would expect. He isn't the sort of guy I would want to piss off. Him or his boss."

"He calls him The Shaman," replied Wang. "Did you know that most Shamans are actually women?"

"He referred to The Shaman as a he. Either way, in my book, I don't want to ever put myself in a position to find out about their early retirement plan."

"Here it comes," whispered Sammy.

"Think you'd end up like that wino in the park?" asked Wang.

"Maybe." There were several seconds of silence before Goldie continued again. "Why they did it or had me deliver him way out there still puzzles me. My own guys, who I used to pick him up, are still looking at me like I'm squirrelly. I said it was a prank to drop off a wino in someone's yard. It all seemed like a big risk for nothing."

"You never asked?"

"Was told it was a need-to-know basis. The whole thing wasn't professional in my books. Totally out of character to the point that it was comical. The fuckin' wino almost ... well, I shouldn't talk about that. Anyway, it gave us both a good laugh after."

"Both? Thought you said there were three of you?"

"The third guy I told you about before. The one wearing a suit. He doesn't laugh at anything. I've never met anyone so cold in my life."

"Like that woman's boyfriend who was going to cut the guy's nuts off tonight?"

"Man, that was nothing compared to the guy wearing the suit. You could see it in his eyes. Black, cold ... like they were dead. Let's change the subject. It gives me the creeps thinking about him. We shouldn't be talking about it, anyway. Especially in a car. How about turning on some tunes?"

"That's it," said Sammy, turning off the recorder and looking at CC. "What do you think? Time for you to string some wire naming Goldie?"

"That's it?" said CC. "There's nothing to say this is even my case. The victim's tox' came back negative for alcohol or illicit substances. He's certainly no wino."

Jack didn't want to say what he thought. *The Shaman? The Enabler? Guys above Goldie. Then some guy in a suit with dead eyes? The wino in the park has got to be Melvin. But why would they kill Melvin? Goldie has proven himself to be a smart businessman … and these others are above him? Nothing makes sense.*

"Maybe it is a coincidence," said Sammy. "Might not be related to your thing."

Jack's mind was still replaying what he heard. *They thought it was comical? Something to laugh about? They'd probably really find it funny if they saw me shooting Winston in the alley.* He realized his fist was clenched and took a deep breath to relax his body. He knew it was one conversation he would not tell Natasha about. She was in enough pain already. He glanced at CC and said, "Melvin looked like a wino. If you didn't take the time to know him, you would think that."

"Goldie's big," said CC. "What? Maybe a size ten to twelve shoe? Sammy might have a point. It could be a coincidence."

"Come on, CC," said Laura. "We traced the gun to Goldie's doorstep, it was used to murder Melvin, and now Goldie talks about a wino in a park who almost escapes? It fits."

CC sighed and shook her head. "I'm sorry. Don't get me wrong. I think we might possibly be on to something. But what *I think* doesn't matter. It's what evidence we have, both supportive and contradictory, that counts. I'm speaking about how the Crown or a judge would view it. I sincerely doubt we could get a wiretap on Goldie based on what we have so far. Not to mention, you heard these guys — they use code names. Also words like product. Even Goldie said they shouldn't be talking about it in a car."

"To be this close to nailing him for murder," said Laura. "It's driving me nuts."

"Close to nailing him for murder!" exclaimed CC. "That's a laugh. Girl, we're a long way from that. Even if we could prove it was Melvin he's talking about, what have we got? It sounds to me like Goldie was only the delivery boy. If the evidence was going against him, all he would have to say is he thought it was all some sort of prank. He even told his guys it was. You know what the judges are like. He doesn't have any convictions. Upstanding businessman. He'd probably end up with probation or at best, a few months served before being released. Hell, if we did catch him, I'd cut a deal with him in a second and let him walk if he'd give us whoever did do it. Even then, without a motive, it would be damned hard and likely impossible to get a conviction. Sorry to break your bubble, Laura, but in my books, we're not close at all."

"A wire on Goldie might give you whoever did it," said Sammy. "Maybe identify The Shaman and The Enabler, or even the guy in the suit with dead eyes."

"Even if we did get a wire on Goldie, do you really think he would ever talk about it and go over the details again with whoever did it? At least in a place where we could hear? I bet this is as close as you would ever get ... and it isn't nearly enough. It would be nice to know who the guy with dead eyes is, though."

"And The Enabler," said Jack.

"You don't know if he was the one laughing in the park with Goldie," said CC. "His name wasn't used to clarify if he was the third guy."

"Goldie thought the idea wasn't professional," said Jack. "He asked and was told it was on a need-to-know basis. It had to be his boss, which is the one they call The Enabler."

CC shrugged and said, "Logical, provided we're even talking about the same incident."

Her choice of words irritated Jack. *Incident?* He knew that was how it would be referred to in a court-room. *Grabbing an innocent man ... sticking a plastic bag on his head and chasing him through the woods to murder him would be simply stated as an "incident."*

"What about a search warrant?" suggested Laura. "Maybe we could find a dirty shoe or boot in Goldie's house that the lab could match with the dirt in the park where Melvin was killed?"

CC frowned and said, "Sorry, I doubt we have grounds for a search warrant, either. And as far as lab evidence, it sounds like you've been watching too much *CSI* on television. Things tend to work a little differently in the real world."

"I know, but occasionally we get lucky with the lab," countered Laura.

"'Occasionally' being the operative word," said CC. "Another issue with courts would be potential motive. Why would someone like Goldie, if he did do it, deliver some wino —" She paused, catching a dark look from Jack before correcting herself and saying, "Okay, homeless person, to a park for a couple of other guys to shoot him? Tell me how you would answer that question to a judge?"

Jack thought about it. He knew CC was right. *Her reasoning was sound. Why would anyone do it? Goldie is wealthy. Whoever he works for must be more so. Is there some past connection to Melvin's life that nobody knows about?* His own choice of words caused him to reflect and think deeper. *Nobody knows about? ... Nobody ... like Ophelia said, "People who got it don't give a shit about people who don't. We're nobodies." Goldie said they were laughing. They wouldn't be if there was a specific reason to murder Melvin. It would have been strictly business. Whatever their reason, Melvin was a random pick. The motive for the crime was the murder itself. The victim could be a nobody. But why would any presumably sane person want to murder an innocent person for no reason? Or is the person behind this whole situation even sane?*

"Well, sorry if I brought you in on your day off for no reason," said Sammy. "It seemed important to me."

"It is important," said Jack. "I need time to go over it in my head. But I'm positive we're on the right track. We've got to identify these three guys. The Shaman, The Enabler, and Dead Eyes."

"And I'm not saying it isn't important," said CC, defensively. "All I'm saying is that so far, don't expect much judicial backing."

"I never expect that," said Jack evenly.

CC gave a sharp glance at Jack. "Don't even think about it!" she said tersely.

"About what?" asked Jack, his voice sounding both innocent and surprised.

"Don't give me that shit! About whatever it is you're thinking."

Jack slowly shook his head and said, "I'm thinking we need to come up with a plan. Something to gather more evidence to support the judicial criteria you need to make a case."

"Are you ridiculing me?" asked CC, her voice tinged with anger.

"No," replied Jack. "I wish I was, but I respect your abilities and your opinion. If you say we don't have enough, then we don't have enough."

By his sincerity and the sadness in his voice, everyone knew that Jack meant what he said.

"We need to keep digging," continued Jack. "And we definitely need to find out who these other guys are. We'll get more evidence ... somehow."

It was the *somehow* that bothered CC. *Which is why I told him not to do whatever he was thinking in the first place! God, here we go. Full circle.*

"Any plan come to mind?" asked Sammy. "Not that it is any of our business. We're concentrating on drugs, but if there is something we can do to help, let us know."

"I appreciate that, Sammy," replied Jack. "If we come up with something, I'll be sure to contact you."

CC looked at Jack. *If we come up with something? Give me a break. You already have.* She took a deep breath and slowly exhaled. *Time to have a private chat with Staff Sergeant Rosemary Wood. I wonder if she knows what Jack Taggart is really all about? Hell, I don't even know what he is all about. Everything with him is smoke and mirrors. Lies and deception ...*

It was late Monday morning and Rose glanced at Jack and Laura as they sat across from her desk while Jack brought her up to date on the investigation. The private meeting she'd had earlier at Starbucks with Connie Crane still weighed heavily on her mind.

"So, from our perspective," said Rose, sounding businesslike, "this investigation, which started out under the auspices of gun smuggling, has changed to ecstasy, meth, and heroin? Knowing of course, that the murder in the park is under I-HIT's mandate."

"The drug investigation is legitimate," replied Jack. *Why is Rose sounding so officious? Not friendly like before ...* "I feel that it is significant enough to fall within our job description."

"I agree," replied Rose. "But I was also at that meeting with Drug Section two weeks ago when they said their budget did not allow them to purchase large enough quantities of heroin to allow them to work their way up to the kingpins. Even if we combined our total budgets between our two sections, the penalty someone might receive for drug trafficking would not be worth the cost."

"I'm well aware of the budget restrictions," replied Jack. "That's nothing new."

"So, with that in mind, are you proposing we enter into a long-term investigation ... likely taking several years, in the hope of nailing some of the kingpins through some type of conspiracy charge? I'm not against that, although again, the cost would be prohibitive for what we would achieve in the way of doing any significant damage as far as organized crime goes."

"No, I agree," said Jack. "The time it would take, including using all available personnel over that time frame, even if successful, would likely see the rise of several other crime families in the meantime. We would end up one step ahead and three back."

"Then what is your solution?"

"They're talking about a man by the name of Woo maybe moving to Montreal and looking for someone to move product. They're hoping to expand operations."

"Are you thinking about working a joint project with our unit in Montreal?"

"No. We don't know for sure that Woo is even going. Even if he does, I don't see that being overly productive to help us out here. I'm not thinking of using them to help. I was thinking of someone else."

Rose caught the sideways glance that Laura gave Jack. *She has her doubts about something … Connie warned me …*

"Are you familiar with the Irish Mafia in Montreal?" asked Jack.

"A little. The Irish Mafia is one of the oldest and makes the top three list for being the most influential organized crime families in North America. In Montreal, they are known as the West End Gang."

"That's the boys," said Jack.

"Some boys," replied Rose. "They also have a reputation for being extremely violent — including dismemberment. Victims have been found minus body parts."

Laura pursed her lips in a small grin. *Dismemberment … like cutting a guy's testicles off with a jackknife.*

"Are you familiar with one of the captains in the West End Gang, a fellow by the name of Happy Jack O'Donnell?" asked Jack.

"I'm not sure," replied Rose. "I haven't heard that name for years. Is he the one the press used to call 'Happy' because he was never convicted of anything?"

"The press called him that. His name came up a lot during a trial years ago when a police agent testified against the gang. There was never enough evidence to even charge O'Donnell, but it was clear he was one of the bosses. A journalist who tried to follow up on the story had his car blown up in his driveway as a warning."

"So, what about him? Or the Irish? What's that got to do with this case?"

"I've got a plan to use him and the Irish Mafia to help us," said Jack.

"You what?" exclaimed Rose, lurching forward and knocking some reports off her desk.

16

Later Monday afternoon, Jack hung up the telephone as Laura entered their office. He waited until she sat at her own desk and said, "Remember our two Russians in May — the ones we tricked into going to Vietnam where they were arrested?"

"They're not getting out, are they?"

Jack smiled and shook his head. "No. Remember the posh penthouse suite they rented that backs onto Stanley Park? Two bedrooms, mini-bar, plasma television, underground parking —"

"Yeah, yeah. What about it?"

"I spoke with Derek. The ex- policeman in charge of security for the apartment."

"Uh, huh."

"It turns out the two Russians paid for the suite one year in advance. The year isn't up until the fall. Derek agreed to us using it, providing we guarantee the

Russians don't come back. I assured him they would definitely not be back for at least the next eighteen years."

"How sweet. Our own little love nest."

"Exactly. We can pick the key up from Derek this afternoon. I've also got two friends, Paul and Katie, who own a forty-five-foot powerboat parked down at the Bayshore West Marina. It's called the *Blue Gator*. I've been in it. It's one hell of a beautiful boat. Very lavish. They are willing to let us borrow it. Paul also happens to be Irish and has the brogue."

"Nice friends to lend us that."

"I met Katie years ago. She used to be a social worker up in Kelowna. Our paths crossed and we have been friends since. Really nice people. I think Katie has seen her share of the bad side of life as a social worker."

"So we have the penthouse, a yacht … this is sounding better all the time."

"The things you have to do when you have champagne tastes and a beer budget."

"So, when do we do this?"

"Tomorrow. Pack a bikini and your winter coat into a suitcase. We'll be off to the airport."

On Wednesday night, Jack and Laura strolled down the street and entered Goldie Locks. Hidden in a van across the street, Staff Sergeant Rosemary Wood took several surveillance photographs of them entering the club. Her portfolio of surveillance photos on Jack and Laura had grown considerably since the day before.

* * *

It was dusk on Friday night when Goldie arrived in the alley behind his club and parked his Aston Martin. He stepped out of his car as a four-door, tan-coloured, unmarked police car pulled up behind him.

The plainclothes officer gestured for him to approach.

"Good evening, Mister Arthur Goldie," she said, somewhat contemptuously. "My name is Staff Sergeant Wood. I am with the RCMP Organized Crime Task Force. You and I need to talk."

"What? What about?" demanded Goldie.

"Hop in the car beside me. We'll take a little drive and I'll tell you what it's about," replied Rose.

"I'm not going with you without consulting a lawyer," replied Goldie, taking out his cellphone.

"Why are you acting so paranoid?" asked Rose. "This isn't about you, particularly. I want to talk to you about two of your customers. I prefer not to be seen by them or have anyone know I talked to you."

"What customers?"

"Get in. I'll only drive a couple of blocks away and show you their pictures. These two aren't who they pretend to be."

Moments later, Rose drove Goldie a few blocks away and drove into an above-ground parkade.

"So what do you think" asked Jack, turning in his chair to look at Laura. "Figure we can get away with it?"

"Think we can rely on Rose?"

"I think so."

"Cost is certainly a factor. Like the narcs say, we can't afford to buy the quantity of dope needed to make the connections."

"You're right. But the Irish Mafia can."

Rose parked the car and turned to Goldie and said, "So, off the top, what can you tell me about Jack and Laura?"

Goldie shrugged and said, "I'm not sure I even know them."

"Bullshit! Take a look at these," said Rose, opening her briefcase and handing Goldie a surveillance photo. "Tell me again you don't know them."

Goldie glanced at a photo of Jack and Laura sitting in the front of their car. Jack was talking to him out the window of the car. "This was last night," exclaimed Goldie.

"Tell me again you don't know them," said Rose.

"I don't! I just arrived at my club and they were driving by. The guy asked if we had any free parking for the club. That's all it was about. Maybe they have been in my club before. The guy likes his martinis … not too many. I'm not saying he drinks too much to drive or anything. Otherwise we wouldn't serve him."

"Are these them for sure?" asked Rose, handing Goldie some more photographs.

Goldie looked at the top picture. It showed Jack and Laura bundled up in heavy coats with a glimpse of the Vancouver Airport arrivals area in the background. Their suitcases were piled at the back of a limousine and the driver was getting out.

"These were taken a few months back when they arrived," said Rose.

Goldie looked at the next picture showing Jack and Laura leaving a fashionable apartment complex.

"This last photo is a little more recent," said Rose, "taken from a restaurant patio overlooking the Bayshore Marina."

Goldie looked at the photo and saw Laura sipping a glass of wine. She was wearing a bikini and sitting on the deck of a luxury powerboat. Jack, wearing a golf shirt and cargo shorts, sat beside her.

"So?" asked Rose. "Do they look familiar?"

"Yes, that is them," admitted Goldie. "They have been in my club a few times. I think the guy told one of my waitresses that they were from Edmonton. Why?"

"From Edmonton? That's a laugh," said Rose. She studied Goldie's face briefly and said, "You really don't know who they are, do you?"

Goldie shook his head and said, "Just a couple of customers. That's all I know."

"Who have they been meeting with in there? Have they been coming in with any other people?"

"Not anyone that I've seen. They seem like a nice couple. Real friendly with everyone. My staff likes them. No complaints. They're not troublemakers."

"Any other customers they socialize with?"

"Not really. As I said, they're friendly with everyone, but don't socialize with anyone in particular."

"If I find out you're lying to me, I'll have the tax man all over your joint. Health inspectors, too."

Jack leaned forward in his chair, peering through the one-way glass in the back of the van. "Looks like Rose is really giving it to him," he said to Laura, without turning around. "She's wagging her finger in his face. Maybe she would make a good operator."

"Yes, playing herself," replied Laura.

"Go ahead," said Goldie defiantly, glaring at Rose. "Call the tax man. I'll give you my accountant's name. And as far as cleanliness goes, my place is tops. We cater to a sophisticated crowd. If you would ever step inside, you would know that."

Rose returned Goldie's stare briefly before lowering her eyes submissively. "Okay," she said. "I believe you. Maybe the son of a bitch has decided to retire." Rose's face brightened and she said, "Makes it easy for us. We can conclude our file. I'm sorry to have bothered you with this. We had to make sure. I'll give you a ride back now."

"Do you mind telling me who they are?"

"Well, I can tell you they're not really from Edmonton. They're from Montreal."

"Montreal?"

"Yup. I don't know how much you know about the Irish Mafia, but Happy Jack O'Donnell is, or I guess was, one of the captains in that mob. One of the oldest and most established crime families in North America. A long history of extreme violence. People who have crossed them have been found dead and missing various body parts."

Goldie's thoughts briefly returned to a mugger outside a convenience store.

"We heard that he might be retiring," continued Rose, "but we didn't know if it was true. We were afraid he might be coming to build connections. Telling people he is from Edmonton makes it seem more like he is hiding his past. It fits the retirement mode."

Jack turned around in his chair again from where he was watching Rose from out of the back of a van and smiled. "Rose glanced our way and made a fist and scratched the bottom of her chin with her thumb nail."

"The old thumbs up," replied Laura. "Must be going well."

"We'll see if he says anything to us tomorrow night when we go in. If he does, I'll thank him and show some appreciation for him telling us."

"What if he doesn't say anything?"

"I'll tell him we know about it and thank him anyway."

"You'll tell him we know about it?"

"If I have to, I'll get my old partner, Danny O'Reilly, to seem like he's dirty and deliver me a fake report. Give the appearance that Irish blood is thicker than justice routine. If Goldie doesn't say anything tomorrow night, we'll still show our appreciation because he didn't tell Rose anything."

"He didn't have anything to say to Rose, even if he wanted to."

"I know. But either way, I'll show him our gratitude. The hook will be baited. I bet we get action soon."

Jack was right on his guess that they would be getting action soon. Later that same night, Goldie met with Wang again in the alley behind Wang's restaurant and told him about his visit from the RCMP.

"How long before Woo moves to Montreal?" asked Goldie.

"Today is Friday," noted Wang. "He told me he moves into a new apartment on the first of August. That's next week so I expect he'll be leaving in the next couple of days."

"Good. I'm not taking anything at face value. Let's check him out pronto. Tell Woo to find an Irish pub and ask around about Happy Jack O'Donnell."

17

It was midnight Saturday night and Jack pretended to look at Laura over the top of his martini glass as he took a sip. In reality, he was looking at Goldie who had wandered out from the rear of the club and was talking to the bartender while aimlessly looking at customers. *There he is. A man who laughs at the brutal slaughter of an innocent person. Can I pretend to befriend him and make it look genuine?*

Laura caught a subtle change in Jack's demeanor and said, "Is he back?"

"Behind you talking to Purvis at the bar," said Jack, wryly. "Laughing about something. He's definitely seen us but is keeping his distance. I'm going to order another martini at the bar and then invite him over."

"Want me to play the bimbo role?"

"Not after your karate demonstration the other night. Pretend you're smart and in the know."

"Pretend? Hey, I take offence to that remark."

Jack would have smiled, but the sight of Goldie laughing in the background made him think of a terrified man trying to escape through some darkened woods. *Running and staggering with your hands tied behind your back. Barely able to see through a plastic bag. Unable to scream. Your breath cut short by tape. The sound of gunshots. Your body feeling the pain. Twisting and turning. More gunshots … falling. Goldie laughing … his diamond-studded tooth glimmering in the light …*

"Jack? Did you hear me," asked Laura.

"Yeah. Wait here. I'm going to tell him I want to talk to him at our table."

A moment later, Goldie joined them and introduced himself as Arthur. Jack and Laura each introduced themselves by their first names.

"Is there a problem?" asked Goldie. "Something you wish to discuss with me?"

"No problem at all," replied Jack, reaching for the gift bag beside his feet. "Quite the opposite, really. I wanted to apologize for any inconvenience I may have caused you last night."

Goldie accepted the gift bag with surprise. He reached inside and pulled out a bottle of Tyrconnell single-malt Irish whiskey. "What inconvenience?" he exclaimed, casting a curious glance at Jack and Laura.

Jack smiled warmly at him and said, "You know, there are those who think the Irish blood is too watered down with Guinness. Let me tell you that is not so." Jack winked and leaned back in his chair and finished the last of his martini.

"I don't understand," replied Goldie.

Jack smacked his lips, savouring the last swallow, before looking directly at Goldie and saying, "Many of the Irish have become police officers, but the Irish blood is thick and they are Irish first." Jack paused as Goldie reflected upon what he said, before continuing, "Shall we just say that I have friends who keep me well informed on such matters. The intrusion in your life by Officer Wood last night did not go unnoticed and I wish to apologize to you for any inconvenience it may have caused."

"I ... I don't know what to say," said Goldie. "I mean, it's not any of my business who the customers are or —"

Jack let out a hearty laugh and said, "Whatever you did say, I owe you a debt of gratitude. They actually think I have retired." Jack turned to Laura and said, "Really, honey, do I look that old to you?"

"Certainly not," replied Laura, frowning. "You don't have a wrinkle on your body. At least, not one that stays a wrinkle for long," she added with a wink.

"But this really isn't necessary," said Goldie, attempting to hand the bottle back.

"It is nothing, really," replied Jack. "I would feel insulted if you did not accept. Besides, I was born in Canada. No Irish brogue and Irish whiskey for me. My taste is for gin and vermouth ... and fresh olives. I'm a great disappointment to my dear old father, I am sure."

"Well ... thank you," replied Goldie, setting the bottle down.

"You wouldn't believe the scurrilous and absolute scandalous accusations the police have made about me and my comrades over the years," said Jack. "Absolute nonsense, I can assure you. I am a businessman. That is all."

"What type of business are you in?" asked Goldie. "I mean, if you don't mind me asking. If it is too personal then —"

"No, I don't mind at all," replied Jack, leaning back from the table as Patty brought him a martini. "Here you go, Patty," he said, tipping her another fifty-dollar bill. "Did I ever tell you I think you have a beautiful name?"

After Patty expressed her gratitude and left, Jack looked at Goldie and said, "I'm an entrepreneur. Investments here and there. Trying to eke out a living."

Goldie smiled knowingly. "An entrepreneur," he said. "I have several friends who are entrepreneurs."

"Ah, alas, there is competition everywhere," replied Jack, raising his glass for a toast. "May you live as long as you want, and never want as long as you live."

"And," added Laura, "as you slide down the banister of life, may the splinters never point in the wrong direction."

"I love it," said Goldie. The diamond stud in his tooth reflected the light as he threw his head back and chortled.

Goldie's action made Jack pause. *I'd like to smash my fist into your face. See how funny you think that would be.* He took a deep breath. *Damn it, get a grip.*

Pretend to smile. He clinked glasses with Goldie and thought of another old Irish toast:

> *Drink is the curse of the land.*
> *It makes you fight with your neighbour.*
> *It makes you shoot at your neighbour.*
> *It makes you miss.*

Jack took a sip of his martini and put the glass back down on the table. *Believe me, Goldie, you're in my sights — I won't miss.*

18

It was two o'clock in the morning when Jack drove Laura home.

"I think it went well tonight," said Laura. "Goldie was pretty friendly. Even bought us a round."

"You're right. No conversation to hint of anything illegal, but friendly. Monday is a stat holiday. Let's take the next three days off. Wednesday morning the narcs have scheduled a meeting. We'll wait until next Friday before going back to the club. See how Goldie acts toward us then."

"You think he's trying to check you out? Maybe with that Woo character that Wang was talking to?"

Jack nodded and said, "In the event something does go awry, I've got my fake ID made with O'Donnell ending in one *L* instead of two. If worse comes to worse, I can make it look like Rose made a mistake and thought I was the more notorious O'Donnell."

"Let's hope they don't check you out beyond old newspaper clippings."

"Oh, I don't know, it could prove interesting," replied Jack.

Laura saw a bemused look on Jack's face. "Okay. What is it?" she asked. "I haven't seen a genuine smile on your face all night until now."

Jack cast a sideways glance at Laura and said, "I presumed Goldie might want to check me out — but think about it. They obviously don't have any real connections in Montreal yet. It would be a little like going to Chicago and asking about Al Capone back in the 1930s."

"So they might hear some bad stories to support your cover story?"

Jack smiled and said, "There is something I neglected to mention to Rose. The real Happy Jack is a bona fide sociopath, on top of which he hates being referred to as *Happy* Jack. It wasn't the media who first named him that. It was a title his enemies bestowed upon him, inferring that he was always drunk. Rumour is he shot someone in the balls once for calling him that."

"No kidding?"

"Guess he has issues. Hope whoever decides to ask about *Happy* Jack has life insurance."

"Oh, man," mumbled Laura. *Here we go again.*

On the morning of the following Wednesday, Jack, Laura, and CC were invited to attend a meeting with Drug Section. When they all arrived, Sammy told them that they were expecting to end their undercover heroin operation within the next two or three days.

"I thought things were going well for you with the targets who hang out at Wang's restaurant?" said CC.

"They are," replied Sammy. "We're using different operators for the ecstasy and meth. We hope to run that one for another month, depending upon whether or not the money holds out."

Sammy passed Jack a couple of surveillance pictures of a man with a ponytail and a black goatee. "This is Jojo. So far he is the biggest fish we've caught. Our operator is going to approach him Friday and see if we can buy a kilo. We can't spend the cash, so if he goes for it, we'll bust him and whoever else shows up."

Both Jack and Laura examined the photos carefully.

"When on Friday?" asked Jack.

"We don't want to give Jojo any time to dick around. The operator will approach him early in the evening. Part of the cover story is that he's a truck driver and has to be on the road by midnight."

"You think Jojo can come up with a kilo that fast?" asked Jack.

"He told the operator he could come up with it on two hours' notice. I don't think Jojo is bullshitting. Last time we ordered a quarter pound from him, he went to Goldie Locks, then met our guy at a McDonald's half an hour later and did the deal."

"Think it will be the same restaurant?" asked Jack.

"Have no idea. The operator is going to try and push him to meet his source. Don't know how that will go, but either way, I'm going to plunk myself in a corner at Goldie Locks before Jojo gets there. If he shows up, I should be in a position to see who he meets. I'll have my cell. If that person goes somewhere, we'll tail him and see if he takes us to a stash."

"What can we do to help?" asked Jack.

"You know a lot of the regulars. I'm hoping whoever he meets might be somebody you can put a name to. You know how these things go. Whoever he meets could end up chatting with someone else and so on. Anything you can do to help identify these pricks the better. If you need to tell me something, make eye contact and I'll meet you in the can."

"We're not in a position to help with any arrests or if something goes wrong," said Laura. "We've got our own thing going on in there."

"Yeah, I know. All I'm asking is for you to be our eyes and ears. Leave any rough stuff to us."

"So why did you call me to this meeting?" asked CC. "You're talking dope. I'm homicide."

"Jojo is currently serving triple probation."

"Triple probation?" asked CC. "How the hell does he do that?"

Sammy grimaced and said, "Very easily, I'm afraid. Welcome to the world of drug trafficking in B.C. He was convicted three times in the last two years for trafficking. He received probation each time and the sentences are overlapping each other. The only thing hurting him is his sides from laughing so much. I'm hoping this time might be different. If we nail him with a kilo, he could be looking at doing federal time. If you want us to try and roll him, we're willing to do so."

"You'd let him walk?" asked CC.

"If he can provide info on a homicide, sure. It's your call."

CC thought about it for a moment and shook her head. "I appreciate the offer, but even if Jojo was somehow connected with Goldie and was able to give him to us, Goldie would serve less time than what Jojo is looking at. As I said before, his lawyer would put him on the stand and have him say he thought it was all a prank — that he didn't really know what was going on." CC slowly shook her head and looked at Sammy and said, "I don't think it's worth jeopardizing what you already have. In this case, it's like having two birds in the hand and wanting to trade for one in the bush. Besides, would Jojo at his level be in with someone like Goldie? What do you think, Jack? Organized crime is your baby."

Jack sighed and said, "Unfortunately, I agree with you completely. Goldie said he used his guys to grab the victim. He also said he told them it was a prank. Even if Jojo was one of those guys, it wouldn't change anything as far as the courts go. Not to mention, whoever The Shaman and The Enabler are, they're above Goldie and that makes them light years out of Jojo's league."

"Those two and the guy with dead eyes who wears a suit, as well," added CC. She looked at Sammy and said, "Thanks for thinking about me, anyway. If something of interest comes up on the UC or wiretap involving Wang's people, let me know."

Once the meeting came to an end, CC asked Jack if she could talk to him in private for a moment.

They found a quiet spot in the hall to talk and Jack

asked, "Any chance we could get a surreptitious warrant for Goldie's home and businesses?"

"Not a chance with what we've got," replied CC. "Better hope what you and Laura are doing will turn up something. That's if it really was the same guy in the park that Goldie was talking about."

"You still don't think it is?"

"The small footprint still bugs me. I'm not completely convinced that it is."

"I am," replied Jack confidently. "So what's up? What did you want to talk to me about?"

CC took a deep breath and slowly exhaled. "I have a confession to make. I spoke to Rose about you the other day."

"You what? What about?"

CC glanced around and said, "You and I — well, you know what's happened in previous murder investigations I've had. You've got to admit, you tend to stick your nose into investigations that you have no right to be involved in."

"It's not like they didn't turn out well."

"No, and I'm sure whoever the Coroners Service hired to keep up with the extra workload appreciates the work."

"It wasn't my fault."

CC put her hand up and said, "Stop. Don't even go there."

"What did you tell Rose?"

"I told her my concerns and gave her my honest opinion."

"Which is?"

"I feel you get too emotionally involved with the victims. I could see it on your face when we listened to Goldie and Wang on the car bug. I understood when it was your niece and nephew. Even when those guys came after your last partner's family, I understood. But with you, it doesn't stop there. This file is just about some homeless guy —"

"That homeless guy has a name. It's Melvin Montgomery."

"See? That proves my point. You're becoming emotional just talking about it. You should stick to whatever it is you do on Intelligence and leave the homicides to me."

"This is organized crime," replied Jack adamantly. "Big time."

"Yeah, maybe we are into that now, but you didn't know that when you first butted in."

Jack silently reflected on his thoughts for a moment. "Okay," he said, quietly. "Melvin was Natasha's patient. She liked him and was afraid the investigation would get swept under the carpet."

"I would never do that."

"I know. I told her so. As far as me being emotionally attached to the victims, you're probably right. Thanks for bringing it to my attention. I'll try to make sure it doesn't affect my judgment."

CC paused as she looked at Jack before saying, "Fuck you. Don't bullshit me. What do you think I am? Internal?"

"I'm not bullshitting. I'm married. My world has changed."

"Yeah? Well, anyway, I wanted to apologize. I told Rose she should keep an eye on you. You're a good cop. I don't want to see you get in shit."

Jack grinned momentarily, then said, "Don't worry about it. I understand your point of view. We're both trying to do the right thing."

"Yeah, I know that. There is one more thing. When I was talking to Rose, I had the distinct impression she knew everything about your previous … uh, episodes. I think somebody else may have already spoken with her. You might want to keep your head up. Or is it down? Whatever. You know what I mean."

"Thanks, CC. Appreciate it."

On their way back to their office, Laura turned to Jack and asked, "What did CC want?"

"She apologized for speaking to Rose the other day. Feels guilty."

"Good," replied Laura.

"Rose said she probably would apologize. She could tell how guilty CC felt."

At 8:30 Friday night, Jack and Laura sat in their usual spot in Goldie Locks. They were barely seated when Jack received a call from Sammy.

"I'll be there any second," said Sammy, speaking rapidly. "Our operator is with Jojo and heading your way. They're only about two blocks behind me. Jojo is going to make our operator wait outside in his car while he goes in to talk with the man. Jojo is really pissed off and doesn't want to do it, but our guy said for the amount he is buying, he wants to make sure he is guaranteed a better price next time and wants to be able to score if Jojo isn't around. Jojo said he would ask, but I bet he doesn't."

"Good luck," said Jack, hanging up his phone. He quickly relayed the information to Laura as Patty approached to take their order.

"Three-olive martini and a Bellini?" Patty asked, with a smile.

"Sounds good to start," replied Jack.

"Uh, Mister Goldie said if I see you to let him know," said Patty.

"Fine," replied Jack. "Tell him we're here."

When Patty placed their order with Purvis and disappeared into the back of the club, Jack saw Sammy saunter in and take a seat on the opposite side of the club. It was a good spot. Between them, they would be able to watch everyone without having to leave their seats.

Moments later, Patty returned with their drinks and said, "Jack, Mister Goldie asked if you would meet him in his office for a moment. I think he is expecting an important call and doesn't want to miss it."

Jack looked at Laura and she said, "That's okay, honey. I'll wait."

As Jack followed Patty he caught a glimpse of Jojo entering the club. He knew that Laura also saw him and continued to follow the waitress down a short hallway to Goldie's office.

"Come on in," said Goldie, looking up over the screen on his laptop and eyeing Jack carefully.

Any warmth Jack had detected in Goldie's voice the last time they met was gone.

"Thanks, Patty," said Goldie. "That is all. Close the door after you."

Once Patty had left, Goldie arose from his desk and gestured for Jack to take a seat in a sitting area in his office that was composed of an overstuffed black-and-white cowhide patterned leather sofa and two matching leather chairs.

A glass coffee table in the centre contained a moss-filled, black clay pot sprouting a cluster of white orchids.

Jack selected a chair and Goldie sat across the table from him on the sofa.

"What is it, Arthur? You seem a little distraught?"

Goldie glared silently at Jack for a moment, his eyes studying Jack's face for a response.

Ah, the psychological games we play, thought Jack. *You bring me into your lair, close the door, and adopt an alpha-male attitude …* Jack eyed the plant on the coffee table and smiled. He leaned forward, slightly turning the clay pot. "Beautiful. The moth orchid. They're such an exotic flower. One of my favourites. A common variety perhaps, but beautiful, nonetheless."

"Yes, it is."

"So," said Jack harshly, pointing his finger at Goldie. "We're not here to discuss flowers. What's on your mind?"

The change in Jack's demeanour caught Goldie off guard and he automatically leaned back on the sofa. "Well … I received some rather disturbing news this morning. Rather upsetting. It concerns you."

"Concerns me?" replied Jack. His tone was friendly again. His face showed surprise, as he turned the pot back to its original position.

Goldie felt a little confused. *How will he respond? Admire my damned plant and smile ... or reach in his pocket for a jackknife?* Goldie took a deep breath, subconsciously crossed his legs and said, "It's about an incident that happened in Montreal two nights ago. You didn't hear about it?"

"I've been out boating for the last few days," said Jack casually. "Haven't stayed in touch with the news. I do have a few calls to return, but no indication of anything urgent. Why? I can't imagine anything that would have any affect on you. Has the RCMP been around again making their usual vociferous and blasphemous accusations? I understood they had finished prodding into my affairs."

"No, it's nothing like that. Well, sort of. It was because of the visit I received from them that —"

"That what?" said Jack coldly.

"That, uh, tweaked my curiosity at little. I happened to mention the incident to a friend. Turns out he knew someone who happened to move to Montreal recently. A Mister Woo. Apparently your name came up in conversation between the two of them. Mister Woo and a friend of his happened to find themselves in an Irish pub two nights ago and Mister Woo took it upon himself to ask about you."

"Mister Woo sounds like a very nosy person," replied Jack. His voice was monotone and he showed no emotion.

"Anyone he spoke to said they had never heard of you."

That's hard to believe. He wouldn't have bothered to call me in if that's all there was to it. "See? It is as I said," replied Jack. "The RCMP are completely wrong in their assumption that I am some type of gangster."

"Later, when they left to go to their car, Mister Woo was attacked by several men and severely beaten with a baseball bat. His friend was told to stay out of the fracas or he would get the same."

"Sounds unfortunate," said Jack. "What with the economy the way it is, many poor people become desperate for money."

"It wasn't robbery," said Goldie with determination. "They didn't steal anything. As they were putting the boots to Mister Woo, their remarks indicated it was because he was rude to be asking questions, let alone insinuating that one of their friends was a drunk. By their accents, he knew they were all Irish."

"He told one of them they were a drunk?"

Goldie shrugged and said, "He was being beaten so badly, plus English is a second language to them, they probably didn't understand."

"What an unfortunate incident," said Jack, lightly. "Perhaps my people thought he was a cop or a reporter or something."

"Your people?"

"Uh … I mean the Irish. Generally speaking. What with the problems over the years with the IRA, the British … you must understand what it was like. Old habits don't go away so easily. Asking too many questions in an Irish pub can be detrimental to your health. I wouldn't advise it, personally. How is the poor fellow? This Mister Woo?"

"He is out of intensive care, but he has two broken arms, a broken collarbone, and his jaw is wired shut. Some of his ribs are cracked, and on top of that, he will be in traction for the next six weeks."

"Sounds like a most unfortunate misunderstanding."

"Misunderstanding! Who are you kidding? It was *your* people."

Jack leaned forward, sticking one finger into the moss at the base of the orchid. "This orchid is far too dry," he said. "It needs a wee touch. Keep this up and you'll have to borrow an intravenous tube from nosy wee Woo to rescue it."

"Did you listen when I told you what they did to him? The poor bastard can't even wipe his own ass!"

"Well," said Jack, calmly, "with his jaw wired shut, it isn't like he is going to be eating much, anyway."

Goldie's mouth gaped open in surprise. He thought about Jack's comment and started laughing.

19

Jack returned to where Laura was sitting as Jojo stood up from a bar stool and pulled out his wallet to pay for his drink. Sammy was still seated in the same place.

"What happened?" asked Jack.

"Think Jojo was jerking the operator around, or maybe killing time. He came in, sat at the bar, and ordered a drink. Kept looking at his watch and now it looks like he's leaving. Didn't talk to anyone else. How did it go with you?'

"Goldie took the bait. Had Woo check me out."

"How did that go?"

"Really well."

"Is Woo dead?"

"Didn't go that well, but he is in hospital. Goldie is going to join us for a drink in a few minutes. I've got to talk with Sammy before he goes. Sit tight."

A moment later, Jack met Sammy inside the washroom.

"Laura tell you?" asked Sammy.

Jack nodded.

"The bastard didn't meet with anyone."

"Use his phone?"

"Nope. Just sat at the bar and had a drink. You find out anything? Where did you go?"

"Chatting with Goldie in his office. Nothing that helps you."

Sammy answered his cell and said, "I gotta go. Jojo is back in his car and the surveillance teams are on the move. Sounds like they're going to another fast food joint."

"The operator is wired?"

"Yeah. With this much cash, we're not taking any chances."

"Let me know as soon as any arrests are made. There is something I want you to do right after."

"Sure, what?"

Jack showed Sammy a picture he had saved on his cellphone.

"What the fuck! That's my ID photo from work," said Sammy.

"I know. After the arrest, I want you to come back and meet with the bartender. His name is Purvis. Say you're a friend of Jojo and warn him that Jojo got arrested."

"Purvis is the man?"

"Has to be. The only guy Jojo talked to was Purvis. I've seen how Purvis dresses. He's got bigger diamond rings on his fingers and more jewellery than a Hollywood mistress. His tips aren't that good."

"Son of a bitch."

"I want you to say that the heat came down as Jojo was talking to you on your cell. Tell Purvis that Jojo sent you back to warn him."

"Purvis will never fall for that."

"I know. Besides, I'm going to burn you with Goldie before you arrive."

"You're what?"

"Come on, it'll help me out. Busting Jojo will make people a little paranoid, especially when it comes out that you were doing surveillance in here. Do this for me and I'll be able to story it in a way to take the heat off of this place. I don't need Goldie thinking he is under the magnifying glass."

Sammy thought about it momentarily and sighed. "Okay, I'll do it. I'll call you on your cell. Guess I better dig my Kevlar out of the trunk," he mumbled.

"Good idea," said Jack, "but let me tell you how I hope it will go down."

Jack and Laura smiled as Goldie joined them for a drink.

"This round is on me," said Goldie. "Consider it an apology for having overly inquisitive friends."

"Jack told me," said Laura. "It sounds like Mister Woo was lucky."

"Lucky?" replied Goldie.

"His body is intact, is it not?" replied Laura. She turned to Jack and said, "They didn't! Tell me poor wee Woo still has his winky!"

"Oh, honey," said Jack, smiling. "The boys didn't do that. They only roughed him up a little for fun. Don't be giving Arthur the wrong impression!"

"For fun?" Arthur noted admonishingly.

Jack's face instantly hardened and his tone became serious as he looked at Goldie and said, "I dislike violence. I'm not a violent man by nature."

The abrupt change in Jack's demeanour caught Goldie off guard. *You may dislike violence, but there is no doubt that you have no qualms about using it ...*

Jack's face softened and a whimsical smile appeared. "I suppose I should apologize," he said. "Maybe send him some candy. Perhaps some toffee to chew on while he reflects upon his nosy ways."

"I'm sure he'll be fine," said Goldie, unsure whether he was supposed to laugh or not. He glanced quickly at Laura before looking at Jack and whispering, "I suppose I should not have made that comment in front of Laura about having overly inquisitive friends."

"It's okay," replied Jack. "Laura is not kept in the dark on such matters. Anything you say to me can be said in front of her."

"I see," said Goldie. "No insult was intended," he added, looking at Laura.

"Just don't refer to me as madam," said Laura.

Goldie looked puzzled. "I'm not sure what you —"

"On the matter of you checking me out," said Jack firmly, changing the subject.

"I wasn't really," replied Goldie. "I happened to mention you to —"

"Listen," said Jack coldly. "There is an old Irish expression that says it is better to have fifty enemies outside your house than one in it."

The comment caught Goldie off guard and he hesitated, unsure of how to respond.

"I understand the need to check people out," continued Jack, sounding matter-of-fact. "I do so myself on occasion. But there are enough troubles in the world without insulting each other's intelligence. If you and I are to become better acquainted, I suggest we start by being honest from the beginning. Agreed?"

Goldie stared silently at his glass. After a moment he looked at Jack and said, "Agreed."

"Good," said Jack, raising his martini. "Then with that I will propose a toast to new friendships."

After the three of them clinked glasses, Jack smiled and raised his glass in Goldie's direction again and said, "May your troubles be as few and as far apart as my grandmother's teeth."

Goldie chuckled and sat back and smiled.

Jack smiled back. *The hook is in, you bastard. Wonder if you would mind if I drove you to a park? Let you run around awhile ...*

The next forty-five minutes passed with the three of them making idle conversation before Sammy called Jack.

"You free to talk?" asked Sammy.

"No, not at all. Just sitting with Laura and ... a friend, having a drink."

"Okay if I talk?" asked Sammy.

"You're not interfering at all."

"We just took Jojo down in a restaurant bathroom," said Sammy. "He was showing the operator the kilo. Went like last time except it was a Tim Hortons. Surveillance saw him pick the kilo up from under a bush outside the restaurant. The restaurant is crowded. I'm sure whoever laid it down is probably watching and will soon see Jojo leave in cuffs. Your end will know Jojo was busted soon enough. Still want me to come back there?"

"Of course."

"Be there in ten minutes. If I get shot, I'm not going down without shooting you, too," said Sammy as he hung up.

Jack still pretended to talk on his cell and said, "The chat room? I think so, hang on." Jack looked at Goldie and asked, "Could I borrow the laptop in your office for a moment? Are you hooked up to the Internet?"

"Sure. I'll bring it out. We're on wireless."

"That won't be necessary. Actually it would be better for you to come with me and talk about something in private," said Jack, glancing around at some patrons sitting nearby. He spoke back into his phone and said, "Two minutes. Get online."

Moments later, Jack used Goldie's laptop while Goldie watched him patiently from his sofa. When Jack was finished, he turned the computer off, shook his head, and snickered.

"Everything okay?" asked Goldie.

"I just found out why the RCMP decided to talk to you about me the other night," said Jack. "Turns out it was a coincidence."

"A coincidence?"

"Yes. They're working on some heroin dealer associated with your club. Guess they started running licence plates in the vicinity and discovered I was a customer. Typical. They jumped to the wrong conclusion and thought I was involved."

"Heroin dealer ... in my club?" said Goldie, looking concerned.

"Nickel-and-dime stuff. Some street urchin dealing a pound or two."

"You call a pound or two nickel and dime?"

Jack continued as if he didn't hear him. "Rather insulting that they would think I would stoop to that level."

"Did your friend say who it was the police were working on?"

"Yes. Some punk. The police realize that my being here was a coincidence. Apparently there was an undercover cop in earlier tonight watching this dealer."

"Did you get the ... uh, punk's name?"

"Oh, I'm sorry. I can't remember. I deleted everything, including the trash bin. It was an odd name. Something like Mojo. Not really important. My friend also sent me a photo of the undercover officer ... hang on, my phone vibrated. Probably it."

Goldie looked at the photo of Sammy on Jack's phone and asked, "Would you mind if I show this to my bartender. Just to see if he's been in?"

"Sorry, no," replied Jack, deleting the photo. "Purvis seems like a nice guy, but I don't want word getting out that I have access to cop photos. It could cause a huge problem for the person who is helping me."

"I trust Purvis," said Goldie. "He wouldn't tell anyone about the photo."

"I had a tough time deciding on whether or not to tell you." Jack paused, as if deciding upon a course of action. "Tell you what, give Purvis a description of what you remember in the photo, but don't tell him you actually saw a photo. Ask him if he knows this Mojo character. Okay?"

"Okay," agreed Goldie.

"I'll wait. If there are any other concerns you might wish me to help you with, I may need to borrow your computer again."

Laura saw Goldie come out from the back of the club and hurry over to speak with Purvis. Seconds later, Purvis used his cellphone, but quickly hung up and slammed his fist onto the counter. Goldie said something to him and then retreated back to his office while Purvis paced back and forth behind the bar.

"Did Purvis know Mojo?" asked Jack when Goldie returned to his office.

"Yes. His name is actually Jojo."

"Jojo! Yes, that was it. If he and Purvis are friends, I would suggest he warn him somehow. But keep in mind that Jojo's phone could be tapped."

"He already tried to call him. Someone else answered."

"Not a good sign," replied Jack.

Goldie eyed Jack carefully and said, "Remember when you said we should be honest with each other?"

"Of course."

Goldie nodded and said, "Let's step out back in the alley for some fresh air. There is something I want to tell you."

"Your office isn't bugged," said Jack.

"You know that? How can you be sure?"

"I'm positive. Otherwise I would not have borrowed your laptop, let alone used this room to tell you what I did."

Goldie eyed Jack curiously and said, "I take it you have a *very* good friend to keep you so well informed?"

"Blood is thicker than water and easier to see," shrugged Jack. "Kinship is important."

Goldie smiled. "I think you and I will become good friends."

"Oh?"

"You see, I also have an entrepreneurial spirit. We have things in common, not to mention that I also use chat rooms for communication. We should get to know each other better."

"If Jojo was arrested, does it affect you?" asked Jack, sounding surprised.

"No, not at all. We've never met. As you say, he is a nickel-and-dime operator. Hardly worth —"

Purvis burst into the room. "He's here! He just walked in!"

"Who?" asked Goldie.

"The ... uh," Purvis stopped talking when he saw Jack.

"It's okay," said Goldie. "Jack is my new friend. He knows you and Jojo are acquainted."

"The guy you described," said Purvis. "The undercover cop. He just came in and beelined straight for me. Says his name is Sammy."

"He didn't try to arrest you?" asked Goldie.

"Not yet. He told me he is in business with Jojo and that Jojo just got busted with a key of smack. He said Jojo got word to him to come and warn me! What the fuck? What should we do?"

"What did you say to him?" asked Goldie.

"Told him my boss wanted something and I'd be back in a second. What the hell should I do? He obviously suspects me from when he was in earlier and saw Jojo meet with me. It could be my neck on the line."

"Perfect," snickered Jack. "Sammy the narc is trying to incriminate you or set you up."

"No shit," replied Purvis.

"Want to get rid of him for good?" asked Jack. "Nice and clean with no heat on you or the club?"

Sammy was surprised when Purvis came back to the bar and smiled at him and said, "You say you're Jojo's partner and he got busted with a kilo of heroin?"

"Yeah," replied Sammy.

Purvis looked nervously around and said, "Give me a minute to look after some other customers. I want to talk to you about it. Would you like a drink on the house?"

"Thanks," replied Sammy, trying to keep his suspicion from showing. "Canadian Club on ice with Coke on the side."

"Sure thing. CC on the rocks with a side of Coke."

Sammy watched carefully as Purvis prepared the drink and passed it to him. He was not taking any chances on being drugged.

Purvis smiled. "I'll be back as soon as I've taken care of the other customers.

Sammy watched as Purvis puttered around at the far end of the bar.

"Come on, Purv', you're slower than hell tonight," complained one of the waitresses.

Sammy's attention was concentrated on Purvis and he did not see the arrival of two newcomers into the club. He was taking a sip when he felt the muzzle of a pistol on his back.

20

It was quarter to three in the morning. Jack and Laura sat with Goldie as one of the bouncers let the last of the other customers out the door before relocking it. Jack saw Patty cashing out at the register while Purvis put away some clean glasses behind the bar.

"I'll be right back," said Goldie. "There is something I would like to talk to you about before you go."

Jack saw Laura's raised eyebrows as she gave him an optimistic grin.

He shrugged in response and said, "I'm going to drop a twenty for Purvis before he goes."

As Jack approached the bar, he heard Goldie say to Patty, "I'm having a party at my house next Saturday night. How would you like to be my date?"

"Oh, I'm sorry, Mister Goldie, but I have a boyfriend," she replied. "Thank you, anyway."

"Not a problem," replied Goldie.

Jack walked to the end of the bar where Purvis was working and reached over to place twenty dollars in a tip glass.

"No, Jack," said Purvis smiling. "Please, I appreciate it, but I feel I owe you tonight."

"Ah, it's nothing," replied Jack.

"Your bill is on the house tonight," said Goldie, as he walked over.

"Hardly necessary," replied Jack.

"Look at it as part of my apology for having nosy friends."

Jack smiled and said, "Apology accepted."

"Now," said Goldie, "may I have Purvis mix us one more round?"

"You're asking an Irishman if he wants a free drink?" chuckled Jack.

"I'll have Patty bring them over. I'll join you in a sec."

As Jack turned to leave, he heard Goldie say to Purvis, "Find a reason to fire Patty. I want her gone within the week."

Minutes later, both Jack and Laura masked their feelings with a smile as Goldie sat across from them and said, "Wow! That was quite a night."

"Hope the action didn't scare off any customers," said Jack.

"Are you kidding?" replied Goldie. "Everyone thought it was hilarious! I bet it will bring us more business."

"That undercover officer must have had the shock of his life," said Laura.

Goldie laughed and said, "I came out just as it happened. Too bad you couldn't see his face! I almost pissed my pants trying not to laugh. Same for Purv'. Damned hard to keep a straight face."

"I don't think he saw it coming," said Jack.

"Those uniformed cops weren't taking any chances," said Goldie. "When they found his gun they had him handcuffed behind his back so fast and face-first down on the bar — I thought he would break his nose."

"Made Purvis look good, calling it in," said Jack.

"It was perfect. Makes the club look good, too. Excuse me, nine-one-one," said Goldie, sounding officious while holding his hand up by his ear to simulate a telephone. "I have a drug trafficker in my club saying he and his partner sold a kilo of heroin a few minutes ago. He said the police showed up and arrested his partner, but he escaped. Perhaps you would like to pick him up?" Goldie then broke down laughing. "Oh, Jack. You're the best. The absolute best!" said Goldie, raising a glass of Tyrconnell on ice in a toast to Jack.

"It must have been embarrassing for the undercover officer to apologize to Purvis," said Laura.

"Oh, that was fantastic," said Goldie. "Telling him he was guessing that Purvis was somehow connected and was only doing his job to find out. His face was the colour of the cherries that Purvis keeps behind the bar. He couldn't apologize enough for all the trouble he caused."

"Enough of that," said Jack, not wanting to be reminded any further of the favour he owed Sammy.

"You mentioned that there was something you wished to talk to us about?"

"Yes," replied Sammy. "I'm throwing myself a birthday party next Saturday at my house. I was hoping you both could come?"

"We'd be delighted to," said Jack.

"We should exchange phone numbers," suggested Goldie.

"Good idea," replied Jack.

"Your birthday is next Saturday?" asked Laura.

"Well, actually on the following Thursday, but I thought Saturday would be better for the party. And please, no gifts."

Jack smiled. *Maybe play a party game. You can dress as a piñata and I'll bring Patty along to beat you with a stick.*

"I've traded in my Aston Martin for a new Ferrari 612 Scaglietti," bragged Goldie. "It should arrive this week. That will be plenty gift enough."

"Turning forty?" asked Laura, with a smile.

Goldie smiled back. "Actually, I'll be forty-four. And I know what you're both thinking. I am not having a mid-life crisis. At least, I don't think I am."

Laura smiled. *Actually I was thinking you are likely compensating for having a small penis.*

Jack didn't smile as he thought, *Buddy, believe me, you are far past "mid" life.*

"I'm heading home," said Purvis as he approached the table. "Wish to thank you again Jack, for a fun night."

"No problem."

"Purvis," said Goldie seriously, "You will be a very good boy for the next few months, correct?"

"Yes, sir. I'm sorry," said Purvis, before leaving.

Jack raised his glass to Goldie and said, "*Sláinte*!"

"*Sláinte*?" asked Goldie.

"Irish for 'cheers,'" replied Laura.

"God, you're a fun group, you Irish," said Goldie.

"You've got no idea," replied Jack.

Another mid-week meeting with Jack, Laura, Sammy, and CC went about as well as Jack expected.

"I ran everything past the prosecutor," said CC. "She reviewed all your notes. There is nothing to confirm that Goldie is personally involved with anything criminal." She looked at Jack and added, "And I didn't raise the small footprint issue. She did, but said regardless, even if it had been an adult-sized print, there are no grounds to substantiate a wiretap application."

"Too bad," said Jack. "He trusts me enough to think his office is free from bugs. It could be good. He told me he uses chat rooms to communicate. I'd love to have spyware on his laptop. You can bet that is how he keeps in touch with The Enabler."

"Sorry," said CC, "unless you come up with something more, warrants and bugs are out."

"Same for drugs," said Sammy. "We never got anything on Jojo's phone to indicate Goldie was involved. In fact, we never even had him call Purvis. Although, from what you said, it sounds like he'll be clean for awhile to ensure there's no heat."

"Maybe The Enabler will be invited to his birthday party," said CC.

"I doubt it," said Laura. "If he and Wang are afraid to even mention his real name when they talk, I doubt they would invite him to a party."

"I agree," said Jack, "but CC, if you're available it might be nice to scoop some plates and see who does show up."

"I'll make myself available," she replied. "So where does that leave you two?"

"Guess it leaves us time to party," said Jack.

Goldie's waterfront home on Lower Bellevue Avenue in West Vancouver afforded a view of Burrard Inlet from the rear. A towering hedge along the front of the property ensured privacy to anyone passing. An interlocking brick driveway wound its way up to the two-storey Tudor-style home.

It was ten o'clock at night when Jack and Laura were let in by one of the caterers, and the house was crowded. They were late, but Jack wanted to ensure that none of the two dozen licence plate numbers obtained by CC belonged to anyone he or Laura knew from their past. None did, although many of the owners were known in police intelligence reports as either suspected drug importers or financial backers for those who did.

"Hey! My Irish rogue!" shouted Goldie gleefully as he pushed his way through the crowd, slopping champagne onto his pants leg as he walked over.

"Looks like he started the party at noon," whispered Laura.

Goldie embraced Jack like he was a missing relative and then leered at Laura and said, "A birthday kiss for an old gentleman, my lady?"

"Certainly," replied Laura, sidestepping away as Goldie lurched forward. "But that will be next Thursday, so you will have to wait."

"Ooow, wicked you are to make me wait," said Goldie, "but I'll hold you to it. Come on in and make yourself at home. I've hired a bartender who you'll find set up in the dining room, and there's plenty of food."

The next two hours went by without incident and Jack and Laura mingled with the crowd, making small talk, while Goldie spent the time draped over a young woman.

"Notice our Chinese friend from the restaurant isn't here," observed Jack, quietly.

"Yes, I noticed dear Mister Wang is conspicuous by his absence."

"I suspect their affiliation is strictly business. Between them and The Enabler," replied Jack.

"Making The Enabler a rather interesting character if he controls two completely different drug syndicates."

"Exactly." Jack nodded toward the young woman who was receiving Goldie's attention. "Any idea who she is?"

"Told me her name is Candy," replied Laura. "Coke slut, I think. She offered me some earlier on the way to the washroom. Her sister is with one of the other guests."

Jack saw Candy giggle as Goldie peeked in the top of her blouse before pretending to slap his hand away.

"Nice," commented Laura. "I was with her for about a minute and she mentioned twice about how rich Goldie must be. Coke slut or hooker. Take your pick."

"Is there a difference?" asked Jack. "Either one will do anything for —"

"To Arthur!" yelled one of the guests. "Hope you have the best birthday ever!"

Goldie seemed to appreciate the applause and his head wobbled around looking at the crowd until he spotted Jack. "Hey, Jack, my buddy! You got one of them Irish toasts you could give me?"

The crowd fell silent as everyone turned to look at Jack. He nodded, raising his glass and said, "We drink to your coffin."

Laura heard the gasp from several people. *Oh, man …*

After a pause, Jack continued, "May it be built from the wood of a hundred-year-old oak tree …" He looked around the room and added, "that I shall plant tomorrow."

Goldie howled with laughter and made his way toward Jack.

Jack looked at Laura and whispered, "You have any idea how much I hated adding that last part?"

"Jack, Laura," said Goldie. "Come with me. You gotta see this!"

Jack and Laura followed Goldie as he led them down a hall and through a door leading into his three-car attached garage.

One spot was empty, one was taken up by a speedboat, and in the third spot was a Ferrari 612 Scaglietti that reflected the overhead light like a shiny black emerald.

"What do ya think?" asked Goldie, beaming while groping inside his pants pockets with both hands at the same time. "Wanna, want ... want me to take you both for a spin?" he said, pulling out a keychain and dangling it in the air.

"Not tonight," replied Jack. "You've had too much to drink. This car is too beautiful to risk damaging."

"Ah, my lucky rabbit's foot will protect us," said Goldie, indicating the white stump of animal hair dangling from his keychain.

It reminded Jack of a three-legged cat in an alley and he unconsciously clenched his fist. He glanced at Laura and saw a quick flash of disgust cross her face before she regained her composure. He knew she felt more compassionate about animals being killed than people. Or at least, some people. *Now I'm starting to feel the same way ...*

"So what say? The cat got your tongue?" asked Goldie.

"No, not tonight," Jack said. "It really is awesome. I've never seen a car like it." Jack then approached the car and slowly walked around it, looking inside as he went.

"Take a look inside," said Goldie opening the car

door. "Go ahead, sit behind the wheel."

Laura felt it might be an opportune time to let Jack talk in private with Goldie so she said, "It's beautiful, but I'm not really into the car thing. I'll see you when you come back inside."

"Laura, wait!" ordered Jack. He glanced at Goldie and said, "Would you show her the car? She won't appreciate it until she sees all the detail. I have to go to the bathroom, but I'll be right back."

"Sure thing," replied Goldie, getting in to the driver's seat. "Laura, hop in beside me," he yelled.

Jack pretended to kiss Laura on the side of her neck as he was leaving. "Keep him busy," he whispered. "Don't let him out of the garage until I get back."

"Not a problem. Did you see his keychain? I'm going to slap a sleeper hold on him, start his car and euthanize him. Why, what's up?"

CC answered her phone and recognized Jack's voice.

"I was just in Goldie's garage. There's a workbench there with a box of garbage bags on it. The clear plastic type. Same as what was over Melvin's head."

"It could be a coincidence," replied CC.

"Yeah, it could be, but what if it isn't? Are you sure we can't get a warrant? If the next bag on the roll is sequential to the one used on Melvin, the lab can match it."

"Goddamn it," muttered CC. "I'm going to call the prosecutor at home. Can I call you back?"

"Hurry."

The minutes ticked by and Jack hoped that Laura was keeping Goldie occupied. *What am I thinking ... Goldie is loving the moment. That's if Laura hasn't killed him.* He answered his phone on the first ring.

"Sorry," said CC. "No can do. Wrong foot size, all that bullshit."

"What do you want me to do?" asked Jack.

"Without a warrant we could never get it admitted as evidence," said CC.

"The bag could be used or gone soon. It has to be the next bag in sequence or there's no use."

"That's if it is from that roll and if it's not already gone," said CC.

"Would you like to find out?"

The seconds ticked past as CC thought it over.

"There is a limited window of opportunity at the moment," said Jack. "Has to be now or never. Going, going —"

"Okay, damn it. Do it!"

21

The RCMP laboratory opened Monday morning. Jack was the first in line. The lab still had the other plastic bag provided to them by CC.

Later that afternoon, Jack received the call from CC that he had been waiting for.

"Jack, the lab says it's a match," said CC. Her voice sounded hollow and empty. "Guess you were right about Goldie. I can forget about my kids theory."

"That's great it matched," replied Jack. "The bastard did bring Melvin to the park. We're on the right track. Now we have to find out who The Enabler is and the guy in the suit described as having dead eyes."

"There's a problem ... huge," mumbled CC. She spoke like she was in pain, as if someone had beaten her stomach and ribcage with a hockey stick.

Jack realized that CC was fighting back tears. "CC? What is it? What's wrong?"

"I fucked up," she cried. "Tree of the poisoned fruit or something. No, that's not it."

"What? You're not making sense."

"Fruit of the poisonous tree. That's it. That's what the prosecutor just told me. The garbage bag, we can't —"

"I know. We can't use it in evidence. We knew that. It's too bad but at least we know we're on the right trail. We'll get other proof."

"No, it's much worse," sniffled CC. "The prosecutor was screaming at me she was so fucking mad. She said that we might as well have given Goldie permanent immunity from prosecution for it."

"What the hell are you talking about?" asked Jack, feeling a sense of dread ooze through his body like a parasitic disease.

"Because we stole the garbage bag, not only can't it be used, but she says any evidence we gather on Goldie from here on in is tainted because we're using illegally obtained evidence as the catalyst to further our investigation. If we didn't know about the garbage bag in his garage as being literally connected to the one at the murder scene, we wouldn't have continued to pursue the investigation on Goldie."

"Bullshit!" yelled Jack angrily. "I was working on the premise from what Goldie said in Wang's car that he was involved. Not to mention, the trail of the gun that Laura and I followed. Even if the garbage bag hadn't matched, I wouldn't have given up!"

"I know. That's how I perceived it. The prosecutor says different ... or at least says a judge would say different. The evidence leading up to stealing the bag is admissible. What was said in the car was under a legal wiretap."

"Yeah, which means squat," replied Jack. "Even you weren't convinced they were talking about the same incident. Jesus! Now you've got me saying it."

"Saying what?"

"Incident. Like, oh, well, guess we have to let this *incident* slide and work on some other incident. These incidents are murder! Now the murderers walk because I stole a garbage bag?"

"It's not your fault. I'm the primary investigator and I was the one who told you to do it."

"Yeah, with me prodding you and putting you on the spot saying we didn't have much time. I knew it was wrong. I just didn't realize how wrong."

"I should have known better."

"What about this Enabler, The Shaman character, or the guy with dead eyes? What if we find out who they are?"

"The angle I think you need to pursue is that you're investigating Goldie for drugs and these others are his bosses. But as far as nailing Goldie for his part in the murder, I think you better forget about it."

"I am investigating them for drugs. By coincidence, Melvin is a priority above and beyond that."

"You don't need to convince me. Save all that for the courts," said CC. "Won't take a defence lawyer long to bring up reasonable doubt to some juror."

Jack stared briefly at the phone in his hand. *So if all goes well, maybe Goldie could get a one- or two-year stint in jail for drug trafficking? How do I explain that to Natasha?*

"What's going on?" asked Laura, once Jack hung up.

"No use explaining it twice," said Jack. "Come on, I better tell Rose how I screwed up."

Both Rose and Laura looked as sick as Jack felt once he finished explaining the situation.

"I'll back you if any complaints come from Department of Justice," sighed Rose.

"I don't give a damn about DOJ," said Jack. "Once I stop to think about it, it's not like Goldie would have received any real time in jail even if we did have a warrant. Defence would have tabled it as a prank gone awry. He really might spend more time in jail on drugs. Will our budget allow Laura and me to continue in that regard?"

"Maybe if you would quit dropping fifty-dollar tips, it might," replied Rose. "No, wait, it seems to me the one you claimed Saturday night was a hundred."

"That was an exception," said Jack. "A young woman by the name of Patty. I think it was her last shift. Besides, we didn't claim any drinks that night, so it balances out."

"Relax," said Rose. "I wasn't really serious, although money is an issue. We're no different than the narcs when it comes to that. Our budget isn't going to let you go out and start buying kilos."

"I'm hoping they think we're above that level," said Jack. "I think if we get an offer, it will be something far more substantial. These guys are definitely worth pursuing. I'm certain that Goldie is about to take me into his confidence. Our priority is to identify whoever is above him."

"I agree," said Rose. "Keep playing it as you have been and keep me in the loop. Once they're identified, we can reassess the situation."

"Will do," said Jack. "I don't think it will take very —" He paused to answer his cellphone and made a slash sign across his throat with one finger as he looked at Rose.

Rose took her desk phone off the hook as she and Laura watched.

"Arthur! Good to hear from you," answered Jack.

22

"What's the name of this spot again?" asked Laura as she drove along West Broadway.

"Regal Beagle," replied Jack. "Keep driving, it's up in the twenty-two-hundred block.

"You pick it, or Goldie?"

"It was my choice. Great spot. Small pub with an Asian restaurant attached to it. For pub food, it has some of the best. One of the owners makes his own pickled green beans that they put in a lot of the drinks."

"Pickled green beans?" said Laura, wrinkling her nose.

"Calls them Blaze's Beans. Beats a stick of celery in a Caesar. Try it sometime. You'll like it."

"I would if I was invited."

"Sorry about that. He was adamant about talking to me in private first. He said once I heard what he had to say, if I still wanted to tell you it would be okay."

"You want me to park out front and sit in the car? A little subservient if we want him to respect me."

"Park a couple of blocks away. I'm not worried about my safety. He won't be searching me in a place like this. I'm going to be packing my piece, so don't fret. I'll tell him you're off shopping, but will be back by five o'clock for drinks and supper. Should be enough time for him to say what he has to say."

"Great. While I'm waiting I think I'll call Natasha and tell her you're off drinking and getting your bean snapped."

"My what? Where did you pick up that expression?" said Jack, chuckling.

It made Laura feel relieved. Jack's mood since CC called him had not been good. He was taking the garbage bag fiasco personally. Too personally.

Jack entered the pub and spotted Goldie drinking a glass of white wine. Jack joined him and ordered a Caesar with two Blaze's Beans. The waiter had barely left the table when Goldie outlined his real business to Jack, starting years earlier when he was arrested at a Burmese checkpoint near the border to Thailand and was saved by a man he called The Enabler. He told Jack his couriers, along with his shipment of heroin, were also detained, but later both the couriers and the heroin were once more on their way.

"And the man you call The Enabler saved you?" asked Jack.

"I probably owe him my life. Since then, life has been one big gravy train. I know you have the connections back east. Jump on the gravy train with me and we'll both get rich together."

"So, if I have it right," said Jack, "The Enabler is a middle man. He knows everyone from the poppy growers up to the drug warlords to the police, customs officials ... everyone."

"You got it. At least as far as the Asian countries go. Specifically heroin. He enables everything to run smoothly and efficiently. All the buyers do is pay a small commission based on how much weight is being transported. Because of the volume involved around the world, he also gets the best price. Even with the commission, you still come out way ahead. Then every dealer down to the five-kilo level pays a commission that is distributed back up the ladder."

"It's a pyramid scheme," said Jack. "The more dealers I would have working for me, the more commission everyone gets, and the more money we make."

"Exactly."

"So in a way, we're all working for The Enabler."

"We are for the one in Vancouver. I understand there are a few other Enablers spread around the globe."

"So The Enabler isn't the top boss?"

"No, there are a couple of people above that level. I've never met any of the other Enablers or the top boss. Only the Enablers know who it is. As things stand now, in a few months the organization wants me to take over The Enabler's role in Vancouver. He is being promoted to the number two man in the organization."

Jack didn't respond as he slowly took his time to crunch through a pickled bean while Goldie leaned forward, waiting in anticipation for his response.

"Damn it, what do you think?" asked Goldie, no longer able to contain his emotion.

Jack stared at him blankly and said, "I'll give you a shot." *And I mean that, literally ...*

"That's great!"

"Small to start with," continued Jack. "Only one ton on the first transaction to make sure everything runs smoothly. And that is only if the price is right, the product good, and you can guarantee safe delivery to Vancouver."

Surprise registered on Goldie's face. "One ton is small to you? Christ, you're tied into the New York markets, aren't you?"

Jack countered with another question, "I'm from the east, aren't you tied into the U.S. markets in the west?"

"Nothing like you are," admitted Goldie. "Purvis has a contact in Seattle, but strictly low level by your standards. Five or ten kilos here and there. The quantity you talk about is huge."

"Perhaps over The Enabler's capabilities?" asked Jack.

"No, certainly not," Goldie hastened to say. "As I said, he controls Asia. We can definitely accommodate that," he added, while figuring out his commission based on a one-ton shipment.

"And the money transaction?" asked Jack.

"The Enabler is well connected to financial institutions. The organization even owns some banks in certain countries. I think we can come to an agreeable method of transferring the money, once we agree on price."

"Before that happens," said Jack, "I would have to meet The Enabler. With the millions we're talking about, I want to know who I'm in bed with."

Goldie's face reflected his sorrow and fear that their intended business partnership could go awry. "Sorry, Jack. I already told The Enabler all about you. He is pleased, but at the same time, is adamant about not meeting you."

"Well, I'm adamant about meeting him."

Goldie shook his head and said, "They're really paranoid about protecting their identities. He described it like protective layers on an onion. Something about it becoming more intense the closer you get to the core. Either way, it won't really matter. In a few months I'll be The Enabler and you and I already know each other."

"So there is no way you could convince him to meet with me?"

"Not a chance. I already tried. I have to admit, I'm impressed with you. I was hoping to introduce you and show you off, but he rejected the idea immediately. Like I said, they are extremely cautious. Hell, do you know that before I become The Enabler they are going to make me take a lie detector?"

"You're kidding?"

"No, I'm not. It was also made clear to me if I fail the test I'm dead. So I'm telling you, once you get in, you better get in all the way. There's no fucking around with these people."

"Well, count me in," said Jack, cheerily.

Moments later, Goldie prepared to leave, but asked, "You mentioned Laura is meeting you for supper later?"

Jack nodded.

"Tell her she still owes me a birthday kiss on Thursday. See you both at the club then?"

"You will. Drive carefully. Don't smack up that new Ferrari of yours."

Goldie smiled and shook his head. "You should feel it go," he said. "Runs like a dream. You barely think of passing someone and the next thing you know it's already happened."

Jack nodded politely and as soon as Goldie left, he paid the bill and called Laura.

"He just left," said Jack. "It went fabulously. He told me everything. Hurry and pick me up. I need to get back to the office. I've got a ton of notes to make."

"Be there in a couple of minutes," replied Laura. "Traffic is heavy. No place to park, so meet me on the curb."

Jack stepped outside. The traffic was congested, but in a car across the street he spotted the familiar mop of brown hair that Laura had described as looking like a dead rat. Jack peered closer and saw Goldie edging forward in the traffic ... driving a red Ford Taurus. Goldie was concentrating on the traffic and did not see Jack.

Jack swore under his breath and pushed redial. "Exactly where are you?"

"Curb lane westbound, a block and a half away. Hold your horses. You only called me less than a —"

"Goldie just left, going eastbound driving a red Ford Taurus. Follow him, but make damned certain he doesn't see you! Lose him if you have to, rather than be burned."

"Why? What is —"

"Talk to you in a sec. Don't hang up. I'm going to commandeer somebody's car!"

Jack waited for an opportunity before seeing a young couple driving a black Pontiac Grand Am stuck in traffic several car lengths behind Goldie. The Pontiac was tucked in tight behind a large truck and Jack knew that Goldie couldn't see it from his position.

Jack used a passing transit bus for cover, darted across the street toward the Pontiac, and tapped on the driver's window. The man driving looked startled, but rolled the window down enough to speak. "I'm an RCMP officer," said Jack, quickly showing his badge. "My name is Jack Taggart and I need your car to follow somebody."

Traffic started to move and someone in a car behind them started beeping their horn.

"Hop in," said the young man, opening his door and leaning forward in the seat so Jack could get in the back of his car.

"No, I want to —" The sound of more horns convinced Jack to quickly squeeze into the back seat. "What are your names?" he asked.

"Hi, I'm Steven Thomas —"

"And I'm Kelly McMahon," said the young woman excitedly. "Who are we following?"

"We? Okay ... Steven, keep going straight."

"If I have to run a red light, will you pay my ticket?" he asked.

"Only if I tell you to do it. Hang on. I need to speak to my partner."

"Jack!" said Laura. "What the heck is going on? He went past me going the other way. I don't think I can get turned around in this traffic in time to catch him. Sounds like you grabbed someone's car?"

"He bought a new sports car. Says it runs great. Why is he driving a red Taurus?" Jack peered out the back window and saw Laura cutting into the centre lane as she looked for an opening to turn around.

"The red car ahead that just made a left turn?" asked Steven.

"What? Yeah, that one," said Jack. "See if you can follow him, but drive carefully. It's not worth anybody getting hurt."

"Must be worth something for you to do this," said Steven.

"Laura, he turned northbound on Burrard," said Jack.

"So why is he driving this car instead of his other one?" asked Kelly.

"His other one is much fancier. Stands out," said Jack.

"So he's doing something he shouldn't be and doesn't want to get noticed," said Steven.

"Uh … exactly. Do you mind telling me what it is you two do for a living?"

"I work for an online advertising agency in Victoria," said Steven. "It's called Neverblue."

"I'm with London Drugs," replied Kelly. "Why?"

"Steven seems rather astute when it comes to bad guys."

Jack caught Steven's smile in the rear-view mirror. "My dad is a retired RCMP officer," he said. "I've heard a few things."

Jack smiled back and said, "Good. Do you know the city well?"

"Vancouver? No way," said Steven, shaking his head. "We've been lost for an hour driving around."

"Wonderful," muttered Jack.

"It's my fault," said Kelly. "We are supposed to meet my dad but I've only been to his new house a couple of times. We're completely lost."

"Pull this off and I'll buy you a tank of gas and lead you there personally," said Jack. "I would only ask that you don't mention any of the details about this to anyone."

"I understand. We won't," replied Steven.

"Is he really dangerous?" asked Kelly.

"Yes, but right now I think he might only be meeting somebody. All I want to do is find out who. He knows my face. Same goes for my partner, so we can't let him see us."

Fifteen minutes later they found themselves in the heart of downtown Vancouver, with Laura still stuck in traffic and trailing two blocks behind. Steven's ability to quickly grasp surveillance was surprisingly good. Soon he made a habit of always allowing one or two cars between them for cover, but weighed it with the option of when to speed up to make the same traffic light as Goldie when needed.

"Your dad would be proud," said Jack, hunched low in the back while peering out between the two front seats.

"Thanks. Is it okay if I tell him?"

"Yeah —"

"He's stopping!" said Kelly. "There, right in the entrance to that alley!"

Jack peered out the window as they drove past the alley and saw Goldie getting out of the car.

"You going to follow him on foot?" asked Steven.

"Can't risk him seeing me," replied Jack. "But this was a great help. He's bound to be meeting someone in a building close by. This helps us narrow it down."

"Yeah, to what? About ten thousand people," said Steven, looking up at the skyscrapers around them.

Jack peeked out the rear window and saw a familiar glimpse of Goldie's moss-green windbreaker in the crowd as he came their way.

"He doesn't know me," said Kelly, opening the door and leaping out.

"Wait, I don't —" Jack knew Goldie would be coming past them within seconds. "Okay, but public places only. Under no circumstances go anywhere unless there are lots of people."

She flashed a pretty smile back at Jack and said, "I'll be careful. This is so cool," she added, closing the door.

"What do you want me to do?" asked Steven.

"Keep circling the block. Does Kelly have a cell-phone?"

"Yes, we both do."

Goldie walked briskly down the sidewalk toward them as Steven sat parked in traffic. Jack saw Kelly appear to be intently examining the front display window of a jewellery store as Goldie walked past her in a throng of people. Jack laid down on the back seat out of sight.

"Dangerous sign," said Jack, watching Steven's nervous face as he stared straight ahead, afraid to be seen by Goldie in case he'd be caught looking at him.

"Dangerous sign?" repeated Steven, nervously, risking a glance at the back of Goldie's head as he passed by on the sidewalk.

"Yeah, I think Kelly is looking at wedding rings."

Steven's smile matched Jack's.

Minutes later, Goldie disappeared around the next corner with Kelly following discreetly.

"We're stuck," said Steven in frustration, gesturing at the traffic. "Maybe I should phone her?"

"Hang tough," replied Jack. "I know it's not easy, but the sound of a cellphone could attract attention and get her noticed. She already has a disadvantage in that category."

"How's that?"

"She's too damned cute. Guys will remember her. What's her ethnic background?"

"Irish."

Jack chuckled.

"What's so funny?"

"Inside joke. Basically this bad guy won't like the Irish when I'm done with him."

Steven had only managed to make one circuit around the block when they saw Kelly standing near where she had been let out.

"The tallest building around the corner," she said breathlessly. "He went to the forty-seventh floor. It is the very top. He told the receptionist that his name was Mister Golden ... or something like that. He said he had an appointment with Mister Lee. That name I'm certain of."

"You went with him in the elevator," said Jack, frowning.

"There were lots of people. There are different elevators for the first thirty floors. Although it was just him and me when we got to the top. I had to get out with him, there was no place left."

"Did he look at you a little strangely when he realized you didn't belong there?" asked Jack.

"The name of the company behind the reception desk is Intrinsic Global Investments. While he was waiting to see Mister Lee, I asked the receptionist if they had any secretarial positions open. She said they didn't. I don't think he paid much attention to me. Then I left."

Jack grinned. "If either of you decide to become police officers, I'll be your reference."

"Law enforcement was one of two occupations my dad said he never wanted me to go into," said Steven.

"You never told me that," said Kelly. "What was the other?"

"To become a defence lawyer," said Jack and Steven in unison. Both men chuckled.

"Do you want to know what Mister Lee looks like?" asked Kelly.

"You saw him?"

"He came out as the elevator door was closing. He's easy to identify. Asian, mid fifties, probably. He was wearing a navy blue suit, red tie, has a bald head, and a diamond stud in his left earlobe."

"Excellent," smiled Jack.

"Oh, yeah, and he is really short and small. If it wasn't for how he was dressed and his bald head, you would think he was just a kid."

Steven and Kelly both saw the startled reaction on Jack's face. He immediately used his cellphone to speak to Laura.

"Just found a match for the footprint in the park," he said quietly.

23

On Wednesday afternoon, Jack and Laura met with Rose to update her on the investigation.

"I'm certain it's the man they call The Enabler," said Jack. "His name is Kang Lee. He is originally from Seoul, South Korea, and is currently in Canada under a work permit as the president of a financial consulting company called Intrinsic Global Investments. He rents a two-bedroom penthouse overlooking English Bay in the west end and drives a new Mercedes-Benz SL500 leased to the company."

"Must be doing extremely well as a financial consultant," said Rose. "I knew I entered the wrong profession."

"CC confirmed that a picture of his shoe print matches exactly the size of the print they found at the murder scene," said Laura.

"What did you do? Mug him and steal his shoe?"

Laura smiled and said, "There are several levels of underground parking in his office tower. The bottom two levels are public parking, but the other levels are reserved spaces for different companies in the building. We went there this morning before Lee arrived. His spot, closest to the elevators, is reserved in his name."

"And?"

"And I smeared a film of dirty engine oil beside where he parks," said Jack. "He stepped in it as soon as he got out of his car."

"After that we placed a ruler beside his print and took a picture," said Laura.

"Too bad he didn't fall on his ass," said Rose. "How about Drug Section? Are they on board with us?"

"Drug Section is using what we gave them to prepare a wiretap application on Goldie. They hope to have it before a judge next week. In the meantime, they're going to start doing surveillance on him. Strictly periodic. They don't want to risk burning anything at this stage."

"And Integrated Proceeds of Crime?" asked Rose.

"I-POC came on board yesterday to follow the money trail. At the moment, they have only done a cursory examination. As they said, for them to track everyone that Lee's company is connected with will be a nightmare. They obtained last month's phone tolls and said there were thousands of calls worldwide."

"And that doesn't include Internet," added Laura.

"What reputation does the company have?" asked Rose.

"So far, they look legitimate," said Laura. "I-POC has made some discreet inquiries. The company has invested wisely into a lot of reputable companies, often at the opportune time. They have made a lot of share-holders wealthy."

"Are poppies listed as one of their commodities they promote for investment?" asked Rose facetiously.

"Nothing that obvious, I'm afraid," replied Jack, "but I am sure we'll find out they are tied in with ship-ping, air, train, and who knows what else. It is still too soon to tell. It will take months, or more likely years, for I-POC to get a basic knowledge of who's who and who's connected to whom."

"Perfect company to launder money and have the connections to ship anything they want worldwide," said Laura.

"If Lee is the president of a company like Intrinsic Global," said Rose, "then who is his boss? The one he calls The Shaman? Logic would dictate that it would have to be someone who is either a silent part-ner, or —"

"Or, as big as Intrinsic Global is," said Jack, "it's only the tip of the iceberg. Perhaps one company of many controlled by The Shaman."

"Jesus," muttered Rose, as she realized the poten-tial scope of the empire.

"Scary to think about," said Laura.

"So buying a ton of heroin from these guys is defi-nitely a possibility," said Rose.

"I figured it would be once Goldie started telling me that they controlled the Asian market," said Jack.

"I thought I better sound big if I was to get an introduction up the ladder. Guess it wasn't big enough."

"What you said is too big already," replied Rose. "There's no way the Force could even come up with a flash roll that big, or if they could, they would never risk losing it. How the hell will you work your way around that without proving you have the cash?"

"I'm going to demand that I see a lot of their operation before spending. Starting from the ground up and taking it as far as I can."

"Sort of like checking out a company before buying into it," said Laura.

"Doesn't sound like they'll ever let you see the corporate boardroom, though," said Rose.

"Not yet," replied Jack, "but once we get the ball rolling, and with what we already know about Lee and his company, maybe we'll figure it out without personal introductions."

"But so far, all this is simply speculation," said Rose. "From what you say, everything we know about Intrinsic Global is legitimate. You're basing all this on one meeting between Lee and Goldie."

"And the size of Lee's feet," said Laura.

"Goldie loves his car almost as much as he loves himself," said Jack. "It doesn't make sense that he would borrow a car, which incidentally belongs to his bartender, to go and meet someone like Lee. It was planned. They wanted to know what my response would be to joining the company. Goldie was being a good little messenger boy by running back and telling him my answer."

"Okay," said Rose, "let's say you're right. I know

your instincts for what you do are finely tuned. But it begs the question, if you are right, then what was someone of Lee's stature doing in a park at night with Goldie and some other guy while one of them is taking potshots at a homeless person?"

"I don't know," replied Jack. "Goldie is being promoted to the Enabler position. Maybe they were impressing upon him that they aren't afraid to murder someone."

"The 'you better stay in line or look what will happen' approach?" said Rose.

"Something like that. Goldie told me they are going to make him take a polygraph as part of his promotion. These guys are professional."

"And what if they decide to put you on the polygraph?" asked Rose. "Think you can lie your way out of that? You may be top-notch at lying to criminals, but it's a different story once you are tied to a bullshit detector with a professional interrogator scrutinizing your every verbal and physical response. Responses you can't control. Forget trying to drug yourself or doing self-hypnosis. These guys know their stuff."

"I know," replied Jack. "When Goldie told me that was what they were going to do to him, my insides cringed thinking about it. The thing is, Goldie has been protected in his heroin importation by these people for years. It is only with him about to learn who is really in charge that he is facing this test. With all the resources we have going for us, I would hope we can discover who The Shaman is long before they decide to slap me on the machine."

"So you and Laura will continue to play things along as you have and see what happens?"

"Exactly. Once we get a wire on Goldie, things may open up a little more. Maybe catch him talking to Lee."

"You might get lucky with a wire but I would be surprised. I think catching Lee will be a huge problem," said Rose. "Your boss, for all intents and purposes, will be Goldie. They're not going to let you climb the corporate ladder any farther than you already have."

"Then we have to get rid of Goldie," said Jack. "Convince the company to have me replace him."

"How? If you arrest him on a drug beef, then you're burned and I bet that Lee, as paranoid as this organization is, will drop him like a hot potato. With the millions that are involved, there is no way that Goldie is going to roll on anyone for the sake of spending a few months in jail."

"I know," replied Jack.

"And if you try and charge him with murder … well, you heard what will happen because you took the garbage bag, let alone trying to convince anyone of a motive. Even at best, he only drove the victim there after telling his guys it was a prank."

"Goldie is the one who had him kidnapped," said Jack, tersely. "He is as much to blame as whoever pulled the trigger. And as far as it being a prank goes, that's a crock!"

"Of course it's a crock, but you and I have been around the block a few times. Defence don't usually pick jurors they think are worldly. A lot of judges are also pretty naive."

"So he walks away from a murder rap because I stole a goddamned garbage bag!" said Jack, bitterly.

"That's justice," said Rose.

"Is it?" asked Jack.

Rose gave a weak smile and shrugged her shoulders.

"Yeah, I don't think *that* is justice, either," said Jack.

Laura reflected upon Jack's comment. *"That" is justice? Oh, man, he's got something else in mind …*

She was right.

24

Later that evening, Jack and Laura returned the wave from Purvis, who was standing behind the bar as they took a seat in a booth. A new waitress served them, and a few minutes later, Goldie joined their table.

"We've only dropped in to ask you something," said Jack.

"Tomorrow is your real birthday," said Laura. "How would you like to come out with us on our boat, the *Blue Gator*, and have dinner while the crew tours us around Vancouver Harbour?"

"That would be absolutely fab!" replied Goldie.

"Perhaps come over to our apartment for a drink first," said Jack, "then you could follow us to the marina."

"Bring a date, if you like," said Laura.

"This is really something. I'm absolutely thrilled," Goldie said, beaming with delight. "I'll bring Candy. She was at my party last Saturday. Perhaps you met her?"

"I did," replied Laura. "Very pretty girl."

"One rule I must insist upon," said Jack. "No drugs onboard the *Blue Gator*. We travel into the U.S. too often to risk some customs dog finding a trace of anything and having my boat seized. Understood?"

Goldie smiled and replied, "I don't do drugs, anyway."

"Neither do we," said Jack.

"Good," replied Goldie. "Leave that stuff for the suckers. I prefer friends who are a little more cerebral."

"You might want to mention that to Candy," said Jack.

Goldie chortled and said, "I don't use her for her brains or friendship. But don't worry; I'll make sure she behaves."

"One other thing," said Jack. "My crew, Paul and Katie ... they're Irish and I don't want you to jump to any conclusions. No business talk in front of them. They think I'm totally legit."

"Understood," replied Goldie.

As Jack and Laura were walking away from Goldie Locks, Jack looked at Laura and said, "So far so good. It's supposed to rain all week, so Goldie should be dressed for it. Tomorrow we can tell the narcs to drop their surveillance. He'll be with us. Also, we'd better do a little window dressing in the apartment. Make it look like we do live there. Same for Paul and Katie's boat. Put up a couple of pictures of us together."

"Why the apartment? I thought you were going to do it on the boat?"

"Gives me two chances. I'm not all that good with a needle and thread."

"Me, either."

"But you will be better at distracting Goldie in case I take too long."

"His new girlfriend may not take kindly to me flirting with him."

"I doubt that how she feels would be a consideration to Goldie."

"If your plan works, he'll never have anything to consider again," said Laura, quietly.

"Fly with the crows, expect to get shot."

Laura's sigh was audible.

"You think this is wrong?" asked Jack.

"No, but it isn't right, either."

"Envision yourself with a garbage bag over your head, running through the woods and being shot. Picture Goldie with his diamond-studded tooth, laughing and —"

"I know, I know. Don't remind me."

"Maybe his lucky rabbit's foot will save him."

"This isn't anything to laugh about," said Laura, frowning. "This will be his last birthday and we're acting like we're his best friends. Instead, we're assassins. Don't you feel dirty inside?"

"No, I don't," said Jack, firmly. "If you feel that way, then take another look at the photos from the park. It isn't anything to laugh about, either."

They walked a little farther and Laura said, "Sorry, I'm okay with it. Just had to talk it out."

Jack nodded. "Good. We're partners. We should talk things out. Are you really okay with it?"

"Yes."

"Great." They walked on and Jack added, "Wish I could see the look on his face when he sees what we gave him as a surprise birthday present."

Oh, man ...

On Thursday evening, Goldie and Candy arrived on schedule. "Welcome!" said Jack, inviting them inside the penthouse.

"And your birthday kiss as promised," said Laura, kissing Goldie on his cheek while giving him a quick hug.

A flicker of disappointment crossed Goldie's face. *Is that all I get? A quick peck on the cheek?* He glanced at Jack and pretended to smile. *Just as well, Jack is bound to have a jackknife lying around somewhere ...*

"Come on in, make yourselves at home," said Jack. "I'll take your jackets and toss them on the bed. Laura, how about showing them around and I'll be back to see what everyone likes to drink. Then in an hour, we can head down to the marina."

Later, after a tour of the apartment, Goldie leaned back on the sofa, with one arm draped over Candy, and the other holding his wineglass as he used it to gesture around the room. "How did you ever find this place? A penthouse backing on to Stanley Park. Two bedrooms, a view of the city. All I can say is, wow!"

"Ah, it's nothing," replied Jack. "It used to be rented by a couple of Russians who I am told ran into some business difficulties. The timing happened to be right for Laura and me to move in. Actually, I think the *Blue Gator* is much nicer, but I find this quieter."

"Your own home is lovely, too," said Laura. "Right on the water. I think it — Jack! Watch it!"

"Shit," muttered Jack, looking down at the red wine he had slopped on himself. "Excuse me, I better change."

Some time later, Jack returned with a fresh shirt on. Laura saw him make eye contact with her as he casually made a fist and scratched his chin with his thumb. *Mission accomplished.*

The rest of the evening continued to go as planned. Once they arrived at the marina, Jack quickly introduced Candy and Goldie to his crew. While Paul and Katie took charge of slowly navigating the waters of Vancouver Harbour, Jack and Laura entertained their guests with glasses of Sauvignon Blanc and a beautiful view of the city lights reflecting off the water. Later, the four of them enjoyed a dinner that Jack prepared, consisting of Caesar salad, Dungeness crab, garlic toast, and plenty more Sauvignon Blanc.

After dinner, Goldie and Candy snuggled together on a sofa, where Candy started kissing Goldie on his neck.

"A toast," said Jack, raising his glass. "Here's to women's kisses, and to whiskey, amber clear. Not as sweet as a woman's kiss, but a damn sight more sincere!"

Goldie looked at Candy and laughed. "Aptly put, Jack. Aptly put!" He stood and grabbed a bottle of wine and said, "Mind if I go up top and offer a drink to your crew?"

Jack shook his head and whispered, "I wouldn't. I told you they are strictly legit, but Paul has got a fearsome reputation. Kind of guy who would start a fight in an empty house."

"Oh, I see," replied Goldie, giving a nervous glance up toward the helm before sitting back down.

Jack hid his smile. Paul had a great sense of humour and was one of the nicest, gentlest people he knew. Too nice a person to be putting up with the likes of Goldie.

The rest of their time together was spent in idle gossip, with much *oohing* and *aahing* over the night lights of the city reflecting off the water. Goldie was not shy about drinking, but several hours later, as the *Blue Gator* approached her berth in the marina, he did order a limousine to take him and Candy home.

As Jack helped first Candy, and then Goldie on with their jackets; he knew he would also have to help Goldie get off the boat without falling in.

"Jack, my Irish rogue," slurred Goldie, reaching for his wineglass one last time. "I think you and me are going to conquer the fuckin' world. You and me, buddy. You and me."

"One last toast," smiled Jack, reaching for his wine glass. "Some Guinness was spilled on the barroom floor, when the pub was shut for the night. When out of his hole crept a wee brown mouse, that stood in the pale moonlight. He lapped up the frothy foam from the floor, then back on his haunches he sat. And all night long, you could hear the mouse roar, 'Bring on the god-damn cat!'"

Goldie tossed his drink back and laughed. If he hadn't had so much to drink, he might have wondered why Jack and Laura's faces momentarily turned to stone as they watched him.

As Jack and Laura stood on the back of the boat, watching Goldie and Candy make their way down the wharf, Jack said, "And there staggers the wee brown mouse. Tomorrow we hunt rat."

"You think Rose will figure out what we were really doing tonight?" asked Laura. "Especially after tomorrow?"

"She might."

"What do you think she'll do?"

Jack shrugged and said, "I guess it depends upon whether she believes in justice."

Laura returned Goldie's wave goodbye, as did Jack.

"He certainly enjoyed himself tonight," noted Laura.

"His next party will be his farewell party."

"Yeah," replied Laura. "Either his or yours."

25

Natasha awoke half an hour before her alarm radio went off, and saw Jack's head on the pillow next to hers, staring at her intently.

"You're awake early," she murmured. "I didn't even hear you come in last night."

"Was around two," Jack replied. "Laura and I were entertaining a bad guy."

"I see ... so if I'm a bad girl, will you entertain me?" asked Natasha mischievously, before kissing Jack first on his chest and then on his mouth.

"Maybe," said Jack, when she finished. "What type of entertainment do you prefer? Were you thinking PG or —"

"Forget that! How about triple X?"

Jack grinned and said, "I don't know if I want the mother of my future children talking like that ... although I have to admit, I am curious. Exactly what is triple X? Is it anything like a triple fudge sundae?"

Natasha put one finger on her chin as if in serious thought and replied, "I suppose it could involve a triple sundae. Might make a mess out of the sheets, though."

"How about a little religious entertainment?"

"Religious?"

"You know, where we each make the other say 'Oh, God!'"

Natasha's grin faded quickly when she felt the fingers on Jack's hand slowly caress up the inside of her thigh, cross her pubic mound, and glide up the side of her ribcage toward her breasts. She closed her eyes as his hand softly trailed back down her body, repeating the process, only now she felt his kisses trailing behind his hand. She tilted her head back as her lips parted in anticipation. Her body pushed upward wherever he kissed, urging him on.

His entry felt agonizingly slow and she relished the feeling, but soon found herself breathing heavily as her hips began to match the rhythmic beat of his and their tempo increased. Their lovemaking soon became a frenzy of soft cries of orgasmic delight as their bodies rolled on the bed, convulsing together as their hands sought each other's backs and buttocks, pulling each other tighter as they felt the climax of their lovemaking reach its pinnacle.

After, Natasha lay with her head on Jack's chest. She felt his fingers brush the hair from her eyes and his lips place a gentle kiss upon her forehead. She moaned when her radio turned on automatically, and, with great reluctance, left for the ensuite to ready herself for the day.

Later, upon re-entering the bedroom, she saw Jack sitting on the edge of the bed, slowly twirling Melvin's plastic rose in his hand. He looked worried.

"What are you doing?"

"Nothing," he said quickly.

It was obvious his mind had been elsewhere and she had startled him. She watched as he put the rose back on the dresser and asked, "What were you thinking about?"

Jack gave a sheepish grin and said, "I was wondering when you would get pregnant. How long it would take now that you're not —"

"Probably at least another month or two," replied Natasha. She smiled and said, "You looked so serious, I was afraid something was wrong?"

"Everything is okay."

"Something happening at work today?" she prodded.

Jack nodded. "Taking care of business," he added.

Natasha knew that meant that whatever Jack was doing, it was dangerous. At one time he would never tell her when he was doing something dangerous, but then she found herself worrying all the time, often needlessly. They talked about it and he agreed he would be truthful about when she should worry and when she shouldn't. It actually worked better. Sort of.

"Will you be late tonight?"

"I don't know."

"Call me when it's over."

"I will. I love you."

"I love you, too."

It was not until Natasha was driving to work that she connected the dots. Why Jack was wondering when ... or if she could be pregnant ... and him doing something dangerous today. *He is worrying about leaving a widow behind. Worrying I could be pregnant at the same time ...*

She stopped at a traffic light and a feeling of panic overtook her. *The rose ... it has to be about Melvin ... and I pushed him into becoming involved. If he dies ...* She felt the tears well up in her eyes.

Her cellphone rang and in her frustration she dumped the entire contents of her purse on the seat beside her to find it.

"I know you're worrying," Jack said as soon as she answered. "Wanted to remind you that I am very good at what I do."

"I know that," she replied, trying not to cry.

"Good. You should also know that since meeting you, my risk scale has dropped considerably. I have too much to live for. Once we have a family, it will be even more so. Just thought I should tell you."

Natasha swallowed as she fought to keep her emotions under control before saying, "But whatever you're doing, I know it involves Melvin and you're doing it because of me."

"No, I'm not."

"You're not?"

"I'm not doing it for you. I'm doing it for Melvin." Jack paused and said, "Okay, maybe for Winston, too."

Natasha was oblivious to the driver behind her

who tapped the horn. She sighed. *This is the guy I married. Would I really want him to be any other way?*

"You still there?" he asked.

"I'm still here," she replied. "I'll always be here for you. Make sure you do the same for me."

It was one-thirty in the afternoon when Laura dropped Jack off in front of the office tower housing Intrinsic Global Investments.

"Perfect weather," said Jack. "Windy, rainy —"

"You sure you want to do this?" Laura asked nervously.

"I think it will work," replied Jack, taking off his windbreaker and tossing it back in the car. "I don't see any other way to get to him. I'll call you in an hour. If I don't, then call me."

"And if things go sideways?"

"Worried about handling Lee?" asked Jack.

"I can handle that little squirt."

"I know you can, but remember, we're supposed to be bad guys. This will work, trust me. Use the ski mask if you have to. It's in the trunk."

"But if it doesn't work? What then? What do you want me to do?"

"Tell Natasha that I'm sorry and that I really loved her."

"No, about me. What should I do if they kill you?"

"Obey your conscience. I know you'll do what's right."

"Okay, if something happens to you, Lee is dead," replied Laura solemnly. "You have my word on that."

"No! That is not what I am telling you to do. You have a life to live. Don't blow it by doing something stupid."

"You mean, like you?"

"What I am about to do will work. It's a calculated risk. Now, promise me you won't do anything stupid."

"Promise me you won't get killed," replied Laura, stubbornly.

26

Kang Lee answered the telephone on his desk. It was the receptionist who worked at the main entrance to Intrinsic Global Investments. Her voice sounded curious in a whimsical sort of way.

"Mister Lee, there is a gentleman here who wishes to see you. He says he has never met you and doesn't have an appointment, but —"

"I'm busy. Book him an appointment in about two weeks or call someone else."

"He, uh, insisted that you would want to see him. He said *The Shaman* would be very upset if you didn't see him immediately." She caught the gasp on the other end of the phone and added, "Do you wish me to call extension 666 to, uh, assist?"

"No!" replied Lee quickly. *Who would dare say 'The Shaman' to anyone outside the circle? It has to be Goldie or Wang ... whichever one will pay dearly.*

"Mister Lee?"

"Security is not necessary," he replied. "A practical joke involving an old friend. I'll be right out."

The startled look on Lee's face was obvious when he stepped into the reception area and saw a stranger.

Jack held his hand out and said, "Hello, Kang. My name is Jack O'Donnell."

Lee's eyes darted nervously around the room as he shook hands.

"Is there a place where we can talk in private?" asked Jack.

"Certainly. Follow me, if you would," replied Lee.

Moments later, Jack found himself in a large, glassed-in corner office that afforded a view overlooking much of downtown Vancouver, including Burrard Inlet. The office included a wet bar and seating area, but Lee sought refuge behind a mammoth black wooden desk with intricately carved legs and panels.

"Beautiful desk," commented Jack.

"I discovered it in Bali," said Lee. "What is it you wish to speak to me about? You mentioned some odd name ... Mister Salmon or something?"

Jack smiled and said, "Oh, get off it, Kang. You know who I am and you certainly know who The Shaman is."

"Perhaps I ... have heard of you," replied Lee coldly. "A mutual friend may have mentioned you."

"If you're talking about Arthur Goldie, he is no longer a friend of mine," replied Jack.

"It was Mister Goldie who had spoken to me about you," admitted Lee.

"In great depth, that I am certain," said Jack, smiling.

"To some extent, yes. I understood that you were his friend?"

"That was before this morning, when a little birdie told me he was working for the police."

"What? Impossible!" said Lee, partially rising from his chair, before regaining his composure and sitting back down. "I mean, what on earth for? What could that possibly have to do with me?" Before Jack could reply, Lee added, "I don't believe it," and folded his arms across his chest.

"Maybe you're right," said Jack. "I only came as a courtesy to warn you. From what Goldie told me, your ... business is not unlike my own. Some day, perhaps, our paths will cross and you might be in a position to do me a favour. After all, you are The Enabler."

A twitch of Lee's eyelid expressed his distaste at Jack calling him that. "I still do not believe that Mister Goldie is the sort of person to, how should I put it, run to the police over some trivial matter."

"From what I heard, it isn't trivial. At least the Yanks don't think so."

"The Americans?" asked Lee. "What do they have to do with this? I'm not even sure Mister Goldie knows any."

"He might not, but a man who works for him by the name of Purvis is well acquainted with an American living in Seattle. Arrests have not been made yet, but the DEA has applied to have Goldie extradited to the U.S. for conspiracy to traffic in heroin. American courts don't like drug traffickers as much as judges in B.C. do. I am told he is looking at a minimum of twenty-five years ... unless he co-operates with authorities. Which, I am told, is the path he has chosen."

"And somehow you think it concerns me?"

"Perhaps the police are correct in their suspicions that Goldie is a liar," said Jack. "In which case, I should not talk to you any further about what I heard. I am sorry if I wasted your time," he added, getting up to leave.

"No! Please ... wait. I do know Mister Goldie and naturally I am a little curious. I am also a cautious man." Lee stared at Jack for a response that he understood.

"I see," said Jack, sitting back down. "Then you would like me to tell you what I have heard?"

Lee nodded silently.

"Two days ago, Goldie was approached by someone from the RCMP Drug Section. Given the circumstances of his connection to a conspiracy charge in the U.S., he said he would inform on those people who were above him."

"And you say that I am one of those people?"

"Yes." Jack then went on to describe to Lee everything Goldie had told him when they had met at the Regal Beagle earlier in the week concerning commissions, enablers, and The Shaman.

"And your 'birdie' told you this is what he told the police?"

"Yes."

"Why should I believe you? I do not think Mister Goldie would go to the police because the whole story is bogus. He told me he had spoken with you last Monday and told me about the ridiculous story he had told you. Apparently he believes you to be ... well, shall we say, connected to some illegal activities. A belief he obtained from what some RCMP Intelligence officer told him. He was hoping to impress you with these lies. For whatever reason, it appears that you are now trying to ruin my friendship with Mister Goldie with this preposterous allegation that he went to the police."

"I see," replied Jack. "Maybe it would help if I told you some things that he didn't tell me or likely include in his conversation with you."

"Such as?"

Jack watched Lee carefully and said, "Such as him telling the police that you ordered him to take a homeless person to a park to be executed. He said there were three of you."

Lee's eyes widened and he put his hands on his lap as if he were about to be castrated.

The response was what Jack had hoped. *The bastard either did it, or was there. But why?* He faked a yawn and looked at Lee and said, "If all this is some bullshit story that Goldie made up to impress me, then you should be aware that he is telling the same story, with a little extra, to try and convince the police not to send him to prison."

"I see," uttered Lee.

"Either way, I would be damned careful if I were you that the next time you see him he isn't trying to put words in your mouth." Jack stood up and said, "Have a nice day," before walking toward the door.

"Please, no, wait," pleaded Lee. "What else did your friend tell you?"

Jack shrugged and said, "That was about it. I'll be talking with my friend later."

"Would you let me buy you a coffee or perhaps a drink? Go some place where we can talk, other than in my office? I think it would help for us to get to know each other better."

Jack glanced at his watch and replied, "I told my girlfriend I was going to meet her but ... what the hell. I'll call her and tell her to go shopping instead."

"Good. Please wait for me in the reception area. I need to cancel an appointment then I'll be right with you."

Jack called Laura from the reception area and said, "Lee is taking me for a drink. Don't know where, but better cover the exit. If we come out together, then hang tough and wait for us to return. If you don't hear from me by three-thirty, I'm in trouble."

Yes, or dead. "How's it going?" asked Laura, deciding it was no use to state the obvious as she checked her watch. It was two-fifteen.

"Exactly as expected," replied Jack.

"Sure you don't want me to follow?"

"No, you'd need sunblock. Also can't risk them grabbing you. You're all I've got."

It took several minutes after Jack hung up for Lee to appear, but when he did, he smiled at Jack and patted him on the back and said, "Come on, we'll take my car."

A smile and personal touch for reassurance ...

okay, asshole, what are you up to? Jack smiled back and followed Lee into the elevator.

From a partially concealed spot, Laura was able to see Lee and Jack leave. Her fingers nervously beat the bottom of the steering wheel as if it were a bongo drum, but she remained where she was. Waiting and wondering was often the hardest part of the job.

Lee drove Jack to a wireless Internet cafe about fifteen minutes away and brought a laptop computer inside with him. Once they were seated, Lee asked, "You said something about the police having suspicions that Arthur is a liar. Can you expand upon that?"

"The police usually offer people the opportunity to inform, in the hope of catching a bigger criminal. Apparently it wouldn't be the first time the police have caught someone who turns out to be the top person — who then fabricates a story to try and make someone else seem like the boss. My source says the police have already made discreet inquiries about you and are dubious that you are involved in anything illegal."

"So they don't really suspect me?" asked Lee, his face brightening for the first time since meeting Jack.

"They suspect that Goldie may have laundered some drug money through your company, likely without your knowledge. They think that is how he met you and is taking advantage of an international financial corporation to throw the police off the trail. The police know it would take years to prove, by which time it would be too late or impossible to charge Goldie if it was then discovered that he was lying."

"Which, of course, he is," said Lee, smugly.

Jack smiled and said, "Given the circumstances and the fact that you do not know me, I would also respond in the same manner that you now are."

Lee looked indignant and said, "I'm telling you —"

Jack put up his hand indicating for him to stop and said, "I could care less if it is true or not. Goldie also talked to the police about me. He told them I am interested in purchasing a ton of heroin as an initial investment. The police ... small-minded as they are," he muttered, "think that quantity is too large to be believable. As a result, they think Goldie is lying about me and that he came up with my name only as a result of some RCMP Intelligence officer having made inquiries about me a few weeks back."

"I heard about that," said Lee.

Jack chuckled and said, "I bet you did."

"And the story about a homeless person being murdered in a park? What of that? Do the police think it is something Goldie may have picked up on the news?"

"No, Goldie would be smart enough not to make such a blunder. It would be too easy for the police to know certain details that had not been released to the media."

"So the police know that Goldie is telling the truth about that?"

"That he may have been there, sure. It is also a reason why they think he is lying about you."

"I don't understand."

"Neither do the police. It doesn't make sense why anyone in your position would be involved in such a ridiculous situation. They think it involved Goldie and his bartender, Purvis."

"His bartender? Why?"

"They speculate that Purvis made a heroin transaction with someone in an alley, perhaps behind Goldie Locks, and then realized that the homeless person saw them. They think it more likely that Purvis took the witness somewhere else to be killed so as not to bring any heat down on the club. Goldie may have gone with him."

"I see," said Lee. "Then I am sure that is what did happen. It certainly did not involve me. As you say, it would be ridiculous."

Jack smiled knowingly, openly betraying his belief that Lee was lying.

"Excuse me a moment," said Lee, while flipping open his laptop. "Your unscheduled meeting interrupted some important business. I have to take care of some loose ends."

It was three-thirty when Laura answered her cellular. *Nothing like waiting until the last minute …*

"Hi, honey," said Jack. "I'll be a little late tonight. I'll call you in an hour."

A couple of minutes later, Laura saw Lee and Jack return to the underground parkade.

Laura breathed a sigh of relief and leaned back in the seat and waited. Her relief lasted until four-thirty before she held her cellphone in her hand. *Come on,*

Jack, call! Five minutes later she dialed Jack's cellular. There was no answer.

She redialed. *Damn it, Jack! Pick up!*

Laura had no idea that Jack had left the parkade an hour earlier. He was driven out in the back of a cargo van, naked, and with a gun stuck in his ear.

27

Once they arrived back in the underground parkade and stepped out of the car, Lee raised his voice to speak to him over the top of the car and abruptly said, "Well, it was certainly interesting meeting you, Mister O'Donnell. Hope you have a pleasant day."

Jack knew he was in trouble and caught movement out of the corner of his eye. He turned to see four Asian hoodlums, two of whom were pointing pistols at him. The closest one held his index finger up to his lips, telling Jack not to say anything.

A cargo van immediately appeared as one of the men placed a band of duct tape across Jack's mouth before securing his wrists behind his back with a plastic zip-tie. He caught a glimpse of Lee casually walking toward the elevator being held open for him by a fifth Chinese man. Seconds later, Jack was hustled into the back of the cargo van and made to sit on the floor.

The van radio was blasting out music that echoed inside the confines of the van, making any conversation difficult, but none of his captors spoke, regardless. Another band of duct tape was placed over Jack's eyes before he was pushed onto his back.

He felt the muzzle of a pistol on his temple, while someone undid his belt and someone else pulled off his shoes. Seconds later, his pants were tugged off. He felt a thin cold flat piece of steel on his stomach and knew it was a knife. *Is that it? Is my life over? Are they going to gut me right here?* Someone yanked on the front of his golf shirt and he soon realized it was being cut off. His captors were not taking any chances by undoing his wrists. He was rolled onto his side and his underwear was pulled partially down and then back up.

He heard the rustling sound of a garbage bag as all his property, with the exception of his underwear and socks, were crammed inside. The sound of the garbage bag moved to the van door, which opened and closed quickly. Tires of another vehicle squealed slightly and Jack knew his clothes had been taken away. The radio in the van was turned off and he was driven out of the parkade. He was still blindfolded and tied up, but now someone was straddling his ribcage with the muzzle of a pistol inserted in his ear.

The van drove for an hour before Jack heard the difference in the sound of the tires when it left the highway and followed a road with an obviously slower speed limit. That, too, changed when he heard the sound of gravel beneath the tires.

* * *

Laura drove into the parkade. Many parking spots were opening up as most of the companies in the office tower ended their day between four and five o'clock. She parked in a spot close to Lee's car and sat and waited. If he came out with someone other than Jack, she would follow him. *If he comes out alone* ... Her eyes caught the reflection of her trunk in the rear-view mirror. "Oh, man," she said aloud, before getting out and going to the trunk and getting a ski mask and shoving it inside her purse.

When she got back inside the car, she continued to dial Jack's number every ten minutes, but there was no answer. By five-thirty, the only car besides hers on the reserved level belonged to Lee, and she knew her position stood out. What few cars did pass through were the occasional shoppers who had been parked in the public parking lot deeper within the complex.

Laura took a deep breath, slowly exhaled, and started her engine. Seconds later, she was parked right beside Lee's Mercedes-Benz.

It was six o'clock and suppertime, but being a farmer did not mean punching a time clock. George Appleton stooped to pick up a staple that had worked its way loose from the barbed-wire fence and fallen in the grass. It was a common problem and he routinely walked alongside his fenceline to ensure he found the staples before one of his Holsteins swallowed it with a mouthful of alfalfa and got it caught in its throat. He was about to hammer the staple back in when the sound of a gunshot came from a wooded area near an entrance lane to one of his fields.

Seconds later, a cargo van emerged from the woods and raced past his field on the gravel road. He was too far away to see the licence plate or clearly see the faces of the two men in the front of the van, but their straight black hair caused him to think they were Asian.

He swore under his breath as he ran toward the wooded area. It was a favourite spot for his cows to rest and he had a sickening feeling that he would find one of them shot. He arrived minutes later out of breath.

It wasn't a cow he found shot lying in the dirt. It was a man. A man who was naked, except for his underwear and socks. His hands were bound behind his back with a plastic zip-tie and duct tape covered his eyes and mouth. A bullet hole through his temple oozed blood. Death had been instantaneous.

It was six-thirty when Lee stepped off the elevator and into the parkade. He smiled politely at the pretty woman in front of him and was about to hold the elevator door open for her. Something about her looked familiar. *Yes! The lady who beat the mugger. Jack's lady* — His thoughts were interrupted by the sheer terror of seeing her point a 9 mm pistol directly at his face.

"Do not speak," she commanded. "Walk in front of me and go to the passenger side of my car and lean on it," she added, gesturing toward her car with a quick jerk of the barrel.

"I beg you to listen," said Lee. "I —"

"I said shut up!" Tears ran down Laura's cheeks and her hand trembled. "Go over to my car ... now!"

Lee wondered whether she might shoot him accidentally and hurried over to her car and placed his hands on the roof. Laura patted him down quickly before ordering him to get in the passenger side of the car and sit bent over with his head down between his legs.

"Don't move until I tell you," she said. "If I see you look up, I will shoot you. If you yell or even talk to me, I will shoot you."

Lee fought the urge to vomit as Laura got into the car and started it up. He expected that she would be driving him away someplace. Instead, she drove him to the basement of the parkade and parked.

"Stay put," she said, before getting out of the car and coming around to his side and opening the door. "Get out and get into the back seat. Hurry!"

Lee was confused, but quickly scrambled into the back seat while Laura got in the front seat, keeping her pistol trained on his face. "Okay, put this on," she said, tossing him a ski mask.

"I don't understand," Lee said, bewildered.

"Put it on!"

Lee put the ski mask on as directed.

"Perfect," said Laura. "Now I am going to call my boyfriend again. If he doesn't answer, I'm going to shoot you. I'll drag your body out of my car and use your blood to write *rapist* on the floor beside you. If the cops ever do find me, no jury in the world will convict me. Now, do you understand?"

"I ... I ... please listen. This is all a big mistake. I —"

"No! You listen! I'm dialing!" Laura pushed the redial and held the phone out so they both could listen.

Lee listened to the sound of each ring from the back seat. He knew his orders had been followed. Jack's phone would not be answered. After six rings, his answering machine came on and Laura hung up.

Lee saw that Laura had quit crying. Her eyes burned pure hatred as she levelled the gun at his face. He gasped when he saw her finger squeeze down on the trigger. "I beg you! No!" he screamed. "He does not have his phone to answer! Please ... you must ... I —"

"I must what? Kill you?" said Laura. "It's too late for excuses."

"No, please. Let me call someone. It is not too late. I thought he would have called you already. It is taking longer than I thought. Please, let me use my phone and call someone."

Laura stared back silently for a few seconds. Seconds that seemed like a lifetime to Lee. Eventually, she nodded and watched as he retrieved his cell and nervously punched in some numbers. "It is ringing," he said, glancing at her. "I think — hello! This is — hello? Hello?"

It wasn't only the ski mask making Lee sweat profusely. "We were disconnected," said Lee in a panic. "The parking lot. The phone doesn't work down here. Please, we need to drive someplace else. I beg you."

More seconds ticked by before Laura responded, "Face down on the seat with your hands behind your head. I will give you one last chance."

Moments later, Laura parked in the upper level and Lee tried again. Laura heard the phone ring and someone picked up and said, "Wang Hui Chinese Restaurant."

"You better not be ordering Chinese food," whispered Laura.

Lee shook his head and held his phone with two trembling hands and said, "My order has not arrived. The delivery person called me twenty minutes ago. It should have arrived then. This is very bad ... wait." Lee looked at Laura and held up two fingers and said, "Two minutes. He will call in two minutes." His eyes then flickered from Laura to the gun she was holding in front of her. He leaned slightly forward, as if to say something else.

"Don't even think about it," said Laura, pulling back and distancing herself from his reach. "The clock starts now," she added, glancing at her watch.

Lee turned his attention back to the phone. "Contact the delivery person again. I must speak to him within two minutes! No longer!"

One minute later, Lee's cell rang and he stared at Laura, as if in a trance.

"Answer it," she said. "Better hope it's Jack and not a wrong number."

Lee answered and said, "Put him on. Quickly!"

Laura cocked the hammer back on the pistol she was pointing at Lee's face while carefully accepting his phone in her other hand. "Please ... be careful what you say," he cautioned. "You never know who is listening."

Laura subconsciously held her breath and brought the phone to her ear. "Hello?"

"Hi, honey," said Jack. "Kind of a long day, eh? You okay?"

The pent-up emotion Laura felt released itself. "Yeah, I'm okay," she said, as tears streamed down her cheeks. "You?"

"Still above ground. Feel a little chilly, but I'm okay. Someone borrowed my cell so I couldn't call. I was worried that you might have gone skiing."

"I … I was going to," replied Laura, wiping her tears with her fingertips. "My friend is already dressed for it."

"Sorry about that. Somebody will be in deep ca-ca for not letting me call. I've, uh, been busy. Tied up until half an hour ago. Just got back into the city. They said I'll have my stuff back in half an hour. The heels of my shoes somehow fell off and are being repaired as we speak. You sure you're okay?"

"I'm fine," replied Laura, feeling more in control. "Just get here."

"You okay to eat?"

"You're hungry? Now? After all this?" said Laura, instantly angry.

"I spoke with Lee about twenty minutes ago. He apologized and offered to treat us to dinner. Being gracious, I accepted his offer. After all, it is just business. Nothing personal. I was supposed to call you but … these gentlemen I'm with didn't understand the urgency. They insisted I would have to wait until I got my stuff back."

Laura paused a moment to collect her thoughts and said, "You sure this isn't a way to ... you know, *get us* together?"

"I'm sure, but hang on. My favourite team is here. Mister Smith and ... gee, I forget the other guy's name. Tell Mister Lee to introduce me so I can shake his hand."

My favourite team? Mister Smith and ... Laura clued in. *Smith & Wesson!* She put her hand over the mouthpiece of the phone and whispered to Lee, "The men with Jack have guns. He would like to be given one," she said, handing him the phone.

Lee's head bobbed that he understood and he spoke into the phone. "You will give him anything he asks for immediately. Anything! Consider him your boss for now." Seconds later, Lee passed the phone back to Laura.

"Thanks, honey. I am now shaking hands with my favourite team. I would suggest that we take Mister Lee up on his offer for dinner. I need to buy a fresh shirt for the occasion as well. We should give everyone a fresh start, don't you agree?"

After hanging up, Laura took a deep breath and slowly exhaled before looking at Lee and saying, "I want lobster. Lots of it. Scallops, too. And take off the ski mask. You look silly."

* * *

At eight o'clock, Jack and Laura accompanied Lee to the Five Sails restaurant in the Pan Pacific Hotel. Laura ordered scallops as an appetizer and then dined on Atlantic lobster. Jack ordered roasted breast of pheasant while Lee contented himself with a meal of pan-seared Alaskan sablefish.

Neither Jack nor Laura discussed what had happened earlier in the day and tried to keep the conversation light.

As they were finishing their meal, Jack noticed that Lee's hand still shook as he sipped on a glass of Chardonnay, "Kang, you have hardly eaten. Was the fish not to your satisfaction?"

"It was fine, thank you. I have simply lost my appetite. So much has happened so fast. My mind is still reeling." Lee noticed Jack's appetite appeared to be fine and asked, "Didn't today's events spoil your appetite?"

"I thought you were a little rude," replied Jack.

"You describe what I did as simply rude?" asked Lee in surprise.

"Perhaps I am being needlessly finicky," replied Jack. "I have been in your position before where such measures were taken, but you could have offered a sweatsuit. I was rather chilly."

"Oh, honey," said Laura. "Quit being a wimp. The two martinis you had as an appetizer surely must have warmed you by now."

"A sweatsuit? That is your only complaint?" asked Lee. "Didn't you find the whole ordeal stressful?"

"Business often is," replied Jack.

"Your ability to ... handle business is remarkable," said Lee.

"You appear to have done well for yourself, also," said Jack. "Perhaps we should see if there would be an advantage for us to go into business together?"

"Absolutely," replied Lee. "We should talk later. Perhaps I can call you early next week."

"That would be fine," replied Jack. "Although, I must admit, if the long hours we put in today are normal, then I should decline such a partnership. You may have noticed that Laura gets a little upset when I do not come home on time."

Lee smiled and said, "I have noticed that."

"I did find today stressful," admitted Laura. "I would suggest we not do that again."

Lee lowered his voice and said, "Not as stressful as it was for Arthur Goldie."

"Oh?" replied Jack. "Did he have a bad day?"

"I have heard," said Lee, "that he had a bug infestation. One was apparently found inside the collar of his jacket."

"I see," said Jack. "Bet he didn't find that funny," he added, glancing at Laura.

"Certainly no laughing matter," replied Laura, seriously, frowning at Jack.

Jack speared the remaining piece of pheasant with his fork, smearing it around in the creamy risotto and wild mushroom sauce before taking a mouthful. "Will Mister Goldie be quarantined?" he asked, after swallowing.

"Quarantined?" replied Lee with an evil grin. "No, I'm afraid the bug he caught was fatal. It is fortunate that I avoided any contamination. You have my gratitude."

"Ah, I didn't really do anything," replied Jack. "I would have handled it myself, but I am new to Vancouver and was afraid you might get the wrong idea. I did not want you to think that my organization was attempting a hostile takeover, if you know what I mean."

"I understand perfectly," replied Lee. He studied Jack closely for a moment and said, "You are a shrewd and knowledgeable businessman. You opened my eyes about someone I thought was a friend. The bug was only part of the evidence of his utter lack of loyalty. I am told that he had surrounded himself by an enemy common to us both."

"An enemy who wears uniforms?" asked Jack.

"Yes, their colleagues are known to do so."

"But you told me Goldie's condition was fatal?"

"It was. His experience was similar to yours, except he did not survive." Lee glanced at Laura and said, "I have come to the conclusion that underground parkades are dangerous to everyone's health." He smiled at Jack and added, "He was not provided with a sweatsuit, either."

"I see," said Jack.

Lee raised his wineglass in a toast and said, "Today, although discouraging in nature, was ultimately successful. You are responsible and I am indebted to you."

Laura clinked glasses and thought, *You have no idea how responsible …*

28

Da Khlot and Sayomi were summoned to meet The Shaman. They bowed at the entrance to his den before entering and standing silently as he gazed out his window at a clump of bamboo. Eventually he turned, waving an arm in the direction of his computer as if to explain it, and said, "We have to go back to Canada." He pointed his finger at Sayomi and said, "Go alert the flight crew and tell them we will leave Sunday morning at nine."

Da Khlot remained standing and watched as The Shaman's eyes followed Sayomi's figure as she left the room. *Even a shaman cannot resist her beauty. But she is still a whore ...*

"There is a serious matter to attend to in Vancouver," said The Shaman. "Mister Lee did not choose wisely for the candidate he named as his successor and enthusiastically supports a new candidate. I am concerned that Mister Lee may be blinded by his rush to correct his error or perhaps by his desire to return home. Either way, Mister Lee's error in judgment and his rapid decision to correct the situation causes me considerable distress. Mister Lee will be provided with a test to give to the new candidate. Should the candidate fail, I believe it would be prudent to sever ties with everyone concerned. Therefore, your services may be required."

"The special suit?" asked Da Khlot.

"No. This will require your personal touch in regard to the new candidate. What Mister Lee is unaware of, is that the results of the test will ... gravely ... affect him, as well. Understood?"

Da Khlot nodded. If the new candidate was not suitable, both Mister Lee and the candidate would fall within the familiar category. *To keep you is no benefit. To destroy you is no loss.*

On Monday morning, Rose was sitting at her desk when Jack called from home.

"Guess who bought Laura and me dinner Friday night," he said.

"Goldie?"

"No. His boss. Kang Lee."

"The Enabler?"

"The one and only. We dined at the Pan Pacific. Don't worry about expenses because he picked up the tab."

"That's unbelievable! How? Fill me in."

"I took a chance on bypassing Goldie and went straight to Lee. Met him Friday afternoon in his office. The meeting went well and he offered to buy us dinner, so we accepted."

"Incredible! You must be a hell of a talker. This guy potentially could be one of the biggest organized crime figures in North America ... and you just waltzed into his office? I never would have believed it. Did you talk business?"

"Very little. I think he was basically feeling us out. He said he would call me early this week to get together."

"This is astounding. Was Goldie at dinner, too?"

"No, it was only the three of us. Actually my timing may have been lucky. By coincidence, it sounds like Lee and Goldie have had a falling out."

The alarm bells sounded in Rose's head as she recalled the assistant commissioner's words in describing Jack. *The Coincidental Corporal* ... "Oh, really? Tell me why you would think that?"

"A casual comment he made. Something about Goldie surrounding himself with an enemy common to us both."

"I'm not an operator. Spell it out for me."

"It means he believes Goldie could be an informant."

"Damn it," muttered Rose. "That's all we need. If he was one of ours, we'd have been told. I'll go through channels and check with VPD. See if it's true. If it is, they may not like us sniffing around."

"Relationships with local police forces are different than back east," said Jack. "We don't hesitate to work with each other. Unlike our brethren in Ontario and Quebec, out west most of us have gone through a stint in uniform."

"What's that got to do with it?"

"Good education when it comes to dealing with people. We don't show up in a province still wet behind the ears from the academy and strut around like plainclothes detectives on a Hollywood movie set. It's bound to build animosity and distrust. The sooner the Force clues in about that, the better. Don't worry about working with VPD. It won't be a problem."

"You sure?"

"Positive. I've worked with them in the past. They've got some really good people. Besides, we're a step up the ladder from Goldie. Now we need to find out who Lee works for."

"Ah, yes. The mysterious Shaman. Any clues?"

"Not yet. One step at a time. Laura and I are going to take today off, unless Lee calls. I'll keep you posted."

"Terrific job, you two. It's absolutely incredible. Can't wait to tell Isaac. After his suspicions about you, it won't hurt to rub his nose in it a little."

"Uh … why don't you hold off until the end of the week. If Lee doesn't call, it could make us look rather bad."

At two o'clock that afternoon, Rose answered another call that was less pleasant.

"Where is that son-of-a bitch?"

"Who is this?" demanded Rose.

"Connie Crane. I warned you! Where the hell is Jack Taggart?"

"Taking the day off."

"Yeah, I bet. More likely he's out in the country droppin' off a body!"

"Care to enlighten me?" asked Rose.

"I-HIT picked up another homicide Friday night out in Langley. Unidentified man, stripped of his clothes and shot in the head. Found by a farmer who thinks some Asians did it."

"Perhaps you're not aware," said Rose, "that Jack is Scottish."

"Let me finish. I didn't get the case, but I saw a picture of the victim and identified him. It's —"

"Arthur Goldie," said Rose, feeling stunned.

"So you already knew? What? You in on this with him? What the hell is going on?"

"No, I didn't know. Just a lucky guess."

"Really?" said Connie sarcastically.

"Yes, really. But the grounds for your suspicions … I was told Drug Section were doing surveillance of him while they were preparing to get a wiretap. Did they see him and Jack together on Friday?"

"I haven't called them yet, but I'm suspicious every time a body shows up with a connection to Jack. I'm calling the narcs and I want a meeting right now with all of us. Including Jack and Laura!"

* * *

"Anything you wish to tell me before we go in?" asked Rose as Jack and Laura arrived outside the boardroom. "Connie is already inside and I have to say, she's steamed."

"No," replied Jack, politely smiling as Sammy and two other Drug Section members arrived. "I think it best that we hear from everyone."

Once everyone was seated, Rose said, "Well, Connie, this is your show. You call it."

"We can make it simple," said Connie. "Jack, tell us what you did on Friday, or do you not wish to speak until you have contacted a lawyer?"

"Oh, CC. You are a character," said Jack, shaking his head. "I'm surprised ... concerned ... but I must deny —"

Two of the Drug Section members laughed outright and one said, "Yup, act surprised, show concern, deny, deny, deny!"

"This is not a time for gaiety," said Rose crossly, "or unsubstantiated accusations for that matter," she added, glancing at Connie. "We have some serious matters to discuss. We will not turn this into a three-ring circus. Jack, out with it."

Jack reiterated the sequence of events that he had told Rose, including that he left Laura in the car as potential backup if it was needed. He said he went to Lee's office and spoke with him directly in the hope of being able to bypass Goldie. He said that Lee was obviously interested and upon leaving his office, took them both out for dinner.

"And you told me that during dinner he said

something about Goldie being an informant," said Rose.

"That's right," replied Jack. "He mentioned words to the effect that he didn't trust Goldie, that he thought he may be surrounded by the enemy, which I understood him to mean the police," said Jack.

After a momentary silence, Connie slapped her hand on the table and said, "Bullshit! First of all, you're telling me that you walk in unannounced to a guy heading one of the biggest criminal organizations in the world with only Laura as backup?"

"Hey!" said Laura.

"No offence, Laura," said Connie. "But this stinks. Shouldn't you have had a complete surveillance team? What could you have done if something went wrong? I mean, really."

"When it comes to my life, I trust Laura completely," Jack replied tersely. "UC is filled with judgment calls. I admit sometimes we make mistakes, but more people means more chances of being spotted. It is not always better."

"Yeah? Whatever ... but I don't believe in coincidences when it comes to murder. Not with you. I don't know how, but ..." Her eyes searched the room for support and settled on Rose. "Damn it, Rose, you know my feelings. I warned you before about him. Jack and Laura call off the narcs on Thursday night and entertain Goldie on a boat. The next day the guy is murdered. Don't tell me that you think it's all a —"

"It is our fault," interjected Sammy. Silence descended upon the room as all eyes stared in his direction. "We got him killed," he added, quietly.

"How? What?" blurted Connie.

"We had surveillance on him yesterday afternoon. At around four o'clock he took off and we followed. Everything was going fine for the first few minutes and then we realized other cars were following him, too. At first we thought our paths had crossed with the City. Then we saw the others were all Asian. About then Goldie drove into an underground parking lot. I called for the team to break off, but I think we had already been burned."

"You're telling me they killed him because you were following him?" said Connie. "That's ridiculous."

"Is it?" asked Rose. "Goldie told Jack last Monday that this organization is so paranoid they were going to put him on the lie detector. Connie, I sent you a copy of his report. Didn't you read it?"

"Yeah, I read it."

"Did you also happen to read the reports outlining how much our office has done to assist you in relation to the murder of the homeless person in the park?"

"His name is Melvin Montgomery," said Jack, sounding irritated.

Rose looked sharply at Jack but continued, "How Jack and Laura traced the gun from the U.S. up to Canada. Right across the country to Goldie's doorstep? Including solid evidence in his garage linking him to the murder? Have you bothered to read those reports? Now you have the audacity to point a finger at him because he's involved in a case where a suspect is murdered? If you're pointing fingers, what the hell were you doing on Friday?"

"Rose, please," interjected Jack, calmly. "I've known CC a long time. I normally respect her judgment. There have been unusual circumstances in the past on unrelated matters. It's her job to be suspicious. She's a good cop."

"Thanks, Jack," replied Connie, automatically. *What the fuck! I just thanked him!* She glared at Jack and then looked at Rose and said, "You have to admit, to kill someone in your organization because he is being followed by the police doesn't seem practical."

"It could be that they will wipe out anyone who they think will lead the police to them," continued Rose. "Or maybe they did put him on a polygraph and he failed. What do you think, Jack?"

"I think I'm glad that I didn't have a cover team following us yesterday," he replied, staring at Connie who purposely avoided looking back.

"Which is another thing," said Rose. "Until this matter is finished, Jack and Laura will not be coming into the office. These people are too dangerous to mess around with. We'll rent a hotel room to meet if necessary."

"Appreciate that," said Jack. "Coming here does put us at risk. I wouldn't have come except for Connie's insistence."

Connie ignored the remark and turned to Sammy and asked, "And you didn't have any wire on Goldie? Nothing to help us?"

"We were working on getting some, but it was still a week away. Sorry about yesterday. Sounds like we really screwed up. Just didn't know how much until now."

"Don't worry about it," said Jack. "You can't blame yourself for their paranoia."

"Yeah, I guess," replied Sammy.

"What about the Chinese restaurant and the dealers down there?" asked Connie. "You said the ones following Goldie were Asian. The farmer said he thought whoever shot Goldie was Asian, as well."

"Our UC operators haven't heard anything. As far as the wire goes, nothing out of the ordinary."

"Nobody making innuendos?" asked Connie. "Sounding angry? Scared? Anything?"

"Nope," replied Sammy. "The closest thing we got to anger was some guy upset that his delivery order hadn't arrived twenty minutes earlier."

Laura felt a light kick under the table from Sammy as he spoke. *He knows!*

"And that was it?" persisted Connie. "No calls about people being followed or a team being put together to whack someone?"

"Nope. Also, for your info, all of us who were on the surveillance team yesterday looked at the mug shots that the Asian Based Organized Crime Unit has. There was nobody we recognized, but we might come up with something once we make arrests from our current UC."

"I appreciate that, thanks," said CC.

"They're big into using laptops," said Jack. "These guys are too professional to use telephones."

"Can you show me the underground parkade where Goldie went?" asked Connie. "I'm betting his car is still there."

"No problem," replied Sammy.

Connie sighed and said, "Guess maybe I do owe you an apology, Jack. Sorry."

"It's okay," he replied. "I feel like I'm made of Velcro as I go through life. Things seem to stick to me. I understand why you would be suspicious."

"Velcro?" snorted Connie. "More like Teflon if you ask —"

"As I said, your apology is accepted," interrupted Jack.

As the meeting broke up, Sammy whispered in Laura's ear and said, "About that guy whose Chinese food was late. Must have been his wife in the background who said, 'Don't even think of it' and 'the clock starts now.'" Sammy grinned and continued, "Now to me, she must have been talking about the order. The strangest thing is, her voice sounded like yours."

Surprise registered on Laura's face.

"Yeah, I know," said Sammy. "Now show concern and deny it. By the way, I drink Canadian Club."

"Jack, Laura!" interjected Rose. "The two of you ... my office."

Rose didn't mince words when the three of them were alone in her office. She pointed a finger at Jack and said, "This has become personal to you. Why?"

"Personal?" replied Jack.

"You weren't content with letting me describe the investigation about the murder of a homeless person. You put a name to it — Melvin Montgomery. You have personalized the issue, I am simply wondering why? Something in your past?"

"Ah, perhaps the two of you should discuss this in private," said Laura, rising from her chair.

"Sit down," said Rose. "You two are obviously a team. Your decisions affect each other. Unlike our meeting a few minutes ago, this isn't an inquisition. I simply want to understand why you take the risks you do and to ensure that your decisions are pragmatic in nature and not skewered by personal bias."

"Everyone has personal bias," replied Jack. "Whether you admit it or are even aware of it. We all come from a past where we have encountered different experiences."

"Yes, and those experiences cause us to be biased in different directions," said Rose. "So what are your personal experiences with someone, say, like Melvin?"

"I'm an operator," said Jack. "I've seen and dealt with many Melvins and Ophelias. Up close and personal."

"Ophelias?"

"Another friend of mine who died recently. A hooker and a junkie. Another nobody in the eyes of society."

"And you met her working undercover," concluded Rose.

"She tipped us off, for free, about a guy she knew who had robbed and murdered an old-age pensioner. She would have been killed if anyone knew she informed."

"So you believe that this nobody in the eyes of society actually risked her life to help society?" replied Rose.

"Jack believes it because it's true," said Laura. "She put Mad Dog and his crew away, as well."

"I see," said Rose.

"Do you?" asked Jack. "It goes further than society not seeing these people. Most don't even want to think they are people."

"What are you getting at?"

"That someone like Goldie, faced with twelve upstanding citizens and a judge, would never have to worry. Not that he could be convicted because I committed a far worse crime by stealing his garbage bag. But even if I hadn't, any sentence he might have received would have still left him laughing."

"Sounds to me like you're admitting to being biased in this matter," said Rose.

"Biased or experienced?" asked Jack. "Knowing the probability of an outcome does not mean you are biased."

"Perhaps, but when it comes to the law, you must be accountable. Bias is something twelve jurors might discuss and reach a balance. Not one or two people deciding the fate of others for themselves."

"When it comes to the law, you are absolutely right," said Jack.

"You agree?"

"Of course I do, but I wasn't talking about the law. I was talking about justice. What are your views on that?"

Rose stared silently for a moment. Briefly, she looked sad. Jack had the feeling she was remembering something. Her eyes met Jack's and she said, "I would compare your views on handling justice to those of someone skating on a river in early April. It is only a matter of time before you fall in and drown." She glanced at Laura and added, "Sometimes drowning people take others with them."

"I'm a good swimmer," replied Laura.

"Interesting analogy," said Jack. "Do you skate yourself?" he asked, watching her intently.

Rose spotted Jack's gaze and her face hardened and she said, "I gave that up. I respect my own life and the people I love. Something you would be wise to consider."

Jack turned to Laura and said, "Guess if we do any skating, we're on our own."

Rose sighed and said, "I'll be back on shore. I may have a rope to toss you, but at the rate you're going, I don't think it will be long enough."

Jack thought about Natasha … and a family he hoped to have. His BlackBerry received a text message from Lee requesting they meet. "We have to go," he said.

29

Lee set his sake down when the sushi arrived and smiled understandingly when Laura requested a knife and fork.

"You seem well acquainted with chopsticks," he commented to Jack, who handled them with ease.

"I love Japanese food," replied Jack. "This is okay, but next time Laura and I decide on the restaurant."

"Agreed," replied Lee.

Da Khlot sat alone at another table and discreetly watched the threesome. *This clumsy Western woman cannot even master the use of chopsticks? Lee said she was dangerous.... With his soft life, he would think a bird with a broken wing is dangerous.*

Da Khlot turned his attention to Jack. *The man perhaps could be difficult. He is tall and does not have the physique of so many Westerners ... like that of a pot-bellied pig. No matter. Much bigger men have fallen.* Da Khlot recalled some of the men he had killed in the past. Big men who towered over him in height and weight. *They do not look so big when they look up at you from the floor. Their eyes wide and their brains confused as to why they are paralyzed. Size is no match for surprise, speed, and experience ... nor is it a match for what The Shaman desires.*

Da Khlot leaned forward to reach for a glass of water and his thoughts changed as he felt the pistol he had tucked in his pants. *Ah, but tonight, there will be no such death for these Westerners. Their deaths will be a bullet to their brain. Lacking the skill of an artist — but effective just the same.*

Da Khlot went over the plan again in his mind. Mister Lee was to give the Westerners the test when they finished their meal. Should they fail the test, Mister Lee was to go to the washroom. Da Khlot had already let the air out of one of the tires on the Westerners' car. He would simply follow them out and shoot them both from behind. To appease Mister Lee, he said he would steal the woman's purse and run away. A ruse to trick the police into thinking that Mister Lee's dinner guests were simply the victims of a robbery. The ten-shot 9 mm Browning semiautomatic pistol provided by Mister Lee would ensure easy completion of his mission.

Mister Lee had volunteered to use his own people for the assassination, but The Shaman said he wished to arrange for a suitable replacement for Mister Lee in Intrinsic Global. As he was back in Vancouver, anyway, it would be prudent to use the services of Da Khlot.

What the unfortunate Mister Lee did not know was that he would not be allowed a second mistake in judgment. He would be killed first when he went to the washroom. Stealing the purse would not be necessary.

Da Khlot felt the presence of the scabbard holding the narrow-bladed dagger strapped to the inside of his left forearm. It was his weapon of choice. Silent and deadly. He would undo the button on his shirt sleeve and walk into the washroom behind Mister Lee. If Mister Lee should see him, Da Khlot would assure him that there was no rush and he simply wanted to ensure that he had received the correct signal. He had, after all, let the air out of one of the tires. There was lots of time. Then he would stab him in the throat and sever his windpipe. There would be no noise to warn the Westerners, who he would shoot immediately after.

As Jack and Laura picked away at the sushi, Lee carefully reiterated what Goldie had already said and explained that his organization controlled the safe delivery of tons of heroin through the Orient. Bringing a ton into Canada was not a problem.

"You do not have a problem clearing customs?" asked Jack.

"It is not as easy as other countries." Lee frowned. "But we have made certain connections who are agreeable to business. Our objective is to expand to the eastern seaboard. Something we know you could assist us with."

"So I would become an enabler," said Jack. "Guaranteed a percentage of commission on who I recruit and on down the ladder to whomever they use."

"Basically, yes," replied Lee. "We guarantee safe delivery from the poppy fields in Burma ... or Myanmar as some call it these days, to the docks in Vancouver. We act as broker to those selling, those buying, and keep the peace with everyone who is involved along the way."

"Sounds too good to be true," said Jack, sounding skeptical.

"I'll say," agreed Laura.

"I assure you, it is true," said Lee earnestly. "From Burma and on through countries like Thailand or Laos and then on to shipping destinations in Vietnam, Korea, China, Japan ... wherever the next available ship can be used."

"And you work for someone called The Shaman," said Jack.

"His identity is secret," said Lee, solemnly.

"But surely not to me," said Jack. "Not if I am going to be working for him."

"I am sorry, but there is no need for you to know his name. You would be reporting to me."

"If you think I am going to be turning over millions of dollars to someone I don't even know, then you must take me for a fool."

"I do not take you for a fool," Lee replied earnestly. "You would be turning the money over to me. I would distribute it as agreed, just like others below you would distribute it up the ladder. There is no need for anyone to know the names of people they are not directly involved with."

"How do I know that this isn't all an elaborate scam?" asked Jack.

"Or perhaps you are really working for the police!" said Laura.

"I am not! If you wish to take me to the washroom and search me, I would not object."

"Honey," said Jack. "Do you mind taking him to the washroom and searching him? If I do it, someone may come in and question my sexuality."

"Men's or women's?" Laura asked Jack.

"What?" replied Lee. "I don't —"

"It's okay," said Jack, giving a quick grin. "Lighten up. All I'm saying is you must understand where I'm coming from. Everything you describe seems too good to be true. It is not just my money that is at risk. If I introduce my colleagues to take part, we are not talking millions, we are talking billions. Not chicken feed like one lousy ton."

Lee's face lit up and his enthusiasm showed in his voice when he said, "You can handle that much?"

"If I couldn't, I wouldn't say so."

"I knew it!" beamed Lee. "You are the ideal man to be the enabler for North America. You have sources inside the police already. We have the same in customs. Join forces and we'll be wealthy beyond belief."

"Forget it," said Jack. "This is all very interesting, but I must decline."

"You're not interested?" said Lee, in a panic. "Why not?"

"How do I explain to my colleagues in New York that I am working for someone I do not know? Then ask them to invest millions because of a deal someone I just met over sushi told me about?"

"You do not believe me," Lee said, matter-of-factly.

Jack shrugged and said, "Let's simply say my friends are a suspicious bunch of guys. If something were to go wrong, my death would be slow and painful. All this is just talk. I haven't really checked you out. In fact, I've never heard of you before."

"Because we are new to the North American market." He turned partially in his seat and yelled, "Waiter! The check." His eyes flickered to Da Khlot, who gave an imperceptible nod. *It is time …*

"It's our turn to buy," protested Jack.

Lee smiled and said, "I picked the restaurant, I buy. Next time you decide on the restaurant."

"Sounds good," replied Jack.

"Now, about our problem of trusting each other," continued Lee. "What if I arranged a personal tour for the both of you … of your shipment literally from the ground up."

"What do you mean?" asked Laura.

"You would be taken to a poppy field in Burma and follow the product from there to a laboratory and on to Thailand. At the moment, I do not know which country would be next, but when that time arrives, if you still have doubts, you could then follow the shipment to the designated port and watch it be placed on a ship. At that point, you would pay for half the shipment before the ship leaves." Lee paused and said,

"Incidentally, what is your preference for how payment is made?"

"My colleagues have a bank in the Grand Caymans. A few phone calls would have to be made, but the money could be transferred to wherever you like. Split and sent to multiple accounts if you prefer."

"Excellent," replied Lee, nodding his head. "I admire your professionalism. So then, once you pay half, the ship usually takes about six weeks to arrive. The balance would be paid upon delivery."

"You would be willing to do that?" asked Jack. "To expose your organization in such a manner prior to the down payment?"

Lee smiled and said, "I was getting to that." He paused to pay the waiter cash for the meal and waited until they were alone again before continuing. "We would meet in Thailand, where it is only a short journey to the Burmese border. There are certain security precautions that would need to take place in Thailand first."

"Such as?" asked Jack.

"Nothing serious. If you are being honest about doing business with us, you would have nothing to fear. It will be made clear to you only then."

Jack shrugged and said, "I'm easy to get along with." *The goddamned lie detector!* He hid his fear and replied, "That would be an important first step, something I could assure my colleagues about, but without knowing the identity of who we would be working for, I doubt that they would give any serious consideration to the matter."

"And why not?" asked Lee, making no effort to hide his frustration and anger. "What I am offering is almost full access to our organization."

"My colleagues are well-connected on an international basis. There have been times when certain groups found themselves in competition with each other — competition that resulted in bloody conflict. We agreed on a system to maintain peace by having disputes handled through an arbitration-type process."

"Wise and sophisticated approach," commented Lee.

"I like to think it is civilized, but how can we do that if we do not know who is the boss of who ... and who is in control of which area of the world? At least I should know the name to be able to make certain recommendations to the arbitrators in the event it becomes necessary to avoid conflict."

"I still don't think The Shaman will —"

"It would be most unfortunate," continued Jack, "to create a war amongst associates who thought someone was infringing upon their territory, when in fact, it could be simply that they were both doing business with The Shaman, a mutual friend. Furthermore, my colleagues may have other business ventures and could use The Shaman's influence. Our commissions would be even greater."

Lee was silent for a moment and said, "I will convey your thoughts. If you meet the security precautions I have spoken of, perhaps he will be agreeable."

"I would not wish to be involved with an organization that did not take security seriously. I would expect nothing less."

"I suspect The Shaman will make his decision after you arrive in Thailand and undergo certain security checks," said Lee.

Jack smiled and said, "Not a problem. I love Thai food. However, I will need time to take care of some business before we leave. When would you propose we go?"

"Would a couple of weeks be satisfactory?" asked Lee.

"Sounds fine," replied Jack, while helping Laura on with her jacket. "And for how long?"

"It is a long flight. It will take us a day to get there. I would suggest we take time to relax and get to know each other a little more once we are there. I think you should count on being gone at least two weeks."

"Sounds perfect. We'll be in touch with you in a few days."

"There is one other matter we need to discuss," said Lee, taking a folded piece of paper from his wallet. "I have talked to you a great deal about my organization, most of which I know Mister Goldie had already told you. What we have not discussed, however, is the price I have been authorized to give you for the safe delivery of your first ton."

"I thought that would be negotiated when I received a sample of the product to ensure purity," replied Jack.

"I can assure you," replied Lee, while pushing the piece of paper across the table towards Jack, "that the product is the most pure you would find anywhere in the world. The skill of the people working in the labs is derived from a science that goes back centuries."

Jack accepted the piece of paper and looked at the numbers. "Pure or not, this is absurd! I'm not paying that! You're at least 20 percent above market rate. Maybe more. For a shipment that large, I expect it to be far less."

"It is reasonable for the first delivery," replied Lee. "Perhaps after that we can adjust the price more to your satisfaction."

"That is not acceptable," said Jack, shaking his head. "The amount we discussed is plenty large enough to rate a twenty percent reduction, not addition."

"I am sorry. I was told there was no negotiation on this first transaction. Take it, or leave it."

Jack threw the piece of paper on the table and said, "Then you have wasted my time."

"You already possess a great deal of information about us," said Lee. "You know what we are capable of."

"You think you are capable of ripping me off? You are wrong. We have nothing further to say to each other!"

Lee stood stone-faced as Jack and Laura left the restaurant.

Da Khlot waited patiently, without emotion. It was ten-thirty at night and the sun had long since set. *Ideal time to kill.*

30

It was seven o'clock the following morning when Rose pushed the buzzer on the intercom and waited outside for an answer. Moments later, Natasha responded.

"Rose Wood," she said. "I work with Jack."

"I know," she replied. "He's not here yet, but called an hour ago to say you would be coming. He didn't come home last night. I guess Laura didn't, either."

"I know. May I come up?"

Rose pushed the button on the elevator and watched silently as the door closed and heard the hum of the cables as she ascended. She went over the phone call she had received last night from Jack, telling her that he and Laura had met with Lee. He said they didn't want to go home last night after the meeting. He told her that he and Laura would be spending the night in the penthouse suite. He was hoping Lee would contact him.

Rose sensed there was something else. His voice seemed edgy and nervous. *He isn't the type to scare easy. So why? Perhaps fearing bad guys might follow him home to his wife would explain his fear. Or is there something else?*

She was familiar with Jack's personal file. Married less than two years — roughly the length of time Rose had been married to her first husband before he had been killed at a crosswalk by a hit-and-run driver.

She remembered the agonizing pain she had felt. In the initial months it had never let up. If she could have even gone thirty seconds without thinking about it, she would have felt some relief. Her doctor had prescribed medication. It made her brain feel fuzzy and did little to block her pain. She slept sporadically and only then through sheer exhaustion. Eventually time helped her cope with the grief enough to carry on.

Then there was the driver. Witnesses obtained the licence plate number, but were unsure about his face, except to say he was balding, with a horseshoe ring of black hair. The owner of the car matched the description and had four previous convictions for impaired driving. The judicial process lasted three years, during which time the driver racked up another impaired charge. Those three years to Rose seemed like an eternity. Then the driver was acquitted. After all, positive identification was in doubt. *Maybe some day I'll tell Jack I know the difference between the law and justice. I've done my share of skating on thin ice. But I've also lost the love of my life and I know how that feels. Not something you would ever want anyone you loved to have to go through.*

She tried to smile as Natasha answered the door and invited her inside. *An attractive woman. Young, bright, enthusiastic. So much in love. So much to lose.*

"I made coffee," said Natasha, cheerily. "Would you like toast or a bagel, as well?"

"Just coffee, thanks," replied Rose.

"Jack said he and Laura will be here soon. Had to do some heat checks first." Natasha paused and said, "That's what you call it, isn't it? Heat checks?"

Rose smiled and said, "Yes, that is what it's called, although usually it's the bad guys' expression. They refer to the police as the heat and often drive in a manner to make sure they are not being followed."

Natasha grinned and said, "With Jack, the police have followed him before, as well. Me, too, come to think of it."

"So I heard," replied Rose.

"Jack said the penthouse he and Laura are staying in isn't that far away. I expected they would have arrived by now. Maybe he's being extra cautious."

"I'm sure he is," replied Rose. "Does it — never mind. I'm sure they'll be here soon."

"You were going to ask if it bothers me that my husband spent the night with another woman?"

"It's none of my business," replied Rose. "Sorry. That was the psychologist in me coming out."

"I would be lying if I said it didn't," replied Natasha. "At least, a little. But I trust my husband and accept that his role as an undercover operative demands it sometimes. I know he loves me a great deal. I've also met Laura. I really like and trust her, as well.

I feel like her and I have bonded. I'm pretty good at reading people."

"I know my husband used to worry about me dealing with some fairly dangerous people."

"Used to?" asked Natasha.

Rose smiled and said, "The lofty position of management keeps me handcuffed to my desk. My work is not dangerous now."

"How do you feel about it? Do you miss the action?"

"I'm content with my decision. I've collected enough wrinkles."

"You don't think Jack will give you more?" asked Natasha, grinning. "I know I've collected a few since meeting him."

"Possibly," admitted Rose. "I worry about the people I'm responsible for. Having two active undercover operators in my section adds to that worry."

"Actually, I don't worry about them all that much," replied Natasha, seriously.

"You don't?"

"Okay, maybe a little, but I keep the worry harnessed in the back of my mind. Jack has told me he is very good at what he does. He said if he had to rewire a faulty lamp he'd probably electrocute himself, but undercover is what he does. It's his specialty. I believe him."

"That he would electrocute himself?"

Natasha laughed and said, "Yes, that, too, but you'll have to excuse me. I have to go to work. Please help yourself to the coffee."

"Thanks, I —"

Rose was interrupted when Jack and Laura arrived. She saw the passionate kiss Natasha gave Jack, before saying goodbye and leaving for work. *Jack is a lucky man ...*

"So what's up?" asked Rose, once Jack and Laura had each poured themselves a coffee and sat down. "You said on the phone that Lee met with you and invited you to go to Thailand and Burma to check out their organization. Fill me in on the details. We need to strategize."

Jack and Laura started from the beginning of when they arrived at the restaurant and used the extensive notes they made later to tell Rose all the details leading up to when they stormed out of the restaurant.

"You did what?" exclaimed Rose when they got to that point. "Tell me it was a negotiation ploy to lower the price. You did go back in, right?"

"Wrong," said Jack.

"Did Lee follow you out to talk some more?"

"No. Haven't heard from him since."

"Damn it," said Rose in frustration. "I can't believe you did this. Sounds to me like you blew a chance to penetrate one of the biggest international crime syndicates around. The intelligence we could have learned would have been invaluable."

"Not at that price," replied Jack. "I wouldn't pay that for it."

"Who cares? We probably can't get authorization for a kilo, let alone a ton. You could still have played along and when the time came, we could have extrapolated you before the money transfer." Rose shook her head in disbelief and said, "Okay, let's hope you didn't offend him and it's not too late. Contact him. Apologize and say you reconsidered."

"No," replied Jack.

"What do you mean, no? Why not?"

"If I was genuine, I wouldn't go for it. We're talking big money. If I have the backing for that much money, it's from being a good businessman. Not a stupid one."

"Jack thinks it was a test," said Laura.

"A test?"

"I think if I had agreed to it, Lee would have later cancelled."

"More like cancelled us," said Laura, frowning. "Tell her your thoughts about our flat tire."

"A flat tire?" asked Rose.

"When we got back to our car," said Jack, "we saw we had a flat tire. It looked like someone had punctured it with a knife." Jack stared at Rose, wondering if she would connect the dots.

Rose said, "You're thinking —"

"Exactly," said Jack. "In my mind, there are two obvious reasons for doing that. To delay us if someone was waiting for a surveillance team to arrive and follow us … but they already think they know where we live and we did go back to the penthouse. So that leaves the second reason."

"You were being tested," said Rose.

"That's my guess."

"And to fail that test meant they weren't going to let you drive away. Someone wanted to assassinate you."

"Just a theory," shrugged Jack. "Maybe it was some punk vandalizing property. It could have been coincidental." He locked eyes with Rose and smiled, before adding, "You know how that is with me — coincidences do seem to happen."

Rose ignored the comment as she realized how dangerous the situation was. She took a deep breath and leaned back in her chair and slowly exhaled before saying, "Now I know why I was never accepted when I volunteered to be an operator. I'd be dead. So what's next? Do we simply wait?"

"The hardest part," said Laura. "Waiting."

"Lee is anxious," said Jack. "He thinks he's found the motherlode with us. My guess is we hear from him by the weekend. In the meantime, Laura and I will carry on like life is one big party. If I think we're being followed, we might visit a travel agent and look at brochures for going to Caracas or someplace else on that continent."

"Venezuela?" asked Rose. "Did I miss something? I thought all Lee's connections were in the Orient. What does South America have to do with this?"

"Nothing," replied Laura, sounding puzzled before pausing and smiling. "But for Lee, it could indicate our money is going to his competition. We might be investing in cocaine instead of heroin."

Jack smiled and gave her a thumbs-up sign.

"I see," replied Rose. "The thing is, you should be followed. By us."

"So we could end up like Goldie?" suggested Jack.

"I don't suggest you use that as an example," said Rose firmly. "I have a distinct feeling that the narcs following Goldie wasn't the only thing that got him killed. And skip the part about pretending to look surprised. I despise being played by anyone."

After a moment feeling uncomfortable, Jack said, "I know policy calls for us to have cover, but these guys are smart. The probability of a cover team being spotted and getting us killed is much higher than it is of them being needed to rescue us. In this case, policy could get us killed. Besides, I think the real testing will come when we arrive in Thailand — a place where us fair-skinned, round-eyes stand out."

Rose briefly massaged her temples with both hands as she reflected upon Jack's instinct for survival. *Natasha was right. These two will be giving me wrinkles.* She looked up and said, "For now, I'll agree to ignore policy on that issue, but I want you packing. The both of you."

"We already are," replied Jack. "Both of us have non-issue weapons."

"Non-issue? You mean throwaway pieces?" asked Rose.

"No, no. My mistake," said Jack. "They're officially issued to operators, but aren't the standard weapons issued to uniform or plain clothes members. No Mountie symbols."

"Oh, good," replied Rose.

"Yes, we wouldn't tell you about the throwaways," said Laura.

Rose looked quickly at Laura and saw her eyes sparkle.

"Gotcha!" said Laura. "You looked as freaked out as my husband did once when I said that to him.

He works Anti-Corruption. I think he believed it for a moment, as well."

Rose grinned, "Okay, you got me. But this is serious. Please be careful. What can I do to help?"

"Let's get our ducks in a row," said Jack. "We have the basic identification to match our aliases, but we'll need passports, as well. Also, permission for foreign travel to the countries Lee has mentioned."

"I'll handle that. What else?"

"I want practice sessions with a polygraph operator. I want to know what I can do to beat that damned machine."

"Don't think you can," replied Rose. "I've heard that the best you could achieve for some of the questions is maybe inconclusive results. No pass, no fail. However, it only takes one question to fail, and the probability of you failing that critical question, even with training, is extremely high."

"Perhaps I can come up with an undercover scenario that might negate me having to take the actual polygraph. But polygraph operators are experts when it comes to body language. They conduct lengthy interviews prior to even using the machine. They usually know long before they put anyone on the machine if they are guilty or not. I need to know how to behave if I am being interviewed by someone like that. What I learn from a polygraph operator would affect the type of undercover scenario I use and add to my credibility."

"If you're being questioned by someone who is a polygraph operator, I'd like a cover team practically holding your hand," said Rose.

"Me, too," agreed Jack. "Lee has been looking to me for all of the business dealings. Drugs are still a male-dominated business. I doubt that Laura would be asked to take a polygraph, and if she was asked, we would refuse. One of us is risky enough, but it still wouldn't hurt for her to learn the basics, as well. Will you arrange it?"

Rose looked deep in thought, but smiled.

"What's so funny?" asked Jack.

"I was imagining the look on Assistant Commissioner Isaac's face when I ask him."

"Sort of like a bad guy asking if he can hold your gun," said Jack, wryly. "Remind him that I really am one of the good guys."

"I think he believes that," replied Rose. "Otherwise you wouldn't be working for me."

"Or perhaps Isaac is simply putting all his naughty fish in one rain barrel," suggested Laura. "Easier to shoot at."

31

Jack and Laura did not have to wait until the next weekend to hear back from Lee. It was only three hours after Rose had left Jack's apartment that he received a text message.

"Perfect," smiled Jack.

"You hear back from Rose?" asked Laura. "Did Isaac go for it?"

"Not Rose. It was Lee. He said there was a misunderstanding. Wants to meet for lunch. Our choice where."

At twenty past twelve, Jack and Laura walked into Ceili's Irish Pub and Restaurant and made their way to the rooftop patio where Lee waited, glancing impatiently at his watch.

"Sorry we're late," said Jack. "Had a flat tire we needed to get repaired," he added, watching Lee for a response.

Lee looked slightly uncomfortable and quickly forgave them for being late. After Jack and Laura each ordered a Guinness to drink and beef stew for lunch, Lee came straight to the point.

"As a result of your displeasure over the asking price," said Lee. "I spoke with my boss, and it occurred to us that you were likely thinking the quantity was a ton, or two thousand pounds. We were thinking in terms of a metric tonne. That would add over two hundred pounds to the quantity that you thought we meant."

"You're right," said Jack, "I wasn't talking metric. However, your price would still be at least ten percent too high. Sorry, I'm not —"

"No, please, hear me out," said Lee. "My boss wishes to apologize for the misunderstanding. No wonder you felt insulted! He is prepared to offer you a metric tonne at twenty percent less than originally asked."

Jack paused as he looked at Laura for a moment. Both their faces remained impassive. He looked back at Lee and stared at him briefly, before smiling and saying, "That, my friend, is an offer too good to refuse. We should drink to our new business venture."

"I thought you would agree," smiled Lee. "I have already taken the liberty of making a reservation for you both in Thailand. It is time, as they say, to get this show on the road."

* * *

The following afternoon, Jack and Laura met with Rose, Connie, and Sammy back at Jack's apartment, where Jack tossed a bar coaster to Rose. On it he had written: *Pavilion Samui Boutique Resort — island in the Gulf of Thailand called Koh Samui.*

"That's the resort where Lee has booked us two weeks of accommodation," said Jack. "We're supposed to arrive in Bangkok on September seventh, which is two weeks from tomorrow. We overnight there and then continue on to Koh Samui the next morning."

"He said once we arrive in Koh Samui that we would be given a week to recover from jet lag and the fourteen-hour time difference before any business took place," said Laura.

"Meaning we can expect to be under the magnifying glass the whole time," said Jack. "However, it also gives us more time to befriend Lee. See if he gets liquored up and says something about what took place in the park with Melvin. Who knows, maybe we'll get to meet the guy in the suit with dead eyes."

"I would definitely like to find out who that is," said Connie.

"You will have a cover team," said Rose, looking at Sammy.

"Four from our office can go," replied Sammy. "I'll be in charge of the cover team and will handle that end of it. We'll arrive one day ahead of you, but remember, we're not allowed to carry weapons over there, so really, all we can really do is surveillance."

"Must be nice," said Connie. "A two-week vacation on a sandy beach in the tropics. Wish I could go along."

"Personally, I feel that four members from Drug Section is too many as it is," said Jack. "We'll presume we're being watched the whole time. Lee picked the resort. They could even have our room bugged."

"Well, that's interesting," said Connie with a smile, looking at Jack and Laura. "You two are supposed to be a happy couple right? Young, virile, in love ..."

"Good point," replied Laura. "What do you think, Jack? Maybe we'd better practise kissing and getting intimate with each other before we go. We don't want to look or sound nervous with each other when we get there."

"Yeah, I guess we should," replied Jack, trying not to smile as Connie's head swivelled back and forth at the two of them, unsure if they were joking or not.

"Hope neither of you talk in your sleep," said Rose, seriously.

"I don't like being plunked into a spot of their choosing," said Jack. "We'll give it a couple of days to recognize faces and then find an excuse to switch hotels."

"Keep the bad guys off balance," said Rose. "Help put everyone on an even playing field."

"Exactly," replied Jack. "Still, we'll have to be vigilant."

"September is their low season over there," cautioned Laura. "I've been to Thailand. Did a UC in Bangkok once pretending to mule drugs. Very few Canadians or Americans go over because it takes so long to get there. Most tourists are European or Russian, with a small smattering of Australians thrown in."

"If that's the case," said Sammy, "and they have

an insider at the hotel, my team is liable to be burned as soon as we check in. Too coincidental with that many Canadians showing up. I'd better split the team and put us up in different hotels nearby."

"Good idea," said Jack. "See what it's like when we get there, but for the most part, I think you should keep as much distance between us as you can. Ensure that everyone going has their cellphones programmed to work over there."

"What about the Thai police?" asked Rose. "We need to have someone with guns if things go to hell."

"My understanding is there are a lot of good ones," said Laura, "but they also have a problem with corruption. When I was there last, we dealt with our Liaison Officer in Bangkok and he arranged for a couple of trusted officers to assist."

"I'll contact the LO myself," said Sammy. "See what we can come up with."

"What do you think your chances are of The Shaman showing up?" asked Rose.

"I'll really push to meet him," replied Jack. "If we do, and we can get the right type of conversation from him to prove he's importing and exporting heroin, we would never have to worry about him again."

"Thailand has the death penalty," added Laura. "Lethal injection. You definitely don't want to be caught trafficking in that country."

"Might also be the death penalty for both of you," said Rose, "if they decide to put you on a polygraph."

"Speaking of which, did you talk to Isaac?" asked Jack.

"I did. He shook his head and muttered something, but he okayed it."

"Perfect," said Jack.

"The only problem is that you will not get permission to travel to Burma," said Rose. "Too dangerous."

"We could find a poppy field and a lab for them," said Jack, feeling frustrated.

"I know. But between the corruption in Burma and guerrilla gangs controlling vast areas, it isn't worth it. You could be telling them something they already know ... or own. You'll have to come up with an excuse to tell Lee that you're not interested in seeing that part of his network."

"Okay," sighed Jack. "I'll tell him that I don't want to visit the lab because if the place is ever raided, he might blame me. Besides, in theory, all we're interested in is the final product. Not how or where it is made. I'll see if we can convince him to let us examine the heroin once it arrives in Thailand."

"Lee did say you can easily take a ferry and drive the round trip from Koh Samui to Burma and back within the day," said Laura. "So if we convince Lee to let us see the heroin when it arrives, it shouldn't take long."

"Good," replied Rose. "Even that has to be arranged and pre-approved."

"Understood," said Jack. "I don't fancy myself receiving a lethal injection."

* * *

The next two weeks went by fast for Jack and Laura. Rose arranged for a polygraph operator by the name of Larry Killaly to work with them.

Jack and Laura soon learned that Larry was acutely aware of even the smallest nuances when it came to detecting liars. On their last session, Larry had Jack prepare an account of what he did on his last two days off. Some of it was made up, while other parts were true. Larry was quick to spot the lies as he questioned Jack about his activities.

"You made eye contact with me about three seconds longer than you should have when you answered that last question," Larry said.

"I thought direct eye contact was an indication I wasn't lying," replied Jack, feeling upset that Larry spotted his falsehoods so easily.

Larry shook his head. "We are taught to believe that as children. So as adults, we think we can deceive someone by maintaining longer eye contact. Also, don't forget to be conscious of which direction your eyes veer to when you are asked to recall something. Remember, for most people, it is opposite directions when they recall something that is true versus using the imaginative side of their brain to fabricate a reply. And if you pause to think about it, I know you're being deceptive, so try again."

At the end of the session, it was clear that Larry had accurately pinpointed many of the lies that Jack tried to tell him.

"And this is before you even put me on the machine," said Jack in amazement. "I knew you were good, but I had no idea how good."

"Don't beat yourself up," replied Larry. "For the most part, you learned exceptionally well. I think you would bring about inconclusive results for the verbal interview and even the majority of the questions you would be asked once you are on the polygraph. Unfortunately, if you are on the polygraph, it would only take a couple of questions, like, have you ever worked for a police force or provided information to the police? You might be able to control your outward appearance, but inside, your body would react. You wouldn't fool a qualified polygraph operator. Every question would be like playing Russian roulette, only they wouldn't stop until every question was answered. There would be no passing the gun. Sooner or later, they would hit you with one of the questions I just asked."

"And there aren't any drugs I can take to prevent or numb involuntary reactions?"

"Dead giveaway," replied Larry, shaking his head.

After Larry left the apartment, Laura looked at Jack and said, "Guess we better find out who The Shaman is before any polygraph operator shows up."

"Finding out who he is doesn't give us the evidence to convict," replied Jack. "We need to meet him. Get him saying something we can use in court."

"I know, but from what Goldie told us, that won't happen without passing the lie detector."

"Guess we better force the issue and demand to meet him before the test, then," said Jack, sombrely.

Oh, man ...

* * *

Rose called Jack on the morning he and Laura were heading to the airport.

"Just a comment from Isaac," she said. "Larry apprised him on the outcome of what would happen if they put you on the lie detector — basically that you would be dead. Guess I don't need to tell you that under no circumstances are you to take it. If push comes to shove and they insist, then we'll get Sammy's team and the Thai police to extract you."

"For sure," replied Jack. "I'm not suicidal."

"Isaac said to wish you good luck. He also suggested that it would be nice if a suspect was brought home in handcuffs rather than a body bag."

32

Lee was all smiles as he met Jack and Laura in the departure level of the Vancouver International Airport. Their conversation was light as they boarded the plane. The first leg of the journey would take over fourteen hours to Hong Kong. There, they were to change planes before continuing on to Bangkok, arriving six hours after that.

Jack and Laura appreciated the comfort they felt as they sat in first class. The role they were playing demanded that they at least appear to be rich, when in fact, every penny spent had to be accounted for. Lee took the comforts of first class for granted.

Sammy, along with three of his colleagues, took the same flight the day before. Jack grinned to himself when he recalled Sammy's tongue-in-cheek demand that he should fly first class with Jack and Laura as part of the cover team. Rose suggested that, based on her experience with the narcs she knew, they were nothing but a bunch of dirty dogs. She told Sammy he was lucky they didn't cage him and put him in the baggage compartment.

Three hours into their flight, Lee placed his glass of Grand Marnier down and said, "I have some unfortunate news I forgot to mention. Some unexpected business arose on an unrelated matter and I have to stay in Hong Kong for a couple of days while you continue on."

"That's too bad," said Laura.

"Only for a couple of days," replied Lee. "I'll arrive either Monday or Tuesday. Besides," he winked, "it is very romantic where you are going. I'm sure I won't be missed that much."

"Did you hear that, honey?" asked Laura, sounding excited. "A romantic getaway."

"I heard," replied Jack. *I'm sure Natasha will be excited to hear about it, as well …*

"I think you will enjoy Samui," continued Lee. "Thai people are nice. Buddism is prevalent, and overall they are a gentle race. Not the type of people you would encounter, say, on the street a block or two from Goldie Locks. Okay, Laura?"

"You heard about my mugging incident?" asked Laura.

Lee smiled and said, "Actually I saw it. I was on my way to meet Goldie and an associate at the time. I was impressed. Where did you learn karate?"

"Just as a kid growing up. I had three older brothers and needed something to give me an advantage," Laura added with a smile.

"And you, Jack? Have you received any training in hand-to-hand combat?"

"Lots," replied Jack.

"Really? The both of you happen to be trained in martial arts?" asked Lee suspiciously.

"Oh, none of that leaping around and chopping boards or bricks for me," replied Jack. "My training was hands-on experience. Not officially recognized as schools. More like barrooms and back alleys. I prefer a baseball bat, broken bottle, or a gun. Trying to chop at somebody with the edge of my hand isn't my style."

"I see," replied Lee. "Perhaps not as impressive to watch as Laura, but the desired outcome is still … brutally attained."

Later, when Lee left to use the washroom, Laura asked, "So what do you think? Why are we being sent on alone?"

"Could be the truth," replied Jack, looking up from his Thai phrase book, "but more likely they want us to think we are alone."

"That's what I'm thinking, as well. They're going to want to be confident that we're who we say we are before showing us the goods."

"So we frolic and play for a couple of days. Act like we don't have a care in the world."

"And hope Lee does show up," said Laura. "Otherwise the bean counters might be a little upset."

* * *

Lee said goodbye to them at the Hong Kong International Airport and assured them that he would see them soon. Jack and Laura continued on to Bangkok, arriving shortly before midnight on Friday night. The following morning found them on a one-hour flight from Bangkok to Koh Samui, where a van from the hotel met them and a forty-five-minute drive brought them to the Pavilion Samui Boutique Resort.

Jack went to the reception desk and said, "Jack O'Donnell. I believe you were expecting us?"

The receptionist was friendly and obliging when Jack requested a room with twin beds.

"He's a kicker," said Laura, with a smile as she wrapped her arm around Jack's waist.

"A kicker?" asked the receptionist.

"When he sleeps, he kicks," said Laura.

On their way to their room, Jack whispered, "Connie would be so disappointed if she knew."

Jack and Laura set out to explore their surroundings. They discovered the hotel was in a small town called Lamai and it was set on the ocean. The long, sandy beach was lined with palm trees and several other hotels, but not so many as to make it overcrowded. Local industry appeared to be either fishing, or catering to the tourists with numerous tailor shops, bars, and souvenir shops.

It was evident that many of the bars catered to prostitution, but with Laura present, Jack was seldom propositioned or annoyed. Jack called Sammy and learned he was booked into the hotel next door to theirs. For now, they would keep their distance.

Jet lag and exhaustion took its toll and on their first night they decided to go to bed early. But not so early that Jack didn't stand and rattle the headboard against the wall. Laura rolled her eyes and said, "I've got a headache. Don't … stop! Jack? Don't … stop." Soon her plea picked up in pace to, "Don't stop! Don't stop! Don't stop!" as Jack increased the rhythm of banging the headboard against the wall. They did not know if the room was bugged, but by the knowing smiles they received from an elderly couple in the adjoining room the following morning, they knew someone had heard.

Over the next two days, Jack and Laura found the Thai people exceptionally friendly. Some were timid at first, but they did enjoy a good laugh, and a little humour went a long way. As did a basic knowledge of their language when it came to the simple niceties.

The Pavilion Hotel catered to the more wealthy tourists, and although the staff were polite, Jack and Laura preferred to frequent the restaurants or locations that the Thai people did. They discovered a bar on the main street in Lamai called The Outback. It was owned by an Australian by the name of Bart and his partner, an attractive Thai woman by the name of Tukta, who acted as bartender. Soon Jack and Laura were on a first-name basis with everyone who worked there.

The bar, like most others, was built with an open front facing the main street. People from all over the world passed by on the sidewalk and in and out through the bar. Short, squat-looking tribal women from various mountain regions of Thailand and dressed in traditional costumes strolled the sidewalk selling handcrafted souvenirs. Transvestites, or what the Thais referred to as "ladyboys," occasionally entered the bar along with other prostitutes. It was a spot where humanity seemed to set their differences aside and accept each other for who they were. It was a great place to people-watch — or be watched.

In the evening, The Outback had a Thai band perform most of the hits from the seventies to the eighties. Jack thought they were exceptionally good, until Laura clued him in that they were lip-synching. After Jack impersonated them, the band had a tough time trying to lip-synch without laughing.

By Monday morning Lee had not yet appeared, and Jack advised the hotel that something had come up and they were checking out. He and Laura took their own suitcases and trudged along the beach for about twenty minutes to another hotel they had located called Bill Resort. It was much less fancy than the Pavilion, but Jack and Laura had discovered that they had great food, a beautiful pool, and more importantly, had the atmosphere of a family-run operation with loyal staff.

Jack called Sammy as soon as they checked in and said, "Well?"

"Yeah, you picked up a tail walking down the beach," said Sammy. "Stocky fellow and taller than most Thai people. He purposely kept out of sight, but was definitely watching the two of you. Wearing navy-blue long pants and a yellow T-shirt."

"A lot of them wear yellow T-shirts," said Jack. "It has something to do with symbolizing their love for their king."

"He also had on a cheap-looking watch with an oversized silver strap."

"Good, we'll keep our eyes open. No sign of Lee yet. He is supposed to arrive today or tomorrow. I left a message at the Pavilion for him to phone my cell."

"We'll keep our distance. Let us know if you want us to move in closer."

Monday night found Jack and Laura back at The Outback. Music was blasting and the place was filling up. They found a seat and each ordered a Thai beer, Chang for Jack and Singha for Laura.

Jack could hear Bart's thick accent as he sat drinking beer with several grey-haired Australian expatriates at a table directly behind him. One of the older men swore and Jack heard Bart say, "Watch it, mate. There's a lady behind you."

"Sorry, I didn't know," he whispered to Bart.

"Well then, turn around and apologize. Better sound like you mean it, or I'll bar you," ordered Bart.

The man turned and apologized to Laura, who claimed that she hadn't heard him.

Jack grinned as he looked around the bar. It was very rustic, but had lots of character. In a glance, he saw an obese Swedish man with eyeglasses that were thick enough to qualify him for being legally blind, stumbling around the pool table with two prostitutes who were trying to teach him how to play. Nearby, a ladyboy was drinking with a young man who Jack suspected would be in for a real surprise later.

Across the room, he spotted a man and a woman who had moved their table aside to jive dance. They were staggering and swaying as they held each other up, while laughing and encouraging each other on in French. Not unusual, except the man was missing a foot and dancing lopsided. His prosthetic foot was sitting on the bar and he saw Tukta smile at them as she moved the foot aside to pour more drinks. *All this and Bart makes a guy apologize for uttering the word* fuck? *Bart, you're a gentleman. Rough around the edges perhaps, but a real gentleman.*

"I like this place," said Jack, smiling.

"You would," replied Laura, shaking her head.

"No, I'm serious. I've been in a lot of bars. This is one of the best. The most fun."

"I know you're serious," replied Laura with a laugh. She leaned over like she was kissing Jack in his ear and said, "Don't look now, but across the street we have a guy in a yellow T-shirt and a gaudy silver watchband loitering about in front of another bar."

"Love you, too," said Jack, when Laura leaned back.

Later, after Bart got up to leave, he stopped by at their table. "Everyone treating you all right mate?" he asked Jack.

"Couldn't be better," replied Jack.

"A bit of a Canadian invasion we have tonight," said Bart.

"Oh?" replied Jack, glancing around the bar while wondering if some of Sammy's team had entered.

"The French couple," said Bart. "Both soldiers from Quebec. Left his real foot in Afghanistan. A bloody shame, that is. The one they gave him to replace it hurts his stump. Last night he forgot it, so Tukta kept it behind the bar until he popped back in at noon to claim it. Tonight when he took it off, we put it up there as a reminder. Mind you, right now I bet he could wear it. Don't reckon much would hurt either of them at this point."

Jack glanced at the couple as a waitress brought them another round. The waitress tried to pour a handful of change into the soldier's hand, but he said, "Keep the shrapnel. I have an aversion to the stuff."

"Do me a favour, Bart," said Jack. "Send them over another round and put it on my tab. Make it anonymous, will you?"

"Sure thing, mate. Aren't you going to say hello to 'em? Fellow Canadians and all. Their English is good. Well, sort of. Seem like a decent lot, although a certain wanker I saw earlier today would disagree."

"A certain wanker?" asked Jack.

Bart smiled and said, "I saw them browsing in a shop down the street this afternoon. They spotted some big ape of a wanker trying to buy a young kid. Bet she wasn't ten years old. The soldier kicked him in the ass with his store-bought foot and put up his dukes. The big wanker backed right off and beat it down the street. The lady soldier followed him for about two blocks, cussin' him out in French and

English. Bet he thinks twice before goin' after the next kid."

"Forget buying them one round," said Jack. "Make it four."

"I'll tell you what, mate," said Bart. "I'll split it with you. You going to join them?"

"Maybe later. They look like they're having too much fun right now."

The truth was, Jack had no intention of talking with them. He hated having to lie about who he really was to decent people.

It was a couple of hours later and not yet midnight when Jack and Laura decided to leave. The town was really coming alive and it was obvious that most of the inhabitants were nocturnal, but jet lag had taken its toll. They decided to do the twenty-minute walk back to Bill Resort and call it a night. Jack noticed that as soon as they stood and paid their tab, the man in the yellow shirt reappeared from the bar across the street and used his cellphone.

Jack and Laura had earlier discovered a shortcut back to their resort. A lane from the main street led between two tall buildings and out across an open field to the beach. From the beach, it was only a ten-minute walk to their hotel.

They purposely walked slow, occasionally stopping to look at various souvenir shops. The man in the yellow T-shirt followed on the opposite side of the street. Jack casually glanced back as they entered the darkened alley, wondering if the he would follow them there.

"Jack!" screamed Laura.

Jack felt a blow to the side of his head and stumbled, but did not fall. In the darkness, he saw two large men, each holding Laura by an arm and pinning her against a wall. A third man delivered a punch to her stomach as she tried to scream again, leaving her gasping for air.

"Hey!" yelled Jack. "You sons of —" He stopped when a fourth man appeared in front of him. Jack raised his fists, but the man delivered a side kick to Jack's ribcage. The blow wasn't hard enough to cause any serious injury, but the man stood between him and the others, beckoning with his hands for Jack to come forward.

"And you, Jack? Have you had any training in hand-to-hand combat?" Lee's words echoed in Jack's brain. *These guys haven't demanded money ... no weapons ... three of them on Laura and only one on me. Son of a bitch! I'm being tested and this is going to hurt!*

Jack stepped forward in anger, which was genuine. His clenched fist swinging in a round arc from the side of his body toward the man's head was not genuine. He left himself wide open and paid for it with a jab to his chest. The man was much smaller than Jack, but by the way he moved and positioned his fists, there was little doubt that he had taken boxing.

Jack purposely eyed the man's groin, announcing his intention before trying to kick. His opponent nimbly stepped aside and did another side kick, landing a blow to Jack's temple. Jack's guess at what his opponent had been trained in changed. *Make that Thai kick-boxing.* He felt dazed from the kick and stumbled.

"*Tabernac*! No way to treat a lady!" yelled a man in a thick French accent.

Jack turned to see a man use the stump of his leg to kick the man in the groin who had been standing near Laura, while swinging his prosthetic foot and clobbering one of the other men in the face. This man let go of Laura's arm and she took advantage of it to punch her other captor in the throat. A second woman, also swearing in French, joined the melee.

The scene also distracted Jack's opponent enough that Jack landed a blow to his nose, spraying blood across his face and making his eyes fill with tears.

Seconds later, the four assailants beat a hasty retreat across the open field and up the beach. Jack and Laura both made a pretense of chasing them for a couple of minutes before returning to thank their rescuers. When they arrived back, the French couple were disappearing down the street in the back of a taxi. Neither Jack nor Laura ever saw them again or found out who they were.

It was mid-afternoon on Tuesday and Jack and Laura were relaxing around the pool at Bill Resort when Lee arrived, with a scowl on his face, about thirty minutes after he had called.

"Why are you here?" he asked, sitting on the end of a wooden lounge chair beside them. "Why did you change hotels?"

"Quite simple," said Jack. "I'm afraid we have some bad news. We have to cancel the deal. It's not safe."

"What? What are you talking about? The side of your face is bruised. Did something happen?"

"Oh, that," replied Jack. "No, that is nothing. Some guys tried to rob us last night. A minor scuffle. We weren't really hurt."

"Another mugging," replied Lee, faking surprise. "That is too bad, but if not that, then what is it then? Why did you change hotels? Why isn't it safe?"

"We didn't like the Pavilion," said Laura. "We definitely prefer Bill Resort."

"But this place is not as luxurious," said Lee. "I don't understand."

"Well," said Jack. "See the man over there talking to the head waiter? His name is Moo. A very astute fellow who usually works up at reception. Speaks good English and has worked here for years. The head waiter, he is Captain Sak. Nice fellow, also has worked here for years. The cook in the kitchen is named Noy and her husband is the sous-chef. His name is also Moo. The gardener over there with the ponytail is called Mong. The maid you see walking past prefers to be called Gee, although her colleagues have nick-named her Rat, as that is the first three letters of her surname. They have all worked here for years. It is like one big family."

"I don't understand," said Lee, "why do you know all their names? These people are merely servants. Not worthy of knowing. What is it about? Why do you think you have to cancel our deal?"

"In our business, I believe it is important to know people," replied Jack. "It is necessary for survival. For instance, the man sitting at the bar over there drinking Heineken is a police detective from Frankfurt, Germany, by the name of Otto Reichartinger."

"He is?" replied Lee, his head snapping around to look.

"No need to worry about him," continued Jack. "I am told he is a regular tourist at Bill Resort. However, did you know that at the Pavilion, there is a staff member who is so new that the others do not know his name. Makes me wonder if it is a staff member or a police officer. There is also something else that is unusual. If you walk through the restaurant behind you and gaze out at the beach, you will see a man loitering about wearing a yellow T-shirt and navy-blue pants."

"The same man who was loitering around us at the Pavilion," said Laura.

"I'm sure he is also a policeman," said Jack. "But, unlike Otto, a policeman who is very interested in Laura and I. Which is why I think everything should be called off. Maybe wait six months or so."

"Six months!" Lee took a deep breath and sighed. "Okay, the man on the beach is a policeman. I should have told you."

"What? You knew we had heat," said Jack angrily. "Why didn't you tell us?"

"No, it isn't what you think. He works for us. We, uh, told him to keep an eye on you to make sure you were okay."

"Well, that's a relief," replied Laura. "Too bad he wasn't around last night when we got mugged."

"Uh, yes, later I will talk to him about that."

"So," said Jack, smiling. "Like me, you also have friends who are policemen?"

Lee nodded and said, "But not yet in Canada. Which is why it is good for us to join forces. Agreed? Everything is okay now?"

"Agreed," said Jack. "But I hate wasting time. I was hoping your boss would be with you."

"He has consented to meeting you," said Lee, "but not for a few days."

Jack tried not to let his excitement show. "Why the delay?"

"As we spoke about before, there are certain security measures to be taken."

"You still don't trust me?" said Jack. "Afraid I'll hit you over the head with a bottle of Guinness and steal the dope?"

"My boss is a careful man. Getting close to him is like peeling an onion. The security is more intense the closer you get to the core."

"I've always preferred garlic, myself," replied Jack. "Tell you what, have him come and witness whatever it is you need to do to assure yourselves that I am being totally honest. He will see the truth for himself. Let's do it and get it over with."

"Actually," said Lee, "that is something he might do."

Later that afternoon, Lee used the Internet to update The Shaman and told him of Jack's impatience.

The reply sounded innocent, but wasn't:

Tomorrow take them to Burma and enlighten them with a sampling of our product and hospitality. A welcoming team has been arranged. If any friends of theirs decide to come, then arrange for them to stay in Burma, as well. Should that venture go well, two days later I will send Mister Sato and Da Khlot to see you. If Mister Sato decides that we should not do business with them, then Da Khlot and his associates will.

Deciphering the message for Lee was easy. He knew that Mister Sato was a polygraph operator. Tomorrow Lee would take Jack and Laura to Burma. If anyone followed them, Jack and Laura were to be killed. If none followed, then in two days Da Khlot would accompany the polygraph operator to meet with Jack. If the polygraph operator decided that Jack wasn't truthful, Da Khlot would kill them.

Lee reflected on the upcoming course of events. Other tests would follow, including the successful transfer of funds to a bank owned by The Shaman. Naturally, any problem with such funding would see a quick end to Jack and Laura.

Lee shrugged it off. There was really no need to worry about Jack and Laura. Briefly, an uncomfortable thought entered his mind. *If something goes amiss at this stage, Da Khlot will kill me, too. Maybe from*

Thailand I could escape — no, I would be trading my life for the lives of my family. I am foolish to even consider the possibility that anything could go that wrong. Jack will most certainly pass the lie detector. Then there is the last remaining test after the lie detector ... but Jack has no doubt murdered before ...

33

Lee joined Jack and Laura for supper at Bill Resort. The restaurant was built partially over the beach and gave a panoramic view of the Gulf of Thailand. Sunset comes early to countries close to the equator, and the crashing of the white foamy waves added a pleasant backdrop to the restaurant lights shining across the sand and palm trees. In the distance, bright lights shone like stars from bobbing boats as the fishermen used the lights to attract and catch squid.

Lee watched as Laura ate her green curried chicken in traditional Thai style, using a fork to push her food onto a spoon before putting the spoon in her mouth. "Some day you must learn to master the chopsticks," he said.

"Why should I?" she replied, sounding upset. "We're in Thailand. It is their culture to use a fork and spoon."

"Ah, yes, that reminds me," said Lee. "You both need to get to bed early tonight. Tomorrow morning at four-thirty I have hired a van to pick us up. We're going to spend the day going to Burma and back."

"Burma?" said Jack, eyeing Laura curiously. "I told you before, there is no reason for us to go there. That part of your operation is not our concern."

"The Shaman insists," replied Lee. "He wants you to see a small sampling of what we can do. Tomorrow you will be shown a hundred kilos arriving into Thailand. Our presence in Burma will be less than two hours. It has been arranged. The Shaman would take it as a personal insult if you were not to attend. He would think that you do not have faith in his abilities."

"I see," replied Jack. *Let the games begin …*

Jack managed to get the pertinent details involving their travel, but Lee would not tell them how the heroin was arriving. "You'll have to wait and see," he said.

After dinner, Jack and Laura excused themselves on the pretext of a romantic walk down the beach before calling it a night.

"Well, this is a fine mess, isn't it?" stated Laura. "What are we going to do? Rose would skin us alive if she thought we were going into Burma."

"It's only for a couple of hours. We can say we thought we were being taken to the border. If we happen to stray into Burmese territory for a couple of hours, we'll say we had no choice. I don't think it'll be a problem."

"I can see it being a problem for Sammy and the others," said Laura abruptly, while gazing out to sea.

"We have to catch a ferry in the morning to leave Koh Samui. Sammy showing up with a surveillance team on the boat would be a dead giveaway. And I mean, dead. Then there's what, a six-hour ride in a van to the other side where we clear Thai Immigration before taking a boat across a river to Burma. Tough for any cover team to follow."

"Exactly," replied Laura. "There is no way I want any Canadians around me, unless it's our two unknown friends from Quebec. Wish we could find out who they were. I'd like to thank them."

"Likewise," replied Jack. "Maybe someday I'll figure out a way, but right now, are you agreeable to going into Burma?"

"I guess, but what do we tell Sammy?"

"Tell him we're going on an elephant trek with Lee tomorrow. We're supposed to be back tomorrow night. Then we'll say Lee sprung it on us as a test. He's an operator, he'll likely know we're lying, but at least he'll understand."

"Yeah, whatever," replied Laura, acting disinterested.

"Okay, Laura," said Jack, grabbing her by the shoulders and spinning her around to look at her face. "What gives?"

"Nothing. What are you talking about? I'm fine," she added defiantly.

"Ever since we came down for dinner, you haven't been acting yourself. If I've done something to make you angry, I want to know. There is enough stress going on as it is. Whatever is bugging you, I want to know."

Laura sighed and kicked at the sand with her toes. "Sorry, it's not you," she replied. "Well, then again, it probably is."

Jack felt his heart sink. *Whatever I did, I never meant to hurt you ...*

"When I was putting makeup on for supper I saw it," said Laura.

"Saw what? I waited out on the porch while you got ready. What are you talking about?"

"Grey hair," sighed Laura, pointing to a place on her scalp.

"A grey hair?" Jack laughed.

"It's not funny! Not just one — a whole group. I've never had any before. Now it's like overnight and wham! Suddenly I have grey hair and am being called madam. I bet you saw it," she added, touching her hair. "If you were a friend, you would have told me!"

"Sorry, I never noticed. To be honest, I have a hard time looking at you too closely."

"Why?"

Jack looked at Laura and gave an intentionally loud sigh and said, "Because you're so damned beautiful. I have to slap my brain daily to keep you in the sister category," he added, sounding frustrated.

Laura looked shocked as she stared at Jack. A moment later she turned so he wouldn't see her smile. *He is such a liar, but I think I'll let him get away with that one for now.*

* * *

At four-thirty in the morning, Lee's van appeared with a driver who appeared to speak little English. They were on schedule, and, at noon, Jack and Laura patiently stood in line at the Thai Immigration Office in Ranong and watched as their passports were stamped.

Jack turned to Lee and asked, "Aren't you getting your passport stamped?"

"No, I am not going with you," he replied. "It is better I wait here while the boat takes you across to Burma. Our people on the boat will look after you. Trust me."

Later Laura had the opportunity to whisper to Jack and say, "He's not coming with us and says to trust him?"

Jack nodded.

"So what do you think? Something's gone wrong and we're going to be executed and he doesn't want to dirty his hands?"

"Maybe. Let's hope we can trust him."

"Trust him? N-F-L!"

Normally Jack would have grinned. The letters stood for *not fucking likely*. It was a phrase the narcs sometimes used, however, not one he had ever heard Laura use before. But at this moment, his sense of humour had disappeared. In the pit of his stomach, he was worried that Laura might be right.

Jack and Laura left the Thai Immigration Office in a van with Lee. The driver took them slowly through a quiet ghetto for another ten minutes before arriving at an abandoned warehouse alongside a river. Lee spent the time talking on his cellphone, and when they arrived at the warehouse, three Thai men were waiting. Lee smiled and gave them the thumbs-up sign.

There was little doubt, Jack knew, that their ten-minute ride through the ghetto had been monitored to detect surveillance.

"Now," said Lee, "it is about a forty-five-minute journey across the mouth of the river to Kaw Thaung in Burma. These three men will take you across and you will be provided with an opportunity to see the product you wish to purchase."

"What if something goes wrong?" asked Jack. "Where will you be to help us?"

"I assure you, my friend, that nothing will go wrong. Part of this exercise is to build trust between us. It is time for you to trust me."

Jack and Laura climbed into the boat, which was like an oversized canoe. It was called a long-tail boat because of a long length of gear shaft that extended from a motor in the back to the propeller. The length of the shaft made it well-suited to handle the large swells from ocean waves without allowing the propeller to come up out of the water. This particular boat did have a canvas canopy overhead to provide relief from either the sun or monsoon rains — both of which Jack and Laura had seen plenty of in the last couple of days.

Only one of the three men, wearing an American Eagle brand ball cap, spoke a little English. Very little, as Jack would discover.

They were soon on their way across a muddy and dirty expanse of water. They passed one more Thai Immigration Office on a jetty opposite a stationary raft in the river holding three Thai soldiers all dressed in camouflage.

Minutes later, Thailand was behind them and everyone was quiet. American Eagle took off his shirt and Jack nudged Laura so she could get a look at his full back tattoo. Jack had the distinct impression that the tattoo was gang-related. As they neared a dock in Kaw Thaung, Jack saw a large sign welcoming people to Burma.

American Eagle put his shirt back on, looked at Jack, and pointed to a plastic bag partially hidden by a pile of rags and said, "You want whiskey, cigarettes, or Viagra?"

Jack would have laughed except the situation was serious. He politely shook his head, but saw Laura cover her mouth to hide a giggle and look away.

"Not allowed for Thai running boat. Okay for tourist. You sure?" persisted American Eagle.

"I'm sure."

The three crewmen moored their boat next to another boat at the end of the dock. "Okay," said American Eagle. "Burma Immigration end of dock. Must hurry. Both get passports stamped and come back. Hurry."

Jack and Laura left the boat and waited to have their passports stamped by Burmese Immigration.

A young man approached Jack and whispered, "You want whiskey, cigarettes, Viagra?"

"No!" said Jack, perhaps a little too loudly.

"Why not?" demanded the young man.

"I don't smoke, I don't drink whiskey, and I don't need Viagra."

"Okay," he shrugged and moved away.

"You sure you don't want me to call Natasha and get a second opinion?" asked Laura.

A few minutes later, they returned to the boat, and as they were getting in, Jack said, "We got our passports stamped. Where to from here?"

"Back to Thailand," replied American Eagle. "As soon as we finish loading."

Jack felt a chill go up his spine. A wooden section of the floor behind the driver had been lifted out and Jack saw numerous plastic-wrapped bricks stowed away. He realized the heroin had come from the boat they were parked alongside.

"Here? With us?" said Jack. "What the hell? I thought we were only going to get a glimpse of it, not smuggle it ourselves."

One look at Laura's pale face revealed her dismay at the situation.

American Eagle gave a command in Thai and they were then on their way back across the river. As they neared the stationary raft with the three soldiers, Jack could see that the soldiers were selecting passing boats at random to come in for inspection.

"Don't worry," said American Eagle. "Never stop us."

As they passed, one soldier yelled to them and waved them to come over. Jack saw the immediate terror in the eyes of the crew and heard their panicked whispers.

American Eagle looked back at Jack and said, "Wrong soldier working today." He put his fingers to his lips and said, "Top secret. Say nothing. Top secret!"

No, shit!

Jack watched as one of the crew members purposely ground the gears on the boat while the other held his hands open in dismay for the soldiers, telling him their boat had trouble with the reverse and they would stop next time.

N-F-L, thought Jack. He was right. The soldiers started yelling, and for a moment Jack wondered if the crew would try to race away. He turned to Laura and said, "If they make a run for it, we're going in the water. It'll be safer than being sprayed with machine-gun fire."

Oh, man …

American Eagle quickly calmed the other two crew members enough to convince them to make a wide arc and return to the raft. As they pulled up to the raft, Jack saw American Eagle pop a handful of breath mints into his mouth and give a big smile as he walked to the brow of the boat to welcome the soldier aboard, before shaking hands with him.

They spoke in whispers for several seconds and Jack saw American Eagle eventually nod his head and gesture to the plastic bag containing the contraband cigarettes, whiskey, and Viagra. The soldier nodded and American Eagle discreetly handed him a wad of money and they were allowed to continue.

Once they arrived back at the warehouse, Jack and Laura rushed off the boat and met with Lee, who was waiting in the van.

"So," said Lee, glancing at his watch. "Right on time. I told you there was nothing to worry about. These boats run tourists back and forth all day to get their passports stamped to allow them to extend their stay in Thailand. Dozens of boats a day and this is only one spot. Upriver there is even less interference from the military, but it is more difficult for me to take you there. Also, too many mosquitoes."

"I hadn't expected that Laura and I would be bringing it back with us," said Jack, vehemently. "You risked us getting caught and receiving the fucking death penalty!"

Lee looked genuinely startled. "There is no risk, that is the point," he replied. "If the soldiers had found something, it would have either been returned to us later, or at worst, one of the crew members would have been charged with it. He would have been executed, not you. Relax, everything is under control."

"You should have warned us," said Jack. "I don't like taking risks I don't need to take."

"I thought you wanted to stay with the product until it was put on board?"

"I don't need to see every step. I'll be happy to see it placed on a ship, and where it is hidden, but I do not need to babysit it every step of the way."

"Good, that makes it easier for us," said Lee. "So everything is okay. You have seen that you can trust me."

"N-F-L," said Jack and Laura in unison.

"You want to watch football?" asked Lee, confused.

It was seven o'clock that night when they turned off the main highway and onto a rutted road leading to Bill Resort.

"You have not asked for a sample," said Lee. "Do you trust us enough to believe the drug is pure?"

"No, I would like to obtain a sample from the shipment as it is loaded on the boat," replied Jack.

"And what would you do with this sample? We will want our down payment before you leave Asia."

"I'll mail it back to Canada," replied Jack. "I've got a friend who can analyze it for me."

"That will take time," replied Lee. "We would require a financial down payment as soon as you see the shipment. Perhaps I could convince you in some other way that our product is ultra pure."

"How?" asked Jack.

"My boss has come up with a somewhat amusing illustration," replied Lee. "We have done this many times before with others who wanted proof of the quality of the merchandise. Let me demonstrate," he said, and took a pen and paper from the glovebox and wrote several names on the paper and handed it to Jack.

"What's this?" said Jack. "Looks like a list of hotels?"

"Hotels and districts in Bangkok," said Lee. "Well-known locations where heroin addicts congregate. Point to one of the districts or hotels. Any one, it doesn't matter."

"What for?" asked Jack.

"You will see. It is like a game. Quite amusing."

Jack looked at the list and randomly pointed to a district called Soi Ngam Duphli. "Now what?" he asked.

Lee smiled and said, "Tomorrow my friend, I will

show you something interesting, but now I need to use the Internet and call it a night. It has been a long day."

Late the following afternoon, Lee met up with Jack as he lay on a lounge chair by the pool. He waved at Laura, who was swimming, and then tossed Jack an English edition of the *Bangkok Post* and told him to turn to a small article buried deep within the paper:

> Eleven people died last night in the Soi Ngam Duphli district of Bangkok. The victims were all believed to be heroin addicts who evidently did not realize they had been sold a very pure form of the drug. Countless other victims were rushed to hospital and treated for overdoses. The police are continuing to investigate as the probability of more deaths is likely to occur over the next few days, before all the addicts know to take extra caution …

"So, Jack," chuckled Lee. "Do you have any more doubts about our product? Or would you like to see this rather amusing display repeated in some other district?"

Jack felt numb as he slowly shook his head. *The real Happy Jack wouldn't have minded.*

"Is everything okay?" asked Lee.

Jack looked up and smiled. "You bet. Your boss certainly has a way of illustrating things. I'm convinced." *Convinced I'm going to kill him.*

"I'm going to get a drink," said Lee. "Would you like one?"

"No," replied Jack, watching as Lee whistled a tune to himself on his way to the bar.

"What's up?" asked Laura, climbing out of the pool.

"I just killed eleven people," said Jack, lamely pointing at the newspaper.

Moments later Lee returned with a pina colada in his hand, sat down beside Jack, and sucked on a fresh piece of pineapple from the rim of the glass. "These are really good. You should have one."

"No, thanks."

"Where did Laura go?"

"To her room. She's feeling ill."

"See? You should move back to the Pavilion where I am."

"The cook there was trained by Bill Resort."

"It is still nicer."

Jack leaned back and closed his eyes. He could hear the wind rustle the newspaper. Ophelia appeared in his mind. Leaning against a doorway. A woman's words came back to haunt him. *"Don't stare, honey. That's just nobody." Was Melvin another nobody, too? Like eleven other nobodies in Bangkok last night? Eleven people who died because I selected their fate.*

34

That night, Jack met with Lee over dinner at The Patio Restaurant in the Pavilion resort, which overlooked a fountain and the ocean beyond.

"Is Laura still feeling ill?" asked Lee.

"Yes," replied Jack, truthfully. "The sooner we are finished business, the better. I want to meet The Shaman. No more jerking us around."

"Tomorrow, you shall," replied Lee.

Jack felt both surprise and elation. "He is coming here? Tomorrow? What time?"

Lee brushed Jack's questions aside with a wave of his arm and said, "He will not meet you until you pass one more small test."

"I'm tired of tests!" replied Jack angrily. "I know you were checking to see if we were followed yesterday to Burma. What kind of bullshit is this? I thought we trusted each other?"

"I do trust you, Jack. Believe me, my life depends upon it. Please do not be angry with me. It is The Shaman who decides these things. Like an onion, the —"

"I know. I've heard that crap before. I want to meet him. Face to face. That is how I conduct business."

Lee sighed and said, "The small test I refer to tomorrow is a lie-detector test. If you do not take it, I can assure you that you will never meet The Shaman."

"Then give me the bloody test," said Jack, coldly. "I'll take it!"

"Once you pass the test, and I know you will," said Lee, smiling, "then you shall be taken to meet The Shaman."

"Taken where?"

"That, my friend, I am not allowed to tell you until you have completed this annoying matter with the lie detector. You and Laura must —"

"Laura! I'll be damned if I'm going to embarrass her by submitting her to such a —"

"No, let me finish. She will not be asked to take the test. But she must come with you and you both must agree to be held incommunicado from the time you are picked up to take the test and until you meet The Shaman. Do you agree?"

Jack sighed and said, "I agree, but there is no need to pick us up. We will walk over from Bill Resort."

"No, the test will be held in a hotel in Chaweng. It is a town a half-hour drive north of us. You will be picked up after lunch and driven. Bring your luggage, as well. The Shaman is arranging for you to stay in another hotel at his expense. A much nicer place."

"Fine by me, but I better be meeting The Shaman right after."

"I assure you that is his wish as well."

Later that night, Jack and Laura walked along the beach and then went through an intricate prearranged jaunt, cutting through pathways and in and out front and rear doors of other hotels. Eventually Sammy called Jack to tell him that they were not being followed. Minutes later, they met in Sammy's room at the Samui Laguna Resort located next to the Pavilion. Also present were three other members of the Vancouver Drug Section, as well as the LO from Bangkok and two plainclothes officers from the Thailand National Police Department.

Jack outlined his meeting earlier that evening with Lee.

"I don't like it," said Sammy. "If they hook you to that damned machine, you're dead."

"The thing is," replied Jack, "The Shaman could be in the next room. I'll try to see him first, but even if they don't let me, you should be able to figure out who it is by watching Lee or his buddies. It's better than giving up."

"But it will be damned difficult to cover you without being burned," protested Sammy.

"What the hell do we have to lose? If we don't show up, we won't identify him. If you get burned then kick the doors in and save us."

"Yeah, that's if we know which room you're in. .

"Polygraph tests start with an interview first. Altogether we're looking at about three hours. Surely by then you can figure out what room we're in."

"Lee thinks I'm sick," said Laura. "Actually, I am, but it's not from the food. I can use being sick to help you figure out which room we're in. Once we're inside, I'll beg Lee or one of his cronies to go to a pharmacy and get me something. If you haven't spotted what room we go to when we first arrive, then that should help. I'll also tell him I'm out of sanitary pads. You see some guy in a pharmacy buying those, follow him."

"It's damned risky," said Sammy.

"I want this guy," said Jack, vehemently. "He's responsible for a mass murder two nights ago. You going to let him walk?"

"I'm with Jack on this one," said Laura bitterly. "If all else fails we can resort to tossing something or someone out a window. That should clue you in as to where we are."

"There is only one road up to Chaweng," said Sammy, "and it isn't very crowded. Too obvious to follow you, turn off at the road into Chaweng and continue along to whatever hotel you go to. These guys are known for spotting surveillance. I don't want the both of you to end up like Goldie."

"Then wait for us on the road leading into Chaweng," said Jack. "I'm told the town itself is crowded. Lots of cover for you. I've also got a map. Most of the hotels face the main road in town that runs the length of the beach. Stagger a few cars along it and wait. We don't need to leave with a parade behind us."

"Will it be the same driver and van who took you to Burma?" asked Sammy.

"I don't know," replied Jack. "If it is, the guy won't be too surveillance-conscious. I think he was only hired as a driver."

"You sure?" asked Sammy.

"As sure as I could be. He didn't speak English and Lee doesn't seem to speak Thai. I think he doesn't know anything about what is going on."

"Okay." Sammy sighed. "I'll leave a guy at Bill Resort to confirm your departure and positively identify the van for us. The rest of us will wait up the highway near Chaweng."

The plan might have worked, except Jack and Laura were not taken to Chaweng.

At three o'clock the next afternoon, Jack and Laura recognized the same van and driver who had taken them to Burma when it arrived in front of Bill Resort. The side door with deep-tinted windows opened up and Lee beckoned for them to come inside. They complied, as the driver tossed their luggage into the rear of the van.

Now there was an additional passenger sitting behind them. It was the man with the yellow T-shirt.

"I believe you have seen my friend before," smiled Lee.

There was little doubt in Jack's mind that the bulge

in the man's T-shirt covering the front of his waistband was not a banana.

Ten minutes out of Lamai, Jack and Laura were both glad they had opted to have the surveillance team wait for them in Chaweng as the van pulled over into the parking lot of a fashionable restaurant located high on a bluff.

They sat and waited in the van for several minutes, watching the highway.

"Please do not be angry with me," said Lee. "It is not personal. Just business."

"I know," replied Jack. "But I am developing a hatred for onions."

"It is time," said the man behind them.

To Jack and Laura's surprise, they were told to get out of the van. Minutes later, they were loaded into a different van, which once more proceeded north. The seating arrangement was the same, except a different man was driving.

"Good move," said Jack, patting Lee on his shoulder.

"Thank you. Again, I apologize. Once The Shaman meets you, I am sure he will trust you as much as I do."

"You okay, honey?" asked Jack, looking at Laura.

She shook her head and muttered, "Feeling crampy. Must be from the food."

Twenty minutes farther down the road, Jack politely said, "Uh, according to the sign, you just missed the turnoff into Chaweng."

"We've located a nicer hotel," said Lee. "The Amarin Victoria Resort. A little farther north, up near the airport."

Jack glanced behind him and the man in the yellow T-shirt edged back out of reach, while placing his hand under his shirt. *Oh, fuck!*

At four o'clock, Jack and Laura were hustled into a hotel room. Inside were four more men. The man who let them in was Japanese and was dressed in a dark suit with a white shirt and a black tie.

The other three men seated in the room looked to be Thai, except their skin was slightly darker. Perhaps Burmese or Cambodian, guessed Jack. Two of them were dressed in long khaki-coloured cargo pants and wore dark blue golf shirts that weren't tucked in.

The third man wore black slacks and a white golf shirt. He stood up and the other two quickly followed suit, both of them standing erect, like they were at attention. It was obvious that they worked for the man in the white golf shirt. Something about him seemed odd. Jack returned his cold, hard stare. He knew he was looking at the man with the dead eyes.

"You will accompany Mister Sato into the bedroom," said Lee. "A table has been set up in there. He has some questions to ask you."

"I would like to meet your boss first," said Jack. "There are some things I would like to discuss with him."

"Please do not delay," replied Lee nervously. "You must answer Mister Sato's questions first. I beg you."

"Laura," said Jack, "I am sure you do not wish to sit in a bedroom with a bunch of men you don't know. Go find the lounge and we'll meet you there for a drink after."

"No," replied the man with the dead eyes. "Nobody is to leave this room until we are finished."

"And you are?" asked Jack.

"Da Khlot. You would be wise to obey."

Laura took a deep breath and shrugged her shoulders indifferently. "I'll be okay, honey." She smiled at Lee while Jack and Sato went into the bedroom and closed the door.

Two of the men took their chairs and moved them between the bedroom door and the entrance door to the room. The third man remained by the window, seated beside Da Khlot.

Laura moved toward the man sitting with Da Khlot and smiled. "May I sit there?" she asked, gesturing with her hand.

The man started to rise.

"No!" ordered Da Khlot, closing the drapes. "You sit on the floor."

"Up yours," replied Laura. "I'll sit where I damn well feel like."

"Please," interrupted Lee, looking at Da Khlot. "Do not treat her like a prisoner. Western women are not accustomed to taking orders." He looked at Laura and said, "Please, sit on the bed with me. We can watch television."

Da Khlot's impassive face did not change, but a slight nod of his head gave Laura permission and she sat on the end of the bed between Lee and the man with the yellow T-shirt.

Lee leaned toward the television remote, but Da Khlot said, "Mister Sato said there was to be no television, no radio, and no talking. We just wait."

Laura waited as the seconds ticked past to eventually become minutes. She strained to listen, but could only hear the murmur of voices from the next room. She could smell the sweat and feel the dampness from the arms and legs of the two men she sat between.

From his chair by the window, Da Khlot continued to stare at her, his face blank as to what he was thinking. It was his eyes that portrayed a sense that he was lacking in any human emotion. *What could cause a person to become like that?*

Laura did not know about children swinging pick-axes, or screaming people turning into corpses in muddy ditches sodden with blood. If she had, perhaps she would have understood. It would not have eased her fear, but she would have understood the true nature of the man she faced.

At five-thirty, the bedroom door opened quietly and Sato appeared. He shook his head, a sign that caused Laura to speculate on her chances of running and diving into the drapes and through a glass window.

"We are not finished," said Sato, looking at Lee. "Only the first part. I need to go to the bathroom and then he will be hooked to the polygraph."

"Is it going well?" asked Lee.

Sato paused, appearing to be in deep thought, but replied, "I do not have an answer for you yet. Nothing definitive. Inconclusive about — well, let me say that we have reached a stage where I can elicit more penetrating questions. You will soon know."

At six o'clock, Sato abruptly flung open the door

and everyone leaped to their feet. He strode across the floor to Lee and pointing his finger back toward the bedroom he said, "That man is either a police officer or is working for the police!"

"No!" cried Lee, as the panic swept across his face. "Maybe you made a mistake?"

"No mistake and no doubt," replied Sato.

Laura felt like she was drugged. Life appeared in slow motion. She rose from the bed and stepped forward, catching a glimpse of Jack in the bedroom, still sitting in a chair, with a strap around his chest and wires dangling from his fingers.

The two men in front of her pulled pistols from under their shirt and pointed them at Jack. Laura felt Da Khlot's hand slip over her mouth and the sharp point of a knife on the back of her neck.

35

At four o'clock that afternoon, Sammy realized something had gone wrong. He sent one car racing north while he took the road south, back to Lamai. The van was not located until five o'clock, parked at the Pavilion resort.

Another tense meeting took place in Sammy's room.

"Goddamn it! Goddamn it! Goddamn it!" Sammy cursed as he paced back and forth. "I knew I shouldn't have let them do it! It's my fucking fault!"

"What are —"

"Shut the fuck up," muttered Sammy to his subordinate. "I'm thinking." He turned to the Thai policemen and said, "Is there a local police officer you trust completely?"

"Yes, several," replied the men.

"I want the driver of the van questioned. Find out what he knows."

"I understood from Jack," said the LO, "that the driver doesn't really know anything. If Jack is wrong, then grabbing him would alert the bad guys. Jack and Laura could be killed."

"Yeah, and maybe they're already dead or dying," said Sammy, turning to the Thai policemen. "Use a hit-and-run scenario."

"Hit and run?" they asked in unison.

"Have the driver interrogated and tell him his licence plate was taken as the result of a hit-and-run accident. Find out everywhere he went today. Please hurry."

It was six o'clock when the Thai police reported back. The driver had been interrogated.

"He swears he was not in any accident and the only trip he made was to pick up two men from the Pavilion and a man and woman from Bill Resort and drop them all off at the Cliff Bar and Grill a couple of kilometres north of Lamai. He thinks they were getting in another van when he left to return to the Pavilion, but cannot recall anything about it. The police officer who questioned him believes he is telling the truth."

"Would you like us to have him question the people at the Cliff Bar and Grill?" suggested the other Thai policeman. "He could pretend to be checking the driver's story that he was not in an accident."

"Yeah, good idea," said Sammy quietly. "Other than that, where would you go to dump some bodies?"

* * *

"Hey! What's the fuss?" yelled Jack, still sitting in the chair.

"You lied!" shouted Lee. "You are working for the police!"

"I didn't lie," said Jack. "Sato! Do you think I lied?"

"No," replied Sato, "I could tell that you weren't lying," he said, adamantly.

"What?" yelled Lee, grabbing Sato by his arm. "You told me Jack worked for the police?"

"That's right," said Jack. "I told him I did. I wasn't lying."

"You work for the police!" said Lee, astounded.

"Of course I work with them. You know that," he chuckled. "So do you. How do you think I learned about Goldie becoming a rat if I didn't have friends on the inside?"

"Oh, my friend," replied Lee, shaking his head. "That is not what we were thinking."

"Jesus! You mean you thought I was *really* working for them? Christ, what kind of guy do you take me for? Sure, sometimes we have to scratch each other's back a little, but come on! If you're trying to find out if I *really* work for the police, let me prepare a few questions of my own that you can have Sato ask me. They should alleviate any doubt."

Jack was brought a pen and paper and quickly jotted down four questions:

Have you ever purposely lied to, or deceived the police?

Have you ever committed crimes that you could be jailed for?

Have you ever disposed of and hidden a body of a murdered man?

Have you ever orchestrated or committed murder?

Sato soon appeared in the bedroom doorway again and motioned for Lee to come over before whispering the results of his findings.

"You are certain?" asked Lee.

"He answered yes to all four questions. With some of the earlier questions, my findings were inconclusive, but with these questions I am positive he is telling the truth. I also asked him how many murders he had been responsible for. He told me he had lost count. I believe him."

"Which questions were inconclusive?" asked Lee. "Anything significant?"

"His answer to transferring money. He believes it to be available, but has some hesitation about his colleagues delivering it. It could be a simple control issue. He likes to have absolute control and lacks faith in others."

"That, or he doubts our ability to deliver," replied Lee. "He did not climb to the top by completely relying on others. What else was inconclusive?"

"The first question when I asked him his name

brought an inconclusive result. I asked him if he has used other names. He admitted he had, but refused to say what they were."

Lee smiled and said, "In his business that is not unusual. The important thing is he sounds like he is suited to work with our organization. Come, it is time to leave."

Moments later, Jack gave Laura a heartfelt hug and looked over her shoulder at Lee and said, "Satisfied? Can we meet the boss now?"

"Your suitcases are still in the van," said Lee. "All we need is you."

At seven-thirty that night, Jack and Laura looked out the passenger window of a Falcon 50EX private jet as it lifted off the runway, leaving the twinkling lights of Koh Samui far behind. They were not told their destination and were still not being allowed to use their cellphones.

Laura felt Jack's reassuring squeeze on her hand. She looked across at Sato and Da Khlot who were both staring at them. *Oh, man …*

In a seat toward the front of the cabin, Lee relaxed while sipping on a Grand Marnier. *Tomorrow Jack will complete his final test. That will not be a problem. He has obviously murdered many times before.*

36

They were in the air seven hours, but with the time difference, it was actually five-thirty Saturday morning when the jet touched down on a foggy, wet runway.

Lee came to the back of the plane, grinning like a Shakespearian theatre mask. He bowed deeply before Jack and Laura and with a flourish of his arm he said, "Welcome to Osaka!"

"We're in Japan?" asked Laura, giving Jack a look like she was accusing him.

"*Kon-ni-chi-wa*," said Lee, carefully annunciating the word. "It means hello."

"Really?" replied Laura. "How about *sayonara* instead?"

"Come on, sweetie," said Jack. He looked up at Lee and said, "She's tired."

A van picked them up and took them to a private room where a customs official quickly stamped their passports. Moments later, they boarded a chauffeured stretch limousine. Once more, Jack and Laura found themselves sitting across from Da Khlot and Sato.

"How long before we're there?" asked Jack.

"About three hours," replied Lee, smiling understandingly at Laura's tired groan.

Jack tried to pay attention to the roads and signs they passed, but had little success, due to his lack of familiarity with Japanese characters. The only two signs he recognized were NISSAN and TOYOTA. He felt uncomfortable under Sato's constant gaze and decided to feign sleeping. But minutes later, he wasn't feigning.

Jack and Laura each awoke about two hours later. The limo was driving through a mountainous area on switchback roads. Sato and Lee were asleep, but Da Khlot sat silently, staring blankly at them.

Eventually the limo arrived at a resort and slowed down, waking those who had been sleeping.

"It is an *onsen*," explained Lee. "A resort that incorporates a mineral hot spring to soak in. Extremely popular in Japan. The food served is also exquisite. Multiple courses, including a wide variety of dishes. Later, you both must try it."

The limo drove past a public parking area and took a small lane up a steep incline behind the resort. The area they drove through looked like an immaculately kept park, dotted with a selection of both bonsai and cherry trees.

"I've heard of *onsens*," replied Jack. "You bath nude in public hot springs, correct?"

Lee pursed his lips in a grin and then said, "I

understand that Westerners dislike bathing naked in public. I should tell you, that for the most part, men and women are separated, each with their own private facility to bathe in."

"For the most part?" asked Laura.

Lee pointed to a small structure of wooden screens and clumps of bamboo strategically located halfway up the hill from the resort. A small stream that billowed steam bubbled out from the ground higher up the hill, flowed down through the structure, then disappeared into the ground again before reaching the resort below.

"There," said Lee, "is a private location for a man and a woman. Popular with honeymooners, but perhaps we can reserve some time for the both of you."

"I would really like that," said Jack, ignoring Laura's heel as she stepped on his toes.

At the top of the incline, the limo parked in front of a four-storey mansion built in traditional Japanese style with an intricate gabled roof and tiled ends.

"This is the home of Mister Fukushima," said Lee. "He owns the *onsen* that you see down the hill. He is the man we refer to secretly as The Shaman."

"And how should I address Mister Fukushima?" asked Jack.

"You should refer to him as Fukushima-*san*.

"I have heard of the title *sensei* following a name in regard to a teacher," said Laura, "or someone teaching karate simply being referred to as *sensei*. I am not familiar with *San*."

"*San* is used in Japan to show respect," replied Lee. "Sort of like *Mister* or *Missus*, except with the Japanese it can also be used after either the first or last name. *San* is not gender specific. You are also right about *sensei* being used in regard to someone like a teacher or perhaps a lawyer. Actually Fukushima-*san* is a master of *kenjutsu*, a form of Japanese martial art involving sword fighting. He does not teach *kenjutsu*, so the use of *sensei* with his name would be inappropriate."

"Handy guy to have in the kitchen," suggested Jack.

"Be careful, Jack," warned Lee. "He is familiar with Western culture, but he is old school when it comes to honour and respect. What may be humour in your culture, may be considered a slap in the face here. If you insult Fukushima-*san* it would be a … fatal mistake."

They were ushered inside into an elevator and brought directly to a bedroom on the third floor. Here, two futons were laid out on bamboo mats, and there were two silk kimonos and slippers at the entranceway. An ensuite off the bedroom offered a bath and shower.

"When do we meet Fukushima-*san*?" asked Jack.

"At twelve-thirty for lunch, after you have bathed and had a chance to rest," replied Lee. "Leave your clothes by the door and they will be taken and cleaned. It will be appropriate to wear the kimonos around the building. Laura, the pale green kimono is yours. Jack, the blue."

"Our cellphones?" asked Laura.

"I am sorry. They will be provided to you later, after you meet with Fukushima-*san*. Should you need anything, there will be two attendants outside your door."

Jack smiled and gave a short bow to the squat, burly-looking attendants wearing kimonos who stood in the hallway. They politely bowed back and Jack caught a partial glimpse of tattoos rising toward the backs of their necks as they bowed. He noticed one of the men was missing his little finger, as was their chauffeur earlier. A self-mutilation he knew, made by some of the Japanese mafia, or the *yakuza* as they are called in Japan, as a symbol of their loyalty. Tattoos are generally seen as anti-social in Japan and are also strongly associated with the yakuza. *Attendants my ass. Thugs is what you mean.*

As soon as they were alone, Laura sat on one of the futons and said, "Ouch, I think a bug bit me."

"Wouldn't be surprised," said Jack, nodding in agreement. "You should get out of those clothes. Lots of bugs in Thailand. Hope you didn't bring any hitchhikers."

Laura then went to the washroom and closed the door.

"It will certainly be nice to meet Fukushima-*san*," said Jack, loud enough, ostensibly for Laura to hear. "From what I have seen, I am suitably impressed with what he has accomplished. I am looking forward to doing business with him."

"That's nice, honey, but I'd respect him a lot more if we could use a phone. I promised my sister I would call her last night. She'll be worried."

"You're right," replied Jack. "Rose isn't the type to sit back and wait. She's liable to end up calling the authorities. Hopefully this afternoon we can rectify that."

Jack walked to a window and looked out. Directly on the ground below, another "attendant" sat staring back at him on a small bench amongst a clump of cherry trees.

Jack retreated back into the room and looked around. He saw a phone jack, but no phone. *Rose will be freaked out. Sammy and his crew will be tearing Koh Samui apart looking for us. Too bad they're looking on the wrong island, let alone the wrong country.*

He heard the shower running as Laura got in, but her voice still carried, "Jack, would you be a dear and bring me my kimono? I'm all wet and don't want to come out."

Jack found Laura standing in the shower stall with her head sticking out the sliding door. She had a towel wrapped around herself and the shower head was pointed at the wall.

"Here you go, hon," he said, before flushing the toilet.

"Make it quick," he whispered.

"What are we going to do?"

"Meet the boss and get details on the shipment."

"He'll want money."

"At that point he'll have incriminated himself. I'll tell him I need to use a phone to make plans to get the money. When I do, I'll call Rose. She can trace the call back to us. I'll also demand to see the dope put on a ship before the final transfer of funds. When that happens, if we haven't already been rescued, we're bound to be in a public place. We escape the first chance we get and call the cavalry. In the meantime, we'll show respect, but we want him to respect us, as well. Maybe keep him a little off balance."

"Good idea, as long as he isn't insulted and decides to kill us."

The sound of the toilet died down and Jack said, "Here, honey, let me soap your back."

Laura slammed the door shut and smiled when Jack left the bathroom. They often used humour to relieve stress. Right now she could use a truckload of it.

Both Jack and Laura felt a little refreshed from their showers and each put on the kimonos and slippers that had been supplied.

At twelve-thirty, Lee came to their room. "Laura, you look great. Jack, you should have the left side of your kimono overlapping on top of the right side. The way you are wearing it is how it would be worn if you were dead."

I might be, soon.

Lee saw Laura with a tissue in her hand, about to shove it inside the sash holding her kimono. "And Laura, kimonos do have pockets inside the sleeves."

Jack and Laura each held an arm up and realized that the large drooping sleeves were sewn in a fashion to form pockets, easily accessible by the opposite hand.

"Everything okay?" asked Lee, as Jack rearranged his kimono.

"Fine," replied Jack, "except for the slippers."

Lee nodded when he saw Jack's heels extending well beyond the length of the slip-on slippers. "Not made for Westerners," he said. "Come, follow me. Fukushima-*san* is prepared to meet you. We will then have lunch, after which he would like to visit with you in private."

"You mean, talk business?" asked Jack.

"Yes, after he gets to know you a little."

They were brought back down to the first floor where Lee led them to a double set of doors comprised of thin, dark wooden slats forming squares of wood over rice paper. Two more attendants stood outside, but both bowed and one opened the door.

They stepped inside and Lee immediately bowed deeply to a man standing inside the room, wearing a black silk kimono. It was emblazoned with five family crests. Jack and Laura took their cue from Lee and also bowed slightly.

"Fukushima-*san*," said Lee, solemnly, while automatically avoiding direct eye contact with his master. "This is —"

"Jack and Laura," said Jack, maintaining his best poker face as he stared brazenly at the man and held his hand out. He guessed Fukushima to be in his early fifties and presumed that his straight, black, collar-length hair had been dyed. He was shorter than Jack, with the top of his head about as high as Jack's chin.

"It is okay," said Fukushima, walking forward and extending his hand. "I went to university in Los Angeles when I was a young man. I am somewhat familiar with your Western culture."

Jack accepted his firm grip and noted that Fukushima moved gracefully as he walked. From behind, Fukushima could have passed for a man in his thirties. It was his rugged face that betrayed his real age. He appeared gentle, but Jack knew appearances were deceptive. *The reality is that he finds killing to be an amusing pastime.*

"Have either of you been to an *onsen* before?" asked Fukushima.

"Never," replied Jack and Laura.

"I think you will enjoy it. After lunch, I will give you a tour and introduce you to the pleasure of soaking in the hot springs. I think you will find it relaxing. We will then talk." Fukushima glanced toward the door and said, "Oh, let me introduce you to Sayomoi-*san*, my personal attendant. Khlot-*san*, I believe, you have already met."

Jack turned to see Da Khlot, wearing a black kimono, entering the room with a strikingly beautiful Japanese woman beside him. Her black hair hung halfway to her waist and she was wearing a red silk kimono that contrasted with a pattern of branches adorned with cherry blossoms. She was in her late twenties and, unlike other Japanese women he had seen, she held her head high and had no qualms about maintaining direct eye contact. She gave the impression and air of confidence, of having been raised in a wealthy family. Her smile, Jack decided, looked contemptuous, particularly when she stared at Laura.

Introductions to Sayomi were made and Fukushima said, "Laura, I understand that you and Sayomi-*san* have something in common. Sayomi-*san* has achieved a black belt in karate and kick-boxing."

"Black belt?" said Laura, with a smile. "Sorry, my achievement in the sport was limited to yellow. Only one step up from white."

"I see," replied Fukushima. "Perhaps on some occasion Sayomi-*san* would be willing to teach you so that your level of skill will improve."

"It would be a pleasure," added Sayomi. "I have taught many older women."

Jack looked at Laura and thought, *Sayomi, you are going to pay for that one.*

Minutes later they were led to another room through another double set of sliding rice-paper doors. The room was large and spacious, with a large, rectangular black marble table in the middle, which was low to the floor. The table was prepared with six table settings placed upon bamboo-thatched mats. A variety of multicoloured silk cushions scattered around the table on the floor substituted as chairs.

Jack was glad to see that a rectangular pit under the table had been made to allow room to put in his legs so that in effect, although he was sitting on the floor it was like sitting on a bench once he put his feet under the table. The Japanese were raised since children to sit on the floor with their legs tucked under them while resting their body on their ankles. Most Westerners found the practice too uncomfortable.

They were each directed to a seat, with Jack, Laura, and Lee on one side opposite Fukushima, Sayomi, and Da Khlot on the other. Two attendants stood quietly at the door while servants appeared, first with hot towels for everyone at the table to wash their hands.

Laura was pleased to see that her setting lacked chopsticks and had been replaced by a fork and tablespoon.

"Thai style, as you prefer," winked Lee.

Laura smiled, but found the knowledge of how close they had been observed a little unnerving.

Their courses consisted of several entrees, including miso soup, rice with prawns, crab cakes, noodles, sea urchin, and tofu dishes. Later, bowls of ice cream were brought, along with a bowl of mandarin oranges, apples, and bananas for everyone to share.

A cultural tradition that Jack and Laura each discovered was that you did not fill your own glass of refreshment. To show respect for each other, it was the responsibility of the person you were dining with to fill your glass for you. They soon realized that when they had enough sake, they had to leave their glasses half full. Any less than that invited someone to replenish it.

Despite leaving the sea urchin on her plate, Laura complimented Fukushima on the fine cuisine.

"Thank you," he replied. "Dining to me is a delight that I feel should enrich one's life and not merely be something one does to survive. In Osaka, I own, amongst other things, a catering business that employs one of Japan's top chefs. I am pleased that you have enjoyed the meal."

Jack glanced around the room. Across from him, behind Fukushima, were the double set of doors and rice-paper wall, where he could see the shadows of the servants come and go as they entered and left the room. Beside and behind him, two more rice-paper walls enclosed the room, while the wall at the far end of the room was made of wood, painted a flat black. There, a potted bonsai tree was in each corner, but a focal point on the black wall was a rack containing two samurai swords, both in bamboo scabbards.

"They are my prized possessions," said Fukushima, realizing what Jack was looking at. "I will show you one of them. Please, remain seated."

Fukushima brought one samurai sword over and held it for Jack and Laura to see more closely. On the scabbard was an intricately carved design of a dragon with its tail wrapped around the scabbard while its mouth breathed fire toward the sword handle.

"Note the craftsmanship on the *tsuba*," said Fukushima, pointing to the hand guard between the handle and the blade. The flat, donut-shaped metal guard consisted of an open design of a miniature samurai soldier in combat with a dragon. "It was made during the Edo period, likely in the early 1800s, by a master swordsmith named Suishinshi Masahide."

Fukushima drew the sword from the scabbard and pointed to some Japanese symbols on the blade and proudly said, "Here is his name, chiselled into the blade."

"Exquisite," commented Jack.

"You may remove it from the scabbard and hold it, if you like," offered Fukushima.

Jack stood and slowly removed the sword while Fukushima held the scabbard. Jack noticed that both attendants, Da Khlot, and Sayomi quickly came around to his side of the table.

"It is held with both hands," said Fukushima, as Jack held the sword awkwardly, away from his body.

"I have never held a sword," said Jack, honestly.

"I'm afraid my knowledge is limited to what I have seen in Hollywood movies."

"There are several different styles of sword fighting," said Fukushima. "The type I engage in is called *kenjutsu.* Unlike other types, such as *iaijutsu,* where the sword starts in the scabbard and incorporates the speed of the draw to defend oneself, *kenjutsu* is different. After the formal bow to show respect, you retrieve your sword and start the challenge with the sword already in your hand. The emphasis is more on attacking, as well as defence."

"I'm afraid I prefer a rifle or a shotgun," said Jack.

Fukushima laughed and said, "So little honour in using a gun, but I know your Western culture reflects that unfortunate trait."

"And I understand your culture finds honour in falling on your sword," said Jack. "What is it called? Hara-kiri? We call it suicide."

"Hara-kiri is more of a slang expression," replied Fukushima. "The proper term is *seppuku.* It is called *oibara* if it is performed because of the death of one's master."

"People would kill themselves because their boss died?" asked Jack.

"Loyalty is admired and respected." Fukushima shrugged. "Either way, the ritual involves plunging the samurai sword into the left side of your abdomen and slicing through to the right side."

"Oh, gross!" said Laura.

"Imagine the degree of honour one must have to perform such a ritual," said Fukushima. "Historically, the samurai were renowned for their code of honour. The true samurai may be gone, but their legacy of honour and loyalty is very much a part of our culture."

"I also believe in honour," replied Jack. "A man's word is extremely important to me, as well, but I must confess, I do not believe I would ever have the courage, or desire, to perform such an act."

Fukushima smiled and said, "By that admission, it does show that you are honest. I believe that few Japanese people would also complete such a ritual. It would take tremendous courage."

Or a complete lack of respect for your own life ... "Please, I realize it is valuable ... also very sharp," said Jack, as he dangled the weapon with his fingers on the handle while gingerly passing it back to Fukushima.

"It is very sharp," said Fukushima, while returning to the far end of the room, where he replaced the scabbard in the rack, but held the sword with both hands. "Khot-*san*! Lee-*san*! Demonstrate for our guests!"

Da Khlot and Lee each snatched an apple from the table and threw them simultaneously at Fukushima, who severed both apples in one single swoop of the sword. His speed, agility, and hand-eye coordination was nothing short of phenomenal.

"Holy Christ," Jack muttered to himself. By Laura's open mouth and wide eyes, he knew she was also stunned by the speed and skill of what they had just witnessed.

Lee turned to Jack and Laura and said, "Now you see why I told you he is a master in *kenjutsu*."

Jack watched as a young man who had been serving them food quickly approached Fukushima and bowed with his hands held before him. Fukushima gave him the sword and the servant bowed again and left the room to clean it. Not a word had been spoken to the servant. There was little doubt Fukushima had performed the demonstration many times before.

After lunch, Fukushima said, "Come, I will show you what other pleasures you may enjoy while you are my guests."

Next to the banquet room there was a steam room, with wide, cedar planks making up the walls, floor, and ceiling, along with a cedar bench. Opposite that was another door which led to the outside and a private patio used to cool down, if one should desire.

The next room down the hall was smaller, but contained two massage tables. Fukushima turned to Sayomi and said, "You and Laura will now enjoy a massage." He looked at Jack, smiled, and added, "It is time for us to talk. Only the two of us. I have a private spa that the two of us can use. It will be more relaxing."

Jack walked with Fukushima to a change room. Fukushima gave an order in Japanese, and Da Khlot, along with two attendants, sat on a bench while Jack and Fukushima stripped completely naked. Jack followed Fukushima's lead and picked up a face cloth and followed him through another door.

Fukushima's spine was completely covered in a tattoo that resembled a spinal skeleton. Jack took a deep breath and slowly exhaled. He knew the yakuza had huge memberships. The largest yakuza clan based out of nearby Kobe was reputed to have 39,000 members. *What are we doing here? This is insane. Get some conversation from him and get the hell out!*

Jack discovered that the next door led to an outdoor pool. The pool, easily large enough to accommodate twenty people, was billowing steam. Hot water, fed from a mineral spring, poured in from an overhang close to the roof. At the opposite end of the pool, a hole covered by a grate allowed water to continue outside into a small stream, where it disappeared into the ground.

Part of the pool was protected by the overhang from the roof, but if one chose, you could also sit in the open. Tall clumps of bamboo, along with wooden screens, provided privacy.

Jack stuck his head out past a screen. He could see the well-manicured grounds. The clusters of bamboo, along with the bonsai trees, made it exotic. The hot springs reappeared a short distance away, revealing its route down the hill with a rise of steamy mist. The stream disappeared around some large boulders into the private honeymoon spa before reappearing farther down the hill and travelling on to the public resort. Normally he would have thought it beautiful. A romantic and tranquil setting, decided Jack, had it not been for the situation they were in.

He followed Fukushima into a small alcove beside the pool, containing a row of six shower heads no higher than Jack's waist. Small wooden stools were in front of each shower head. Jack followed Fukushima's example of sitting on a stool and soaping and washing his entire body before entering the pool.

"Is there a Missus Fukushima-*san*?" asked Jack.

"Yes, she lives with my two sons in Tokyo. Both of my sons are in university there." Fukushima eyed Jack carefully and said, "You and Laura do not have any children yet?"

"We both want to."

"I feel more comfortable doing business with a man who has a family. I believe him to be more stable."

Right, someone you can go after if things go wrong. "Does Lee-*san* have a family?"

"Yes, also in Tokyo."

Jack felt the hot water soothe his body. Had he been there with Natasha, it would have been wonderful. Sitting in a mineral spring with a mass murderer who was the head of an organized crime syndicate was much less appealing.

"Are you enjoying it?" asked Fukushima. "It may interest you to know that you are the first Westerner to ever step foot in my private spa."

"I would enjoy it more," replied Jack, "if business was out of the way. I have not had access to any communication for over twenty-four hours. There are people who will be concerned, not to mention financial arrangements that need to be made."

"As far as financial arrangements go, I am a patient man and would expect that such arrangements may take a week or so. The product you are purchasing will be available for you to view within two days. It will be loaded on a ship in Kobe, not far from here. Naturally, you and Laura will be my guests until such time as I have received the first payment."

"Viewing a ton of heroin makes me nervous," replied Jack. "I would hate to end up in a Japanese prison, or any prison, for that matter."

"I would never dishonour myself with your arrest if I was not absolutely certain," replied Fukushima. "I guarantee your safety. You have my word on that, although I understand that you come from a culture where people lack honour. Should you not want to view the product yourself, you may choose a representative who will be taken to see it. However, I must stress that such a representative would be blindfolded coming and going from where the product is located. We may trust each other, but it is more difficult to always trust one's employees."

"Understandable," replied Jack, "but I must phone some people to start the process."

"Before you go to bed tonight, such services will be returned to you. Tomorrow, if you and Laura would like to go shopping, or perhaps visit the popular nearby tourist destination of Kyoto, I will gladly arrange for a limousine and driver to take you."

"Great, so why not return my phone now?" asked Jack.

Fukushima paused, staring at Jack intently for a moment before saying, "On that subject, let me ask you a question. What would you do if you discovered that an employee had been stealing money from you, or perhaps your customers? How would that be handled in your Western culture?"

"If it was my business," said Jack, assuming the role of the Irish mobster, "I suspect I would handle it the same way as you." He smiled, using his hand to make a slashing gesture across his throat.

"Exactly," replied Fukushima. "I spoke to Mister Sato after he interviewed you in Koh Samui. I understand that you are personally familiar with performing such a task."

Jack shrugged, acting indifferent.

"There is a final test I wish you to perform," said Fukushima.

"Another test! I have already passed the lie detector. What more could you possibly ask?"

Anger appeared on Fukushima's face. He was not used to being spoken to so harshly. "For you it will not be difficult," he said sternly. "I have an employee who works for me at my catering company in Osaka. He has been stealing from us."

Despite the heat from the mineral springs, Jack felt goosebumps spread across his flesh.

"After work he will be put in a van and brought here. He will arrive at nine o'clock tonight. You will kill him."

Jack felt stunned as his mind raced, trying to figure out how to respond. "Why should I kill him?" he finally asked.

"You must understand," said Fukushima, "that we know little about you. Initial inquiries made in Montreal resulted in a severe beating. Further, more discreet inquiries were made. Rumours exist of the ... shall we say, *magnitude* of your success in business and the close ties you have to families in New York. There are many rumours. Some say you are no longer active. Others say you are still living in Montreal."

Jack smiled and said, "Good, I prefer my enemies to never know exactly where I am."

"I understand that," replied Fukushima, "although you must have few enemies."

"Why would you say that?" asked Jack.

"You do not have a bodyguard. Certainly," he smiled, "you have Laura. I also have Sayomi-*san*, but I also ensure I have someone like Khlot-*san* nearby. His talents are extraordinary."

"How so?"

"He was taken in by the Khmer Rouge as a child. He is well experienced and is an expert with a knife. He knows a spot on the back of a person's neck where he can sever the spinal cord in one thrust. Death for some of his victims can be a long time in coming. Now I usually find a more expedient need for his services."

"Such as?"

"He is useful to have around in some countries where it is difficult to carry guns."

"I see," replied Jack.

"I know from your polygraph test that you are personally experienced in these matters, but your personal experience has not become our personal experience."

"After passing the lie detector, I must say, I feel insulted that you still do not trust me," said Jack. "I am a Westerner, but I assure you, I am a man of honour."

"It is not because you are Caucasian that you must do this." Fukushima paused to wipe his eyes with a facecloth before continuing. "I had Mister Lee perform the same task for me not long ago in your country.

There it took place in a park. Here, the sauna room will suffice. It is private and the wooden flooring is easily replaced if necessary."

"And who did Mister Lee kill?" asked Jack.

Fukushima waved his hand as if it was insignificant and said, "It was nobody."

Jack heard himself inhale sharply at Fukushima's choice of word in describing Melvin.

"It is the act of murder that is important to display loyalty," continued Fukushima, "not who." He smiled and added, "Mister Lee is not experienced in such tasks. He worried so much about getting blood on his clothes that he placed a plastic bag over the man to shield himself. He should have worried more about his aim. I trust for you that aim will not be a problem."

So that is why Melvin was murdered, thought Jack. *Destroy a human life as a display of loyalty. Your only concern is to not soil your clothes from the blood.* He stared sullenly at Fukushima. *I want so bad to wrap my hands around your throat. Press my thumbs into your windpipe and hold you under —*

"Is there a problem?" asked Fukushima suspiciously.

Jack sighed and said, "If Mister Lee is so inexperienced in such matters, I am surprised that he did not refuse."

Fukushima laughed and said, "He would never refuse anything I ask. If someone did that, then it would be their body found in a park."

37

"It is about three-thirty," said Fukushima, getting out of the pool. "Dinner will be at seven. Would you like to enjoy a massage? There is plenty of time."

"Actually," replied Jack. "I would prefer to enjoy the hot mineral waters with Laura in private."

"I understand," smiled Fukushima. "Such beauty should be enjoyed. I will send for her. If you decide there is anything either of you would like, such as chilled wine or a beverage, simply call one of the attendants waiting in the next room."

The minutes ticked by as Jack sat alone, waiting for Laura to arrive. He knew they had to escape, but how? He climbed out of the pool and peered past a wooden screen toward the resort below. *Choke the guards unconscious, steal their clothes, and do a dash down the hill? We would never make it. Even if we did, they would find us within a minute.*

Then he heard it. Voices of a young couple carried softly up the hill. "Akiyo!" said the man, "I'll get you for that!" It was followed by the sound of splashing and laughing. Whoever the man was, he spoke again, but in Japanese. *Did I really hear what I think I did?*

"Jack?" said Laura, peeking out the door behind him as he stood naked, with his back toward her. "You, uh, want me to join you?"

Jack turned his head quickly and saw Laura, with Sayomi looking over her shoulder.

"Yes, honey. It's beautiful in here," he added, getting back into the pool as Laura found a sudden need to turn her head and wipe her eye with a finger. Sayomi's stare indicated she was not shy about her curiosity.

"I thought it would be romantic, just the two of us," added Jack.

"I'll wait with Khlot," said Sayomi. "But if you are too long, I will join you."

Moments later, Laura slowly stuck her head out the door again and saw Jack standing in the pool with his back toward her as he stared at the wooden screen. He waited until he heard her in the pool before turning around.

"I don't happen to be in the mood for romance," she whispered tersely.

"This is one place we can talk," whispered Jack, "without having to worry that the room is bugged." He proceeded to speak quickly, telling her what Fukushima had said, pausing once and putting his finger to his lips to silence Laura when he heard the faint sound of laughter from the young couple down below.

"We need to escape!" said Laura.

"The couple we heard laughing from down at the resort," said Jack, indicating the direction with his thumb. "I'm positive the guy spoke English a moment ago."

"You sure?"

"I think so. I was trying to listen when you first arrived," said Jack, climbing back out of the pool.

"You look at me and I'll tell Natasha," said Laura, climbing out with him.

They both peered out from behind the screen and heard the murmur of voices again.

"It's not from the resort," said Laura. "It's the honeymoon spa, halfway up the hill."

Jack saw two of Fukushima's thugs between them and the spa. One man was still sitting on the bench under the window of Jack and Laura's bedroom while the other was strolling around.

"I have to sneak down there," said Jack. "If it's some tourist and he's English, it may be our only hope."

"And if it's someone who works for Fukushima, we're dead," replied Laura.

"We will be, anyway. I don't see any other choice."

"You think you can streak down there without being seen? Good luck, not to mention the screaming when some naked man busts in on a couple on their honeymoon. Or do you figure we should both go and slap sleeper holds on them if they start to yell?" she added, dubiously.

"I think I can make it by crouching low or crawl-ing through the stream bed," said Jack. "Your problem will be to make sure Sayomi or Da Khlot don't walk in and find me gone."

"Oh, man. We could be risking other people's lives."

"It's our only hope," said Jack, "and neither guard is paying much attention. They hardly expect us to walk naked down to the resort. "If the guy is English, it shouldn't be a problem to convince him to go back to his room and make a phone call for us. The bad guys won't know anything is up until the cavalry charges in. It's a calculated risk, but one I think we should take."

Laura nodded silently.

Jack crouched as he ran toward the small stream, diving on his belly like a baseball player coming into home plate as he skidded the remaining distance into the shallow trench etched out by the water.

It didn't take him long to make his way to the structure containing the exclusive spa. On the other side of a large boulder he could hear the couple talking softly to each other in Japanese.

"Hello?" said Jack. He heard the startled whisper of the young woman in Japanese.

"Hello," responded the young man. "I believe we still have fifteen minutes booked on our time."

"I'm not here for the spa," replied Jack. "I need your help. Where are you from?"

"We're from Osaka."

"You sound English?"

"I'm Canadian, but my wife and I live in Osaka."

"Thank Christ," mumbled Jack. "I'm also Canadian. My name is Jack Taggart. I'm an undercover Mountie.

Is it okay if I come around this boulder and talk to you? It is literally a matter of life and death and I only have a couple of minutes. By the way, I'm also naked."

Moments later, Jack was invited to come closer and he saw a young couple comprised of a Caucasian man and Japanese woman. The woman was wearing a kimono and crouched down beside the stream near where the man was sitting up to his neck in water.

He introduced himself as Mike and his wife as Akiyo.

Jack quickly told them as many details as he figured they needed to know. "What I need," said Jack, "is for you to call my boss in Canada and tell her exactly where we are and get the Japanese police to rescue us. Her name is Rose Wood. Our bedroom is on the second floor down from the top on the far side of the building up there," said Jack, pointing in the direction of Fukushima's mansion concealed behind some wooden screens. "Describe its location to her so she can pass it on to the Japanese police.

"Then we can see your room from ours," said Mike. "We look out over the back of the resort."

"I know my boss's phone number," said Jack. "Do you think you could memorize it and phone her for me?"

"I got my degree in computer software engineering," replied Mike. "Believe me, I'm good with numbers."

"Perhaps this would be of assistance," said Akiyo, slipping her hand inside the sleeve of her kimono.

Jack gave her the biggest smile he believed he had ever given anyone in his life. Akiyo was an exceptionally beautiful woman, but that was not the reason her image would remain etched in his memory forever. It was the sweet look of genuine concern on her face as she held her arms outstretched with her palms up. In her upturned hands she was offering a cellphone.

Moments later, with Mike's assistance, Jack dialled the numbers necessary to make a long-distance call and connect with Rose.

"Yes, we're still above ground," said Jack, as soon as she answered, "but we won't be for long if you don't let me explain."

Jack spoke rapidly, pointing out the urgent necessity to have backup immediately. "Rose, the couple who are helping me, Mike and Akiyo, their room faces ours. Perhaps the police could use it for an observation post?"

Mike nodded in agreement.

"If the police hold off on rescuing us until a van from the catering company shows up with a hostage," said Jack, "it should provide good evidence to convict Fukushima. At the moment, all we have is my word against his."

"What if something goes wrong before then?" asked Rose.

"We're dead if the police aren't here," replied Jack. "But if they are, tell them to hang a towel outside Mike and Akiyo's window to let us know. If something is going wrong, I'll make an excuse to go back to our room and do likewise as a sign we need help. Other than that, if they hear the sound of breaking glass or see someone flying out a window, take it as a sign we need help."

"You can keep the phone," said Mike.

"I heard that," said Rose, "but it still sounds damned risky to me!"

"The police should be here by seven," said Jack. "That gives us two hours before the van with the hostage arrives. We need more evidence and the hostage should provide that. As far as risk goes, we're operators. That's what we do. We're already in hot water, so to speak, we should be able to handle another couple of hours."

Rose reluctantly agreed and said she would immediately contact the RCMP Liaison Officer in Tokyo.

"Has Natasha been alerted that we're missing?" asked Jack. "Or Laura's —"

"No."

Jack breathed a sigh of relief and replied, "Good. Tomorrow is Sunday. She's expecting me to call. If somehow I can't, uh, you know, get to a phone, please tell her I love her."

Rose sighed and said, "You damn well better make sure you call her yourself. Right now I have something more urgent I need to know. Exactly where the hell are you?"

Jack handed the phone to Mike to explain.

Minutes later, Jack made it back to where Laura was waiting and carrying on a one-sided conversation. He glanced over his shoulder as he entered and saw Mike and Akiyo walking into the resort below.

"So anyway," said Laura, "you sit there ignoring me like you haven't heard a word I said. Don't you have anything to say?"

Jack grinned and held the cellphone in his hand, before using the face cloth to conceal it. "I guess I can say I love you," he said.

"Oh, baby," replied Laura, "I love you, too."

It was quarter to seven when Jack and Laura once more entered their bedroom washroom and used the noise of the shower and the toilet to cover the sound as Jack turned on the cellphone and called Rose.

"The LO in Tokyo says Fukushima heads one of the biggest yakuza families in Japan," said Rose. "He has over fifteen thousand guys working for him. The Japanese police are ecstatic. They can't believe a foreigner could penetrate Fukushima to this level."

"Being a foreigner is probably why we did," said Jack.

"They've got a team who should be in the observation post any minute. They've also spotted the catering van coming in your direction and are doing a loose surveillance of it. Still about two hours away. If you can, they would like you both to make an excuse and go to your room around eight-thirty. They'll rush the place ten minutes later. I can give you a direct number."

"I feel safer going through you. You're on redial and I know it works. English is your native tongue. If I call, I may have to speak in code."

It was five minutes to seven and Jack and Laura knew they had to go downstairs for dinner. They were turning from their window when another window opened on the resort below and a towel was draped over the windowsill.

Jack and Laura smiled at each other. *Help has arrived! We're going to be okay!*

The next fifteen minutes would prove them dead wrong.

38

Jack and Laura met Fukushima, Da Khlot, Sayomi, and Lee as they entered the banquet room. Everyone bowed toward each other before taking the same seating arrangement they had previously, with Lee, Laura, and Jack on one side and Da Khlot, Sayomi, and Fukushima on the other. The only difference, Jack noted, was that while all the rest were dressed in kimonos, Da Khlot wore an expensive tailored suit.

Same as before, two attendants stood by the door while servants brought in the first course, a soup consisting of chicken broth, mushrooms, bamboo shoots, celery, and parsley.

Considering that someone was to be murdered in two hours, Jack thought Fukushima seemed rather cheery, making light conversation about the weather in Canada and the quantity of available golf courses.

Fukushima's behaviour abruptly changed after he

set his porcelain soup spoon down and answered his cellphone. He only uttered one or two words as he listened.

"Excuse me," he said, looking at Jack and Laura when he hung up. "Lee-*san*, Khlot-*san*, come with me. A business matter needs to be addressed. It will only take a minute. Please, continue to enjoy your soup."

Fukushima uttered a command in Japanese and the two attendants followed the trio out the door. Jack could see the men's shadows on the rice-paper doors as they stood whispering in the hallway. The shadow of an attendant quickly disappeared down the hall, only to return moments later, in the company of others.

Jack smiled politely at Sayomi while nudging Laura with his knee under the table. He felt her nudge back. Something was wrong and they both knew it.

If they had any doubts that it involved the two of them, they were were quashed when the doors slid open again. The trio returned with six attendants. Fukushima barked an order at the servants and they quickly disappeared from sight.

"I am afraid that dinner must be interrupted," said Fukushima, briskly walking to the far end of the room and removing a samurai sword from the scabbard.

Da Khlot's face held his usual impassive look as he bent over and whispered in Sayomi's ear. She looked startled, quickly glancing at Jack and Laura as she scrambled to her feet. Lee stood to one side, his head bowed toward the floor as his body trembled.

"That is most unfortunate," said Jack. "The soup is excellent. Is there a problem?"

"No problem," replied Fukushima. "Simply an alteration in plans. Your task that you were to perform at nine o'clock will be performed now."

"The, uh, person from Osaka is here already?" asked Jack.

"No," replied Fukushima. "I have selected some-one else."

"I see," replied Jack. "Then if you will excuse me for a moment, I need to go back to my room and use the washroom. I shall return in a moment," he said, getting to his feet.

"You will not be going anywhere!" said Fukushima, allowing his rage to show.

Jack swallowed. *They know. It is Laura and I who are to be executed!* "There obviously appears to be a problem," said Jack, pretending to sound surprised. "Is there something we should discuss?" he added, with genuine concern.

"You do not know what that problem is?" said Fukushima sarcastically.

"No, I don't," said Jack, wanting an opportunity to deny any accusations.

"Perhaps you don't," replied Fukushima, as a wicked smile appeared on his face. "The problem is with Lee!" he said, pointing the end of the samurai sword in Lee's direction.

"With ... Lee?" said Jack, feeling both astounded and briefly relieved. Fukushima was no longer using the polite version of *san* at the end of Lee's name.

A glance at Lee showed a face with bulging dark eyes contrasting with a face that was pasty white.

"Yes," replied Fukushima. "You will kill him immediately," he said menacingly.

Jack glanced at Lee, who now remained bowed as his body shook.

"But why Lee?" asked Jack. "Surely you don't —"

"You will not ask me questions," said Fukushima. "If Lee is not dead within one minute, you and Laura will be."

Jack heard Laura's gasp as they both glanced around the room in panic. All six attendants and Da Khlot withdrew pistols and quietly started fixing silencers to the ends.

"I do not understand," said Jack, "but it is obvious that you have your reasons. If someone would be so kind as to lend me their pistol, I will take Lee next door to the sauna room and carry out your request. It would be rude and lack dignity to conduct such an action in a place where people eat, not to mention in the presence of two ladies."

"You really believe that I would have my men hand you a loaded pistol?" said Fukushima angrily.

"I am not about to hack at the poor man with a sword," replied Jack. "One bullet is all I need. Surely, with the army you have present, that would not make you afraid?"

"So you would do that?" said Fukushima, with a hint of disgust in his voice.

"It would not be the first time I have had to perform such an act to gain someone's trust," replied Jack. "Obviously you have heard something that has caused you not to trust us. Perhaps this act will restore that trust? With my people, we refer to it as the Sophie Solution," he added with a sideways glance at Laura.

"I have never heard of that," replied Fukushima, curiously.

"Simply a test of loyalty," said Jack. "What you have others perform for you. All I ask is that I carry out the task next door. We have been respectful of your culture, now I simply ask that you be respectful of mine. Your men may check the body immediately after, but my belief is that his body should be left in solitude for an hour to allow his spirit to leave peacefully."

"You believe in spirits?" asked Fukushima skeptically.

"You are asking me to commit murder— is it such a difficult request to grant in return?"

Moments later, Jack found himself in the sauna room with Lee kneeling on the floor in front of him. Jack held a pistol in his hand with one single round. He crouched over Lee from behind, holding the back of his collar with one hand and pointing the pistol at the back of his head with the other. Da Klot and four attendants stood a short distance behind him, all pointing their pistols at Jack, with the exception of one attendant whose pistol had be given to Jack.

Jack whispered in Lee's ear and said, "I'm not going to kill you. Pretend you are dead and when you get the chance, slip out through the patio door. Police are watching from a room at the resort down below. Run for help and scream when you reach the resort."

"No!" gasped Lee in panic.

"Son of a bitch," muttered Jack, slipping an arm around Lee's throat so his next attempt to speak resulted in a gurgle. Jack used his other arm in a pincer move to cut the flow of blood in Lee's carotid artery. "Trust me," Jack whispered. He felt the body slump and knew he would have less than a minute before Lee awoke.

"What are you doing?" asked Da Khlot, moving closer.

Jack spun Lee around, slamming him down on the floor, while sitting on his chest. His body blocked the view of Lee's upper torso as he smashed his nose with the butt of the pistol before quickly firing a round into the crack made by two adjoining cedar planks on the floor. As he got up, he smeared his hand across Lee's bloody face.

The attendant who had provided Jack with the pistol approached and looked down at Lee, before speaking in Japanese.

"He says you killed him," said Da Khlot, bluntly. "Are you finished?"

"Of course," replied Jack. "Shall we go back and continue our dinner now?"

Jack, followed by Da Khlot and the others, entered the banquet room where one attendant bowed toward Fukushima and spoke in Japanese.

Fukushima looked at Jack in surprise and said, "You actually committed murder! You really would do anything to survive," he continued, more to himself than to Jack. "I thought you were a man of honour and would stick to your values."

Da Khlot pointed at Jack and spoke in Japanese. Fukushima smiled and nodded his head knowingly.

"What did he say?" demanded Jack.

"He said that you only pretended to kill him by using a — how did he describe it? — yes, a sleeper strangulation hold on him."

"Ridiculous!" replied Jack, realizing in the pit of his stomach that his little charade had not fooled Da Khlot in the least. His mind raced … *Lee was left alone, maybe he did escape to seek help.* He knew Fukushima would have realized that, yet had not countered with any orders to his men. Jack decided to ask. Anything to stall for time. "If what Da Khlot said was really true, why would everyone leave Lee alone where he could escape? I don't understand —-"

"Escape?" said Fukushima. "I think not —"

The sound of Lee's cry from the other room interrupted the conversation. Seconds later, he burst into the room, talking rapidly in Japanese to Fukushima while keeping his head bowed.

"Now do you understand?" asked Fukushima, a bemused smile played upon his lips as he looked at Jack. "Lee-*san* is a man with honour," he added, once more pointing the tip of his samurai sword in Lee's direction.

"Lee," said Jack quietly. "Why didn't you run?"

Lee did not answer.

Fukushima said, "He honours his family name. Is that not right, Lee-*san*?"

Lee nodded, but his eyes remained fixed on the floor.

"Honour," said Fukushima, "is something that you, Corporal Jack Taggart and Constable Laura Secord, know little about."

Both Jack and Laura stared blankly back at Fukushima. *It's over. He even knows our names.*

"Yes, I know," said Fukushima. "I do have my own sources. I am told that the Japanese police are at the resort. It may interest you to know that they will also detain the van when it arrives, but it will do them no good. The man who is being delivered believes it is to bring a special food order. The police will find nothing to prove anything is wrong."

"You kill us and they'll have plenty of evidence," said Jack.

"Evidence such as this?" asked Fukushima, stepping forward and swinging the samurai sword.

Laura put her hand to her mouth and gasped, emitting a sorrowful cry as Lee's severed head bounced off the marble table and rolled on the floor. His body fell over in a clump with the heart still beating a gusher of blood out through the neck.

She looked up at Fukushima in a daze as he raised the sword over her head.

I'm next.

39

"You are a coward!" screamed Jack. "You have no honour!"

"It is unfortunate that you have to die," said Fukushima, looking down at Laura while ignoring Jack. "You are a pretty lady."

"You will go to jail for this," she replied bitterly.

Fukushima smiled. "No, you do not understand. I have eight witnesses to say Corporal Taggart went berserk and killed you. It was only after the poor unfortunate Mister Lee tried to intervene and was also killed by Corporal Taggart that one of my men shot him."

"Is that your way out?" yelled Jack. "You call that honour, killing a defenceless man?" he said, pointing at Lee's decapitated body. "You would even attack a defenceless woman? Is this the samurai code of honour you profess to admire? You are truly the biggest coward I have ever seen," he said, spitting in Fukushima's direction. "If I had a sword you would turn and run like a little boy!"

The tendons in Fukushima's neck grew taut and his face reddened. "You?" he shouted. "You dare to challenge me to fight to the death with these?" he added, brandishing the sword. "You are a fool!"

"Perhaps, but unlike you, I am not a coward. If I die, it will be with honour."

Fukushima walked quickly over to Jack and said, "You will die. The both of you."

Jack saw Fukushima's arm twitch as he thrust out the samurai sword. He jerked his head back, but not fast enough. Fukushima sliced the end of Jack's nostril faster than his reflexes could react.

"If I had wanted to take your entire nose off, I would have," said Fukushima, sneering at Jack, who stood with blood running down across his lips and dripping off his chin.

"As I said," replied Jack defiantly. "You are very brave against an unarmed man."

"You know you could not possibly win," said Fukushima. "If you continue to insult me like this, I might accept your challenge."

"Are you sure you have the guts for that?"

Fukushima's red face deepened to a purplish hue and he replied, "I will grant you your dying wish. Your death will be slow as I remove your less vital body parts one at a time. You saw the demonstration I did with the apples."

"If I were an apple I would be truly afraid," replied Jack. "It is a little different when you fight man to man. Of course, that is presuming you are a man."

"Go ahead!" Fukushima yelled. "Get the other sword."

"Should you die," said Jack. "I would expect that your men would not kill us. That we would be free to go. It would be the honourable thing to do."

Fukushima unexpectedly laughed and said, "I will tell my men that if you win the challenge, you are their new boss."

Jack walked over to where Laura sat and said, "I know you *disagree*, but we will show them that we have honour. We may die, but they will never forget the courage we displayed."

Laura swallowed. *This is insane ... What is he trying to tell me? To disagree?* "Committing suicide is not courageous," she said, with uncertainty. "You are wrong to do this."

"You do not speak to me in such a manner!" said Jack, sounding angry. "You will show respect! If I lose, you will show respect to Fukushima-*san*!" he added, while reaching across the table and picking up a bottle of sake. "The Japanese think we have no honour? We will prove them wrong. Fukushima-*san* and I will bow to each other with respect. We will then retrieve our swords and fight to the death. If I die, it will be with honour. At that time —"

"We will die," said Laura. She sounded matter-of-fact. It was not a plea for help. It was simply a statement of what she believed.

"Shut up and lower your face when I talk," ordered Jack harshly.

Laura lowered her eyes as Jack raised the sake bottle high over her head. He looked around the room at everyone's faces and shook the bottle to emphasize his point, before looking at Laura and saying, "When the battle is over, you will show respect and honour by pouring the winner a drink!"

Laura stared quietly down at the table. She heard Jack's words, but only now became aware of what Jack would try to do. She slowly lifted her eyes toward Jack and asked. "After, do you want me to *take them all out* for dinner, too?"

Jack's eyes revealed his thoughts to Laura. *She understands … I wish I could hug her.* Instead, he glared and said, "I do not believe it possible under the circumstances, but you could extend the invitation. It would show class. Now stand up! What is important is that you honour and obey my command."

"Sounds like a wedding vow," muttered Laura, slowly getting to her feet. "Except you forgot the bit about *until death do us part*. Or did you?"

Jack solemnly handed Laura the bottle before straightening his kimono and walking out to the middle of the room. Fukushima uttered a command in Japanese and one of the attendants retrieved the other samurai sword from its scabbard and held it with both palms facing up and his arms extended. Fukushima passed his sword to another attendant, who held it in the same fashion.

Fukushima paused to glare at Jack before walking briskly to the centre of the room to stand face to face.

"You have honour," conceded Fukushima, "but

your barbarian tongue will also be taught respect before I let you die."

Jack stared back in silence before bowing deeply, as did Fukushima.

A quick upward thrust of Jack's hand and a flash of metal alerted everyone that something was amiss. It takes two seconds for the body to respond to a given stimulus. By then, Fukushima's terrified scream filled the room, as Jack, using a dinner fork with both outer prongs bent down, pierced his eye socket with the two inner prongs, popping his eyeball out like a plump grape.

Fukushima tried to leap back, but Jack's other hand held the back of his head as he rotated the fork, before moving and wrapping his arm around Fukushima's throat from behind, while his other hand positioned the bloody fork close to Fukushima's other eye.

Laura was the first to react. She had seen Jack take her fork a moment before while the others were looking at the bottle of sake being waved above her head. She now turned and smashed the end of the bottle on the table.

Sayomi's reflexes responded at this moment, jumping and throwing a side-kick aimed at Jack's temple. Her mind was focused, blocking out the sound of chaos around her as her body moved to deliver the fatal blow.

It was not until the broken end of a sake bottle rammed deep, twisting into her face that Sayomi's brain connected the reason why Laura smashed the bottle when Fukushima first screamed.

Sayomi's kick flailed in the air as she felt Laura's arm around her throat from behind as they fell to the floor. Laura quickly rolled over on her back, using Sayomi's body on top of her for cover.

Sayomi struggled and felt the sharp edges of the broken bottle on her mouth and nose. She tried to grab at the bottle with her fingers but Laura twisted it deeper into her already shredded lips and broken teeth.

"Don't try it, karate girl," warned Laura. "Or this older woman will show you something you don't want to learn."

Da Khlot, along with the others, pointed their guns toward Jack, who was hunched low over Fukushima. Sayomi was not their concern.

"Back off!" yelled Jack, over Fukushima's screaming, "Or I pop his other eye and ram this fork through his brain!"

Fukushima raised his hand to cup his eyeball dangling from his eye socket.

"Put your hand down," warned Jack, "or I'll shish kabob your eyeball and your brain!"

Fukushima lowered his hand and Da Khlot stared at the eyeball dangling and swaying across Fukushima's cheek. He saw the desperate and determined look on Jack's face as their eyes met and Jack started to twist the fork into the corner of Fukushima's remaining eye.

"Okay, stop," yelled Da Khlot, before turning to the others and shouting a command in Japanese. Some of the men hesitantly lowered their guns, while two didn't. Da Khlot yelled again and the remaining two immediately obeyed.

"He won't die from what I've done," said Jack.

"I know that," replied Da Khlot in a monotone voice. "Let him go and it will be easier on you."

"Like hell I will!" yelled Jack. "All of you get the fuck out of here! Now! Close the door behind you!"

Da Khlot shook his head so Jack put more pressure on Fukushima's eye.

"Do what he says!" spluttered Fukushima.

The men quickly filed out of the room as the sound of Sayomi's crying and babbling became louder.

"Let her go, too, Laura," said Jack.

Sayomi ran for the door with her bloody hands covering her face.

"Remember," yelled Laura, "youth, vitality, and speed are no match for wisdom, experience, and treachery!"

Jack, in shock, stared briefly at Laura. *Make sure I never piss a woman off about her age.*

As soon as the three of them were alone, Jack told Laura to get his phone and call for help.

Laura connected with Rose and yelled, "Help — Jack, behind you!"

Jack spun around and saw he had moved dangerously close to the back wall. Da Khlot's shadow faded from view on the other side as Jack quickly backed toward the centre of the room.

"Rose, we need help," yelled Laura. "Tell them we're in the banquet room. Main level."

"Leave the phone on, put it on the table, and grab a sword," said Jack. "Crouch down close to the door. If someone comes in, do what you can to take them down and grab their gun."

"You are a barbarian," sputtered Fukushima. "You have no honour."

"Guess you're right," replied Jack.

"You will die!" seethed Fukushima, as his pain was transgressed by rage. "The both of you will die."

"We all will someday," replied Jack. "You first, I bet."

"You are Canadian police officers," said Fukushima. "You should not even be here."

"You had Lee murder a Canadian citizen," replied Jack, "who, for your information, was an honourable man. Gives us plenty of reason."

"You are here because of him?" replied Fukushima in disbelief. "He was nobody! Why does it matter about him?"

"Nobody?" said Jack harshly. "Do not use that word! He was somebody! Somebody's son. He was a friend of my wife and was a much better human being than you could ever —-"

The sound of a police siren pierced the air from down the hill, bringing an epiphany of shouts and yelling from outside the banquet room. Shadows from a group of men appeared through the rice-paper walls and doors on the opposite side of the room from where Jack stood hunched over Fukushima.

Da Khlot crouched and waited behind the wall separating him by slightly over an arm's length from where Jack held Fukushima inside the room. He used his cellphone to whisper an order to his men.

Jack saw the doors slide open a crack and automatically reefed Fukushima backward when he saw a glimpse of a pistol as a man peeked through. Laura crouched to one side, out of sight, holding the samurai sword at the ready.

"Close it!" screamed Jack. "Or fuck-you-shima dies!"

Fukushima felt the two prongs from the fork on the outer corner of his eye socket slide over the last bump of bone as it began to travel inside his eye socket. His command screamed in Japanese caused the doors to slide shut again.

Da Khlot caught a glimmer of Jack's larger figure draped over Fukushima, but it faded from view again. He could hear the words clearly through the walls as the men argued.

"I want you to know something, Jack Taggart," said Fukushima. "I gave the command to my men. Whoever fills the honour of killing you will be greatly rewarded. If you do not have the honour to die tonight, you should know that whatever family you have — mother, father, wife, or children — they will be found and take your place."

"Is that why Lee was so loyal?" asked Jack. "Is that what you call honour and loyalty? You pompous ass! You are not only a disgrace to the Japanese people; you are a disgrace to the human race."

"Who are you to say that?" replied Fukushima. "A lowly policeman. A servant for the people. You are nobody."

"I told you not to use that word," said Jack, angrily.

Da Khlot knew that a bullet in Jack may penetrate through to Fukushima, but he had no such worry about the knife he held in his hand. The only worry was the element of surprise. If Jack would move closer, it would be easy to stab through the rice-paper wall and penetrate the top of the spinal cord, paralyzing Jack before he could react and plunge the fork deep into his master's brain.

If that opportunity presented itself, he would bust through the wall simultaneously while carrying out the second penetration, plunging the knife into the side of Jack's neck. He would grab his falling body by the hair with one hand and use his other hand to slash through to the front of Jack's throat, severing his jugular in an outward motion from behind. Death would be unavoidable and would take place within a few gurgling seconds as he lay on the floor while his brain tried to comprehend.

When the others opened the doors for a peek, Da Khlot almost had that chance. If his men yelled and rattled the doors again, it might give him the opportunity. The police vocally announced their arrival into the main entrance of the building. He had little time.

Da Khlot whispered once more into his cellphone before putting it down. Seconds later, the walls shook from hands slapping and banging on the walls and doors on the far side of the room. Sounds and vibrations made by men running and commands being screamed by the police added to the din.

Da Khlot saw his chance when Jack's towering shadow came into view, brushing his back against the wall in front of him. He did not give Jack the opportunity to move away. He lunged forward, his knife making a crisp sound as the tip sliced through the rice paper and deep into Jack's neck.

Da Khot heard the sound of the vertebrae as he twisted the knife before withdrawing it. The head nodded and rolled to one side and the body went limp as Da Khlot smashed through the wall, grabbing Jack by the hair while stabbing deep into the side of his neck and slashing outwards, severing the jugular. His momentum caused all three men to fall to the floor.

Screaming from across the room announced the arrival of a squad of police officers. Da Khlot looked at Jack's face ... awash in blood. It was the first time Da Khlot had truly smiled since he was eleven years old.

He obeyed the police command to drop his knife and stand with his hands in the air. He was not concerned. *The Shaman will look after me. Everything would be okay. He is, after all, The Shaman.*

It was not until Jack stood up that Da Khlot stepped back in horror. He stared down at The Shaman, who lay gasping and gurgling as his severed jugular sprayed blood onto Da Khlot's pant legs.

Da Khlot's brain tried to unscramble the unfathomable. *It ... it is not possible! The Westerner's shadow ... I saw it.* Da Khlot trembled as he stared down at his master, whose twitching lips and one bulging eye expressed a silent terror as he died.

40

It was late the following Friday afternoon when Rose was summoned to Assistant Commissioner Isaac's office. He waited until she sat comfortably in the chair in front of his desk before asking, "How are Corporal Taggart and Constable Secord doing?"

"Remarkably well, sir, considering the trauma they both went through," replied Rose. "They took the week off, but both said they would be in on Monday. It seems a little premature to me. Jack also has to schedule some appointments with a cosmetic surgeon in regard to a slice taken out of his nostril."

"Have they seen the Force psychologist yet?"

"Scheduled for Monday afternoon."

"He may decide that they're not ready to return to duty yet."

Rose smiled to herself and said, "I suspect he will

decide whatever Jack wants him to decide. Laura, too, quite likely."

"Meaning?"

Rose shrugged and said, "Meaning they're both good operators. They're good at controlling situations and people to produce the results they want."

Isaac nodded in agreement and said, "What you said does support a theory I have about what happened leading up to Fukushima's murder."

"A theory?" replied Rose. "I have read the report our LO sent from the Japanese police. It seemed pretty thorough to me. One of Fukushima's bodyguards tried to kill Jack, but instead stabbed his boss to death."

"Yes, and when the bodyguard made that mistake, Corporal Taggart was present."

"Jack was not to blame! His presence was just coincidental to the mistake the bodyguard made."

"Coincidental? Coincidence? Where have I heard those words before?"

"Sir, it *was* a coincidence. The bodyguard has already confessed to the Japanese police."

"I am aware of that," replied Isaac. "Several Japanese police officers actually witnessed the murder as they entered the room. Although they were so appalled and shocked at seeing Lee's severed head and body, along with Fukushima getting his throat slashed, that I understand they were in a state of confusion as to exactly what was taking place and by who."

"They did see it, though," replied Rose. "There was no doubt that the bodyguard murdered Fukushima.

He confessed to everything, including giving a detailed account of the murder here."

"The murder of the homeless person in the park," said Isaac, nodding his head.

"Sir, his name was Melvin Montgomery," noted Rose.

Isaac looked curiously at Rose and asked, "Sounds like you have a personal interest?"

"No," replied Rose. "It just sounds more decent giving him a name." *God, I'm glad Jack isn't here. He'd never let me forget it.*

"I agree," replied Isaac. "In any event, the Japanese police found a video of Melvin Montgomery's murder in a safe in one of Fukushima's estates in Tokyo. It clearly shows Lee as the murderer. They also found a host of other files showing who was being bribed around the world and for how much. It included one of their higher-ranking police officers. They were able to prove it was the same officer who called Fukushima to tell him who Corporal Taggart and Constable Secord really were, and of the impending arrests."

"The LO told me the Japanese police are very upset," replied Rose. "Bribery is relatively rare amongst their department. To have a situation develop that nearly cost the lives of two foreigners is extremely embarrassing for them."

"Yes, I understand they wish to formally apologize to both Corporal Taggart and Constable Secord," said Isaac. "I have even heard talk that the Japanese ambassador wishes to present them each with a samurai sword as a token of their appreciation."

"That's nice to hear, although from a psychological point of view, I'm not sure if the sight of a samurai sword would speed up their recovery."

"Good point," mused Isaac.

"However, given the extraordinary circumstances and extreme danger Jack and Laura both faced, it was only through sheer courage and presence of mind that they survived. Naturally, I'll be recommending them both for Commendation as well."

Isaac stared at Rose silently for a moment, before leaning forward and saying, "First, perhaps you could ease my mind about something."

"Sir?"

"It is the circumstances leading up Fukushima's murder that have me slightly confused," said Isaac. "Fukushima was a small man, was he not?"

"I guess so," replied Rose. "Jack was able to control him. Mind you, it takes the fight out of someone to have their eyeball popped out with a fork."

"Yes, which adds to my theory," said Isaac. "You are aware that Corporal Taggart used a sleeper hold on Lee earlier to make it look like he was dead?"

"Yes, sir," sighed Rose. "And I know members have been forbidden to use such holds since an incident years ago where a man died trying to swallow a bundle of heroin while being choked. But what choice did Jack have? Surely you don't plan to reprimand him over —"

"No, the use of the sleeper hold ... on Lee ... does not concern me. Can you explain to me why someone of Corporal Taggart's stature, size, and training, with his arm wrapped around the throat of a small man who had lost his eye, was unable to control him?"

"I don't understand what you mean," said Rose. "He did control him up until the bodyguard smashed through the wall and stabbed him in the fracas that followed."

"Yes, and according to the eyewitness reports," continued Isaac, "at that time Corporal Taggart was no longer holding Fukushima from behind. He was crouched in front of him and holding him up high by the front of his kimono. One police officer even thought Fukushima may have been unconscious at the time, but opened his remaining good eye when he was stabbed."

Rose stared silently as her brain replayed the scenario of what she now realized had happened.

"The Japanese police did not figure it out," said Isaac, "although they should have, with the other clues they were left with."

"Other clues, sir?"

"They found the results of a polygraph test that Corporal Taggart took. They are extremely impressed with his ability to deceive the polygraph operator who worked for Fukushima. Particularly where he convinced the polygraph operator that he had lied to the police, hidden the body of a murder victim, and … let's see … what were the exact words … yes, fooled the polygraph operator into believing he had 'orchestrated or committed murder.'"

"Sounds like he owes our polygraph operator a

debt of gratitude prepping him enough to save his butt," replied Rose. "I'll tell him he should buy Larry Killaly a drink."

"Is that what you believe saved him?" asked Isaac.

Rose paused, wondering how to respond.

"Exactly. Glad to see you decided not to lie to me." Isaac leaned forward, lowering his voice and said, "You know Corporal Taggart's history. Could he have really been telling the truth?"

"Fukushima was an extremely dangerous man," said Rose, quietly. "Statements indicate he not only threatened Jack and Laura, but their families, as well."

"I am aware of that," sighed Isaac. "So I have a proposition. How would it be if I keep my suspicions to myself and you forget about recommending them for Commendation?"

A tiny smile crossed Rose's lips and she said, "Agreed. Knowing Jack and Laura, they aren't the type who would care."

"Good, I would have great difficulty in presenting it to him and pretending to be a fool."

As Rose stood to leave she said, "Sir, the Japanese police said Fukushima had an army of over fifteen thousand strong scattered around the globe. If you were in the same circumstances as Jack and you heard the threats Fukushima made regarding your family, what would you have done to save yourself or your loved ones?"

"I certainly wouldn't do what you are suggesting," replied Isaac.

"Sir?"

"Forget about telling Corporal Taggart to buy our polygraph operator a drink. Larry Killaly doesn't drink."

Rose grinned all the way back to her office.

Jack caught the shimmering reflection of the candle-light in Natasha's eyes as she glanced up and smiled at him from where she sat at their dining-room table. She savoured the last mouthful of peach flambé that Jack had made for dessert, then reached over and held his hand.

"You okay?" she asked.

"I'm not okay," replied Jack. "I'm great. I love you so much."

"I think you're great, too."

"And?" said Jack.

Natasha smiled and said, "And I love you, too." She gestured to the open patio doors and said, "A full moon tonight. You know what that's good for?"

"Howling?"

"You are such a beast. No, it's good for making babies."

"I thought a full moon was when hospitals were busy delivering babies, not placing the orders."

"I'm a doctor. Are you questioning me?"

"No."

Natasha leaned forward to blow out the candle but stopped. She stared at the faded plastic rose in the crystal vase in the centre of the table and then picked it up, turning it slowly in her fingers. "Maybe we should call our first son Melvin."

"I was leaning toward Mike or Steve," replied Jack, "if it's a girl, I love Brenda."

"Maybe you're right. Melvin was one of a kind. He was a real somebody."

Epilogue

Criminal conduct by informants has often been a cause for serious debate. If criminals could eliminate informants from their midst by testing them to commit a criminal act, or by their refusal to commit such criminal acts as they had prior to being an informant, then criminal organizations would seldom be penetrated.

In September 2006, defence lawyers argued in a British Columbia Supreme Court that the conduct of an RCMP informant by breaking the law constituted an abuse of process. On March 16, 2007, the RCMP won a significant victory in British Columbia Supreme Court when it was ruled that the illegal conduct of a million-dollar police agent did not violate the rights of the accused.

Unfortunately, in British Columbia, on average, criminals committing the same acts and who share a similar criminal history receive a sentence that is approximately three times lower than they would elsewhere in Canada. British Columbia continues to remain a favoured location for criminals to operate from, or, if apprehended in another province, an ideal location to move to for the purpose of pleading guilty in a British Columbia court.

There is a Commission for Public Complaints (CPC) created by Parliament to ensure that complaints made by the public about the conduct of members of the RCMP are examined fairly and impartially. The CPC is not part of the RCMP. The CPC make findings and recommendations aimed at correcting and preventing recurring policing problems. The CPC's goal is to promote excellence in policing through accountability.

The CPC is a vital part of our democracy. It would greatly benefit society if our judiciary would face the same type of accountability on a national level.

More Jack Taggart Mysteries by Don Easton

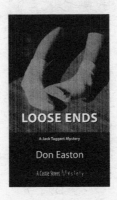

Loose Ends
A Jack Taggart Mystery
978-1550025651
$11.99

Jack Taggart, an undercover Mountie, lives in a world where the good guys and the bad guys change places in a heartbeat. Taggart is very good at what he does. Too good to be playing by the rules. The brass decide to assign a new partner to spy on him. Taggart's new partner discovers a society dependent upon unwritten rules. To break these rules is to lose respect. To lose respect is to lose one's life. *Loose Ends* is terrifying. It is a tale of violence, corruption, and retribution, but it is also a story of honour and respect.

Above Ground
A Jack Taggart Mystery
978-1550026818
$11.99

For RCMP undercover operative Jack Taggart, the consequences of his actions in *Loose Ends* linger. His deal with Damien, leader of the Satans Wrath motorcycle gang, has put him in a bind and has jeopardized an informant in the gang. Meanwhile, other members of the gang, led by a mysterious figure known only as "The Boss," have been working to eliminate Taggart by destroying the lives of anyone with connections to him. And if the bad guys aren't enough of an obstacle, there are problems to be found on the force itself. With Jack's life and career on the line, *Above Ground* is a tough and gritty follow-up that will more than satisfy readers who were pulled into the dark Vancouver underworld by *Loose Ends*.

Angel in the Full Moon
A Jack Taggart Mystery
978-1550028133
$11.99

In this sequel to *Loose Ends* and *Above Ground*, Jack Taggart continues as an undercover Mountie whose quest for justice takes him from the sunny, tourist-laden beaches of Cuba to the ghettos of Hanoi. His targets deal in human flesh, smuggling unwitting victims for the sex trade. Jack's personal vendetta for justice is questioned by his partner, until he reveals the secret behind his motivation, exposing the very essence of his soul. This is the world of the undercover operative: a world of lies, treachery, and deception. A world where violence erupts without warning, like a ticking time bomb on a crowded bus. It isn't a matter of if that bomb will go off — it is a matter of how close you are to it when it does.

Available at your favourite bookseller.

DUNDURN PRESS
w w w . d u n d u r n . c o m

What did you think of this book?
Visit *www.dundurn.com*
for reviews, videos, updates, and more!